Blade rolled to the right in an effort to dislodge the Hatchling. He ducked his head to thwart the talon swipes at his eyes.

The hybrid increased the pressure on the Warrior's neck.

Blade was on top now, the Hatchling pinned under his back. He tried to land a blow with his right elbow, but missed. Frustrated, envisioning the Hatchling tearing into him with those wicked fangs at any moment, he dropped the M-16 and went for his knives. Drawing both Bowies, he rolled again, heaving himself erect, his leg muscles straining as the mutant clung to his neck. Once upright, he plunged his Bowies down and around, driving the gleaming blades to the rear, hoping he would connect.

OUTLANDS STRIKE

Something buzzed past Blade's right ear, and he automatically threw himself to the bank. He landed on his left side and rolled to a squatting posture, the stock of the M60 pressed against his thigh.

There was a hint of movement in a large tree thirty feet away.

Blade squeezed the trigger, the M60 thundering and bucking, the heavy slugs ripping into the foliage and sending leaves flying in all directions, the tracer rounds showing he was right on target.

A harsh shriek greeted the Warrior's volley, and an indistinct shape dropped from the tree into the undergrowth below . . . .

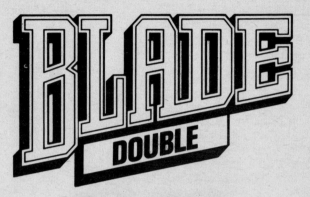

BLADE

DOUBLE

FIRST STRIKE/
OUTLANDS STRIKE
DAVID ROBBINS

LEISURE BOOKS   NEW YORK CITY

A LEISURE BOOK®

January 1992

Published by

Dorchester Publishing Co., Inc.
276 Fifth Avenue
New York, NY 10001

Printed in the United States of America.

FIRST STRIKE

Dedicated to
Judy and Joshua and OOPS! —
SHANE! SHANE! SHANE!
And to the memory of Ivan T. Sanderson,
a true pioneer.

PROLOGUE

It was now or never!

The woman eased from the squat wooden hut, keeping her slim frame close to the south wall, her long brown hair stirred by the gusting breeze, her brown eyes wide with fright. She eased the door shut behind her and gingerly walked toward the dense forest 40 yards distant to the east.

A sliver of moon hung suspended in the heavens, well on its westward descent. The stars sparkled and flickered, animating the inky sky.

Had her gamble paid off?

The woman hunched over as she cautiously moved toward the trees. Her skin was crawling, and she expected to be challenged at any moment. She could only fervently hope the celebration had taken its toll on the inebriated guards. If they were all unconscious or too dazed from the alcohol they'd imbibed to function effectively, she stood a chance of escaping. But if just one of them was still on patrol, then she was as good as dead.

A twig snapped to her left, to the north.

Terrified, the young woman crouched and peered into the night. Nothing moved at the periphery of her vision.

Was it safe?

Motivated by her fear, she impulsively rose and sprinted for the beckoning shelter of the timber. Once she was screened by the vegetation, she felt confident she could elude the guards. The human ones anyway. And since the Hatchlings were pre-occupied with feasting on the sacrifice in the tower, the human sentries were her primary concern. Out of habit, she crossed the first two fingers on each hand, a superstitious reaction to her desperate plight, her eyes fastened on the forest now 20 yards off, anxiously praying to the God her mother had told her about years before, to the Supreme Being of all Creation for her deliverance. She hoped her deduction was correct and all of the human guards were out of commission.

But they weren't.

The woman instinctively dropped and flattened as a harsh cough rent the night to the north.

Someone was moving out there!

She was panic-stricken, and her fingers dug into the compact earth, a sharp rock gouging her left knee just below the hemline of her crude brown homespun dress.

Another cough punctuated the darkness.

The woman could see an indistinct form walking slowly along the edge of the woods to the north, strolling in her approximate direction. At least one of the guards, then, was not drunk. Would he spot her lying on the ground and open fire? She held her breath, her thin lower lip quivering in fright.

The guard was wearing the customary black uniform, and there was a sticklike object slung over his left shoulder.

The woman tensed. She knew what the object was: an automatic rifle!

Ambling in a haphazard fashion, the guard was drawing nearer, but he was staying close to the trees and would miss her by a good eight to ten yards if nothing went wrong.

Something did.

Her nostrils abruptly flared and she experienced an urge to sneeze. Instantly she clamped her right hand over her nose, suppressing the impulse, her nostrils tingling.

The guard was almost abreast of her position.

She felt the tingling cease and she tentatively released her nose, assuming the urge was gone. Without warning, before she could pinch her nostrils a second time, to her utter horror, she sneezed.

The guard abruptly stopped, facing the clustered huts, his arms a vague blur.

The woman knew the sentry had unslung his weapon. Had he seen her yet? Or was she invisible to him, camouflaged by the grass and the night?

"Who's there?" the guard demanded.

The woman's flesh erupted in goose bumps.

"Jim, is that you?" the guard asked, walking several paces toward the wooden huts, toward her.

Her heart seemed to be pounding in her chest.

"Jim?" the guard repeated uncertainly, slowly advancing.

The woman recognized the voice of the guard known as the Sadist, a wicked bastard who delighted in inflicting pain and suffering on the captives, a small man with a pallid complexion and a jagged scar extending from the corner of his left eye to the tip of his pointed chin. Of all the human guards, the Sadist was hated the most.

"Who the hell is there?" the Sadist angrily snapped.

She could see him surveying the huts, evidently perplexed. Not once did he glance at the ground, at her. If only he would pass her by or resume his patrol!

"You'd better speak up or else!" the Sadist warned, but his tone lacked conviction, as if he wasn't completely positive of what he'd heard.

The woman saw him pause, and she could readily imagine his train of thought. He knew no one had ever successfully escaped from the Spider's clutches. There had been a number of attempts decades ago, but the Hatchlings and the human guards had tracked the escapees down and slain them. Or so the captives were told. The woman had often wondered if the guards were telling the truth or concocting lies intended to discourage any bids for freedom. In any event, no one had tried to flee during the seven years of her captivity. All of the women were acutely aware of the dire consequences of being outside their assigned hut after lights-out. So the Sadist wouldn't be expecting anyone except another guard or a Hatchling to be outdoors at such a late hour.

"Is anyone there?" The Sadist was five feet away.

The woman inadvertently trembled.

"Must be hearing things," the Sadist mumbled, looking over his right shoulder at the woods.

Two more steps and the son of a bitch would trip over her! She twisted, reaching her left hand downward and grabbing the

rock gouging her knee, elated to discover it was loose and about
the size of her palm.

The Sadist looked at the huts. "Maybe it was one of the
bitches," he speculated, and proceeded forward.

The woman was ready for him. She saw him take one stride,
then lift his left leg for a second. He was almost on top of her,
his crotch directly above her head. She swept the rock up and in,
lunging to her knees, driving the unyielding stone into his groin.

Startled, overwhelmed by agony, the Sadist doubled over, his
right hand covering his genitals.

"Take this, slime!" the woman exclaimed triumphantly,
swinging the rock in an arc and clipping him on the jaw.

The Sadist grunted, sagging to his knees in front of her.

"And this for everything I owe you!" she cried, unable to
contain her pent-up emotions. Her loathing, the sheer
repugnance accumulated over seven years of emotional,
physical, and sexual abuse, surged to the surface. She bashed him
again and again with the rock, five times in all, each blow
delivered with all of her force to his chin and cheeks.

Groaning, the Sadist toppled to the left, landing on his face.

The woman jumped erect, glancing at the huts, then at the
tower. No one was in sight. Yet. She raced to the forest and
plunged into the trees, heedless of the limbs and the brush
tearing at her arms and legs.

She'd done it!

They'd never catch her now!

A strident horn blast suddenly sounded from the direction of
the tower.

The alarm! The sound chilled her blood and lent speed to her
legs. The alarm meant the other guards would be after her
within minutes! And the Hatchlings! Dear God! The Hatchlings!

Loud yelling broke out behind her.

The woman flinched as a branch gouged her right cheek,
drawing blood, stinging terribly. She pressed onward, scared to
her core, determined to put as much distance as possible between
herself and the Spider's lair, forgetting, for the moment, her
original plan to travel due south. Several minutes elapsed, her
breathing becoming labored, the strain of her pell-mell flight
taking its toll on her undernourished and fatigued body. The
ground was sloping upward.

What the hell was she doing?

The thought brought her up short. She gasped for air, gazing skyward in an endeavor to get her bearings. She had to get a grip on herself! She needed a clear head if she was to survive! Shock numbed her mind as she abruptly realized she was going the wrong way! She was supposed to be heading due south, but instead was making to the east.

The east and the cliffs!

She doubled over, tears of frustration forming in the corners of her eyes. To be so close! And then to blow it because she was too stupid to head in the right direction! What an idiot!

A pronounced click-click-click wafted on the breeze, coming from the rear—an odd, eerie sound, as if someone with thick lips was smacking their lips together.

The Hatchlings!

The woman straightened and fled, still going to the east, knowing her pursuers would easily cut her off if she tried to alter course and bear to the south. Her sandals pounded on the hard ground. The chill, late January air caused her perspiration to become clammy and cold.

More clicking reached her ears.

How far to the cliffs? she wondered. She'd seen them as the plane had glided to a crash landing on the ridge seven years ago. The impact of plowing into the forest had shorn the wings from the aircraft and killed the pilot, impaling the hapless man on a jutting piece of metal from the crushed front of the plane. She had counted herself fortunate to be alive, albeit battered and bruised, and she had crawled from the wreckage confident she could signal a passing aircraft and would be home in Los Angeles within a matter of days. But that very night the Hatchlings had captured her, initiating her into a nightmare existence of slavery and torture.

Seven years of hell! Seven years of being too afraid to try and escape! Seven years of being at the Spider's beck and call! Merely thinking of the monstrosity prompted her to moan in despair.

She'd die before she'd go back there!

There was clicking off to the right.

Her legs were rapidly tiring, but she refused to give up, to surrender without a struggle. The penalty for trying to escape was death, the most horrid demise imaginable. Being consumed alive was a revolting prospect. As she dashed up a rise, she speculated on whether her final decision to flee had been inspired by suddenly acquired genuine courage, or if the knowledge she was slated to be the next sacrifice had mobilized her faltering resolve.

Click-click-click. To the left this time.

The Hatchlings were closing in. They must believe they had her cornered and weren't concerned about disguising their pursuit.

The woman reached the top of the rise and came to an abrupt, petrified halt. In her haste she'd almost fallen to her death! She was perched on the very rim of the cliffs, silhouetted against the stars. Stiff wind whipped her hair. She crouched and whirled, debating which way to go.

A squat black form detached itself from the surrounding vegetation and stopped ten feet away.

A Hatchling!

She tensed, raising the rock in her left hand in a defensive gesture, knowing the futility of using her weapon on a Hatchling. She could see its four hairy arms waving in the air and sensed, rather than saw, its flat, dark malevolent eyes boring into her.

What was it waiting for?

The Hatchling moved toward her, its bulky body rising and lowering in the awkward gait so typical of the hybrids.

So close, and yet so far!

Furious at her failure, she drew her left arm back to toss the rock at the Hatchling. Its tough epidermis would hardly feel the blow, but she needed to do *something* to demonstrate her defiance! Her left foot inched backwards as she braced herself for the throw, and she unexpectedly lost her balance as the gravel under her left foot gave way. She tried to regain her footing, but her left leg dropped from under her and she fell backwards. Her arms flailing wildly, she involuntarily screamed as she perceived her mistake and her predicament. She had stepped too close to the edge of the cliff!

Her scream rose in volume as she pitched over the rim and plummeted into the gloom below.

PART ONE

THE TRAINING

CHAPTER ONE

The giant folded his muscular arms across his massive chest and idly gazed upward, watching the VTOL descend. A brisk breeze off the Pacific Ocean rustled the Free State of California flag adorning the 20-foot pole atop the airport terminal behind him. He glanced over his right shoulder at the flag, speculating on the significance of the solitary red star in the upper left corner, the bright red border along the bottom, and especially the grizzly bear depicted in the center. Why a grizzly bear? he wondered. As far as he knew, there weren't any grizzly bears in California, and there hadn't been for hundreds of years.

"Which one is coming in, Blade?" asked the giant's companion.

Blade turned to the left, his massive physique rippling with raw power and radiating physical force. At seven feet in height, he towered over his six-foot-three friend. Blade's black leather vest, green fatigue pants, and black boots seemed scarcely able to contain his imposing form. The sunlight glinted off the hilts of the matching pair of Bowie knives strapped around his waist, one on each hip. He brushed at the comma of dark hair hanging above his gray eyes with his right hand. "His name is Spader. He's the one the Moles picked to represent them."

"What do you know about him?"

"Not much, Boone," Blade answered. "He's supposed to be one of the best fighters the Moles have."

"Which isn't saying much," Boone commented. His lean frame was clad in buckskins. Buckled around his slim waist were a pair of 44 Magnum Hombre single-action revolvers. The wind tossed his shoulder-length brown hair as he tilted his head, his brown eyes squinting as he followed the progress of the aircraft.

"I'll admit the Moles aren't known for producing top-quality fighting men," Blade conceded. "But we shouldn't prejudge this man. We'll give Spader a chance to prove himself."

"I just hope he proves himself before we go on a mission," Boone remarked. "I don't like the notion of laying my life on the line and not knowing if the other members of the Freedom Force will back me up when the chips are down."

Blade frowned. "I know what you mean," he agreed, his mind filling with a myriad of thoughts. The Freedom Force. The elite tactical squad formed to nullify any threat to the Freedom Federation. Was it only two weeks ago that the Governor of California, Governor Melnick, had proposed the formation of the strike squad? What were the words Melnick had used? They came back to him in a rush: "As allies in the Freedom Federation, we will be ready to band together should any one of us be beseiged. We will stand together against any invader. . . . Our treaty should serve to deter any agression on a widespread scale. But what about isolated incidents? What about localized problems within the boundaries of each Federation member? . . . I propose establishing a special strike force . . . a mobile force organized with one purpose in mind. Namely, to deal with just such trouble spots as we've been discussing. If a localized problem develops anywhere within the Freedom Federation, or outside of our boundaries for that matter, this strike force will be dispatched to deal with the situation."

And here I am, Blade thought, in charge of the Freedom Federation's elite fighting unit. Which meant countless lives depended on his performance, on his judgment in critical situations. All the members of the Freedom Federation were relying on him. The Flathead Indians in what was once Montana; the people known as the Moles, residing in their underground city in north-central Minnesota; the Cavalry, the indomitable horsemen controlling the Dakota Territory, of which Boone had been second-in-command until selected to serve on the Freedom Force; the residents of the state of

California, one of the few states to retain its administrative integrity after World War Three; the Clan, the refugees from the ravaged Twin Cities now living in a small town in northwestern Minnesota; the Civilized Zone, the area in the West encompassing the former states of Kansas, Nebraska, Wyoming, Colorado, New Mexico, Oklahoma, portions of Arizona, and the northern half of Texas; and, finally, his own people, the renowned Family, located in their survivalist compound in northern Minnesota. These were the seven factions constituting the Freedom Federation, and they were depending on him to train a combat unit capable of eliminating any menace to the Federation's security.

The responsibility was awesome, and he felt uncomfortable being responsible for the safety of so many. Before, it had been different. His life had been much simpler. As the Family's head Warrior, he had been entrusted with the preservation of the Family and the safeguarding of their compound, their 30-acre retreat called the Home. Seventeen Warriors had been under his command, and together the Warriors had been accountable for protecting the lives of less than a hundred Family members. Less than a hundred. And now how many might perish if he failed in his duty? Millions. The realization was sobering and not a little distressing.

"When will the others arrive?" Boone asked, intruding on Blade's reflection.

Blade gazed at the Cavalryman. "The other VTOL is picking up the volunteers from the Flatheads and the Clan and should arrive here tomorrow morning."

"What about the Civilized Zone?" Boone queried.

Blade nodded at the descending jet. "This VTOL is going right back out and will collect the soldier the Civilized Zone is sending. He should get here by tomorrow night."

"Kind of strange, isn't it?" Boone asked, his eyes on the VTOL hovering 50 yards above the tarmac.

"What is?" Blade responded.

"This Freedom Force thing was Governor Melnick's bright idea, right?" Boone noted. "And didn't the Federation leaders figure the Force should be made up of a volunteer from each Federation faction? So why haven't we met the volunteer from California yet? I mean, we are *in* California. It was Governor

Melnick's brainstorm to base the Force in L.A., right? So where's his man?"

Blade shrugged. "I don't know. But I was told we could expect him in a day or so."

"So we'll all be together by tomorrow night?" Boone said.

"Maybe," Blade stated. "We'll have to wait and see."

"I can hardly wait," Boone commented sarcastically.

Blade pursed his lips, troubled by Boone's attitude. He had known the Cavalryman for years, and he'd never seen Boone betraying such pessimism. The Warrior determined to get to the bottom of Boone's odd behavior at the first opportunity.

Its engines whining, the VTOL was slowly settling to the ground 30 yards away. The sleek jet was an impressive testimonial to the wisdom exhibited by California's previous leaders. After World War Three, after the devastation unleashed on the environment, after the country was plunged into turmoil and the transportation systems were totally disrupted, those in charge of California had decided to concentrate on maintaining their aircraft instead of wasting precious resources in an effort to keep their cars and trucks running. Because California was so large, and because travel overland was fraught with danger due to the proliferation of mutants, looters, and the Raiders, the government of California had opted to utilize aircraft as the principal conveyances in the state. The two VTOLs were the pride of the California military, and understandably so. Modified to carry up to five passengers and outfitted with extra fuel tanks, and with their vertical-take-off-and-landing capability, the VTOLs were ideal for flying a weekly shuttle service between the Federation factions or making special trips, such as this one to retrieve the volunteers for the strike force.

Boone hooked his thumbs in his gunbelt. "I'll never get used to that contraption."

Blade knew what the Cavalryman meant. The development of sophisticated technology, with a few notable exceptions, had pretty much died out with the war. The VTOLs California possessed were a throwback to the preward times, to an ancient culture and an antiquated social system. One hundred and five years might not seem like a lenghty stretch of time when viewed in relation to eternity, but in the context of the drastic and radical changes inflicted by the nuclear exchange between the so-called superpowers, Blade tended to view the prewar society as an alien way of life. He had studied the prewar civilization in the Family school, and he had been astonished by the lack of wise leadership, the moral and spiritual emptiness of the people, and the government intrusion into the lives of its citizens, whether that government was communistic or socialistic or capitalistic.

The VTOL landed flawlessly, and was immediately converged upon by the ground crew.

"Do you miss the Family?" Boone unexpectedly asked.

Blade's mouth turned downward. He wished Boone hadn't reminded him of his dearest friends, of the tightknit group he had lived with all his life, of the men and women he affectionately regarded as his brothers and sisters. He missed several of his fellow Warriors in particular: Hickok, Geronimo, Rikki-Tikki-Tavi, Yama, and Bertha. "Yes," he replied.

"I miss Dakota," Boone disclosed. "I miss my buddies in the Cavalry." He sighed wistfully. "You're lucky. At least you have your wife and son here in L.A."

The mention of Jenny and Gabe made Blade smile. "I guess I am," he admitted. The idea of being alone in L.A., of not being near his beloved wife and son, was depressing. He silently thanked the Spirit for his good fortune, and suddenly he realized what was bothering Boone.

"Here comes our recruit," Boone said.

A man was climbing down a ladder from the VTOL. He was slightly under six feet tall, slim and wiry in appearance.

Blade studied the newcomer as the man approached, noting the unkempt black hair, the pale, angular features, and the man's clearly bored expression. The recruit was wearing ragged brown pants and a faded green shirt. Black shoes with holes in the toes covered his feet.

"I figured as much," Boone muttered. "I bet he bathes about once a year."

Blade was deeply disappointed. All of the Federation leaders were fully aware of the importance of the unit he was forming. All of them had been asked to select a top fighter for the Force. Since the Freedom Force would be handling extremely hazardous assignments, the Federation leaders were supposed to call for volunteers and pick the best of the lot. Was this the best the Moles had to offer?

The Mole reached them and stopped, his green eyes roving from one to the other. "Is one of you clowns named Blade?" he asked.

"I'm Blade," the Warrior responded gruffly.

The Mole didn't appear to notice. "I'm Spader," he announced. "I was told you're the bozo I'm to see."

"I knew it," Boone quipped. "Why did the Moles send someone with mush for brains?"

Spader instantly bristled. "Are you talking about me, mister?"

"You see any other jackasses around here?" Boone rejoined.

Spader clenched his bony fists. "I don't have to take this crap! I was sent here to join the Fart Force, or whatever the name of the chickenshit outfit is!" He indicated Blade with a jerk of his right thumb. "I know who this yo-yo is," he snapped at Boone. "But who the hell are you?"

Blade's right hand lashed out and clamped on the Mole's shirt. He effortlessly hoisted the Mole into the air, his right arm bulging.

Spader gawked at the immense Warrior. He swatted at the hand holding him aloft, to no avail. "Hey! Let me go, you asshole!"

Blade's gray eyes became flinty. "Let you go? Sure, I'll let you go!" He shoved the Mole from him and released the green shirt.

Spader tumbled onto his back, landing hard on the tarmac, wincing as pain lanced his shoulders and hips. He rolled, ready to rise, when steely fingers locked onto the nape of his neck and he was hauled into the air once again. "Let me go!" he cried angrily.

Blade started shaking the Mole, and he continued shaking until Spader was pleading for mercy.

"Please! Let me go!" the Mole wailed. "I didn't mean nothing by what I said! Honest! Please!"

Blade dumped Spader onto the tarmac and stood over him. "Shut your mouth!" he commanded.

Spader, braced on his haunches, glared at the giant. "No one tells me to—" The remainder of his sentence was strangled off as the Warrior's right hand seized his throat. He gurgled and gasped for air.

Blade leaned over the Mole's reddening face. "When I give an order, you will obey it immediately," he stated brusquely.

Spader was trying to talk, but he blubbered inarticulately.

"I repeat," Blade reiterated. "When I give an order, obey it. Now shut your mouth and listen up!"

Spader wanted to strike at the Warrior, but evidently thought better of the idea. He lowered his right fist, glowering, wheezing but calm.

"Good." Blade loosened his grip and straightened. "You're not to speak unless spoken to. Do you understand?"

Spader nodded, rubbing his sore throat, enraged but unwilling to antagonize the Warrior further.

"You're learning," Blade said. "Now let's get a few facts straight. You're here to join the Freedom Force, not the Fart Force. And since I'm in command of the Force, you will do as I say, when I say it, or suffer the consequences. Do you follow me so far?"

"Yeah," Spader croaked.

"You will refer to me as Blade," the Warrior directed. "Not as a clown, or a yo-yo, or an asshole. Should you ever do it again, you'll be in the market for new teeth. Do you get my drift?"

Spader studied the Warrior's awesome physique. "I get you," he declared.

"Fine," Blade said. "Now stand up."

Spader scrambled to his feet.

"How old are you?" Blade inquired.

"What's that got to do . . ." Spader began, then hastily replied, "Twenty-seven, sir!"

"Call me Blade," the Warrior admonished. "Not sir."

"Yes, si . . ." Spader stopped. "I mean, yes, Blade!"

"Why are you here, Spader?" Blade asked.

Spader appeared puzzled by the query. "What do you mean? I'm here to join the Freedom Force."

"But why you?" Blade pressed him. "Why did the Moles send you? You act like you're none too happy about being here."

"I'm not," Spader confessed.

"Then why are you here?" Blade repeated.

"Wolfe asked for volunteers," Spader said.

"And you volunteered?" Blade asked skeptically.

"Not exactly," Spader replied. "Wolfe called a meeting of all the Moles. He explained about this Freedom Force deal, and that one of us would need to join. But when he said the volunteer would have to travel all the way to California, there wasn't any great rush to join up." He paused and sighed. "So Wolfe volunteered me."

"Wolfe selected you to come here?" Blade asked.

"Yep."

"And he didn't give you any say in the matter?" Blade questioned.

"Nope," Spader said. "I wouldn't be here if he had."

Blade's lips compressed in annoyance and he stared at the ground. Now he understood! Of all the Freedom Federation factions, the Moles came closest to being run by a dictator. Wolfe, the Mole leader, was a haughty, arrogant man who ruled the Moles imperiously. It would be just like Wolfe to pick someone if he didn't get the volunteers he wanted.

"May I say something?" Spader ventured to ask.

"What?" Blade said.

"I don't want to be here, but I can't go back either," Spader said. "Wolfe said I would have to stay here for a year. Is that right?"

"Each recruit serves for a period of one year," Blade confirmed.

"I don't have much combat experience," Spader revealed. "I know this Force is going to be flying all over the place, getting involved with more trouble than I care to think about. And I want to survive my year here. I want to make it back home again." He gazed into Blade's eyes. "I won't give you no more grief. Wolfe said we're going to undergo some training. Is that true?"

Blade nodded. "I'm responsible for your training. We will spend two months preparing for our first mission. I want us to function as a precision team, and that will take lots and lots of hard work."

"I'll do what you say," Spader said. "My life is in your hands. I didn't mean to fly off the handle the way I did. But I was really pissed off about being here. I guess I just took it out on you two."

"We won't hold it against you," Blade said. He nodded at the Cavalryman. "This is Boone. He's from the Cavalry."

Spader and Boone shook hands.

"I got off on the wrong foot, didn't I?" Spader queried.

"You could say that," Boone acknowledged.

"Where's your bag?" Blade asked.

"What bag?" Spader responded.

"Didn't you pack some extra clothing? Bring your weapons? Anything?" Blade probed.

"Wolfe said you would supply all that," Spader said.

Blade was looking forward to the next time he encountered the Mole leader. He had a few choice words he wanted to say to Wolfe.

"So what's next?" Spader wanted to know.

"We go through that terminal there," Blade said, pointing at the building to their rear. "I have a jeep parked in the lot on the other side. We'll drive out to our training facility."

"Where are the others?" Spader inquired. "I was told there would be seven of us."

"There will be," Blade affirmed. "Two more will arrive in L.A. tomorrow morning, and another one tomorrow night. I don't know about the last one."

"Are you sure seven will be enough?" Spader asked. "I mean, who knows what we'll be running up against?"

"California only has two VTOLs," Blade commented. "Each one can carry five passengers. What with seven of us, plus all the gear we might require, seven is the maximum number we can include in the Force."

"You've got all this worked out, haven't you?"

Blade pursed his lips. "I think so."

"I've heard about you," Spader said. "Hell. Who hasn't? I know all about your rep. I figure I'm in good hands."

Blade was rather surprised by the Mole's abrupt turnaround. One minute Spader was ready to spit nails, the next he was bending over backward to be friendly. Either the man was mature enough to own up to a mistake when he made one, or he was unstable emotionally and thus might pose a threat to the Force.

"Before we take off, is there somewhere I can take a leak?" Spader asked.

"Inside the terminal," Blade informed him. "To the left."

"Thanks." Spader hurried toward the structure.

"Well, the Freedom Force is off to a rousing start," Boone

remarked.

Blade noted the sarcasm in Boone's tone, and he had to agree. Spader was not the sort of man he would want to rely on in a firefight. The Mole was inexperienced in combat, and Spader resented his coerced service in the Force. Such a negative attitude would adversely affect his performance. Come to think of it, Blade realized, the Cavalryman's attitude wasn't much better than the Mole's. Boone would much rather be in Dakota than in L.A. And although the Cavalryman had made a name for himself in the Dakota Territory, and was considered to be fast and exceptionally accurate with a handgun, what good would Boone be if his mind was distracted?

Boone walked toward the terminal. "Coming?" he asked over his left shoulder.

Blade sighed and followed.

Boone glanced at the Warrior's troubled countenance. "Is something wrong?"

"I was just wondering about something," Blade remarked.

"Like what?"

"Like why you volunteered for the Force if you didn't want to come to L.A.?" Blade inquired.

"Kilrane asked me to," Boone divulged.

Blade stared at the Cavalryman. Kilrane was the head of the Cavalry. "He only asked you?"

"No. Kilrane asked for anyone who wanted to volunteer to do so," Boone said. "But he told me he'd take it as a personal favor if I volunteered along with the others, so he could formally pick me."

"Why you?" Blade questioned.

Boone shrugged. "He said he wanted someone he could trust, someone who would serve with honor and distinction." Boone shook his head. "For some reason, he had this harebrained notion I could fill the bill."

"But I get the impression you don't want to be here," Blade commented.

"I don't," Boone said.

"Then why'd you accept Kilrane's proposal?" Blade queried.

Boone looked the Warrior in the eyes. "Because Kilrane is my best friend."

Blade nodded his understanding. The Family Elders taught

that the demonstration of loyalty to true friends was one of the higher virtues. But now he had two men on the Force, neither of whom wanted to be on it. Two out of seven. What about the rest? More to the point, what in the world had he gotten himself into?

CHAPTER TWO

Governor Melnick had ordered a special training facility to be constructed for the Freedom Force north of Los Angeles, slightly to the northwest of Pyramid Lake. The facility would also serve as the headquarters of the Force for all future operations. While the VTOLs would be based on the L.A. airport, a runway and small hangar were built at the facility so the Force could be picked up on a moment's notice. The entire headquarters compound embraced 12 acres and was enclosed in an electrified fence topped with barbed wire and patrolled by regular California Army troops. Occupying the southern section was the runway, a concrete pad 50 yards square. With their vertical-ascent-and-descent capability, the VTOLs did not require a lengthy runway. In the center of the compound were three buildings, actually concrete bunkers positioned in a straight line from west to east. In the middle was the command bunker, Blade's HQ; to the east was the long barracks for the Freedom Force members; to the west was the supply bunker. The northern part of the facility was kept in its natural, wild state and would be utilized for training purposes.

Blade mentally reviewed the layout the next morning as he stood next to the gate situated in the middle of the south fence. The sun had been up in the sky for an hour. Birds were singing and the breeze was warm.

"Here they come, sir."

Blade grinned to his left at the speaker, one of a pair of regular Army troops assigned to gate duty. "You can call me Blade," he advised.

"Yes, sir, Blade," the trooper responded. Like his counterpart, he was standing at attention near the swivel bar in the center of the gate.

Blade stared down the asphalt roadway leading to the facility. A green jeep was rapidly approaching. Inside should be the volunteers from the Flathead Indians in Montana and the Clan in Minnesota. He hoped they would be more enthusiastic about their assignment than Boone and Spader.

The jeep slowed as it neared the gate, then braked on the far side. An officer clambered from the vehicle and scrutinized the compound critically.

Blade resisted an inclination to frown. He recognized the officer—General Miles Gallagher, Governor Melnick's personal liaison with the Freedom Force. Gallagher was a stocky man with brown eyes and a crew-cut brown hair, a bulldog of an officer notable for his tenacity and popularity with his troops. Gallagher had made no secret of the fact he disliked California joining the Freedom Federation, and he was skeptical of the elite unit Governor Melnick was forming. While he had expressed his reservations to Melnick, Gallagher was too good a soldier to go public with his disapproval. His eyes locked on the Warrior. "Morning, Blade," he greeted the giant, cordially but with a cold undercurrent.

"General," Blade said, nodding.

Gallagher looked at the two gate guards. "Open this damn gate!" he barked.

The troopers promptly obeyed, raising the swivel bar and pulling the gate wide. They stepped to one side, at attention, saluting as the general entered.

Gallagher walked up to the Warrior. "I've got two more recruits for you."

"I've been expecting you," Blade said.

"I wasn't able to meet the one yesterday," Gallagher stated. "What's the Mole like?"

"Well . . ." Blade began, searching for a tactful reply.

Gallagher chuckled. "You don't have to tell me. I can see it on your face." He gazed at the jeep and motioned with his right arm for the vehicle to drive inside. "Wait until you see the pair

I've brought." He snickered.

"What's wrong with them?" Blade asked, his gut muscles tightening reflexively.

"Nothing eight weeks of basic training wouldn't fix," Gallagher said. "Oh, the Indian doesn't look half bad. He might work out. But wait until you see the moron the Clan sent!" He smirked.

The jeep braked alongside the general and the Warrior.

Blade watched as two men climbed from the vehicle. The first was the Flathead Indian. He appeared to be about 25 or so, with black hair down past his broad shoulders. Two braids, one hanging over each ear to his neck, framed his oval face. His features were handsome, almost noble in the strength of their lines and the fearlessness of his dark eyes. He wore a fringed buckskin shirt and pants and moccasins. In one respect, the Flathead Indians and the Cavalry were alike; after World War Three, with store-bought clothing a thing of the past, both had reverted to wearing the typical frontier garb so popular with their ancestors—durable, easily acquired buckskins. He carried a green canvas bag.

The second man was a striking contrast to the Flathead. He was several inches shorter than the six-foot-tall Indian, and he was heftier of build. His long hair was blond, and had been slicked and shaped until peculiar spikes projected from his head. Silver earrings adorned his earlobes. He wore a black leather jacket with bright studs circling the edge of the sleeves, dotting his shoulders, and forming a large V on the front. Black leather pants and black boots completed his apparel. In his left hand was a brown suitcase.

"Blade, I'd like you to meet the two new members of your Freedom Force," General Gallagher announced. He indicated the Flathead. "This is Thunder."

The Flathead offered his right hand and the Warrior shook. "My given name is Thunder Rolling in the Mountain," the Indian said, grinning. "But you may call me Thunder."

"I'm pleased to meet you," Blade said.

"I have heard much about you from Star," Thunder mentioned.

"How is she?" Blade asked. Star was the leader of the Flatheads, a beautiful young woman possessed of extraordinary wisdom and courage.

"Star is well," Thunder said. "She requested me to relay her greetings."

The blond took a step forward. "Like, hey, man. When do I get to feed my face?" he interrupted.

Blade glanced at the volunteer from the Clan. "And what might your name be?"

"The name, dude, is Kraft," the blond stated.

"You'll get to eat shortly," Blade told him. He looked from Kraft to Thunder. "There's something I need to know. Did both of you volunteer for the Freedom Force?"

"I did," Thunder answered first. "Twenty-one Flatheads volunteered to come here. Star put us through a series of rigorous tests to determine which one would receive the honor."

"And you came out on top?" Blade inquired.

Thunder nodded.

"What about you?" Blade questioned the Clansman.

"Yep. I volunteered. I heard a lot of stories about California. They say there are a lot of heavy-duty foxes out here. I'm looking to groove on some fuzz. You know what I mean?" Kraft said.

General Gallagher laughed.

"You came out here to find some women?" Blade asked in disbelief.

"Why not, dude? A little squeeze never hurt nobody," Kraft said.

"You *do* know the real reason you're here, don't you?" Blade asked.

Kraft nodded. "Sure, man. To waste a few stiffs for you. No big deal." His green eyes twinkled.

"Why did the Clan select you?" Blade inquired.

"Zahner, our head honcho, said he needed somebody who doesn't mind killing," Kraft said.

"And you have no compunctions about killing?" Blade questioned.

"I don't know about no compunctions," Kraft said. "But when it comes to killing, I like it."

Blade frowned. "You like to kill?"

Kraft beamed. "Sure do. Doesn't everybody?"

Blade stared at the ground, concerned his exasperation would show on his face. As if he didn't have enough problems already! This was just what he needed! A psychopath!

General Gallagher cleared his throat. "I've brought a present for you."

Blade looked up, his emotions under control. "A present?"

"Yeah. And I think you'll like it," Gallagher said. He moved to the jeep and pounded on the top. "Now, sergeant," he said.

Another man emerged from the vehicle. This one was a professional soldier, six feet tall and close to 200 pounds in weight with every inch solid muscle. He wore combat boots, fatigue pants, and a green T-shirt revealing his muscular arms and chest. His black hair was cropped close to his head. His eyes were a penetrating blue.

"Blade, let me introduce Sergeant Havoc," General Gallagher said. "He's a gift from Governor Melnick."

"A gift?"

"The governor ordered me to find the best soldier I could for the Freedom Force," Gallagher disclosed. "Havoc is the man for the job. He's thirty-four, and he's been in the Army since he was eighteen. He's a qualified marksman and an expert in hand-to-hand combat, with black belts in karate and judo and a brown in Aikido. Name any weapon and he's proficient in its use. You couldn't ask for a better trooper," he declared proudly.

Blade liked the traits he saw reflected in Havoc's rugged features: honesty, dedication, and a supreme sense of duty. He extended his right hand. "I'm very pleased to meet you."

Havoc shook, his grip firm and hinting at latent power. "I'm looking forward to this assignment, sir."

"You can call me Blade," the Warrior said.

"Whatever you say, sir," Havoc responded.

"Sergeant Havoc is all military," General Gallagher commented. "He goes by the book." He paused and glanced at a watch on his left wrist. "I must be heading back to L.A. Governor Melnick is holding a meeting with his chiefs of staff later and I must attend." He looked at Blade. "The show is in your hands. Don't drop the ball."

"I won't," Blade responded, a touch testily.

General Gallagher was about to enter the jeep when he stopped and gazed at the Warrior. "Almost forgot. I'll be back here tonight with the volunteer from the Civilized Zone. The VTOLs ETA is seven. I should be here between eight and nine."

"I'll be expecting you," Blade said.

Gallagher climbed into the jeep, and a moment later the vehicle executed a U-turn and left the compound.

The gate guards closed the gate.

"Follow me," Blade said to the others. "We'll go to the barracks. Your training session will begin in an hour. Until then you can rest or grab a bit to eat. There's a kitchen in the barracks. You'll be responsible for preparing your own food."

"We cook our own food?" Kraft asked.

"That's right," Blade said, turning to the north.

"You got to be kidding, dude," Kraft said. "I don't know how to cook."

Blade glanced at the Clansman. "How'd you get by all these years without knowing how to cook?"

"I've always had a squeeze handy for that," Kraft mentioned. "I mean, cooking is women's work, right?"

"No one is going to wait on you hand and foot here," Blade informed him. "You've got to learn to fend for yourself. Self-reliance is one of the keys to your survival."

"Well, this sucks," Kraft muttered.

Blade faced the Clansman. "You volunteered for this assignment, so you'll take the consequences without griping. From now on there will be no talking back. When in training, you will not speak until necessary."

"Hey, dude, chill out," Kraft said. "I didn't come here for this crap. Zahner never said nothing about all this military bullshit."

Sergeant Havoc's eyes narrowed.

"This bullshit, as you call it, could save your life," Blade said to the Clansman. "I don't want any more grousing out of you."

Kraft dropped his suitcase on the asphalt. "And what if I do? What are you going to do about it?"

"I'm in charge of this unit," Blade stated. "And I will enforce discipline. You will listen, or else."

"Or else what?" Kraft snickered. "You don't scare me. I can take care of myself."

"Can you now?" Blade asked flatly.

"I know you're supposed to be a real bad dude," Kraft said. "But you aren't the only one with a rep, man. I can handle a knife too, you know."

"You can?"

Kraft's right hand reached into the right pocket of his leather jacket and came out clenching a closed folding knife. "Sure can, sucker." He grinned and pressed a small silver button, and the blade snapped out with a metallic click. The gleaming blade and the handle were both the same length, about five inches.

"A switchblade, huh?" Blade said.

Kraft smiled. "My favorite, dude. I could gut you in a flash with this."

"You think so?"

"I know so," Kraft replied confidently.

"Then let's see just how good you are," Blade said. "Your training will begin right now. Try and gut me."

"Are you for real?" Kraft asked in amazement.

"Try and gut me," Blade repeated.

Sergeant Havoc spoke up. "Allow me, sir. I'll teach this punk a lesson he'll never forget."

Blade glanced at the soldier. "This punk, sergeant, is part of the same unit you are in. You both belong to the Freedom Force now. You must learn to work together, to cooperate, or you'll jeopardize the lives of all of us. Understand?"

Sergeant Havoc nodded somewhat sheepishly. "Sorry, sir. It won't happen again."

"And now," Blade said, staring at Kraft, "let's get this over with. Or are you all mouth?"

Kraft reddened, then lunged, sweeping the switchblade at the Warrior's midriff.

Blade backpedaled, avoiding the slashing knife. He twisted and dodged, measuring Kraft's ability. As the Clansman pressed him, he found himself grudingly admiring Kraft's skill. The man wielded his switchblade with flair, never making any reckless moves, never leaving himself open.

For his part, Kraft was frustrated by his failure to connect. Try as he might, he couldn't so much as nick the weaving Warrior. He used every trick he knew, feinting and using reverse thrusts, always on the attack, but it was as if the giant knew his next move in advance. Only a master at knife fighting could evade an attack so deftly.

Blade admired the determination on Kraft's face. The Clansman's initial anger had subsided and been replaced by a calculating resolution. He waited another minute before making his move.

Kraft saw the Warrior stumble and fall onto his back. He

closed in, grinning, thinking he had his man. Too late, he perceived the fall was a ruse. The Warrior had turned and was rolling toward him! Kraft felt Blade's legs slam into his shins, and he toppled forward onto the asphalt. His right arm was wrenched downward, and the switchblade was torn from his grasp. He abruptly found himself on his stomach with the Warrior straddling his back and his own knife pressed against his neck.

"Now I want your word, Kraft," Blade stated. "I want your word you will obey me. Each time, every time. Without griping."

"You've got it, dude," Kraft said.

"No more of your grief?"

"No more grief," Kraft promised.

Blade rose, using his left hand to haul Kraft erect. He reversed the switchblade and extended the knife. "Here."

Kraft seemed surprised. "You trust me with this?"

"Like I told the sergeant," Blade said, "you're part of our team. We must all learn to trust one another. We have to depend on each other if we're going to survive."

Kraft took the switchblade and replaced it in his coat pocket. "I gave you my word, dude. Whatever you want, you get."

"Then let's head for the barracks," Blade directed.

"That was very impressive, sir," Sergeant Havoc commented. "I was told about you, but I had no idea."

Blade acknowledged the compliment with a curt nod. He glanced at the Flathead and noticed Thunder's forehead was furrowed, his eyes troubled. "What's wrong?" he asked.

"You wouldn't understand," Thunder replied.

"You let me be the judge of that," Blade declared. "We're a team now," he reiterated. "If something is bothering you, I need to know about it."

"You wouldn't understand," Thunder repeated.

"Try me."

"I was just wondering what I've gotten myself into," Thunder divulged.

All three recruits were mystified when the Warrior burst out laughing.

"Did I say something funny?" Thunder queried, puzzled.

"If you only knew!" was Blade's reply.

CHAPTER THREE

$\mathbf{B}$lade sat back in his metal folding chair in the HQ bunker, relaxing. The day had gone well. All five recruits had fraternized with a minimum of fuss. After Thunder and Kraft had rested from their flight and eaten, he had called all of them outside and detailed the purpose behind the formation of the Freedom Force. They had listened in rapt silence.

The afternoon had been spent in target practice. He'd had them stake out targets, and had issued an M-16 to each man, then tabulated the results. Not too surprisingly, Sergeant Havoc had scored highest with the automatic rifle. At 100 yards, Havoc could consistently place ten out of ten rounds in the bull's-eye. Thunder and Boone had also performed in the superior range, averaging nine out of ten. Kraft had managed to hit the target near the bull's-eye about four times out of ten. With a lot of practice he could become quite deadly. But Spader had been lucky to even hit the target, and not once had he come within an inch of the center.

After the M-16 exercise, Blade had dispensed handguns. Everyone but Boone had taken a pair of Colt Stainless Steel Officers Model 45's. The Cavalryman had stuck with his revolvers, preferring the Hombres over the automatics. With good reason. Boone had displayed an uncanny expertise with his handguns. At 25 yards, he could draw and fire ten shots with dazzling speed, clustering all ten rounds in the center of the target. Sergeant Havoc had come in a close second, averaging eight out of ten. Thunder was third. The Flathead wasn't as comfortable with a handgun as with a rifle, and he'd never shot an autoloading pistol before. Still, he'd dotted the bull's-eye or come near it about half the time. Kraft had shot the 45's on a par with his ranking with the M-16; four times out of ten he'd come close to center or hit it. Spader, again, would have been better off clubbing the target with a stout branch.

Blade gazed at the clock on his desk. Almost nine o'clock. General Gallagher and the recruit from the Civilized Zone would be arriving at any minute. He hoped the leader of the Civilized Zone, President Toland, had sent someone the equal of Sergeant Havoc, Boone, or Thunder. Someone with a knack for killing, someone who could hold their own in any situation.

His wish was granted.

The sound of a jeep grinding to a stop outside the bunker was followed by the slamming of a door and the thud of boots on the stairs leading down to the office.

Blade stared at the open doorway.

General Gallagher tramped inside. "I have your recruit," he announced, glancing around the office.

"Hello to you, General," Blade said.

Gallagher stared at the Warrior. "Sorry. I forgot my manners." He paused. "Say, you wouldn't happen to have anything to drink here, would you?"

"I do," Blade replied.

"What?" Gallagher asked eagerly.

"Water and milk," Blade responded.

Gallagher frowned. "That's it?"

"That's it."

"No hard liquor? No beer?" Gallagher asked.

"I don't drink. You know that," Blade reminded him.

General Gallagher rubbed his chin. "Pity," he remarked.

Blade sat up, his curiosity aroused. The general was behaving in an uncharacteristically nervous fashion. "Where's the recruit?"

Gallagher licked his thin lips. "I left him out in the jeep."

"Why didn't you bring him in?"

"I wanted to prepare you," Gallagher said.

Blade leaned forward. "Prepare me? For what?"

"I think you'd better see for yourself," the general stated, wheeling and striding from the office.

"Wait!" Blade called, but Gallagher was already gone. What was going on here? He stood and moved to the front of his desk, watching the doorway.

Moments later footsteps filled the short stairway.

General Gallagher entered the office first, quickly stepping to one side so the figure behind him could enter. The general was clearly jittery.

Distracted for a moment by the general's unusual conduct, Blade didn't look up until the new recruit sent by the Civilized Zone was a full yard into the room. When he did, his hands automatically dropped to his Bowies, and despite his years of experience as a Warrior, despite continually striving for total self-control, his mouth slackened in amazement and his gray eyes widened.

"What's the matter?" the newcomer asked in a low, raspy tone. "Ain't you never seen a mutant before?"

Blade had. Many, many times. Mutants had become commonplace since World War Three, and were divided into three distinct categories. The two most numerous groups had been spawned by the weaponry unleashed during the war. Ordinary mutants were wild creatures born with their genetic code scrambled. Their condition was believed to be the byproduct of the tremendous amounts of radiation the war had saturated the environment with, producing animals with two heads and six legs or any other quirky combination of genetic traits.

The second form of mutation was the consequence of chemical warfare. These were called mutates instead of simply mutants, and they were as different from mutants as night from day. Once afflicted—and only mammals, reptiles, and amphibians had been infected so far—they transformed into hideous monstrosities with insatiable appetites. Their bodies would become covered with pus-filled sores, and like ravenous shrews they would roam the countryside seeking prey.

The third category was the smallest numerically, but the sight of one belonging to it was enough to give any ordinary person a fleeting shock, if not more, because they so closely resembled humans. This category embraced the genetically engineered mutations, created in a scientist's test tube. Genetic engineering had been all the rage prior to the war. Scientists everywhere wanted to be the first to develop new, genetically improved species. Patents were granted. Enormous amounts of money changed hands. Headlines were made when the very first genetically engineered animal was produced, a "super mouse" to be used for research purposes. Next a "super rat" was bred, resulting in dire ramifications when a few of the super rats escaped from a lab and mated with their feral brethren occupying a sewer system underneath a major American metropolis. The result had been a new breed of nearly indestructible sewer rat with a superior intelligence and less fear of humans. Within a year the city had been overrun, and the scientists, predictably, had attempted to solve the problem by creating a breed of "super cat." And on and on it went.

Blade was intimately familiar with genetically engineered creatures. Several resided at the Family compound in Minnesota. They had defected to the Family years ago during the war against the nefarious scientific genius known as the Doktor.

"Cat got your tongue?" the new recruit queried mockingly.

"No," Blade blurted out, scrutinizing the creature before him.

The mutant was a fascinating hybrid, a cross between a human being and a bear. The genetically engineered mutations were produced by tampering with a typical human embryo, and with the right combination of elements a scientist could create any crossbreed desired: cat-men, dog-men, monkey-men, anything. This one was a bear-man, a biped with a human voice but decidedly ursine features. He wasn't all that tall, about five feet eight in height, but he was built like a powerhouse. His torso and limbs gave the impression of a certain density, a thickness derived from the possession of layer upon layer of muscles, and suggested incredible strength. The shoulders and upper arms especially were broad and endowed with bulging contours. His entire body, from head to toe, was covered with a short, light brown coat of fur. The face was singularly arresting: slightly concave cheeks, a pointed chin, elongated nostrils lightly coated with the fur, deep dark eyes, and a receding brow, all framed by a pair of small circular ears. The mutant's mouth was large, his lips thin, and when he spoke he revealed a set of tapered teeth.

Blade recovered his composure and walked up to the hybrid, his right hand outstretched. "Hello. Please forgive my rudeness. My name is Blade."

The mutant cocked his head to one side, studying the Warrior. "You're serious," he stated.

"About what?" Blade asked.

"About your apology," the mutant clarified.

"Of course," Blade assured him. "I shouldn't have gawked at you. It won't happen again."

"I believe you," the mutant said, finally shaking the Warrior's hand. He was wearing a black loincloth, but nothing else.

Blade smiled. The mutant's grip was firm. He glanced down and noticed the hybrid's hands were topped by unusually huge knuckles. The fingers were unusually thick and covered with light fur.

"I'm called Grizzly," the mutant said, introducing himself.

"I wonder why," Blade said, smiling.

Grizzly eyed the Warrior. "You sure are one of the biggest son of a bitches I've ever met! You wouldn't happen to be part mutant, would you?"

Blade snorted. "No. I doubt it."

"I know some of the mutants are giant suckers, just like you," Grizzly commented.

"In my case it's a matter of clean living and lots and lots of exercise," Blade said.

"We should arm-wrestle sometime," Grizzly suggested. "I haven't met a human yet I couldn't beat."

Blade stared at the mutant's shoulders and arms. "I'll bet."

General Gallagher stepped forward. "If you don't need me, I think I'll be getting back to L.A."

"We don't need you," Blade stated. "Not unless you want to stick around until tomorrow and observe our training sessions. In the morning we're conducting stealth tests."

"Stealth tests?" General Gallagher repeated.

"I want to see how quietly the recruits can move," Blade explained. "Their lives may hinge on how silently they can move during a mission."

"I don't need no stealth test," Grizzly remarked.

Blade looked at him. "All the recruits will take the test."

"I don't need one," Grizzly reiterated. "If I wanted to sneak up on you and cut your throat, you'd never hear me coming."

"Maybe. But you'll still take the test. None of the recruits are exempted from any of the exercises," Blade elaborated.

"I can see you're different from most humans," Grizzly commented. "You don't back down. Most humans are such wimps it's pitiful."

General Gallagher turned toward the door. "I'll be back in three days to check on your training progress. If there's anything you need, any way I can help, just let me know."

"Will do," Blade promised.

Gallagher took several strides, then stopped and glanced back. "Oh. I almost forgot. I have your uniforms in the jeep."

"Uniforms?" Blade said.

"The ones the Freedom Force will be wearing," Gallagher detailed. "Camouflage jobs. There are several for each of you."

"We probably won't be needing many of them," Blade mentioned.

Gallagher turned. "What are you talking about? This is a military unit. Everyone in the Force will wear a uniform."

"I'm in charge of the Force," Blade stated. "And I'll decide what we'll wear. If any of the recruits want to wear one, that's fine with me. But it won't be mandatory."

"That's stupid," Gallagher said, frowning. "Uniforms are essential to the maintenance of discipline, to instilling uniformity in the ranks."

"I don't want to instill uniformity," Blade declared.

"How do you expect to succeed as a unit if you don't?" General Gallagher queried skeptically. "Trust me on this. The military has been my life. I've spent almost thirty-five years in the Army. I know what I'm talking about."

"And so do I," Blade said.

"How so?" Gallagher asked.

"I'll use the Warriors as an example," Blade expounded. "The Warriors have successfully protected the Family and defended the Home for over a century. The Warriors function superbly, whether individually, in their respective Triads, or as a team. As head Warrior, I continued the practices established by my predecessors. Although I worked at maintaining discipline, I deliberately encouraged all Warriors to develop their unique skills and express their personality as they saw fit. The Warriors don't wear uniforms. Each Warrior wears the clothes he or she prefers. And the same holds true with weaponry. Each Warrior uses his or her favorite weapon or weapons. We have found that Warriors can be far more effective, far more deadly, if they're able to assert their personalities." He paused. "If you stifle individuality, you limit a person's capability."

General Gallagher shook his head. "I think you're making a mistake, but this is your show. The system you use at the Home has worked so well because there are only eighteen Warriors, not an entire army. The size makes a big difference."

"I agree," Blade said.

"You do?"

"Of course. I don't have an army at my disposal. There are only seven members of the Force, counting myself. I'll use the same techniques here I used on the Warriors," Blade stated.

General Gallagher shrugged. "Your choice. But don't say I didn't warn you if something goes wrong down the line. I'll leave the uniforms in the supply bunker, just in case."

"Thanks," Blade remarked.

Gallagher wheeled and departed.

"What you said makes sense to me," Grizzly commented. "I can't wear a uniform anyway."

"Can't or won't?" Blade questioned.

"Can't," Grizzly said. "You have no idea what clothing does to us mutant types. With all our fur or hair, clothing makes us itch like crazy. There's no way I'd wear a uniform."

"Then you won't have to," Blade assured him. He motioned at the door. "Why don't I escort you to the barracks and introduce you to the rest of the crew."

"Fine by me," Grizzly said.

They exited the office and climbed the stairs. The outer door swung open and they were enveloped by the cool night air.

Blade led the way to the east, the north wind ruffling his hair.

Grizzly sniffed the breeze, inhaling deeply. "I think I've found my supper."

"What?"

Grizzly pointed to the north. "There's a rabbit about twenty yards that way. After I meet the boys, I'm going to enjoy some fresh rabbit." He said the word "boys" sarcastically.

"There's food in the barracks," Blade disclosed. "There's no need to go hunting."

"I like to hunt," Grizzly mentioned. "I like the thrill of stalking and killing. And most of all, I like fresh, raw meat dripping in warm blood. Do you have any in the barracks?"

"No," Blade admitted.

Grizzly chuckled. "Didn't think so. I don't see how you humans can spoil your food the way you do."

"We spoil our food?"

"You sure do," Grizzly asserted. "You cook the meat and ruin the taste. And the sight of blood makes some of you sick! To top it off, you humans like to eat all that leafy green garbage. How disgusting!"

"You don't eat vegetables?" Blade inquired.

"I eat wild greens," Grizzly said. "Natural food. I won't eat anything you humans grow."

"Why not?"

"I've seen the gardens you humans plant," Grizzly stated. "You go to all the trouble to dig up the ground and plant a little seed and give it the water it needs, but then you spoil the whole thing by spreading horse shit or cow manure all over it to 'fertilize it,' as you call it. Yuck! How can anyone eat something grown from horse shit?"

Blade grinned. "I never thought of it that way."

Grizzly gazed at the barracks, about 40 yards away. "Where will I be sleeping?"

"In the barracks with the men," Blade answered.

"I thought you'd say that," Grizzly said. "Thanks, but no. I'll sleep out in the woods."

"What's wrong with the barracks?"

"Nothing, I guess. But I tend to make humans uncomfortable. It might be better for your men if I stay outside. I don't mind. I like the outdoors better anyway."

"But you're part of a team now," Blade remarked. "You should learn to live and work together."

"Aren't you the one who's so big on individuality?" Grizzly asked.

"You can sleep in the woods if you want," Blade said. "But I'd appreciate your giving the barracks a try. The men have to get used to you, and the sooner, the better."

"I'll think about it," Grizzly offered.

They walked in silence for ten yards.

Blade looked at his companion. "I wasn't aware there were

any mutants like yourself left in the Civilized Zone. I thought all
of them had been killed."

"Not by a long shot," Grizzly said, somewhat bitterly.
"There's a few dozen floating around."

"I'd like to ask a question," Blade said.

"What's stopping you?" Grizzly rejoined.

"I don't want to pry into your personal life, but there's
something I need to know," Blade stated.

"Like what?"

"A while back, my Family was involved in a war against a
man known as the Doktor. He was a scientist, a genetic
engineer. He had created hundreds, maybe thousands, of
genetically produced mutants like yourself. Three of them now
live at the Home." Blade paused. "I'd like to know if you were
created by the Doktor?"

"Yep," Grizzly responded, his tone slightly strained.

"Do you mind telling me about it?" Blade queried.

"What's to tell?" Grizzly rejoined. "The damn Doktor made
me, grew me from a cross between a human embryo and a
grizzly bear embryo, or some such bullshit. I don't understand
exactly how he did it. But the bastard did, and here I am."

"How did you survive the war?" Blade asked.

"I was in prison in Denver during the war," Grizzly divulged.
"I wasn't released until after your Family won the war, and after
President Toland became leader of the Civilized Zone."

Blade pursed his lips, reflecting. During World War Three,
after most of America's leaders were killed in a preemptive strike
on Washington, D.C., the government had withdrawn to
Denver, Colorado, and reorganized. A dictator had assumed the
reins, and the area he controlled had become known as the
Civilized Zone. The dictator's bloodline had ruled for a century,
until terminated by the Warriors. The people of the Civilized
Zone had established a representative form of government and
elected Toland as their President. As one of the members of the
Freedom Federation, the Civilized Zone was a staunch ally.
Blade knew Toland well. One of Toland's early acts after
being elected was to release all of those unjustly imprisoned by
the last of the dictators and the Doktor. "Why were you in
prison?" he inquired.

"The Doktor created his merry band of mutants for one

reason," Grizzly said. "To serve him hand and foot." He made a low growling sound. "Only I didn't cotton to being a slave, so he had me thrown in prison."

"Why did you volunteer for the Force?" Blade probed.

Grizzly sighed. "Because I wanted out of the Civilized Zone. I couldn't stand it there anymore."

"Why not?"

"The people were driving me nuts," Grizzly said. "Their attitude. There is a lot of resentment toward mutants because of what the Doktor and his loyal flunkies did. I could see the dislike on their faces. I could *feel* it!" he concluded bitterly.

"Do you think the people in California will be any different?" Blade asked.

"I doubt it," Grizzly said.

"But you came anyway," Blade noted.

"I figured I owed Toland for letting me out of that miserable prison," Grizzly stated. "Besides, I hear this Freedom Force will be kicking ass right and left." He smiled. "I like to kick ass."

They completed the walk to the barracks. Blade opened the door and descended to the living quarters. The building was 20 yards long by 15 wide, solidly built to withstand a direct mortar strike, constructed of concrete. Spacious accommodations were provided for the occupants. The entrance was located at the west end. Two rows of beds were near the entrance, allowing for a swift departure if necessary. Three of the beds were aligned along the north wall, three along the south. Beyond the sleeping section was the kitchen, amply stocked, where the Force members could fix meals to their own satisfaction. The easterly portion of the barracks contained the showers and toilet facilities.

The recruits were socializing, getting to know one another, slinging the bull while seated on the ends of their respective beds or on one of the chairs scattered about the room. Blade was pleased to see them getting along. Boone was sitting on the edge of the bed nearest the doorway along the north wall. Then came Thunder. Sergeant Havoc was seated in a chair next to his bed, polishing his combat boots. Along the south wall, Kraft was closest to the entrance. Spader occupied the next bunk. The last bed along the south wall was empty. The men looked up as the Warrior entered.

"What's this?" Kraft said, speaking up. "Are you here to tuck us in?" He laughed and Spader joined in.

"What's up, Blade?" Boone inquired.

Blade stayed framed in the doorway, obscuring their view of the mutant behind him. "I'm here to introduce your new teammate," he told them.

"The one from the Civilized Zone is here?" Sergeant Havoc remarked.

Blade nodded.

"Where is he?" Thunder queried.

"Right here," Blade said, and stepped to the right.

Grizzly nonchalantly strolled in.

Blade saw everyone in the room tense up, their expressions frozen in amazement. Sergeant Havoc recovered the quickest, composing himself almost instantly and nodding at Grizzly. Thunder seemed horrified. Boone did a double take, then smiled at the mutant. Kraft and Spader were speechless, and Spader's mouth was gaping wide enough to swallow his foot whole.

Kraft came up off his bed, his right hand in his coat pocket. "What the hell is this shit, dude?" he demanded curtly.

Blade indicated the mutant. "This is Grizzly. He is joining the Force."

"The hell you say!" Spader snapped.

Grizzly swung toward them, but otherwise didn't react.

"Grizzly is a part of our team," Blade said. "I expect you to show him the same respect you'd show me."

"I don't work with muties!" Kraft declared.

Grizzly sneered at the Clansman. "The feeling is mutual, jerk-off. I don't much like working with pissant humans!"

Kraft scowled. "Look at this! The freak can talk! Can you do any other tricks, freak?"

Grizzly took a menacing step toward Kraft. "Don't call me a freak," he warned.

"I'll call you any damn thing I want, freak!" Kraft rejoined. His right hand came out of his coat pocket, the switchblade snapping open, the blade gleaming in the glow from the four overhead lights powered by a generator housed in a small shed on the north side of the barracks.

Grizzly reacted in the twinkling of an eye, his furry body a blur as he closed in on Kraft. His left hand grabbed the front of

Kraft's black leather jacket and dangled the Clansman above the floor, while his right hand, the fingers and thumb rigid, swept to within six inches of Kraft's face.

Blade, standing slightly to one side, saw the Clansman's green eyes widen as the mutant's hands suddenly sprouted tapering claws. The claws materialized from the tips of Grizzly's fingers, the nails seeming to slide out of their full five-inch length, the tips an inch from Kraft's eyes.

"Say your prayers, turkey!" Grizzly snarled.

Blade took a step toward them. "Grizzly! Don't!"

"Why not?" Grizzly retorted, his feral gaze locked on Kraft. "I want to turn his brain into a pincushion."

Kraft, ever defiant, wagged the switchblade in his right hand. "Just try it, bastard!"

Grizzly snickered. "You thinking of sticking me with that toothpick of yours? Go ahead. You won't even faze me!"

"Grizzly! Release him!" Blade barked. "And that's an order!"

Grizzly glanced over his right shoulder. "An order?"

"You're in the Freedom Force now," Blade stated. "You volunteered. Like it or not, you're under my command. And I'm telling you to let him go."

Grizzly glared at Kraft. "You're one lucky pissant, you know that?" He opened his left hand and the Clansman dropped and almost fell.

"Kraft!" Blade directed. "Put the switchblade away!"

Kraft hesitated.

"You gave me your word earlier," Blade reminded him. "Or doesn't your word mean anything?"

Kraft frowned, but he closed the switchblade and replaced the knife in his pocket.

Grizzly relaxed his right hand, and as his fingers slowly slackened the claws retracted into the tips of his thick fingers.

Blade walked up to Kraft. "What do you have against mutants?"

"What's it to . . ." Kraft began, then stopped.

"I want to know what you have against mutants," Blade repeated.

"Nothing," Kraft mumbled.

"Nothing?" Blade didn't believe the Clansman for a moment. Kraft's hatred was genuine. There was something eating at him inside, something concerning mutants.

"Nothing," Kraft reiterated.

"If you don't want to tell me, that's your business," Blade said. "But Grizzly is part of the Force, whether you like the idea or not. He's your teammate, and you'll treat him the same way you treat the others. If you have any problems, you'll come to me. Understood?"

"Understood," Kraft replied gloomily.

Blade turned to the mutant. "And I don't want you turning anyone into a pincushion. Got it?"

Grizzly nodded.

"And what about you?" Blade asked, facing Spader. "Why don't you want Grizzly on the Force?"

Spader scrunched up his mouth. "Mutants give me the creeps!"

"That's it? That's your only reason?" Blade demanded.

"Can you think of a better one?" Spader responded.

"I can," Kraft snapped sullenly and marched off toward the kitchen.

"I knew this would happen," Grizzly said disgustedly. He walked to the doorway.

"Where are you going?" Blade queried.

"I'm going to sleep outside," Grizzly stated. "It'll be best for everybody."

"You don't have to," Blade said.

"Yes, I do," Grizzly disagreed. He departed.

Blade placed his hands on his hips and sighed in frustration.

"This isn't like being the head Warrior back at your Family, is it?" Boone asked.

"No," Blade admitted.

"Maybe you should look at the bright side," Boone suggested.

"What bright side?" Blade wanted to know.

"This can't get any worse," Boone said.

"Want to bet?" was Blade's rejoinder.

CHAPTER FOUR

The morning sun was just topping the eastern horizon when Blade emerged from the HQ bunker and stretched. Governor Melnick, at General Gallagher's request, had designed comfortable living quarters in the east end of the HQ for Blade's use. When he'd first seen the setup, Blade had asked to be housed in the barracks. General Gallagher had nixed the idea, claiming a commander should never reside in the same domicile as the troops. Propriety and all that. Blade had reluctantly agreed, only because the barracks had been designed to accommodate six people without overcrowding.

Something crunched to his right.

Blade glanced in the direction of the sound, surprised to find Grizzly already up and about. The mutant was crouched on his haunches at the edge of the trees, eating something. Blade walked over.

Grizzly looked up. He was feasting on a squirrel. His lips and chin were coated with blood, as were his hands. A chunk of stringy flesh protruded from his mouth. His dark eyes locked on the Warrior, his nose twitching.

"Morning," Blade said. "I didn't expect to find anyone up yet."

Grizzly gulped the mouthful of squirrel. "I've been up for an hour. I was beginning to think you were going to sleep the day away."

Blade grinned. "Do you always get up this early?"

"Always," Grizzly said. "When you sleep outdoors, you can feel the morning coming long before you see the sun. Haven't you noticed how the birds and other day animals are up way before sunlight?"

"I've noticed," Blade replied. "I like the outdoors."

Grizzly gazed at the forest to the north. "So do I," he stated fondly. "Sometimes I think I'd like to chuck all this civilization crap and go live in the woods somewhere."

"Why haven't you?" Blade asked.

Grizzly frowned. "Because part of me is human, and my human self wants to fit in. I consider it my curse."

Blade studied the mutant. "I get the impression you're not very fond of humans."

Grizzly laughed, a short, harsh burst. "You've got that right! Humans are the scum of the earth."

"Why do you feel that way?" Blade probed. "Because a lot of humans don't like you?"

"I couldn't care less!" Grizzly declared testily.

"Then why don't you like humans?" Blade pressed him. If he was going to effectively function as the Force leader, then he needed to know what made his recruits tick. He wanted to learn their motivations for joining. In Boone's case, it was out of loyalty to his best friend, the head of the Cavalry. Spader had been compelled to enlist. Thunder, thankfully, had volunteered. Kraft had volunteered, but only because he wanted to meet women and indulge his taste for violence. Sergeant Havoc had joined out of a sense of patriotism. And Grizzly had claimed he owed a debt to President Toland. But did the mutant have an ulterior motive?

"I don't like humans for a lot of reasons," Grizzly said.

"Name one," Blade prompted.

"I'll give you more than one," Grizzly declared, rising, forgetting about the partially consumed squirrel. "Humans think the world owes them a living. They're selfish, vain, and arrogant. I can't stand the stench of them!"

"We're not all that bad," Blade commented.

"Aren't you? Who was responsible for World War Three? Humans?" Grizzly asked.

"Humans," Blade conceded.

"So the lousy humans wiped out half of their kind on the

planet," Grizzly said. "And in the bargain they polluted the world for centuries to come. How can you stand there and tell me humans aren't scum?"

"There are some rotten apples," Blade acknowledged. "But you can't judge the entire human race by the actions of a few."

"A few?" Grizzly snickered.

"Compared to the total, yes," Blade went on. "The majority of humans are fairly decent. They go about their daily lives trying to put enough food on the table for their loved ones. They don't want to hurt others."

"They did a good job, though, didn't they?" Grizzly noted. "Where were all the good humans when the bad ones destroyed their civilization?"

"The bad ones were in power," Blade observed. "My Family has thoroughly researched the period. The power-mongers ruled the people with an iron hand, and the majority of the populace didn't even know it."

"So humans are stupid as well as scum!" Grizzly declared.

"Not all humans," Blade said. "My Family has done a remarkable job over the past century of fostering the higher ideals of love and faith. We are a very spiritual group."

"Spiritual? Does your Family believe in God?" Grizzly inquired.

"Of course," Blade answered. "We are each encouraged to develop our own consciousness of the Spirit Source."

Grizzly chuckled. "And here I thought you had a head on your shoulders!"

"I don't?"

"Not if you believe in God," Grizzly said. "There is no God!"

"There is," Blade asserted.

Grizzly suddenly became angry. "Don't give me that! If there's a God, then why did we have World War Three? Where was this high and mighty God of yours when millions and millions were dying, melted in their tracks by the nuclear blasts or slowly poisoned by the radiation? Where was God when the Doktor attacked your home? Why did God let the damn Doktor create misfits like me? Part human, part animal, and we don't fit in either world!"

"You can't blame God for all the suffering in the world," Blade stated.

"Can't I?" Grizzly snapped.

Blade's forehead creased. He had inadvertently touched a nerve in the mutant. Grizzly was furious. But why? What was simmering below the mutant's surface?

Grizzly crammed the remainder of the squirrel into his mouth, chewing noisily, his teeth crunching the bones, blood spilling over his chin.

"I'll go wake the others and we'll begin our training," Blade said. He walked toward the barracks, wondering what his day had in store.

Little did he know.

Two hours later, after breakfast and a period of rigorous calisthenics, Blade led the recruits to a knoll in the northern third of the compound.

"What are we doing here, dude?" Kraft asked.

"This is where we will conduct our first training exercise," Blade explained.

"I hope we don't have to do more push-ups," Spader commented wearily. "I'm not used to all this shit."

"No more push-ups," Blade assured him. "This will be a stealth test."

"Like what's a stealth test?" Kraft queried.

"I'm going to sit on the top of the knoll," Blade said, pointing at the crest approximately 20 yards distant. "I'll have my back to you. When I call your names, you will take turns trying to approach me without being heard. It's that simple."

"What will we do next?" Kraft quipped. "Play hide-and-seek?"

Blade started up the knoll. "Now remember. Wait your turn. If I hear you, I'll let you know. Come back down and wait with the rest."

"What's our prize, man?" Kraft inquired jokingly.

"You might live a little longer if you learn to reach me without being heard," Blade said.

"I was hoping for some doughnuts or cookies," Kraft remarked. "There isn't any sweet stuff in the kitchen."

"Sweets pollute the system," Blade mentioned. "They interfere with your bodily functions."

"Yeah, but they taste so yummy," Kraft said, licking his lips.

Blade walked to the top of the knoll and sat with his back to the recruits. He glanced down once, noting Grizzly was standing aloof from the group. Then he faced due north. "Spader!" he shouted.

"What?" Spader yelled up.

Blade peered over his right shoulder, his eyes narrowing. "Start up the hill!"

Kraft was laughing at Spader.

"Oh! Right!" Spader called. He moved upwards.

Blade turned away, sitting cross-legged, listening. He could hear birds to the west and the wind rustling the trees. Closing his eyes, he concentrated on detecting the faintest sound. He doubted the Mole would get very far, and a minute or two later he was proven right.

A twig gave a loud snap.

Blade looked over his shoulder, spotting Spader 15 yards away circling a dead bush. "Spader! Back down!"

Spader stared at the Warrior in astonishment. "You heard me?"

"Let me put it this way," Blade said. "An elephant would have done a better job!"

Spader's shoulders slumped and he returned to the bottom.

"Kraft! You're next!" Blade ordered, putting his broad back to the slope. He tilted his head, breathing deeply, his hands in his lap, waiting for the Clansman to betray his ascent. The minutes seemed to drag.

Something thudded to his rear.

Blade gazed over his shoulder again.

Kraft was over ten yards below. The Clansman had tried to cross a stretch of ground strewn with small rocks. He had dislodged one of the stones and sent it tumbling down the bank.

"Back down!" Blade instructed.

Kraft, clearly disappointed, ambled toward the bottom.

"Boone next!" Blade bellowed.

The Cavalryman did much better than the Mole and the Clansman. After cautiously advancing to within five feet of the Warrior, he took a hasty step.

Blade heard the crackle of a dry blade of grass and spun, grinning. "Not bad."

"It wasn't good enough," Boone remarked. "I'd be dead right now if you were an enemy."

"You'll do better next time," Blade said. "Send up Sergeant Havoc next."

"Will do."

Blade settled himself, straining his senses. He was saving the best for last. Boone was an outstanding gunman, but the Cavalryman didn't have much experience at clandestine maneuvers. Havoc, Thunder, and Grizzly, on the other hand, should do extremely well.

They did.

Minutes later, Blade detected the faintest of disturbances immediately behind him and whirled.

Sergeant Havoc was a mere foot away, reaching for the Warrior. Caught unawares, he straightened. "You heard me, sir?"

"I sensed you," Blade stated.

"First you handle Kraft like he's an amateur, when we both know the loudmouth is pretty sharp with that switchblade of his, and now this," Havoc commented by way of a compliment. "I'm looking forward to training under you. I think you can teach me some new tricks of the trade."

"Thanks," Blade said. "I'll do my best." He paused. "Tell Thunder to give the test a try next."

Sergeant Havoc nodded and headed down the knoll.

Blade resumed his original position, draining himself of all internal distractions, focusing on the rhythms of the forest and synchronizing his breathing accordingly. He lost all track of time, his mind drifting, his senses primed. The breeze caressed his skin. Suddenly he knew he wasn't alone on the knoll; he felt another presence close at hand and he spun.

Thunder's right hand was mere inches from the Warrior's spine. The Flathead smiled at being discovered. "The Warriors are all I have heard they are," he mentioned.

"You're as good as any Warrior," Blade said. He stared at the group below. "Would you send up Grizzly?"

"Yes," Thunder responded, "but there is a trifling matter we must discuss before I do."

"What is it?" Blade queried.

"It concerns the one called Grizzly," Thunder said.

"I saw the look on your face last night," Blade noted. "You didn't seem too happy about Grizzly being here, but at least you didn't say anything."

"I would not cause dissension," Thunder stated. "But I am troubled, and I feel I can talk to you frankly and openly."

"Why are you troubled?" Blade inquired.

Thunder gazed at the mutant. "Are you very familiar with Indian ways?"

"One of my best friends is an Indian," Blade divulged. "His name is Geronimo. He's a Warrior, like me."

"Then maybe you know about our affinity for nature, the respect in which we hold all life, and our reverence for the Supreme Being," Thunder said.

"Your people and my Family have a lot in common," Blade observed.

"My people also believe in omens and signs," Thunder stated. "And the mutant among us is a bad sign."

"Grizzly is just a mutant," Blade pointed out.

Thunder looked at the Warrior. "True, and not true. Many of my people consider the mutants to be demons. They are not part of the order of things, of the natural way. Mutants were not created by the Spirit-In-All-Things, but by white men for vile purposes. Years ago the Doktor sent his mutants against us and we were nearly distroyed." He paused. "I repeat. The mutant is a bad omen. I do not like him among us."

"I understand you," Blade said. "But I can not ask Grizzly to leave. If you want to go, though, it's okay by me. The Flatheads are welcome to send another volunteer."

Thunder drew himself up to his full height. "I will not bring dishonor to my people by leaving. I have said what I had to say, and I will say no more." He turned and walked off.

Blade put his back to the group again. Now he had three men who didn't want Grizzly in the force. What was he supposed to do? He certainly couldn't boot Grizzly out; the mutant deserved a chance to prove himself as much as anyone else. Should he send Kraft and Spader back to their homes? No. Doing so would only aggravate the problem. The Clan and the Moles might refuse to send someone to replace them. Maybe if he gave the recruits enough time they would come to accept the mutant. Maybe. But it was a long shot.

He'd better concentrate on the job at hand.

Blade closed his eyes, repeating the focusing technique he'd used before, waiting for the mutant to make a mistake. He waited. And waited. And just when he was beginning to wonder if Grizzly had decided not to take the test, someone tapped him on the shoulder.

"I knew you woke up too early," quipped a familiar raspy voice. "What are you doing? Taking a nap? I didn't think we could sleep on the job."

Blade swiveled to face the mutant, grinning. "Congratulations. I never heard you."

"What did I tell you last night?" Grizzly asked.

"What I said then still goes," Blade said. "Just because you are more skillful in some regards does not excuse you from the training exercises."

"I just hope I don't get bored to death," Grizzly cracked.

"If you die, it won't be from boredom," Blade predicted.

"So what's the next test?" Grizzly queried. "Thumb sucking?"

"Unarmed combat."

Grizzly grinned. "Now you're talking my kind of language."

"I thought you'd like it," Blade said, rising.

The hand-to-hand combat session was held in the early afternoon. Blade had ordered mats to be brought from the supply bunker and aligned in front of the HQ. He deposited his Bowies on the north edge of the mat, then faced the recruits. They were seated in single file along the southern edge, Grizzly off to one side, to the east. "The purpose of this session is to see how you'd hold up without your weapons," Blade began. "There will be no actual training. All I want you to do is to try and hit me. Any questions?"

Kraft laughed. "All we have to do is knock your block off?"

"That's it," Blade said.

Kraft bounded to his feet. "Then take me first, dude. I want to make up for yesterday."

"Dream on," Boone interjected.

Kraft strutted onto the mat. "You know what they say. The bigger they are, the harder they fall."

"Yeah, I know what they say," Boone chimed in. "Ignorance is bliss."

Kraft chuckled. "Just watch me, smart guy." He shifted his legs apart and assumed a crude horse stance.

Blade, his arms folded across his chest, nodded. "Whenever you're ready."

"I was born ready," Kraft retorted. Evidently, he had received some martial-arts instruction. He closed in on the Warrior and aimed a vicious side kick at the giant's left knee.

Blade effortlessly evaded the Clansman's sweeping right leg. He gripped Kraft's right ankle and tugged, upending the cocky recruit and unceremoniously dumping Kraft onto his posterior.

Spader was tittering.

Kraft rose to his feet, a study in indignation. "Let's go for two out of three," he proposed.

"Take a seat," Blade directed, glancing at Spader. "You're next," he instructed the Mole.

Spader walked onto the mat while Kraft sat down. "I'm not much of a fighter," the Mole admitted.

"Give it your best shot," Blade urged.

Spader came in swinging his fists like a wild man.

Blade sidestepped the Mole's flailing arms, then hooked his left leg behind Spader's legs and did a reverse sweep.

Spader was dumped onto his back.

Kraft cackled. "And I thought I did bad!"

Blade pointed at Boone. "Let's go."

The Cavalryman approached the Warrior slowly, his fists upraised to protect his chin and his stomach. He closed in, darting and weaving, boxing.

Blade reacted in kind, blocking the majority of Boone's blows. The Cavalryman did not wield his fists anywhere near as expertly as he did his revolvers, but he was no slouch either. Twice Blade was struck, once a glancing blow to the ribs and again a flicking jab on the chin. After several minutes Blade disengaged, stepping to the right and smiling. "Where'd you learn to box?"

"My dad taught me," Boone replied.

"Do you know any of the martial arts?" Blade inquired.

"Never had any call to learn," Boone said. "I can use my fists, but I prefer to let my Hombres do my talking."

Blade glanced at the Flathead. "Your turn."

Thunder slowly rose and stepped onto the mat, rubbing his palms together, while Boone sat down.

"What style do you like?" Blade asked.

"I am not much of a boxer," Thunder revealed. "But I do like wrestling."

"Then we'll wrestle," Blade said. "The first one to pin the other wins."

They grappled, rolling and tumbling on the mat, working up a sweat. Blade was clearly the larger and the stronger, but Thunder wrestled with a sinewy, elusive skill, narrowly evading pin after pin. Once Thunder succeeded in applying a full nelson to the Warrior. Before the Flathead could savor his seemingly inevitable victory, Blade's shoulders and arms bulged as he strained against the hold. Try as he might, Thunder was unable to retain his grip. His hands were forcibly wrenched from the nape of Blade's neck, and the next instant the Warrior whirled and bore Thunder to the mat, pinning him.

"Not bad," Blade commented, standing and offering his right hand.

Thunder allowed himself to be hauled to his feet. "If you keep this up," he joked, "you're liable to give me a complex."

Blade grinned, then faced Sergeant Havoc. "You're up next."

Havoc's blue eyes sparkled. "I've been looking forward to this. How do you want to do it?"

"Try and take me out," Blade instructed.

"Brace yourself," Havoc warned, and promptly closed in.

Blade was compelled to retreat several paces by the furious flurry of hand and foot blows Sergeant Havoc delivered. He realized General Gallagher had not exaggerated; Havoc was indeed an expert in hand-to-hand combat. But Blade's prowess was likewise exceptional. All of the Warriors had been exhaustively trained in the martial arts by one of the Family Elders. Some of them relied on the martial arts more than others in combat situations, and one of the Warriors, a diminutive Oriental by the name of Rikki-Tikki-Tavi, was the undisputed unparalleled martial artist of the Family. While Blade wasn't quite the equal of Rikki where the martial arts were concerned, he was second to no one else.

Sergeant Havoc had waded into the Warrior full of confidence and optimism. In dozens upon dozens of regulation matches and tournaments throughout California, he had proven his superiority time and again. He was virtually a legend in the California Army, and he was not accustomed to finding an opponent capable of withstanding his aggressive tactics. So when he perceived, after two minutes of sustained sparring, that he could not penetrate Blade's guard, his frustration caused his undoing.

Blade ducked and slid to the left, avoiding a spinning back kick. He expected the sergeant to assume a defensive posture, perhaps the Kokutsu-tachi or the Neko-ashi-tachi, but instead Havoc swung his left leg in a Mawashi-seashi-geri, a roundhouse kick, providing the opening Blade needed. As Havoc's left foot swished past Blade's chin, the Warrior closed in, driving his left instep against the back of the sergeant's right knee. Havoc, perched on only his right foot, was carried forward by his own momentum, falling onto the mat. He rebounded immediately, shoving himself erect.

"Damn!" the sergeant exclaimed. "You did it to me again."

"I was lucky," Blade said.

"Yeah, sure," Havoc said, obviously disappointed in his performance. "I think Thunder is right. If you keep this up, you're going to give all of us a complex."

"I won't," Blade assured him. "I promise."

Havoc grinned. "I hope not." He marched to the edge of the mat.

Blade turned toward the mutant. Grizzly was seated on the ground near the mat, his chin in his hands, a look of boredom on his face. "Do you think you can do any better?"

Grizzly smirked and stood. "You must be joking." He casually strolled onto the mat. "You won't beat me."

"I will," Blade declared, his simple response laced with conviction.

Grizzly chuckled. "What did you do at lunchtime? Sniff glue?"

Blade smiled. "Do you have a style you prefer?"

"I don't go in for any of that fancy footwork," Grizzly stated. "And I'm not much for wrestling or boxing. I like the direct approach." So saying, he raised his right hand, his fingers rigid, and his claws popped into view.

"I've been meaning to ask you about those," Blade said. "How do they work, anyway?"

Grizzly walked up to the Warrior, extending his right arm. "Watch," he directed, starting to relax his hand. As he did, the five-inch claws automatically retracted into his fingers, sliding *over the fingernails*.

Blade's gray eyes narrowed. His initial observation had been wrong! The fingernails were *not* part of the claws. "I thought your nails were the tips of your claws," he remarked.

"They're not," Grizzly confirmed. "I haven't dissected my fingers or anything, you understand. But as near as I can figure, this is the way they work." He tapped his large knuckles. "The claws are housed behind my knuckles. There must be tubes of some kind running from my knuckles to the tips of my fingers. Do you see this?" He used his left hand to carefully pry open a flap of skin and fur located behind the fingernail on the middle finger of his right hand, revealing a hole the width of one of his claws.

Blade understood. "So your claws are fitted into the upper part of your hand, between your knuckles and your wrist. When your fingers go stiff, the claws slid down the sheaths in your fingers and come out those holes behind the fingernails," he deduced.

"That's the way I see it," Grizzly agreed.

"It's like having five built-in knives in each hand," Blade marveled. "I've never seen anything like it."

"Me neither," Grizzly said. "I know other mutants who have claws and talons and such, but none of them just pop out like mine."

"How sturdy are your claws?" Blade inquired.

"Sturdy enough," Grizzly replied. "They will break, but only under massive pressure. I broke one once when I was in prison. I tried to cut my way through a metal door."

"Your claws will cut metal?" Blade queried in disbelief.

"They'll hold their own against swords and knives," Grizzly said. "But I found out the hard way they won't cut through metal. They will cut a human to ribbons."

"I can imagine," Blade remarked. He wheeled and walked over to his Bowies, scooped them up, and replaced the big knives in their sheaths. "Let's put them to the test," he suggested, facing the mutant.

"What?" Grizzly responded.

"A little test," Blade said. "Your claws against my Bowies."

"How will we tell who wins?" Grizzly asked.

"If you're as good as you claim you are," Blade replied, "then you should be able to break through my guard and nick me on the arm, no problem."

"That's the craziest idea I've ever heard," Grizzly declared.

"What's wrong with the idea?" Blade countered.

"What if one of your Bowies slips? What if my claws slip? What if I miscalculate? You could lose an arm," Grizzly said.

"Every day we live we encounter risks," Blade mentioned. "Some are greater, some lesser. Either way, life goes on."

"I still say you're nuts," Grizzly opined.

Blade shrugged. "That's okay. If you don't want to do the test, I understand. There's no shame in admitting you couldn't win."

"I never said I couldn't win," Grizzly noted.

"You don't want to do it," Blade said. "That's the same thing in my book."

"Oh, it is, is it?" Grizzly held his left hand aloft, then his right, his fingers tensed, and his claws snapped free, gleaming in the afternoon sun. "I was just thinking of you, dummy. I kind of like you, and I didn't want to hurt you." He stared at the Warrior. "But no lousy human challenges me like you did and gets away with it. So let's get this over with."

Blade drew his Bowies and crouched, wondering if he'd bitten off more than he could chew. His job as the head of the Force required him to assess the abilities of each recruit. Goading the mutant into a mock duel might not be the brightest idea he'd ever had, but at least he'd discover, firsthand, the extent of Grizzly's capabilities.

Grizzly grinned as he sprang for the Warrior, his claws slashing.

Blade backed up under the onslaught, deflecting each swipe of those deadly claws with his Bowies. The mutant's reflexes were superb, and Blade was hard pressed to evade Grizzly's lashing strikes. The Bowies and the claws produced a clicking and scraping noise as they met and slid apart.

"Come on, Blade!" Kraft cheered from the sidelines.

Blade concentrated on blocking the mutant's blows, seeking an opening, but Grizzly's streaking claws were everywhere. During his training for Warrior status, and over the course of his years as a Warrior, Blade had engaged in countless training exercises with his fellow Warriors. Many of the practice drills had involved the use of edged weaponry: knife fights, sword duels, ax contests, and more. Blade had fought with the best of the best. Or so he'd believed.

Until now.

Grizzly was incredible. His speed and strength was uncanny, and added to those traits was his inherent ruthlessness. The longer he fought, the more bestial he became, his visage distorted by a snarl, his eyes focal points of ferocity.

Blade backpedaled, thwarting the mutant's rain of claws. In the recesses of his mind a doubt began to form, a doubt Grizzly would ever make a mistake. If he was going to win, he needed a clever strategy to turn the tide. But what? Inspiration struck a second later.

Grizzly lunged, bringing both powerful arms around in an arc, aiming a crisscrossing pattern at the Warrior's broad chest.

Blade reacted by extending his arms, his Bowies clashing against the mutant's claws and locking for a moment. The pair strained, their arm muscles rippling. And that was when Blade saw his chance. He took the mutant by surprise by doing the completely unexpected; he released his left Bowie. The abrupt letup of pressure caused Grizzly to lose his balance. The mutant started to fall forward, and before Grizzly could regain his balance the contest was over. Blade drove his left hand down and in, locking his fingers on Grizzly's throat, even as he flashed his right Bowie toward Grizzly's face.

Grizzly instinctively tried to recoil from the glittering blade.

Blade stopped his strike with the tip of his Bowie barely touching the mutant's nostrils. He grinned and tapped Grizzly's nose. "I trust you won't hold it against me if I don't draw blood," he commented.

Grizzly was dumbfounded. He gaped at the Bowie near his nose, then at the Warrior. "No one's ever beat me before," he blurted out in astonishment.

"There's always a first time for everything," Blade remarked, straightening.

Grizzly held his claws in front of his face. "I must be slowing down."

Blade chuckled as he replaced his right Bowie in its sheath on his hip. He spotted his other Bowie on the mat and retrieved it.

Someone began clapping from the sidelines.

Blade glanced over Grizzly's right shoulder.

Boone had risen and was clapping, a grin creasing his features. "That was the greatest exhibition I've ever seen," he said, commending them.

"Me too," Sergeant Havoc added. "And I've seen more than my share of combat."

Kraft made a show of stretching and yawning. "I've seen better," he commented. "It was no great shakes, man."

"I've never been beaten before," Grizzly mumbled to himself, sounding dejected.

"Don't take it so hard," Blade advised. "It was just a training exercise."

Grizzly studied the giant. "I know there are other Warriors where you come from. Are they all as good as you?"

"Some are better," Blade replied.

"Better?" Grizzly repeated skeptically.

"Each Warrior possesses individual strengths," Blade said. "Most of us have tended to specialize. I like Bowies. One of the other Warriors is partial to Colt Python revolvers. Another uses a tomahawk. And still another prefers a katana. They are better with their weapons than I could ever hope to be."

"I'd like to meet them some day," Grizzly remarked.

"Maybe you will," Blade said. He gazed from one recruit to the next, pleased at the expressions he beheld. With one exception, Kraft, they were staring at him with varying measures of respect in their eyes. Perfect. His plan had worked. He'd needed to garner their respect if he was to entertain any hope of leading them. With their respect would come obedience. He could have intimidated them into complying with his commands, but earning their respect was wiser. Now he would also have their loyalty, and loyalty was preferable to fear any day. Give him another two months, and he would whip them into a crack fighting unit.

But he wasn't to get the two months.

CHAPTER FIVE

Blade was at his desk, reviewing the makeup of his team and analyzing their respective weaknesses, when he heard a jeep pull to a stop outside. He looked at the clock on his desk. Ten-fifteen. Who would be arriving at such a late hour? General Gallagher? But Gallagher had said he would not return for three days. So who could it be?

Moments later the general strode into the office without knocking. "Hello, Blade," he greeted the Warrior somberly.

"Hello, General," Blade said. "This is a surprise. I wasn't expecting you for a few days."

"And I wasn't planning to come back so soon," Gallagher stated. "But something came up." He crossed to a chair in front of the desk and sat down.

"What could be so important?" Blade asked, leaning back in his metal chair.

"How did your training go today?" General Gallagher inquired.

"Fine," Blade answered. "The recruits show promise."

"How long will you need to get them ready for their first mission?" Gallagher probed.

"Our agreement was I could have two months, minimum," Blade reminded the officer. "Governor Melnick said I could have more time, if needed."

"That wasn't what I wanted to know," Gallagher said. "How long will you need to get them ready?"

"I intend to take the full two months," Blade informed the general. "I'm not about to take these men out into the field unprepared."

"I can appreciate your sentiments," Gallagher stated. "But you don't have two months."

Blade sat up. "What? Why not?"

"Because something has come up," General Gallagher disclosed. "You'll need to get them ready sooner."

"How much time are you talking about?" Blade asked.

Gallagher hesitated before responding. "Two weeks."

Blade came up out of his chair. "Two weeks! Are you insane! I can't have them ready in two weeks!"

"You must get them ready," Gallagher said. "It's imperative."

"No way," Blade reiterated.

Gallagher sighed. "I knew you'd say that. I even told Governor Melnick you wouldn't go for the idea. But he insisted. He said the lives of dozens of women are at stake."

"What women?" Blade questioned.

"Why don't you calm down and have a seat," Gallagher suggested. "I'll explain everything."

Blade sat back down. "I'm listening," he announced gruffly.

General Gallagher cleared his throat. "Like I said, something has come up. Something requiring our immediate attention."

"Like what?"

"Are you familiar with northern California?" Gallagher inquired.

"No," Blade admitted.

"The country is real rugged up there," Gallagher detailed. "There are a lot of mountains and rivers and the densest forest you'd ever want to see. It's all very remote, and in some places almost inaccessible. There weren't a lot of people there before the war, and now there are even less."

"Does your Army patrol this area?" Blade interrupted.

"We patrol around it," Gallagher responded. "Going through it would take weeks, if not months. As far as we know, there aren't any Raiders operating in the area because there are so few towns to raid. There are a lot of wild mutants, and we keep them away from the inhabited outposts."

"Are there any big towns at all?"

"There are a few along the coast, but that's at the west end, and the part I'm talking about is the Marble Mountain Wilderness in the center of the state. The nearest town is called Yreka. It has a population of about six thousand," Gallagher said, then paused, frowning. "About two weeks ago a young woman was brought into Yreka by a family living in Ft. Jones, a small community of about five hundred southwest of Yreka. You see, Yreka has a doctor and Ft. Jones doesn't, and the young woman was badly in need of medical attention. She was starving to the point of wasting away and had a touch of pneumonia. The doctor reports she was on her last legs, but she has recovered pretty much since."

"Was this woman from Ft. Jones?" Blade queried.

"No," Gallagher replied. "She was pulled from the Scott River near Ft. Jones by a fisherman and his son. She was close to drowning when they found her."

"If she wasn't from Ft. Jones, then where did she come from?" Blade questioned.

"No one knew where she was from until she was able to talk," General Gallagher said. "And this is where the story starts to get hairy. Her name is Athena Morris, and she was officially declared dead seven years ago."

"Dead?" Blade repeated, puzzled.

"Dead," Gallagher affirmed. "She was a journalist from LA on her way to Yreka to do a story when the plane she was in went down. The CAP launched a search for the plane, but they never found a trace of the wreckage. According to her, the plane developed mechanical problems and crashed on a ridge in the Marble Mountain Wilderness, killing the pilot."

"So where has she been for seven years?" Blade asked.

"I'll get to that," Gallagher promised. "We've run a background check on her. She was a top reporter for the *Times*, on her way to Yreka to cover the extensive flooding they had there seven years ago. She had a reputation for honesty and accuracy. I've met her. She's the independent type, a very strong woman. She must be if she survived the hell she went through."

Blade leaned on his elbows, all attention.

"Morris claims she was captured and held prisoner in a secluded valley in the Marble Mountain Wilderness. She says there are other women still being held there. About two dozen," General Gallagher divulged.

"Being held prisoner by whom?" Blade wanted to know.

"I'd rather let her tell you that," Gallagher said.

"Is she here now?" Blade inquired.

"She's in LA," Gallagher stated. "If you're willing, I will come back tomorrow morning with Morris and Governor Melnick. Hear her out. Maybe let her address your men. It's their lives on the line if they go on this mission."

"Why didn't she come along now?" Blade asked. "Why wait until tomorrow?"

General Gallagher stared into the Warrior's eyes. "Because I didn't want to spring this on you cold. I could have phoned, but I wanted to see your reaction when I told you. Governor Melnick wants to rescue the other women as quickly as possible. If you could have your unit ready in two weeks, you can go in after them."

"I don't understand," Blade confessed. "Why us? Why the Force? Why not send in some of your commandos or regular Army troops?"

"There are a couple of reasons," Gallagher mentioned. "First, we don't know the exact location of this remote valley. Morris has a vague idea where it might be, but that's it. So your unit stands as good a chance as any of ours at finding the site, maybe even better because you have an Indian with you. Thunder told me he's an excellent tracker. Secondly, another of your team is ideally suited for the job, considering what you might be up against."

"Who? And what?"

"You'll understand better tomorrow," Gallagher said.

"I have an idea," Blade observed. "Why not search for this valley from the air? Why not drop in your soldiers by parachute? Why go in on foot?"

"Because the site is camouflaged and hidden from the air," Gallagher replied. "They have lookouts on the ridge and can see a plane coming for miles. Morris doubts we could find them from the air. They'd take cover before we got there."

"I still don't like using the Force for this," Blade said. "The recruits haven't been trained to function as a team yet."

"Then that's another reason to use them," General Gallagher

commented.

"What do you mean?" Blade queried.

"This mission could be extremely dangerous," Gallagher stated. "None of you could come back alive. Have you ever noticed how danger has a way of drawing people closer together? Your recruits don't function as a team now, but if they survive the mission I can guarantee they'll be one."

"Do or die, huh?"

Gallagher shrugged. "Life is rough. What can I tell you?"

"You can tell me I'm asleep and dreaming all of this," Blade said.

"Sorry. So what's your decision? Do I bring Morris and the governor up here tomorrow morning, or what?" General Gallagher asked.

"If it was up to me, I'd say no," Blade responded. "But you're right. The men must decide this one. Bring Morris up. We'll hear what she has to say."

General Gallagher rose, smiling. "I knew I could count on you. Thanks. You won't regret this?"

"I hope you're right," Blade said gloomily.

Gallagher walked toward the door. "Don't worry about it. Try and get a good night's sleep," he advised.

"You must be kidding."

CHAPTER SIX

Athena Morris was a singularly attractive woman. Her appeal
was not so much her figure, which was slim and athletic, but the
quality of assurance she projected. Her fine brown hair fell past
her shoulders, accenting her yellow blouse. She also wore tan
slacks and brown shoes. Her alert brown eyes scrutinized the six
recruits standing five yards in front of her.

Blade stood to the woman's right, his hands clasped behind his
back. To the woman's left was General Gallagher and Governor
Melnick, a hefty man with dark hair, blue eyes, and perpetually
congenial features, wearing an immaculate blue suit. Blade gazed
from the governor to Morris, appraising her profile. Her cheekbones were high and prominent, her lips thin. He thought he
detected a certain toughness about her.

The six recruits were eyeing the woman speculatively,
obviously wondering what in the hell was going on. Blade had
told them nothing. After their morning workout and meal,
Gallagher had arrived with his visitors. Blade had formed a single
file in front of the HQ: Havoc was on the left, then Grizzly,
Boone, Thunder, Kraft and Spader.

"So what's the deal, cutey?" Kraft unexpectedly addressed the
woman. "Are you a nurse here to give us an exam? You can start
with my privates!" he suggested lewdly.

Spader cackled.

Governor Melnick reddened, General Gallagher frowned, and Blade took a step toward Kraft.

Morris held out her right arm, halting the giant. She looked up into his eyes. "There's no need," she said. "I can handle this."

"Whatever you want," Blade said.

Morris stared at Kraft, her gaze frigid. "I am not a nurse," she informed him. "And as for your privates, I stopped playing with marbles years ago."

Boone, Grizzly, and Spader burst into laughter. Sergeant Havoc, standing at attention, couldn't suppress a grin. Thunder smiled.

Kraft glared at Morris. "I don't think you know who you're messing with, lady."

"I'm beginning to have my doubts," Morris stated. "I was told you men are known as the Freedom Force, that you're professionals. But maybe they confused you with a grade-school class."

Boone slapped his right thigh in merriment.

"She's got your number," Grizzly said to the irate Clansman. Spader tittered.

Blade took two strides forward, his gray eyes sweeping the line. The men promptly sobered, straightening to attention. Kraft's jaw twitched, but he stayed silent. "I don't want any remarks out of any of you until the time comes for you to speak," Blade directed. "The next one who does so will answer to me."

No one spoke.

"General Gallagher explained the situation to me," Morris said to Blade. "Do you want to start the ball rolling, or should I?"

"I will," Blade offered, his gaze still on the recruits. "This lady is Athena Morris," he introduced her. "I want you to listen to every word she has to say, because in a little while you're going to be asked to make a decision. How you decide could mean the difference between life and death for you." He paused. "Ordinarily you would not have a say in whether or not you go on a mission. You volunteered to serve for a year, come what may. But this is a special case. Governor Melnick here wants us to go on our first mission within two weeks. That's not much time to train. So whether we go or not will depend on you. It's your lives we're talking about." He nodded at Morris.

"Thank you," she said, facing the recruits. "I'll make this short and sweet. For seven years I was held captive, along with approximately two dozen other women, in a valley deep in the woods in northern California. Like these other women, I was a slave. I only recently escaped, and I want to see the party responsible punished and the other women released. That's why I'm here, to talk you into going. Any questions?"

Sergeant Havoc glanced at Blade.

"You can speak now if you want," Blade said. "Any of you."

Havoc stared at Athena Morris. "There's a lot you haven't told us, Ms. Morris. For instance, how were you caught? And who caught you?"

"I was a reporter for the *LA Times*," Morris replied. "I was on assignment at the time, and my plane crashed. That's when I was taken prisoner. As for who caught me . . ." She hesitated, her mouth downturned. "It was the vilest, most loathsome creature you'd ever want to see."

"Creature?" Havoc repeated.

Athena Morris looked at Grizzly, her forehead furrowed, as if she was debating whether to continue. Finally she appeared to gird herself. "I was held prisoner by a mutant," she disclosed.

Grizzly cocked his head, peering at the woman.

"This mutant is called the Spider," Morris hastily continued. "He is a monster, a tyrant. He controls all of the valley I mentioned. The Spider's Kingdom, they call it. The Spider has been there for decades. I don't know how many. His underlings roam the countryside for him, taking women as captives. These women are kept in huts in the valley. I know their lives firsthand. During the day they work in the fields growing crops. At night they're confined to their huts, all except for one. She is chosen to go to the Tower."

"What's this tower?" Boone asked.

"The Tower Of The Spider," Morris said. "Where the Spider lives. He never comes out of it. All his food, anything he needs including the women, are taken in to him."

"What does he do with the women, ma'am?" Spader tactlessly inquired.

Morris frowned. "The Spider uses them for reproduction."

Boone, Sergeant Havoc, and Thunder exchanged glances.

"The Spider uses a different woman every night," Morris disclosed. "He wants them to bear his offspring, the Hatchlings. Those women who can't bear children become sacrifices."

"Sacrifices?" came from Thunder.

Morris blanched. "Those women unable to have the Spider's children are periodically sacrificed." She paused. "They are fed to the Hatchlings."

Blade saw a ripple of tension pass along the line of recruits, all except for Grizzly. The mutant was immobile, his indeterminate countenance seemingly chiseled out of granite.

Spader did a double take. "You mean these Hatchlings *eat* the women?"

"That's precisely what I mean," Morris confirmed.

"What's this Spider like?" Boone inquired.

"I don't quite know how to describe him," Morris responded. "He's hideous, a cross between a spider and a human. You must see him to believe it." She shuddered at the recollection.

"What about the Hatchlings?" Boone probed.

"The Hatchlings are somewhat more human than the Spider," Morris detailed. "But they're still grotesque. They have two legs, but four arms, and they have these huge fangs. Their fingers are like talons, and they can use them to communicate by clicking them, signaling back and forth. They relish eating human flesh."

"How many Hatchlings are there in the Kingdom?" Sergeant Havoc queried.

"Nineteen," Morris answered. "And that's not all."

"There's more?" Boone asked.

Morris nodded. "The Spider also employs human guards to take care of the menial chores like watching over the women. There are eleven of them."

"So the opposition includes eleven guards, nineteen Hatchlings, and the Spider," Sergeant Havoc tallied. "Thirty-one, all told. Is that right?"

"That's correct," Morris confirmed.

"Thirty-one of them and seven of us," Boone remarked. "That's what I like. Even odds."

"There will be eight of us," Morris amended.

Blade glanced at the journalist. "Eight?"

Morris nodded. "Didn't General Gallagher tell you? I'm coming along."

Blade slowly turned toward the general, his expression reflecting his disapproval. "What's this?" he demanded sternly.

General Gallagher mustered a weak grin and looked from Blade to Morris and back again. "Oh! Did I forget to mention you'll be taking Morris with you if you decide to go on the mission?"

"Such a minor detail," Blade said sarcastically. "I can see how you might have overlooked it."

"We'll discuss it later," Gallagher stated.

Athena Morris scanned the recruits. "Do you have any more questions?"

"Why use us?" Sergeant Havoc queried. "Why not locate the valley from the air and drop in Special Forces to mop up?"

"May I answer that one?" General Gallagher interjected, stepping forward. "As I already told Blade, the huts, the tower, and the tilled fields are camouflaged from aerial survelliance. They also have lookouts posted on a ridge above the valley. Finding the site from the air would be a fluke, and might take months. Sending you in on foot, we feel, increases the likelihood of success."

Sergeant Havoc gazed at the general. "Sir, is there a time limit on this mission?"

"No," Gallagher replied. "You'll go in, and you'll take as long as is necessary to get the job done."

Havoc nodded. "Then I take it, sir, this mission is TWEP?"

"It is," General Gallagher declared.

Blade looked at the general. "What does TWEP stand for? It's a new one on me."

"TWEP is an abbreviation for terminate with extreme prejudice," General Gallagher explained.

"In other words," Boone chimed in, "we don't take any prisoners."

"None," Gallagher said.

There were several seconds of silence.

"Are there any more questions?" Athena Morris asked.

"Blade said something about going in two weeks?" Spader noted quizzically.

"Two weeks should be long enough for you to learn the

basics," General Gallagher mentioned. "In two weeks the VTOLs will transport you to the drop zone we've selected. You will land and proceed into the interior on foot. You'll be supplied with a radio and any other equipment you might need. We can easily airlift additional supplies to you if necessary."

"Sir," Sergeant Havoc asked, "will an aerial search for the Kingdom be conducted in the meantime?"

"Negative," Gallagher responded. "A sudden increase in aerial traffic might make them suspicious and cause them to relocate. If that happened, we might never find them."

"Any more questions?" Athena Morris inquired.

None of the recruits ventured any.

"There is something important I would like to add," General Gallagher said. "We wouldn't be sending you in if we didn't feel you could accomplish the assignment. Thunder is a first-rate tracker, as competent as any we have in Special Forces or the commando units. If there's any sign to be found, he'll find it." He paused and glanced at Grizzly. "You also have someone on your Force particularly suited to fight mutants. Always fight fire with fire, is my motto."

Blade stared at the mutant. Now he understood Gallagher's underlying motive in using the Freedom Force; the Force included a mutant. If anyone could ferret out a colony of degenerate mutants, it would be another hybrid, someone with the same enhanced senses and augmented instincts as the quarry. Fight fire with fire. Fight mutants with a mutant.

"And now, men," General Gallagher proclaimed, "Governor Melnick would like a few words with you."

The governor walked up to the general's side. "I simply want to impress upon you the importance of this mission. Not only would you save the lives of two dozen women, not only would you rescue these unfortunates from an existence of torture and degradation, but you would render an invaluable service to California, indeed to the entire Freedom Federation and the Outlands."

Blade saw the recruits eating up every word. As with prewar politicians, Melnick's pitch was as smooth as silk.

"If you complete this assignment," the governor was saying, "you will be sending a message to our allies and a warning to our enemies. The message you will send our allies is that we are ready and willing to meet any and all threats to the Freedom Federation. And you will be warning our enemies to take heed, to leave us in peace or suffer the consequences. This mission is not merely a test to prove yourselves. This mission is for the people of the Freedom Federation, for your people—for the Cavalry, the Flatheads, the Clan, the Moles, the Civilized Zone, for California and the Family. You are helping them to sleep easier at night knowing you are here to protect them." He paused. "That's all I wanted to say. May God speed you on this enterprise."

"Okay," Blade declared. "You see what you're up against. This is the first and only time you, as a group, will decide whether we accept a mission or not. Go over there a ways," he said, pointing to the east, "and talk this over. When you have reached a decision, let us know."

"Sir," Sergeant Havoc stated. "Must the decision be unanimous?"

Blade observed General Gallagher about to speak and quickly cut him off. "Yes. We either go as a team, or we don't go at all."

Gallagher frowned.

"You're on your own," Blade told them, motioning to the east.

The six recruits moved about 15 yards away and formed a circle.

Blade swung on General Gallagher. "Now what are you trying to pull? What's this nonsense about taking Morris with us?"

"I can speak for myself," Athena Morris responded stiffly. "I am going on the mission for two reasons. One, I am somewhat familiar with the country. I can recognize certain landmarks. You'll stand a better chance of finding the Kingdom with me along."

"And what's the second reason?" Blade queried.

"It's personal," Morris replied.

"Oh, great!" Blade exclaimed in disgust, looking at Gallagher. "You want us to take along a woman out for revenge? Are you nuts?"

Athena Morris moved between Blade and the general. "Why are you talking to him? Why don't you talk to me, face to face?"

"Fine," Blade said, annoyed by her arrogance. "I'll give it to you straight, lady! You're not coming on the mission! You want your vengeance more than anything else, and vengefulness is hardly the ideal frame of mind for going into combat."

"What the hell is the matter with you?" Morris countered. "Of course I want my revenge after what those bastards did to me! So would you, if the situation were reversed! But I won't let my thirst for revenge interfere with my performance."

"Yeah, sure," Blade muttered.

"Give me a chance to prove myself," Morris proposed.

"I'd like to," Blade said, "but I can't. We'll have enough to do without baby-sitting you!"

"Uh-oh," General Gallagher mumbled.

Athena Morris bristled. She poked her right forefinger into the Warrior's stomach. "Baby-sitting? For your information, bozo, I won't need any baby-sitting! I was raised in the country! I can shoot and ride as well as any *man!* And I know how to live off the land! So don't give me any crap about baby-sitting!"

Blade glanced at Gallagher for support. "You know I'm right."

"I'll tell you what he knows," Morris snapped. "He knows you don't stand a snowball's chance in hell of finding the Kingdom without me along! So if you want to save those women, you'd better think twice about taking me along!" She spun and stalked off to the west, her fists clenched in anger.

"Quite a little firebrand, isn't she?" General Gallagher commented.

"She's a regular Lynx," Blade remarked cryptically.

Gallagher stared at the Warrior. "You really don't have any choice in taking her. You realize that, don't you?"

Blade sighed. "I wish there was another way."

"All of this may be moot if your men decide to decline the mission," Governor Melnick noted.

"Speak of the devil," General Gallagher said, looking past Blade.

Blade turned. The recruits were returning. "That was quick," he said as they assumed their original positions.

"We have made up our minds, sir," Sergeant Havoc declared.

"So what's it going to be?" Blade asked. "Do we go or not?"

"Let me put it this way," Sergent Havoc said. "Where can we get some first-class tickets for the VTOLs?"

PART TWO

THE MISSION

CHAPTER SEVEN

"I'm so sick of trees I could puke!" Kraft declared, pushing a limb aside as he plodded wearily along.

Blade glanced over his right shoulder. "No talking!" he ordered.

"Ahh, like who's going to hear us, dude?" Kraft retorted. "The trees don't have ears, you know."

Blade halted and turned. The Force was strung out behind him, advancing through the undergrowth to the west. Spader was a few feet away, then Kraft. Beyond the Clansman were Sergeant Havoc, Grizzly, Thunder, and Boone. They all drew to a stop. "It isn't the trees I'm concerned about," Blade said to Kraft. "It's who, or what, might be on the other side of those trees."

Kraft snorted. "The only thing on the other side of those trees is some mangy bear taking a shit."

Spader was leaning on his M-16. "Can we take a break now? We've been hiking for hours!"

"Hours my ass!" Kraft cracked. "In case you can't count, we've been at this bullshit for seven days!"

Blade walked back to Kraft. "When I say no talking, I mean no talking! If you don't shut your face, I'll shut it for you."

Kraft's lips compressed and his eyes narrowed.

"What's the matter, cutey?" taunted a female voice from the front of the column. "Where's your marbles?"

Blade gazed at Athena Morris, her slim figure attired in tight fitting camouflage fatigues. He had been following her for the better part of an hour, ever since she had announced she thought the terrain looked familiar.

"What about a break?" Spader reiterated.

Blade nodded. "Fifteen minutes," he informed them, moving to the head of the line.

Athena Morris was leaning against a tree, her back to the trunk. "I see that look in your eyes again," she told him.

"You shouldn't goad Kraft," Blade advised. "You're only making this worse than it already is."

"I can't help myself," she said. "I'm tired of all his whining. I don't see why you let him into the Force."

"I had no control over the quality of the recruits," Blade mentioned. "I must make do with those who volunteered, Ms. Kraft."

"Will you quit calling me that?" she rejoined. "How many times must I tell you. Call me Athena."

Blade surveyed the dense vegetation ahead. "Do you still think you know where we might be?"

Athena chewed on her lower lip for a moment. "I don't know," she admitted. "That ridge in the distance looks like one I saw on my way out."

"The one above the Kingdom?"

"No," Athena said. "But the next one over."

Blade peered at the ridge in question, visible through the canopy of trees. In all his travels, he'd never encountered vegetation as thick as the growth in northern California. His mind flashed back to the drop-off a week ago, when the VTOLs had deposited the Force in a large clearing adjacent to the Scott River and northeast of the Marble Mountain Wilderness. They had stuck with the river for only a few hours, until Athena had found the stream she wanted. Then they had struck off to the west, into the Wilderness, staying close to the stream. Now, after a week of pursuing the stream's meandering course to the west, he was beginning to wonder if Athena had selected the wrong tributary. He gazed to the right at the flow of cold water, not ten feet away. "Tell me about your escape again."

"You want to hear that again?" Athena queried, puzzled. "You've heard the story a dozen times so far."

"Humor me," Blade said.

Athena sighed, running her right hand through her hair, her left clutching her M-16 with the stock pressed against her left thigh. "I escaped on one of the feast nights. Whenever one of the women who can't bear the Spider's children are sacrificed, the occasion is turned into a big feast, a big celebration. After the sacrifice, the Hatchlings carry the body to the Tower to consume." She stopped, breathing slowly, clearly disturbed.

"If you'd rather not talk about it again . . ." Blade began.

"I'm okay," Athena said, resuming her narrative. "The human guards always overdo their celebrating. They usually drink themselves into a stupor. Most of them, anyway. I counted on that for my escape. With the Hatchlings occupied in the Tower, and the majority of the guards out like a light, I figured I could sneak from my hut into the woods and get away. But I ran into some trouble. One of the guards almost caught me. And instead of fleeing to the south until the ridge ended, then skirting to the east, I stupidly blundered straight up the ridge. The Hatchlings came after me." She glanced at Blade, her brown eyes conveying a haunted aspect. "They would have had me too, but I fell off the cliffs bordering the east side of the ridge. Ironically, the fall saved my life. I landed in a deep pool of water at the base of the cliffs, so deep I didn't even hit bottom. I made it to the surface, and I remembered clinging to a boulder on the shore, coughing and thanking God for my deliverance."

"You had a narrow escape," Blade remarked.

"My ordeal wasn't over," Athena said. "The pool fed a stream." She pointed at the nearby brook. "That one, I believe. I knew the Hatchlings would come after me, and I knew they have an excellent sense of smell. They can track a human by scent. I reasoned my best chance was to stick with the stream, to stay in the water and follow it wherever it might lead. After all, the Hatchlings can't track a scent through water. So that's what I did."

"And the stream eventually fed into the Scott River, and you followed the river to the east until you were rescued near Ft. Jones," Blade concluded.

Athena nodded. "I almost didn't make it. I was too scared to stop and find something to eat. I was weak and exhausted, but somehow I kept going." She shook her head in amazement. "I can't believe I'm alive."

"And yet you're going back?" Blade mentioned.

Athena looked into his eyes. "I've got to go back. I owe it to all the women I left behind, and to myself. I've got to see the Spider dead. My motive is more than mere revenge. I will never enjoy another good night's sleep as long as I know the Spider and his brood are alive. Can you understand this?"

"I think so," Blade said, nodding, admiring her courage. "There is one thing I'm still not clear on."

"What's that?" she queried.

"I'm trying to envision the area we're seeking in my mind," Blade stated. "Correct me if what I say is wrong." He paused. "The ridge we're seeking runs from north to south, with cliffs on the east side and a slope on the west. Right?"

"Right so far," Athena confirmed.

"The valley, the Kingdom of the Spider, is located on the west side of the ridge," Blade said.

"Yes," Athena verified. "There is a gigantic, desolate ravine bordering the valley to the west. To the north is a series of hills and more ravines. To the south the land is essentially flat."

"And where is the Tower in relation to everything?" Blade questioned.

"The Tower of the Spider is in the center of the valley," Athena disclosed. "It stands about seventy feet high and is about forty feet in diameter."

"What's it made of?" Blade inquired.

"Wood," Athena said. "Surrounding the Tower are the huts, ten of them, all made of wood. One hut, the biggest, is used by the guards. The rest are occupied by the women. We were forced to sleep on mats on the dirt floor. There was no indoor plumbing, so we had to cart our water from a well near the Tower. There's a creek on the west side of the valley used to irrigate the crops the women grow."

"How do they hide everything from the air?" Blade probed.

"They use these large green nets to camouflage the tilled fields," Athena detailed. "The nets are propped up on poles. From the air, the fields must appear to be covered with grass."

"What about the huts and the Tower?"

"The huts are painted green, and they were designed so the roofs form a dome instead of slanting. I'd imagine they look like mounds from high up," Athena said. "As for the Tower, I must admit they were rather ingenious. They packed earth around three-fourths of the Tower, encasing the structure in dirt up to the fifty-foot level. The rest of the Tower is painted green, like the huts, and the Tower also has a domed roof. Anyone looking down from a plane would simply see a valley of green grass with a few mounds and a big hill in the middle."

"Are there any walls or fences?" Blade asked.

"None," Athena divulged. "They don't need any. The kingdom is so far from civilization, I doubt many women have made a break for it over the years. I only heard of a few, and they were all reportedly killed."

"About these women," Blade remarked. "Where do they come from? How does the Spider get them?"

"The Hatchlings are sent out every now and then to acquire new blood," Athena related. "They range far afield. They bypass the nearest towns, like Yreka, and travel further east to steal the women they need. They also venture to the coast, and I was told they even go up into what was once the state of Oregon and capture women from the outposts and towns there. The Hatchlings aren't stupid. They don't arouse suspicion by taking more than one woman from any community, and they usually don't hit the same community again for five or six years. By selectively picking their targets, they minimize the risk of being discovered."

"I'm surprised someone hasn't noticed a pattern of some kind," Blade commented.

"Back in the old days they would have," Athena stated. "Back then almost everyone had social security numbers, or those mandatory national identification numbers the government issued shortly before the war, or some method of keeping track of the population. Missing persons were usually promptly reported to the authorities." She sighed. "But today it's different. Many of the towns and hamlets are isolated. Telephone service is generally restricted to the urban areas, and the people don't travel as much as they once did. And you've got to keep in mind how rugged this country is. Disappearances are not uncommon. So if a woman vanishes from a mountain settlement, although a search will invariably be launched, no one has any cause to suspect deviate mutants are swooping down on helpless women and abducting them."

"Incredible," Blade said.

"The Spider only wants young women, breeding females as they are called. The typical victim is between fifteen and forty years of age. If a woman reaches forty in the Kingdom, whether she's borne an offspring or not, she's sacrified."

"These offspring," Blade observed. "Are they all Hatchlings?"

"No," Athena answered. "Many turn out human."

"What happens to them?"

Athena's expression soured. "I don't know. We were never told. I assume they're eaten."

"You mentioned something once before," Blade noted. "About the Spider killing women unable to bear him offspring. How does he know if they can or they can't?"

"Let me explain how his system works," Athena offered. "The average number of women held in the Kingdom at any one time, during the time I was there, was sixteen. For some reason, the Spider decided to increase that number a few months before I escaped. There are twenty-four there now." She frowned. "The bastard uses a different woman every night. So a captive would find herself taken to the Tower once every sixteen to twenty-four days, depending on how many women were in captivity or pregnant. Once a woman became pregnant, the Spider wouldn't touch her. With so many women at his disposal, the bastard could afford to bide his time in trying to impregnate any one woman. The standard give-birth-or-die period was seven years. If a woman hadn't become pregnant within seven years of her capture, she was sacrificed."

Blade's forehead creased. "And how long did you say you were there?"

"About seven years," Athena replied.

"Oh," Blade said softly, electing to change the subject. He gazed at the ridge in the distance. "That ridge up ahead. It's not the one we want, but it could be located just to the east of the one we want. Is that correct?"

Athena glanced at the ridge. "That's right. It's yet another barrier shielding the Kingdom from the rest of the world. The stream should cut through a gorge in the middle of that ridge. On the other side we'll find the pool and the second ridge, the ridge with the cliffs, the ridge overlooking the Kingdom."

"We'd better get going," Blade declared, facing his men.

The recruits were spread out over a 20-yard stretch, resting. The past week had taken its toll on their physical condition and morale. Seven days of pressing into the virtually impenetrable wilderness, seven days of forcing their passage through inconceivably dense vegetation, seven days of constantly combatting ensnaring vines, of forging through a wall of brush and limbs, had sapped their energy and affected their emotions. Spader and Kraft were particularly hard hit. Neither was accustomed to the outdoors to any great degree. Kraft was becoming increasingly irritable with each passing day.

Before leaving their facility north of LA, Blade had offered the recruits the uniforms General Gallagher had provided. He had assured them wearing a uniform was not mandatory. Not too surprisingly, Grizzly had declined. So did Boone and Thunder; they preferred their buckskins. Sergeant Havoc always wore a uniform, although he was partial to brown, green, or camouflage T-shirts instead of a regulation fatigue shirt. Spader, whose clothes were on the shabby side anyway, opted to wear the new fatigues and a pair of combat boots. And Kraft had decided to wear fatigues on this mission instead of his usual black leather apparel. Each one had a green web belt and canteen.

The recruits had been issued ample weaponry. Each one, even Grizzly, had received an M-16, but the mutant had adamantly refused to wear a pair of Colt automatics strapped around his waist. Boone had likewise declined the pistols, opting for his Hombre revolvers, leaving Blade, Thunder, Kraft, Spader, and Sergeant Havoc to pack a pair of Stainless Steel Officers Model 45's. Blade carried his in shoulder holsters, one snug under each arm, his Bowies on his hips. In addition to the guns, each recruit carried a concealed boot knife or, in the case of Boone and Thunder, a knife tucked underneath knee-high moccasins. And Blade, as a backup to his Bowies, had slid a Panther survival knife with a 15-inch blade and a leather sheath under his belt in the small of his back. The Panther was hidden by his black leather vest and might not be discovered during a body search by an enemy should he be captured.

Each recruit was toting a backpack constructed of a waterproof camouflage material containing their necessities, their rations and one change of clothing and their explosives. As if the

guns and knives weren't enough, General Gallagher had issued a
packet of plastic explosive, a detonator, and a timer to each
recruit. Blade had insured they were thoroughly instructed in the
use of the explosive. The orders he received had been quite
specific: Not only was he to eliminate the Spider, the
Hatchlings, and the Spider's human henchmen, but he was to
totally destroy the Kingdom, to blow the Tower, the huts, and
everything else to kingdom come. When General Gallagher used
the expression "terminate with extreme prejudice," he meant
exactly that.

"On your feet," Blade directed. "We're moving out."

Kraft sighed. "Here we go again. I bet that ditsy bitch doesn't
even know where the hell we are!"

Blade reached the Clansman in four strides. He towered over
Kraft, glaring down at him. "I'm getting tired of your griping. I
thought the Clan sent me a man, not a wimp. All of us are tired.
All of us want to get this mission over with. But you're not
helping matters with your lousy attitude. Change it or clam up.
Do I make myself clear, mister?"

"Yeah," Kraft responded testily. "I hear you."

Blade returned to the front of the column behind Athena.
"Lead on."

Athena nodded and tramped to the west.

Blade glanced over his left shoulder to verify his men were up
and ready to go. Boone, at the rear, smiled and waved. Blade
grinned in response, then followed Athena Morris.

"You haven't told me much about yourself," she commented
as she skirted an enormous boulder in their path. She kept her
voice low, barely audible.

"There's not much to tell," Blade said.

"That's not what I hear," Athena mentioned. "You have
quite a reputation."

"People like to exaggerate," Blade said. "They enjoy telling
tall tales."

"And I haven't seen many taller than you," Athena quipped.

"Healthy hormones," Blade rejoined.

"General Gallagher thinks highly of you," Athena remarked.
"He said he couldn't think of anyone better qualified to lead the
Force."

Blade wondered if his ears were functioning. "General
Gallagher said that?" he asked in disbelief.

"Sure did," Athena confirmed.

"The same General Gallagher we both know?" Blade queried.

Athena smiled. "The same one. Why?"

"I was under the impression he doesn't much like me or the Freedom Force," Blade observed.

"Don't let Gallagher fool you," Athena said. "He's rough around the edges, but deep inside he's a pussycat."

"Now I know we're not talking about the same man," Blade cracked.

"So how about it?" Athena stated. "Tell me a little bit about yourself."

Blade opened his mouth to speak when he happened to glance to his right, idly gazing across at the stream at a low hill beyond. His keen gray eyes caught a glimpse of movement in a clearing near the top of the hill. "Down!" he hissed, dropping to his knees, reaching out and pulling Athena next to him.

The men of the Force promptly obeyed.

"What is it?" Athena whispered.

Blade nodded at the hill. He could see seven figures crossing the clearing. Their features were indistinct, but one of them was definitely a woman. The other six were another story; they were squat black forms whose gait and body movements seemed oddly unnatural.

"Hatchlings!" Athena said in horror.

Blade estimated their distance at approximately a thousand yards off. The Hatchlings and the woman were proceeding in single file, the woman in the center. They were bearing to the west, toward the same ridge Athena had targeted, confirming her judgment.

"They've captured another woman!" Athena exclaimed quietly.

"Maybe she's your replacement," Blade commented.

"What?"

"Maybe she was caught to take your place," Blade noted.

Athena appeared shocked by the possibility. "You could be right," she mumbled.

Blade looked at his men. All of them had spied the procession on the hill and were watching the Hatchlings. Blade stared at the far off clearing again in time to see the Hatchlings and their captive disappear in the trees below the clearing.

"Let's go!" Athena urged. "We can follow them to the

Kingdom.''

"Not so fast," Blade admonished her. He scanned his men, debating. Grizzly was his first choice, but no, he couldn't. Thunder could handle the job, but the Flathead was near the end of the line, lugging the radio, their sole link to civilization. Speed was essential.

"What are we going to do?" Athena demanded.

Blade motioned for Sergeant Havoc, and a moment later the noncom was by his side.

"Sir?" Havoc said.

"I want you to follow them," Blade ordered, pointing at the hill. "Stay on their trail, but don't let them see you. We'll come along in a few minutes. I'm relying on you to warn us if they stop for any reason."

"Understood, sir," Havoc acknowledged.

"And Havoc," Blade said.

Sergeant Havoc was already starting to rise. "Yes, sir?"

"Don't get yourself killed," Blade warned.

"No way, sir," Havoc stated, grinning. He cautiously moved to the stream, his camouflage T-shirt and fatigue pants blending in perfectly with the foliage he passed. The water was only three feet in depth. He quickly waded across and was lost to view in the woods on the opposite side.

Blade gestured for his men to join him and they hurriedly closed in. All of them were somber. Even Kraft, for once, was silent. "You all saw them," Blade said. "We're going to trail them to the Kingdom. I've sent Havoc on ahead to keep tabs on them. Thunder, I want you to take the point. Keep in sight. Don't lose Havoc's tracks. And keep your eyes peeled. If those Hatchlings stop, Havoc is going to let us know so we don't blunder into them. Get going," Blade instructed, then added, "but first hand the radio to Spader."

"Me? It was my turn yesterday!" Spader protested.

"And it's your turn again now," Blade declared.

Thunder rose, unslinging the small portable transmitter and receiver from his back. The radio was designed to be carried alongside their narrow backsacks.

"I don't see why I have to be the one," Spader mumbled as he grudgingly accepted the radio.

"Take off," Blade commanded.

Thunder nodded, hefting his M-16. He walked to the stream and forded, then waited for them on the other side.

"Come on." Blade stood and led the rest, Athena right behind him, then Spader, Kraft, Boone, and Grizzly. He reached the stream, gauging the rapidly flowing current, and entered the frigid water. He was soaked from the knees to his boots when he stepped onto the far bank.

Thunder was visible 15 yards into the trees, his eyes on the ground, tracking Havoc and the mutants.

Blade walked a few feet from the stream, watching the rest of his team negotiate their passage. Athena forged straight across, but Spader balked, perched on the bank, his green eyes showing trepidation.

"Come on!" Blade promised him.

Spader nervously licked his lips.

"What's wrong? It's only about six feet wide," Blade noted.

"I can't swim!" Spader whispered in response.

"The water is only three feet deep," Blade said. "It will only come up to your waist, if that."

"What if I fall in?" Spader queried.

"We don't have time for this!" Blade told him. "We can't let them get too far ahead."

"I don't know . . ." Spader wavered.

"Oh, hell!" Grizzly suddenly exclaimed. He came around Boone and Kraft, his M-16 in his left hand, and before Spader quite knew what was happening Grizzly grabbed the Mole around the waist with his right arm, bodily lifted Spader from the ground, and entered the water.

Spader uttered a strangled gasp.

Grizzly speedily surged through the current and climbed onto the bank, walking up to Blade and depositing a petrified Spader at the Warrior's feet. "Anyone want a pissant?" the mutant quipped.

Blade waved for the others to hurry, and within a minute Boone and Kraft had reached them. "Stay alert," he cautioned. "And no noise from here on out."

Thunder was over 20 yards to the west, crouched beside a log, obeying Blade's injunction to stay in sight.

Blade hastened after the Flathead.

Thunder straightened and resumed his tracking.

How far ahead were the Hatchlings? Blade wondered. At least fifteen hundred yards, he guessed. How sensitive were the Hatchling's senses? Athena had said they possessed a keen sense of smell, but what about their hearing? Blade doubted the Hatchlings would be able to detect the presence of the Force.

But he miscalculated.

CHAPTER EIGHT

Sergeant Havoc crept through the verdant undergrowth, angling his pursuit to coincide with the descent of the Hatchlings. He had seen the seven forms vanish in the woods below the clearing, and he assumed they were moving down the west slope of the hill toward the distant ridge. He hurried as quickly as possible, his M-16 held in front of his body, ready for action.

The terrain presented imposing obstacles. Gullies and ravines sliced the landscape. Dead trees littered the ground. And although the month was January, the plant growth was prolific. Large boulders dotted the earth.

Havoc bore to the northwest, hoping to cut the Hatchlings' trail, then follow them. He advanced for ten minutes and began to worry. By all rights, he should have seen or heard some sign of his quarry. But so far, nothing.

The forest was eerily still.

Havoc paused on the south side of a triangular boulder rearing ten feet into the air. He squatted and deliberated his next move.

A twig snapped.

Havoc tensed and flattened his back against the boulder. The sound had come from the far side of the boulder. He held his breath, listening intently. Had an animal made the noise? Or something else? Something far worse?

There was an abrupt spurt of clicking.

Havoc's blue eyes narrowed. What had Athena Morris said about the Hatchlings? "Their fingers are like talons, and they can use them to communicate by clicking them, signaling back and forth."

The clicking ceased.

Havoc slowly exhaled, biding his time. He counted to 50, then eased to the dank ground and crawled around the west end of the boulder. He'd hit the jackpot!

The six Hatchlings and their female prisoner were 25 yards to the west. The hybrids walked with a strangely stiff shuffle, as if their legs lacked the flexibility of a human. Their four arms were held close to their torsos. A coat of fine black hair covered every inch of their skin. They weren't very tall, but had heavy forms.

Havoc had seen a number of mutants in the past, but the Hatchlings were markedly different. There was a perverse aura about them, an almost palpable air of sheer evil. They gave him the creeps.

The last Hatchling in line unexpectedly turned, surveying their back trail, revealing a pair of cruel, circular black orbs.

Havoc froze, afraid he'd been spotted. A small bush partially obstructed the Hatchling's view, and he hoped the monstrosity wouldn't distinguish him against the backdrop of vegetation. An eternity seemed to elapse before the hybrid pivoted and continued its trek. Havoc breathed a sigh of relief.

The last Hatchling shambled from sight around a pine tree.

Havoc rose to a crouch and carefully dogged the hybrids. They were moving at a slower pace than he'd anticipated, which was why he had almost blundered into them and ruined the mission. But no harm had been done, and all he had to do was stick with them like glue. He discovered a Hatchling footprint in a soft section of dirt and paused to examine the print. The impression in the earth was oval, with three protruding claw marks extending for three or four inches from the front of the imprint. He estimated the length of the foot at ten inches.

A scream pierced the forest up ahead.

Havoc quickened his steps, skirting the pine tree, seeking the hybrids. Seconds later he found them, gathered around the woman they'd abducted. She was lying on her back, her hands tied together at her waist, gaping at her captors in stark fear. He noticed her long hair was a sandy blonde and she was wearing jeans and a tan blouse.

What were the hybrids doing?

Havoc stealthily snuck to within 15 yards of the creatures, concealing himself behind a great log, a remnant of one of the forest's gigantic trees.

Someone was speaking in a curiously sharp, metallic tone, the words clipped and precise.

Havoc rose on his elbows and peeked over the top of the log. With a start, he realized *one of the hybrids was doing the talking*! Because of their clicking signals, he had taken for granted the Hatchlings couldn't communicate verbally. Obviously they could when they wanted, although their speech pattern suggested they experienced difficulty in doing so. The clicking of their talons, he perceived, might be their special, secret technique for communicating when they wanted to stay in touch with a minimum of noise, a kind of code.

"One more time," the Hatchling was saying, "and you will perish on the spot."

"I'm sorry," the woman wailed. "I just tripped! I couldn't help myself! You haven't let me rest in two days!"

"You will rest when we reach the Kingdom," the Hatchling said. "Not before."

The woman nodded. "Why are you doing this to me? Who are you? *What* are you?"

The Hatchling doing all the talking glanced at one of his companions. "These human wretches are pitiful."

The second Hatchling grinned, displaying a mouth packed with glistening white fangs, two of which, the eye teeth, were an inch longer than all the rest.

The terrified woman sniffled.

Sergeant Havoc frowned, wishing there was something he could do to assist the woman. But if he helped her, if he tried to take out all the Hatchlings, he ran the risk of one escaping and warning the Spider. All he could do was bide his time and keep tabs on the bastards, just like Blade wanted.

The head Hatchling leaned down and examined the trembling woman. "You will do nicely," it commented. "The Spider will be very pleased with you."

"Who's the Spider?" the woman made bold to ask.

"You will meet the Spider tomorrow night," the Hatchling informed her.

"The Spider is our father," added another hybrid.

"Dear Lord!" the woman exclaimed. "Save me!"

The leader of the mutants laughed, a sort of high-pitched, flinty titter.

Havoc wondered why the six hybrids were wasting so much time in idle conversation. And suddenly his mind shrieked a silent "Look out!" as his brain belatedly registered the discrepancy in his count.

There weren't six mutants surrounding the woman!

There were only five!

Where was the sixth?

Sergeant Havoc whirled, knowing he'd been duped, perceiving the reason the other five hybrids were stalling, bringing his M-16 up, hoping he wasn't too late and mentally berating himself for his stupidity.

The sixth Hatchling was a foot away, its four arms upraised, its talons poised for a strike. Its two hairy right arms grabbed the barrel of the M-16 and wrenched the weapon from the noncom's grasp before the trigger could be squeezed.

Havoc rolled to the right as the Hatchling pounced, evading the hybrid's raking talons. He began to rise, going for the 45's around his waist, but he was way too slow.

Although only five feet in height, the Hatchling made up in bulk what it lacked in stature. And the creature utilized its weight to an advantage as it sprang again, slamming into its adversary's abdomen and bowling the human over.

Sergeant Havoc suddenly found himself flat on his back, each wrist pinned to the ground by two of the creature's hands, the Hatchling straddling his chest. A sensation of revulsion washed over him as the mutant's fetid breath assailed his nostrils. He stared upward into the most inhuman orbs conceivable and repressed a shudder.

The Hatchling smirked, exposing its lethal fangs.

Havoc was astounded by the creature's strength. Try as he might, he was unable to dislodge his wrists from the hybrid's hold. He saw the thing lean toward him with its mouth wide, a yellowish saliva dripping from its teeth, and a fleeting flicker of panic paralyzed him. But only for a moment. The next instant his years of training and extensive combat experience came to his rescue, supplanting the incipient, uncharacteristic dread with a cool, calculating resoluteness.

The Hatchling's fangs were six inches from his throat.

"Eat this, ugly" Havoc growled, sweeping his forehead up and in, connecting with the mutant's large, thin nostrils. He felt the cartilage crunch under the impact.

Hissing, the Hatchling recoiled, its nose flattened to a gruesome pulp.

Havoc pressed his intiative, bucking his body, temporarily throwing the creature off balance. He swept his legs up, his ankles clamping on the sides of the hybrid's squat neck, and twisted his legs to the left.

The Hatchling tumbled to the left, springing to its feet next to the log.

Havoc was already rising, his right hand on his right automatic. He intuitively sensed a new threat to his rear and spun.

Another Hatchling was charging toward him, mere feet away.

Havoc executed a lightning left hook kick, aiming at the mutant's throat while simultaneously shifting to the right to avoid the hybrid's rush. His left combat boot connected with the Hatchling's neck below the chin, snapping the creature's head back as its feet left the ground.

The second Hatchling fell onto its right side.

Havoc drew his right pistol. He had to warn Blade! A couple of shots would do the job! But before he could fire, the first mutant pounced, plowing into the base of his spine and knocking him to his knees, the jolt causing the Colt to almost slip from his fingers. A tremendous blow was delivered to the left side of his head, above the ear, and he swayed, dazed.

A third Hatchling entered the fray, leaping over the log and ramming into the human.

Sergeant Havoc was rocked by the collision. He toppled backwards with the mutant pummeling his face, only dimly aware of his plight. His right fist instinctively smashed the mutant on the left cheek, enraging the creature.

Two more Hatchlings vaulted over the log, and in conjuction with the first three they piled on their victim.

Havoc was buried under a mass of hairy black shapes. Talons

sliced his arms, chest, and legs, tearing the fabric of his clothing and drawing blood. The Colt was gone. He attempted to fight his way free of the mutants, but he was hopelessly outnumbered. They rained punch after punch upon him, effortlessly dodging his futile counterstrikes.

"We have him!" one of them declared.

Havoc knew the damn thing was right. He could feel his limbs losing their vitality and his head was ringing. Self-reproach enveloped him. He had failed Blade and the Force. Worse, he had disgraced his father and his grandfather. Both men had served illustrious careers in the military. His grandfather had passed on, but his father would hear about his blunder, would know he had sullied the Havoc name. A numbing hit was delivered to his right temple and he nearly lost consciousness. His eyes closed and he went limp, hovering on the brink of sentience.

"That's enough!" a Hatchling barked, as if through a long tunnel. "He's out."

"He certainly was a tough one!" commented another mutant.

"The son of a bitch broke my nose!" complained the one with the crushed nostrils.

"Should we kill him here and now?" queried yet another.

There were several seconds of silence.

"No," stated the apparent leader. "Disposing of him now would be a waste of prime meat. We'll take him to the Kingdom. Father will decide his fate." The Hatchling chuckled. "We may have our next feast sooner than we thought."

"Do you think there are more like him?" asked one of the other mutants.

"There could be," the leader said. "He might be part of an Army patrol."

"What would a patrol be doing in this area?" interjected the second hybrid.

"Maybe they're on to us," suggested the mutant with the busted nose.

"No way," declared the leader.

"How can you be so certain, Dox?" asked the second creature.

"How would they know about us, Syph?" Dox rejoined. "We never leave any trace behind after a raid."

"What about the human who escaped, the Morris female?" Syph mentioned.

"We don't know if she escaped," Dox said. "She was probably killed in the fall from the cliff."

"But we never found her body," Syph noted.

Sergeant Havoc was losing consciousness, his mind swirling. He tried to eavesdrop on the Hatchlings' conversation, the effort draining him even more.

"If the female escaped we still have nothing to worry about," Dox stated. "The Kingdom is too well hidden for the humans to find. The odds against the female being able to lead anyone to our valley are astronomical. The humans never venture this far into the forest."

Havoc felt something nudge his right shoulder.

"This one did," one of the mutant's commented. "And where there is one filthy human, there are more. They make rabbits look like a celibate species."

"If there are more humans nearby, whether an Army patrol or not, we can't afford to allow them to leave," Dox said.

"What should we do, big brother?" Syph inquired.

"Half of us will escort the woman and this soldier to the Kingdom," Dox directed. "The rest will wait here. If the patrol shows up, slay them."

"Who gets to go?" asked another hybrid.

"Myself, Syph, and Rhea because he has been injured," Dox said. "Siad, you and the others will secrete yourselves and await more humans."

"How long must we wait?" Siad questioned.

"Until sunset," Dox instructed. "If no humans have arrived by then, return to the Kingdom."

"We will wait until sunset," Siad pledged.

Sergeant Havoc was fading fast. He strained to hear some more.

"If more humans do arrive, should we spare any at all?" asked a mutant.

"You heard me," Dox said. "Kill them. All of them."

"You don't care what we do with the bodies?" Siad inquired.

"Do what you want," Dox stated, his bizarre voice growing fainter as he moved off.

"Good," Siad commented. "I could use a snack."

Sergeant Havoc made a supreme effort to remain awake, but was enshrouded in a benighted gloom.

CHAPTER NINE

The Freedom Force advanced ever so slowly to the west.

Blade could see Thunder crouched next to a big triangular boulder 30 feet distant. The Flathead was minutely examining the earth at his feet. Constantly scanning the dense undergrowth for a telltale hint of trouble, Blade threaded his way to the Indian's side. "What do you have?" he asked.

"Havoc was here, maybe ten minutes ago," Thunder said. "He got down on his belly and crawled in this direction." He moved around the boulder.

"Any sign of the Hatchlings' trail?" Blade queried.

"Not yet," Thunder replied. He walked a half-dozen yards from the boulder. "Ahhh. Here it is. They are heading to the west. Havoc intercepted them here, then followed."

"Take the point," Blade ordered. "Signal if you find anything."

"Will do," Thunder promised.

"And remember," Blade added. "Go slowly. We want them to get a few thousand yards in front of us, give us a little breathing space."

"I understand," Thunder said, and was gone.

Blade grinned, pleased his plan was working. By proceeding at a snail's pace, he minimized the risk of being discovered by the Hatchlings. Added insurance was provided by Sergeant Havoc, who would warn them if anything went amiss. The mission was shaping up nicely. All he needed to do was let the Hatchlings lead the Force to the Kingdom, then mop up. A few explosives, properly placed, would demolish the Spider's domain.

"Is it safe to talk yet?" Athena asked from right behind him.

Blade glanced over his right shoulder. His men were trudging through the brush to the rear of Athena. Grizzly was next in line after the journalist, then Spader, Kraft, and Boone. "It's okay to talk if you keep your voice low," Blade advised. "I doubt they can hear us this far away."

"I've been thinking," Athena mentioned. "You could have some problems up ahead."

"Like what?" Blade questioned.

"They keep lookouts posted on the ridge above the Kingdom," Athena reminded him. "They cover all the approaches. If you try to follow those Hatchlings we saw into the Kingdom, you'll be spotted."

"Then we'll follow them as far as we can," Blade said, "and go in later, under the cover of darkness."

"That's when the Hatchlings are most active," Athena divulged. "They don't come out a lot during the day. The ones we're following must be eager to reach the Kingdom."

"We go in the first chance we get," Blade stated.

"Just thought I'd let you know," Athena commented.

They marched in silence for a minute.

"You never did tell me about yourself," Athena remarked.

"Like I told you before, there's not much to tell," Blade said.

"Do you have a family?" Athena queried.

Blade nodded, smiling at the memory. "I have a lovely wife and a little son."

"What are their names?"

"My wife's name is Jenny," Blade said. "We called our son Gabriel."

"How old is your little one?" Athena questioned.

"He turned three this past December," Blade replied proudly.

"Any plans for any more?"

Blade looked at her. "Are all journalists so nosy?"

"Yep," Athena said. "Nosiness is our stock in trade. That, and a healthy dose of curiosity."

"Will you go back to being a journalist when this is all over?"

Blade inquired.

"I don't know," Athena admitted. "I haven't given the matter much thought. I can't think of anything except making the Spider pay for what he did to me."

"Do you think you'll be able to sleep easier once this Spider is dead?"

"I hope so," Athena said wistfully.

"Don't worry," Blade counseled. "Everything will work out."

"I stopped believing in fairy tales years ago," Athena mentioned bitterly.

"Don't allow the Spider to sour you on life," Blade recommended. "You've been through a terrible ordeal. There's no denying that. But you've got to look at the bright side."

"What bright side?"

"I have a friend by the name of Joshua," Blade said. "He's the spiritual sage in my Family, and twice a week we gather to hear him speak about truth, love, and faith. He said something once which applies to you."

"Like what?" Athena asked.

"Adversity is the crucible from which wisdom is derived," Blade quoted.

Athena snickered. "You missed your calling. You should be a preacher instead of a Warrior."

"I'll leave the spiritual teaching to Joshua," Blade said. "I'm content being a Warrior."

"Is everyone at the place you come from, the Home I heard about, so religious?" Athena inquired.

"Yes," Blade said.

"Everyone?"

"Yes," Blade reiterated.

"Amazing," Athena stated. "Tell me something. How can you believe in truth and love and all that, and go around killing others for a living? Seems inconsistent to me."

"If the spiritual do not protect themselves from the unspiritual," Blade intoned, "the spiritual will be wiped off the face of the earth."

Athena laughed lightly. "What fortune cookie did you get that out of?"

"Fortune cookie?"

"Yeah. A crisp cookie with a slip of paper inside. They're

supposed to tell your fortune," Athena elaborated. "Haven't you ever had one?"

"We do not have fortune cookies at the Home," Blade said.

"The last one I had was right before I took off for Yreka and my plane went down," Athena commented. "We had stopped in San Francisco enroute and I did some sightseeing. I ate at a fantastic Chinese restaurant in the Bay Area."

"What did your fortune cookie say?" Blade asked.

Athena snickered. "Detours delay the soul on its path." She stared up at the sky. "I always thought that was appropriate, given what happened later."

"You mean the plane crash?"

"What else?" Athena retorted.

"Perhaps the fortune cookie referred to your inner path, not your outer one," Blade suggested.

"What's the difference?" Athena queried.

"The inner path can lead your soul to wisdom," Blade said. "The outer can lead you astray."

"Is that what your Joshua teaches?" Athena inquired.

Blade nodded. "Joshua and the Elders."

"I wish there was a way to export fortune cookies to your Home," Athena wisecracked. "Your Family would eat them up. I'd make a ton of money."

"No, you wouldn't," Blade told her.

"Why not?" Athena asked.

"My Family doesn't own any money," Blade informed her.

Athena gazed at the Warrior's broad shoulders as he walked past a black cottonwood. "You're putting me on, right?"

Blade's attention was riveted on Thunder. "I am serious. We believe money, or specifically the *love* of money, only breeds evil. Our Founder advised us to avoid money at all costs."

"But how do you obtain whatever you need? Does your wife make all your clothes? And what about your food?" Athena questioned.

"We have a system set up where we can get anything we need," Blade detailed. "For instance, if a Family member needs new clothes, all they must do is go to the Weavers and request them. Or if food is needed, the Family Tillers will provide it. Don't misunderstand me. The Elders cultivate self-reliance in all Family members. We're taught how to sew our own clothes and grow our own food. But frequently our duties prevent us from attending to such affairs, and we can request them to be done for us."

"Incredible," Athena said. "But such a system would not work in the outside world, in the real world. When you have a large population, you need a medium of exchange."

"I agree," Blade said. "Fortunately, the Family is small enough, with less than a hundred members, that we can operate our Home on the simple principle of sharing."

"No money," Athena marveled. "You don't know how lucky you are! Money can be a real pain in the ass. California has its own mint, you know. Without money, the state's economy would grind to a halt."

"We studied the history of money and the various economic systems in the Family school," Blade mentioned. "Money was responsible for a great deal of misery in the world. People would kill for it. Wealthy individuals were always plotting to gain more wealth. Whether the economic system was capitalistic or communistic or some phase in between, the leaders of any given country were invariably part of the affluent elite who manipulated their respective governments into taxing the lower financial classes into the poorhouse."

"I don't know if it was as bad as all that," Athena commented. "Not all the prewar leaders were greedy for money or power. There were some honest, decent ones."

"Very few," Blade said. "If there had been more honest, spiritual leaders, we would never have had World War Three."

Athena smiled, delightfully surprised. She had expected the giant Warrior to be a typical muscle-head. Instead, he was articulate and intelligent, able to discourse on religion, politics, and economics knowledgeably. Here was a guy considered to be one of the deadliest men on the planet, and he was interested in ideals like truth, love, and faith. Would wonders never cease! Too bad he was married, because she definitely wanted to get to know him better.

Blade abruptly stopped.

Athena almost bumped into him. "What's wrong?" she whispered.

"Thunder," he said.

The Flathead was on his knees, inspecting a stretch of ground near a large log, his expression reflecting concern.

Blade hastened to the Indian's side. "What is it?"

"Trouble," Thunder responded. "There was a fight here."

"Havoc?" Blade asked.

Thunder's dark eyes surveyed the tracks and indistinct impressions. "He's been captured. See these marks here?" He pointed at a pair of shallow lengthy depressions in a few feet of dirt adjacent to the log. "Havoc was unconscious. Two of the mutants dragged him off in that direction." He nodded to the west. "One other mutant went along, leading them."

"What about the other three mutants?" Blade inquired, glancing at his men. They were clustering around him, listening, their attention briefly diverted from the surrounding forest.

"Most strange," Thunder remarked. "One went to the south, one to the north. I don't know about the third. He could be anywhere."

"But why would they split up?" Blade asked, perplexed. Why would three of the Hatchlings take off on their own? What reason would they have for separating? Were the mutants hoping to throw off any pursuit? The Hatchlings must suspect Havoc was not alone. What would he do in a similar situation? Grab the prisoners and take off? Head for the Kingdom as fast as possible? But only three of the Hatchlings had gone west. Which meant the other three might have been deliberately left behind to distract any pursuers. Or attack them.

No!

In a flash of insight, Blade perceived his blunder. He saw his men gathered in a semicircle around him, Athena in the center, and not one of them was paying any attention to the wall of vegetation hemming them in. Not one of them was on vigilant guard.

"Beats me why they split up," Thunder was saying, still on his knees, his back close to the log.

"Take cover!" Blade commanded. "This could be a trap!"

It was.

One of the Hatchlings popped up from behind the log, Havoc's M-16 in two of its hands. The hybrid hissed as it swung the rifle like a club, crashing the stock into Thunder's head and sending the Flathead sprawling even as it shifted its grip and leveled the barrel at the Freedom Force.

Blade was already galvanized into action, leaping and tackling
Athena and bearing her to the ground underneath him.

The Force members started to scatter. Grizzly was the
quickest, bounding into the underbrush in two streaking strides
in the time it took the Hatchling to aim the M-16. Boone was
turning, making for cover. But Kraft and Spader reacted
sluggishly, startled by the mutant's unexpected appearance.
They were standing four feet apart.

Blade saw the Hatchling cut loose with the M-16.

Spader was stitched from his crotch to his face, his body
jerking as the slugs hit home. Thump-thump-thump, with blood
and flesh bursting out and spraying the ground to his rear. He
gurgled and staggered as the mutant continued to pour rounds
into him.

Kraft finally came alive, but instead of fleeing he charged,
taking three running steps and vaulting into the air, launching
himself at the hybrid.

The Hatchling swiveled the M-16 toward Kraft.

Boone saved the Clansman's life. His M-16 in his left hand, in
the act of racing for a nearby tree, his body twisted away from
the mutant, he drew his right Hombre in midstride. His right
hand streaked to the big revolver, his arm a blur as the Hombre
cleared leather and boomed.

The Hatchling about to shoot Kraft was struck in the right
shoulder, the impact wrenching its bulky body sideways as it
squeezed the trigger. The shots went wild.

Before the Hatchling could recover, Kraft was on it. The
Clansman plowed into the mutant and they toppled from view
behind the log.

Blade started to rise, his eyes on Spader. The Mole was flat on
his back, riddled with holes, blood drenching his uniform, his
eyes open.

Boone was running back toward the log.

Blade caught a movement out of the corner of his right eye
and he pivoted.

Another Hatchling, unarmed except for its talons, fangs, and
prodigious strength, was coming at them from the south, closing
on Boone. Although their limbs lacked the dexterity of a human,
the Hatchlings were capable of supernatural speed.

Blade tried to bring his M-16 to bear.

The second Hatchling slammed into Boone from the side, bowling the Cavalryman over. They went down in a jumble of arms and legs.

Blade took a step toward them.

"Look out!" Athena suddenly shouted. "Behind you!"

Blade was jarred by a brutal attack from the rear. He felt a hurtling form ram into his legs and he was knocked off balance and fell forward, landing on his hands and knees, his M-16 clasped in his left hand, the third Hatchling on his back. Two hairy hands clamped on his neck, talons digging into his flesh, while two more swiped at his eyes.

"Blade!" Athena screamed.

Blade rolled to the right in an effort to dislodge the Hatchling. He ducked his head to thwart the talon swipes at his eyes.

The hybrid increased the pressure on the Warrior's neck.

Blade was on top now, the Hatchling pinned under his back. He tried to land a blow with his right elbow, but missed. Frustrated, envisioning the Hatchling tearing into him with those wicked fangs at any moment, he dropped the M-16 and went for his knives, drawing both Bowies as he rolled again, to the left this time, onto his side. He heaved himself erect, his leg muscles straining as the mutant clung to his neck. Once upright, he plunged his Bowies down and around, driving the gleaming blades to the rear, hoping he would connect.

He did.

The Hatchling screeched as the Bowies pierced its body, each knife imbedding to the hilt.

Blade felt a sticky substance on his fingers, and then the mutant released his neck and pushed itself away from him, wresting loose from the impaling Bowies and falling to the ground. Blade spun, glimpsing Boone on his back with the second mutant on the Cavalryman's chest. And there was Grizzly, claws extended, going to Boone's rescue. Blade took all of this in in an instant, and then he was face-to-face with his own foe.

The Hatchling glared up at the giant, its features distorted in bestial fury. A pale yellow fluid was pouring from the knife wounds in its side. It hissed and raked its talons at the human's genitals.

Blade retreated a step, debating whether he could capture the creature alive, whether taking the mutant prisoner might yield useful information. Capturing one would not be easy. The Hatchlings weren't much over five feet in height, if that, but their bodies were very thickset and astonishingly powerful. Added to their brute force were their talons and their fangs. Taking one of them prisoner would be like trying to contain a rampaging, rabid beast; the rewards didn't justify the risks.

The Hatchling pressed its assault, its talons lashing at the human before it. Unable to reach the giant's neck or face because of his height, the mutant was trying to disembowel its adversary or dismember him.

Blade retreated several yards before the mutant made a mistake, lunging too fast and too far, missing and exposing its head and throat for a fraction of a second. Which was more than enough time for Blade to angle his left Bowie in an underhand loop. He saw the point slice into the Hatchling's neck just under the chin, and he drove the Bowie all the way in and up, then promptly released the knife and stepped back.

The Hatchling stiffened, hissing and snarling, futilely attempting to pull the Bowie free. Yellow blood spurted over its hands and chest. It glared at the giant as it slowly sank to its knees, wheezing. The mouth twisted wide, baring the fangs, and it pitched onto its face.

Boone and Grizzly!

Blade twisted, ready to go to their help, but his assistance wasn't required.

Boone was still on the ground, his right Hombre in his hand, gawking at the battle royal a few feet off.

Grizzly and the second Hatchling were going at it tooth and nail. The Hatchling was trying to match its talons against Grizzly's claws, giving stroke for stroke, slash for slash. Grizzly was bleeding from a dozen wounds, the Hatchling from even more.

Blade was about to join in, to kill the Hatchling as quickly as possible, when the tide of battle abruptly shifted in Grizzly's favor. He saw the Hatchling trip.

Grizzly pounced. His razor claws raked the hybrid once, twice, three times in all, directly across the Hatchling's face, turning the hybrid's countenance into serrated strips of gory flesh and hair. The Hatchling tried to flee, starting to turn, but

Grizzly wasn't about to allow his opponent to escape. He took one stride and brought his claws up in a savage arc, burying them in the Hatchling's head, one hand on either side next to the ear.

The Hatchling bubbled and thrashed, then collapsed.

Blade glanced down at Athena Morris. She was sitting up, staring at the carnage in unrestrained horror.

Grizzly contemptuously tossed the Hatchling aside. "Tough little bastard," he commented.

Boone stood. "Thanks for lending a hand," he said to Grizzly. "It caught me off guard."

Grizzly looked at Boone. "Not too surprising. Most human reflexes are as slow as sap."

"Maybe one day I can repay the favor," Boone said.

"Nothing ever catches me off guard," Grizzly stated. "But I appreciate the thought."

Blade bent down, flipped over the dead Hatchling he'd slain, and yanked out his left Bowie. He wiped the blade clean on the mutant's body, then placed both Bowies in their sheaths. He saw Thunder prone on the earth near the log, and hurried to the Flathead's side. A check of Thunder's pulse confirmed the Indian was alive.

"Is he all right?" Athena asked, rising.

"I don't know," Blade said. He squatted on his knees and rested Thunder's head on his legs, then ran his fingers over the rear of Thunder's cranium. "There's some blood and a nasty bump."

Boone came over and knelt alongside Spader.

"Is he dead?" Athena queried.

Boone, frowning, nodded. He reached out and closed Spader's eyelids. "I'm afraid so, ma'am. And the radio is shot to pieces."

Athena glanced around. "Where's Kraft?"

Blade gently eased Thunder to the ground, then stood to peer over the log. The last he'd seen, Kraft had disappeared behind the log fighting a Hatchling. But now there was no sign of either.

"Is he there?" Boone questioned, standing and coming over.

"He's gone," Blade said.

Athena joined them by the log. "But where could he be?"

Blade gazed into the forest beyond. "My hunch is the Hatchling captured him. I don't see any blood, so Kraft might still be alive."

"Now they've got Havoc and Kraft," Boone commented acidly.

Grizzly walked up. "Not only that, but the sons of bitches know we're coming. From here on out, they've got the advantage."

Blade turned, scowling. Grizzly was right. The Hatchlings did have the edge now. And all because he'd been stupid and careless. He should have been more alert. So what if he had assumed the Hatchlings were a mile ahead of the Force? He'd moronically thrown caution to the wind and paid the price. How could he have allowed himself to be distracted by his conversation with Athena? If this was the best he could do, perhaps he should consider resigning as leader of the Freedom Force. He squatted, removing his canteen from his belt.

"Do you want me to take off after them?" Grizzly asked.

"No," Blade replied. "From here on out we'll stick together." He opened his canteen, then rolled Thunder over.

"I can catch up with them," Grizzly said. "Why not let me go?"

Blade looked up at the mutant. "Because I said so," he responded irritably.

Grizzly shrugged. "This is your show," he remarked.

Blade splashed some water on Thunder's face, but the Flathead wouldn't revive. He lightly slapped Thunder's chin, with the same result.

"He could be hurt internally," Athena mentioned. "A concussion perhaps. Or worse."

Blade sighed. This was just what he didn't need! He couldn't afford to waste precious time waiting for Thunder to revive. And he wouldn't desert the Flathead. So what should he do?

"I can carry him," Grizzly offered.

"No," Blade said. "He'd slow us down, and you'd be vulnerable with him in your arms." He pondered for a minute.

Boone was reloading the spent round in his Hombre. "I'm glad you're the one making the decisions," he observed. "I wouldn't want to be in your boots."

"Sometimes *I* don't want to be in my boots," Blade said, rising. He reflected for a bit more. "Okay. Here's what we'll do. Athena, I want you to stay here with Thunder—"

"Forget it," Athena said, cutting him off.

"What?"

"You heard me," Athena declared. "I like Thunder as much as you do, but I'm not staying behind. Not when we're so close. You need me."

"We can get by without you," Blade told her.

"Who do you think you're kidding?" Athena snapped. "The only reason you want me to stay here is because it'll keep me out of danger. You think you're doing the right thing, but you're not. Who else can lead you straight to the Kingdom? Who else knows the layout of the Kingdom like I do? Who else knows where the lookouts are posted?" She paused. "You need me, and you know it."

Blade hesitated. Her knowledge of the Spider and the countryside was a definite asset, but he didn't want to see her harmed.

"I'll stay," Boone volunteered.

Blade glanced at Thunder. "I don't know. . . ."

"You do need Athena," Boone noted. "And Grizzly can hold his own against those Hatchlings. I'm the logical choice. Besides, Thunder and I have become friends. We have a lot in common."

"Okay," Blade said, relieved to be off the hook. "You stay with Thunder. If he revives and he isn't seriously injured, come after us. Otherwise, stay here until we return."

Boone motioned toward the trees. "Where can I go?"

Blade capped his canteen and hooked it on his belt. He noticed Grizzly was staring at the Hatchling dispatched by his claws, grinning. "What are you so happy about?" he asked.

Grizzly chuckled. "Did you see the way I carved that sucker up? I haven't had this much fun in ages!"

CHAPTER TEN

Ooooohhh! His aching noggin!

Sergeant Havoc slowly regained consciousness. For a minute he experienced the illusion of being on a boat, of feeling the rise and fall of the craft on the swelling waves. And then he vividly recalled everything: following the hybrids, being played for a fool, and being captured. His eyes snapped open.

"The human is awake," a Hatchling promptly declared.

Havoc took his bearings. The Hatchlings had bound his hands and feet to a stout branch. Two of the hybrids were carrying him, each bearing one end of the branch on their shoulder. His body dangled from the bough, swaying with every step the Hatchlings took. A throbbing pain engulfed his head. His temples were particularly sore. The front of his camouflage T-shirt had been cut to shreds. His arms sported crimson gashes, and his fatigue pants and legs had been ripped and slashed. All of his weapons were gone. So was his backpack.

The two Hatchlings halted, and the one supporting the front end of the branch half turned and gazed at the soldier. "What is your name, human?"

Havoc licked his dry lips before replying. "Up yours!" He was facing the direction of their travel, to the west, and he could see the hapless woman prisoner several yards away. Walking past her, toward him, was a third mutant. Probably the leader, he guessed.

The third hybrid reached Havoc and stopped. "I am Dox," it stated.

Havoc defiantly stared into the Hatchling's round orbs. "Who cares?" he responded.

"What is your name?" Dox asked.

"You don't get beans out of me," Havoc said.

"I do not want beans, human," Dox reiterated. "I want your name."

"Go play with a live grenade," Havoc quipped.

Dox pointed at the woman. "Do you see her?"

"Of course."

"If you don't cooperate," Dox threatened, "I'll rip her eyes out!"

The woman cringed.

Havoc hesitated. Was Dox bluffing? He couldn't afford to find out.

"What will it be?" Dox questioned. "The information or her eyes? Speak up?"

What harm could revealing his name do? "Havoc," he disclosed.

"Your rank?"

"Sergeant," Havoc answered.

"How many others came with you, Sergeant Havoc?" Dox interrogated him.

"I was alone," Havoc lied.

"If you insult my intelligence again, the female will suffer," Dox vowed. "Now, how many others came with you?"

Havoc looked at the Hatchling called Dox. "Thirty-four," he answered with a straight face.

"And why were you sent?" Dox asked.

"We heard reports of Raiders in this area," Havoc fibbed. "We were sent to investigate." The Raiders were bands of human scavengers, outlaws who preyed on travelers and small communities in isolated regions. Most of the Raiders operated in eastern California and in the mountains in the south.

"There are no Raiders in this area," Dox said.

"That's not what we heard," Havoc declared.

"You are lying," Dox said. "You came after us."

"Hell, you freak. I don't even know what you are," Havoc claimed.

Dox leaned closer. "Don't ever refer to me as a freak again!

Ever!"

"Touchy, aren't we?" Havoc rejoined.

The Hatchling raised its two right arms overhead, about to strike.

"We don't have time for this!" interjected the mutant bearing the front of the limb. "We must warn Father."

"I agree," concurred the hybrid holding the rear of the branch.

Havoc craned his neck to see the third mutant. He recognized his sparring partner with the busted nose. "Hi, ugly! Remember me?"

"I remember you, human," the Hatchling responded, anger in his tone.

Dox suddenly jabbed Havoc in the ribs. "Pay attention."

Havoc grimaced, focusing on the leader.

"We are going to untie you," Dox detailed. "We can make better time if we don't have to carry you. But be advised. Any attempt to escape, any tricks at all, and the female pays the price. Do you understand?"

"I understand you, all right, creep," Havoc replied.

"And if you persist with the insults, I will tear out your tongue," Dox vowed menacingly.

"Me? Insult little old you?" Havoc taunted. "I wouldn't think of it."

Dox nodded at his two companions.

Havoc was suddenly dumped onto the ground, branch and all. A rock gouged his left shoulder blade and intense agony racked his head. "Damn!" he fumed.

Dox leaned over, smirking. "Ahhhh. I'm sorry. Did we hurt little old you?" He straightened, tittering. "Syph. Rhea. Untie this digusting slug."

Syph and Rhea bent to their task, and a moment later Havoc was free.

"On your feet!" Dox barked.

Havoc slowly rose, rubbing his sore wrists.

"Remember what I told you," Dox warned. "Any tricks, and the female bears the consequences."

Havod glanced at the woman. "What's your name?"

"Leslie," she replied. "Leslie Reese."

"Don't worry, Leslie," Havoc assured her. "We'll get out of this mess in one piece."

The three Hatchlings laughed.

"Human stupidity never ceases to amaze me," Dox commented.

Havoc wanted to tell Dox where to go, but he held his tongue.

Dox moved to the head of the line. "There's still an hour of daylight left. We'll ascend the cliffs before dark, and we should be home in a few hours." He looked back. "Havoc, you will walk with the woman. Syph and Rhea will be right behind you."

"Can I untie Leslie's hands?" Havoc ventured to ask.

"How touching!" Dox baited the human. "No. Leave her hands tied. If she experiences difficulty scaling the cliffs, help her."

"What harm can it do to untie her hands?" Havoc said, pressing the issue.

"Don't argue with me, human!" Dox stated, moving out, bearing to the west.

"Sorry. I tried," Havoc said to Leslie.

She mustered a feeble smile.

Havoc allowed her to proceed first. He used the interlude to get his bearings. They were still in the forest, but the vegetation appeared to be thinning. He glanced over his right shoulder, spying a ridge several hundred yards to their rear. Gazing ahead, he spotted another ridge, this one with towering cliffs comprising its visible side. The crags were steep and formidable, and he couldn't believe the Hatchlings intended to climb those palisades.

"I'm scared," Leslie confided softly, giving him a fleeting look.

"Who isn't?" Havoc responded.

"You don't seem the type to be scared of anything," Leslie said.

"Looks can be deceiving," Havoc noted.

"I'm just glad you're here," Leslie stated. "I feel better having you along."

"That's me," Havoc joked. "A knight in shining armor."

They unexpectedly emerged from the trees into the bright light of day. Twenty yards distant, situated at the base of the cliffs, was a pool of blue water 40 yards in diameter.

Dox led them to the right, walking along the edge of the pool toward a cleft in the rocks.

Havoc tilted his head, staring upward. The precipice was at

least five hundred feet high, mostly sheer stone. The Hatchlings had to be crazy if they expected to climb the face of the cliffs.

Dox reached the cleft and stopped, turning.

Havoc indicated the rearing palisade with a jerk of his right thumb. "You're not serious."

"Of course I am," Dox stated.

"How do you expect us to climb *that*?" Havoc queried.

Dox peered upward. "Very carefully," he responded.

"I'll never make it," Leslie interjected. She took a deep breath, her lower lip trembling.

"If you make it to the top, you live," Dox said. "If you don't reach the top . . ." He shrugged.

"You're not going to force her to climb with her hands tied, are you?" Havoc demanded.

"I'm not?" Dox rejoined.

"How can she climb without her hands?" Havoc asked angrily.

"You will be her hands," Dox said. "You will assist her in scaling the cliffs. I've assisted others before. You can do it."

Havoc studied the wall of rock leading to the top of the ridge. "What if I blow it? What good is she going to be to the Spider dead?"

Dox cocked his head, his mouth twitching. "And how would you know about the Spider? You claimed ignorance of our identity?"

Havoc realized he had slipped up. Again. "I heard you talking earlier," he hastily explained. "Right before you jumped me."

"That's possible, I suppose," Dox said. "But somehow I doubt it. I suspect you know a lot more about the Spider than you're letting on. We will find out the truth."

"You think so, huh?" Havoc couldn't resist countering.

"I know so," Dox asserted. "Our father will pry the truth from your lips, human." He looked at the cleft. "We could go around these cliffs, but we're in a hurry. If neither of you fall, you'll reach the top in half an hour."

"How? By sprouting wings?" Havoc questioned sarcastically.

"By walking," Dox stated. "Follow me." He entered the cleft.

Havoc smiled encouragement at Leslie and went after Dox. Leslie stayed on his heels.

The cleft was surprisingly spacious. Even more fascinating was the narrow ledge slanting upward across the cliffs, starting in the cleft and disappearing above.

Dox indicated the ledge. "No one knows about this except us. Passage is perilous, but the ledge goes all the way to the top. Just don't look down if you're afraid of heights."

"Why should you care if we live or die?" Havoc inquired.

"I don't," Dox said. "But my father will be very pleased if you arrive in the Kingdom alive."

"We'll try not to disappoint your old man," Havoc declared.

Dox gingerly stepped onto the ledge and began ascending, his four hands clinging to whatever cracks and protuberances were available.

Havoc frowned as he eased onto the ledge. Portions of the ledge seemed a natural part of the stone, while other sections appeared to have been chiseled out of the rock. The width varied from only six inches in spots to over a foot elsewhere.

Leslie Reese stayed by Havoc's side.

"Lean inward," he advised her. "Keep your body as close to the cliff as you can. Don't look down and don't lean back. I'm right here if you need me."

Leslie nodded.

The climb was a harrowing experience. Havoc was in a cold sweat before he had gone twenty feet. He clutched at every nook and cranny he found, tentatively placing one foot after the other. The higher he went, the stronger the wind became. He kept his eyes on Leslie, his left hand never straying far from her shoulders. She tucked her chin into her chest and gamely followed him.

"You're doing fine," Havoc encouraged her every so often.

Leslie would grin in response.

Havoc forgot all about the discomfort in his head and the gashes on his body. His total concentration was focused on the arduous task of scaling the cliffs. He lost all track of time, except for noting the daylight was progressively dimming. The prospect of being caught on the rock wall when night fell was too disturbing to contemplate.

"Did I mention where I'm from?" Leslie abruptly asked when they were almost halfway to the summit.

"Don't talk," Havoc advised her.

"I've got to," Leslie said. "I must do something to take my

mind off this nightmare."

"Where are you from?" Havoc inquired.

"Weed," Leslie answered.

"Weed? Is that the name of a town or did you sprout from a seed?" Havoc joked.

Leslie shuffled one foot after the other, sticking by him. "Weed is a town, silly. Near Mt. Shasta. Haven't you ever heard of it?"

"Nope," Havoc admitted. A protruding spike of stone forced him to lean out from the wall as he negotiated a thin section of ledge. He paused, gripping her shoulders to brace her. "Be careful."

Leslie blanched and gulped. She nervously sidled past the spike.

"Not bad," Havoc said. "Maybe you should take up mountain climbing as a hobby."

"No way," Leslie declared.

They continued in silence for many minutes.

"Are you from California?" Leslie inquired at one point.

"Born and bred," Havoc replied. "Why?"

"Just asked," Leslie said. "You never heard of Weed."

"Do you realize how many small towns and communities there are in California? I'm lucky if I've heard of half of them," Havoc stated.

"You'd like Weed," Leslie commented. "It's quiet and peaceful. Now and then we have mutant trouble, but mostly we go about our business without having to worry about being attacked. There aren't any Raiders in these parts."

"I'll have to visit Weed some day," Havoc mentioned.

"I'd like that," Leslie said. "I'll bake you some cookies."

"Oatmeal?"

Leslie grinned. "If you like."

"Oatmeal cookies are my favorite," Havoc explained. "My mom used to bake them when I was a kid. I could smell them in the oven miles off. They were the world's best cookies."

"Does your mother still make them for you?" Leslie questioned.

"No," Havoc replied. "My mom died when I was twelve."

"Sorry to hear that," Leslie commiserated.

"I try to visit her grave once a year," Havoc said. "She's buried in my hometown."

"Where's that?"

"Three Rivers," Havoc disclosed. "In southern California."

"Never heard of it," Leslie remarked.

"Are you sure you're from California?" Havoc asked.

Leslie giggled.

Havoc felt his confidence building. He began to believe they would reach the pinnacle without mishap.

He was wrong.

There was a scraping noise and a rustling from above.

Havoc looked up as dust and small stones pelted his shoulders. There was a large crack about four feet above his head. The crack was about eight inches wide and two feet long. Jutting from the lower portion was a profusion of dry sticks, weeds, grass, and bark. A bird nest. He knew a lot of birds constructed their nests in cliffs, talus slopes, and the like. But he doubted the nest was occupied. February was not a normal breeding month, so far as he was aware. But what had caused the dust and stones to fall? He cautiously moved past the crack, then reached for Leslie. "Be careful," he advised.

Leslie smiled at him.

Havoc's left hand was on her right shoulder, steadying her.

"We're going to make it," Leslie asserted.

A small mottled gray bird suddenly darted from the crack, its wings flapping furiously, sending a rain of dust and broken bits of nest into Leslie's face. She instinctively drew her head back, her eyes stinging, involuntarily coughing. And slipped.

Havoc's gut muscles tightened as he felt her start to go. He lunged, clutching the fabric of her tan blouse near her shoulder, trying to restrain her.

Leslie's terrified blue eyes locked on his as her upper torso tilted over the edge, her left foot sliding from the ledge.

"*No!*" Havoc shouted, digging his fingers into the blouse material and tugging.

The blouse ripped.

Havoc's right arm, his hand in a groove in the rock, bulged as he frantically attempted to bear her weight.

Leslie Reese screamed as she plummeted from the ledge. Her blouse tore loose from Havoc's grip, and then she was plunging toward the base of the cliffs.

Havoc, horrified, watched her fall. He saw the pleading look on her face and the O her mouth formed as she screamed. For a hopeful instant he thought she might be safe, might land in the pool at the bottom, but his hope was forlorn. The pool was too far to the left.

Too far.

Leslie was still screaming when she smashed onto the boulders below. One moment she was a living, breathing woman; the next she was a pulpy pile of gory flesh and crimson.

Havoc was shocked to his core. She had relied on him! Depended on him to see her through! He gaped at her shattered figure, his mind dazed.

"What happened?" demanded a grating voice to his right.

Havoc didn't bother to turn. "She fell," he said softly.

"I can see that, you imbecile!" Dox snapped. "Why?"

"A bird," Havoc mumbled. "A little bird."

"Our father will not be pleased," Dox stated. "She may have been trash, but we wanted her alive."

Havoc twisted, glaring at the Hatchling, his expression grim. He wanted to take hold of the mutant and leap from the edge. He felt he deserved such a fate for failing the woman.

"No, the Spider will not like this at all," Dox mentioned, peering downward.

The Spider! The bastard responsible for all of this! Havoc sneered at Dox. If it was the last thing he ever did, he was going to see they paid for their atrocities!

"Why are you looking at me like that?" Dox asked in annoyance.

"Can't you guess, *imbecile?*" Havoc countered, his tone tainted by his rage.

"I warned you about your insults," Dox said.

"What are you going to do about it?" Havoc responded.

Dox scrutinized the soldier for a moment, then glanced over the ledge. "Nothing. For now."

"I didn't think so," Havoc said, mocking the hybrid.

Dox resumed climbing. "But there will be a reckoning, human! You can count on it!"

Sergeant Havoc nodded. "I am."

CHAPTER ELEVEN

K raft came awake with a start, his arms aching, flat on his back.

The heavens were filled with stars and a cool breeze was blowing, refreshing him. Close by an owl hooted. He noted the moon had risen.

Where the hell was he?

In a vivid rush of memories he recalled the fight with the Hatchlings. He remembered tackling the mutant behind the log and tumbling to the turf, trying to draw his switchblade from his right pocket. A hard object had slammed into his head and he'd gone down.

That was it.

So why was he still alive?

Kraft went to sit up and discovered his wrists and ankles were tied, his hands behind his back. And his guns and backpack were missing!

He was a prisoner!

But where were Blade and the others?

An inky form materialized before him. "So, human! You are awake!"

Kraft recognized the hideous outline of a Hatchling. "Are you the one who caught me?"

"I am Siad," the hybrid stated.

"Where am I? Where's my blood?" Kraft queried.

"In your body," Siad said. "You are not bleeding."

"Not that kind of blood, Franky," Kraft stated. "I mean my brothers on the Force. Where are they?"

"How should I know?" Siad replied.

"I don't get this, man. How come I'm still kicking?" Kraft inquired.

"Would you prefer to be dead?" Siad rejoined.

"Cut the crap, jerk!" Kraft snapped. "Come clean."

"I bathe regularly," Siad said.

Kraft shook his head. "This ain't for real! This can't be happening!"

"This is happening," Siad remarked.

"Where are you taking me, Franky?" Kraft asked.

"I told you my name is Siad," the hybrid declared. "Why do you persist in calling me Franky?"

"Can you read?" Kraft questioned.

Siad didn't respond.

"Can you read, Franky?" Kraft repeated.

"Yes, I can read," Siad stated curtly. "Although why bother? All there is to read is human drivel."

"Well, I can read too," Kraft said proudly. "My dad taught me. You see, I spent most of my childhood and teen years in the Twin Cities. Do you know where that is?"

"Who cares?" Siad replied.

"The Twin Cities are in Minnesota," Kraft detailed. "Minneapolis and St. Paul, they were called. They're a wreck now. I was raised there."

"Of what interest is this babble to me?" Siad asked.

"You wanted to know why I call you Franky," Kraft reminded the mutant. He was eager to continue the conversation, to buy time while he worked on the rope or whatever bound his wrists.

"I'm sorry I asked," Siad quipped.

"Years ago gangs took control of the Twin Cities," Kraft went on. "They were always fighting over their turf. I belonged to one of those gangs. The Porns."

Siad raised his head and sniffed the air. "I trust there is a point to all this?"

"Yeah. There is. I came across this far-out deal once in the basement of a demolished house. It wasn't exactly a book. I don't know what it was. There were a lot of color pictures, drawings, and stuff in it. I'd never seen anything like it. Books and magazines were scarce in the Twins. Most of them had been burned, used for fuel during the winter. The one I found was a real turn-on," Kraft said.

Siad yawned.

"Part of the front page was missing," Kraft went on. He was rubbing his wrists together, striving to loosen the loops binding them. "It was titled Something-Illustrated. And the story was about this dude named Frankenstein. He was a scientist, and he put together this groddy monster. The thing was inhuman." He paused, glowering. "Just like you, Franky!"

Siad glanced down. "Don't push your luck. I'm grateful for the opportunity to escape. They'll think I'm dead. But be nice, or else."

"Be nice!" Kraft practically exploded. "I'll give you nice, shithead! Cut me loose and I'll rack your ass!"

Siad squatted next to his prisoner. "I take it you're not fond of mutants."

"Fond? Mutants are sludge! Every damn one should be wiped off the face of the earth! *I hate mutants!*" Kraft thundered.

"And I'm not very fond of most humans," Siad said. "But at least I have a reason."

"So do I!" Kraft bellowed.

"Prejudice is not a reason," Siad stated.

"It has nothing to do with prejudice!" Kraft retorted.

"Then why?"

Kraft leaned toward the hybrid, his features contorted in rage. "Because a mutant killed my sister! Is that reason enough for you?"

"Your petty feelings don't matter to me," Siad responded.

Kraft strained against his bonds, to no avail.

"Don't worry, human," Siad said. "I will put you out of your misery before too long."

"I'm surprised you haven't killed me already," Kraft noted scornfully.

"Not yet," Siad stated. "Not until I get hungry."

"I hope I give you gas!"

Siad rose and walked to a nearby tree. He sat down with his

back against the trunk. "Get some rest, human."

"Why should I?" Kraft rejoined.

"Because we have far to travel tomorrow," Siad disclosed. "I have not slept for two days, or we would be traveling now."

"Where are you taking me?"

"North," Siad answered.

"You mind telling me why?" Kraft wanted to know.

"Yes. Now rest." Siad fell silent.

Kraft glared at the mutant. His arms were aching and he was chafing his wrists, but he was determined to stay up all night working on the rope. And as soon as he was free, there was going to be one less mutated monstrosity running around!

CHAPTER TWELVE

"Thank goodness for the moon," Athena commented.

Blade gazed skyward at the bright full moon, seeming like a beacon in a firmament of starry supplicants. The lunar illumination was sufficient to light up the landscape 15 to 20 yards in every direction. He glanced over his right shoulder at the ridge silhouetted against the heavens. Athena's memory had served them in good stead. She had led them to the first of the two ridges located due east of the Kingdom, the same one they'd seen earlier. In the middle of the ridge had been a gorge. They had vigilantly moved through the rocky gorge and found a stretch of forest beyond.

"There are the cliffs," Athena mentioned.

Blade faced front. The moonlight bathed the second ridge, the one with the cliff wall comprising its eastern side, in a diffuse white glow. Once over that ridge, they would find the Kingdom.

"The pool should be up ahead," Athena said.

Blade followed her as they threaded their way through the underbrush. He looked over his left shoulder to insure Grizzly was still with them. The mutant's ability to glide furtively through the densest vegetation was astonishing. Grizzly was only a yard behind him, but Blade never heard a sound. He knew he shouldn't be surprised, not after Grizzly's performance on the stealth test.

The trio wound a path through the murky woods for several minutes.

"There!" Athena exclaimed, pointing.

Blade saw it too. A large pool of water, slightly to their left.

"That's what saved my life," Athena stated. "That's what I fell in after I went over the top of the cliffs."

Grizzly came up alongside them, scrutinizing the palisade. "How the hell are we going to get up that?"

"Is there a way up?" Blade asked Athena.

"None that I know of," Athena answered. "We'll have to go around, to the south. We can bypass the cliffs."

"But it will take us longer," Blade noted.

"Can't be helped," Athena said.

Blade stared at the rim far above. "Can the lookouts see us from up there?"

"No," Athena replied. "The lookouts are posted on the west side of this ridge, closer to the Kingdom. Their main purpose is to prevent the women from escaping. The Spider doesn't bother posting sentrys on this side of the ridge. Who would be crazy enough to try and climb those cliffs? Lookouts on this side aren't necessary."

Grizzly took several steps toward the cliffs, inhaling deeply.

"Do you smell something?" Blade asked.

"Blood."

"Blood?" Blade hefted his M-16 and moved forward. "Where?"

Grizzly indicated a cluster of boulders at the base of the cliffs about 60 yards to the right. "There. I detect fresh blood."

"We'd better investigate," Blade stated.

"It's human blood," Grizzly added.

"You can tell what type from the scent?" Athena inquired doubtfully.

"The nose knows," Grizzly remarked.

"Lead the way," Blade directed.

Grizzly padded toward the boulders, hunched over, his arms at his sides, his fingers partially tensed.

"Stay behind me," Blade advised Athena.

"I can take care of myself," she responded.

"Stay behind me," Blade reiterated, hastening after Grizzly.

The mutant slowed as he neared the boulders, lifting his nose to the wind. He skirted a cluster of huge circular boulders, then stopped next to a jagged flat one about seven feet across. The top of the flat boulder was four feet from the ground.

Blade reached Grizzly's side. "Where . . ." he started to ask, and then he saw the body on the flat boulder. Or what was left of the body. He turned to warn Athena away, too late.

"Dear God!" she blurted out, standing to Grizzly's left.

Blade bent down, studying the remains. He could distinguish a solitary arm jutting upward from a mushy mass of pulverized flesh and broken bones.

"Is it Sergeant Havoc or Kraft?" Athena queried in horror.

"It's a woman," Grizzly divulged.

Blade spotted strands of light-colored hair at one end of the grisly remains. "It's the woman the Hatchlings abducted," he said. "The one we saw them with."

"What could have happened to her?" Athena questioned.

Blade glanced upward. "It should be obvious."

"But how?" Athena questioned. "If the Hatchlings went around the cliffs, they wouldn't go anywhere near the top above these boulders."

"If they went around the cliffs," Blade observed thoughtfully.

"What are you saying?" Athena asked.

Blade gazed up at the rock wall. "Maybe she didn't fall from the top. Maybe there's a way up we don't know about."

"Up that?" Athena said, nodding at the cliffs. "You're nuts."

"Am I?" Blade responded. "There's no other explanation for the body being here."

"So what if there is a way up?" Athena stated. "We're certainly not going to climb up in the dark, are we?"

Blade began walking to the left. "I'm thinking about it."

"You're insane," Athena told him.

Blade grinned. "There are those who might agree."

Grizzly was examining the face of the ridge. "We could save time."

"You're insane too!" Athena commented. "Up *there*? At *night*?"

Blade followed the base of the cliffs to the left, in the direction of the pool. If the woman had fallen from part way up, and not the top, then there had to be a means of ascending, a ledge or shelf of some kind. He hadn't seen any indication of hand-and footholds chiseled into the rock. But a ledge might blend in, be indistinguishable at close range.

"There's no way I'm going up there at night!" Athena said nervously.

"You can stay here," Blade suggested. "Wait for Boone and Thunder to catch up."

"I'm not staying here by myself," Athena declared.

Blade was almost to the pool when he spied a dark space between two rocks. Curious, he crossed to the spot and discovered a cleft. "Well look at this." He entered the cleft and there it was, a ledge angling up the cliffs.

Grizzly and Athena came into the cleft.

"We found what we need," Grizzly said.

Athena walked up to the rock wall and studied the ledge. "This is the way to the top?"

"Appears so," Blade confirmed, slinging his M-16 over his right shoulder.

"We could wind up like that poor woman," Athena commented.

"That we could," Blade agreed.

"And you still intend going up?" Athena pressed him.

Grizzly slung his M-16 over his left shoulder.

Blade glanced at the mutant. "I've been meaning to ask you. Why didn't you use your M-16 on that Hatchling earlier? Why did you go after it with your claws?"

Grizzly grinned. "I like the personal touch."

"If we make it to the Kingdom, I hope you won't be shy about using the M-16," Blade said. "And your explosives, for that matter."

Grizzly checked the straps on his backpack. "I'm not an idiot. When the odds are stacked against me, I'll use whatever is available."

"Good." Blade turned to Athena. "What will it be? Up with us, or wait here for Boone and Thunder?"

Athena swallowed hard as she arched her neck, staring at the ridge far above. "Why can't we just go around?"

"I think you know the answer," Blade said. "Havoc and Kraft have been captured. There's no telling how long the Hatchlings will let them live. So the sooner we reach the Kingdom, the better."

Athena was clearly in turmoil, torn between her fear and her duty.

Blade gently placed his right hand on her shoulder. "If you don't want to come, we'll understand. There's no stigma attached if you stay here. You're not in the Force. I don't expect you to lay your life on the line."

"But I want to be there when the Spider gets his," Athena said. "I'll never sleep at nights if I don't see him dead with my own eyes."

"Don't let that worry you," Grizzly offered. "I'll bring back this Spider's head for you, if it's necessary."

Athena stared into Grizzly's eyes. "You surprise me."

"How so?" Grizzly responded.

"You seem so eager to kill."

Grizzly smiled. "I was bred to kill."

"But the Spider is a mutant, just like you," Athena mentioned. "You don't mind killing another mutant?"

"I killed a Hatchling, didn't I?" Grizzly asked.

"You know what I mean," Athena stated.

Grizzly slowly nodded. "Yep. I guess I do. And I'll answer your question as honestly as I can. It's no secret I'm not fond of humans. By the same token, I consider most mutants superior to humans in every respect. But this Spider could prove me wrong." He paused, glancing at Blade, then Athena. "Like I told Blade, I believe humans are scum, a blight on the planet. Humans have perpetrated every manner of evil. Your species almost destroyed all the life on this world!"

"And what about mutants?" Blade interrupted. "Your record is hardly stainless. Remember the Doktor, the genetic engineer responsible for creating you and your kind? He had an entire army of mutants at his disposal, and they killed thousands upon thousands during his reign of terror. So where do you get off claiming humans are any worse than mutants?"

"Those mutants the Doktor bred, like me, were specifically reared and trained for one purpose. To kill. And you well know the Doktor snuffed out or imprisoned any mutant who opposed him," Grizzly noted. "Those mutants were merely fulfilling their biological imperative, as the Doktor liked to say. But you humans, on the other hand, weren't produced from test tubes. You weren't raised to function solely as killers. Yet that's what

most of you are. Whether you admit it to yourself or not, as a
species you'll kill anything and everything that gets in your way.
Even yourselves, when you don't see eye to eye."

"Bull," Blade said. "Sure, we've had more than our share of
mindless wars. And granted, many humans do seem ready to
shed blood at the slightest provocation. But by and large the
majority of humans are peace-loving, kind individuals."

"Tell that to the millions who were nuked during World War
Three," Grizzly countered. "I'm sure they'd agree."

"You still haven't told me how you feel about the Spider,"
Athena interjected.

"He puzzles me," Grizzly confided.

"Why?" Athena inquired.

"Because if the Spider is everything you say he is, then he's no
different than you humans," Grizzly said bitterly. "He's just as
warped as the worst of your species. And if that's the case, then
everything I believe in is all wrong. If this Spider is the scumbag
you paint him to be, then I might need to rethink my outlook
on life."

"Why do you keep saying 'if' all the time?" Athena inquired.
"Do you think I would lie?"

"I don't know you that well, lady," Grizzly said. "All I have is
your word about the Spider."

"But you saw the Hatchlings!" Athena protested. "*They*
attacked us! Surely you can see how evil they are!"

"I don't see nothing of the kind," Grizzly rejoined. "For all I
know, they attacked us because we've invaded their territory.
They might like their privacy, and I can appreciate that."

"But they killed Spader!" Athena noted shrilly.

"Spader was a jerk," Grizzly said. "And we killed two of
them. So if you ask me, the slate is about even."

"And what about the woman?" Athena demanded, her anger
rising. "You saw she was their prisoner!"

"All I saw was a woman walking with a half-dozen Hatchlings
over half a mile away," Grizzly stated. "How do I know she was
their prisoner?"

Athena clenched her left fist and shook it at the mutant. "I
can't believe you, you know that! I can't believe anyone can be
so stupid!"

"Watch your mouth," Grizzly advised her.

Athena glanced at Blade for support. "What's with you? Why haven't you said anything? Did you know he felt this way?"

"No," Blade acknowledged. "Not all of it anyway." He looked at Grizzly. "I do need some clarification."

"About what?" Grizzly queried.

"Your motive for coming on this mission," Blade said. "You volunteered, just like the rest of the Force. But I gather your motivation might have been different. The others agreed to come because they wanted to save the women from the Spider's clutches. But you, I take it, came not so much because you want to rescue the women as you want to prove something to yourself. You want to prove the Spider isn't the despicable despot everyone claims. Am I right?"

Grizzly nodded. "That's it in a nutshell."

Athena snorted contemptuously. "Now I've heard everything! All mutants must be off their rockers!"

"Don't judge us by your standards," Grizzly mentioned harshly. "We're not the same."

"Thank the Lord for that!" Athena retorted.

"I should have known you'd be religious," Grizzly muttered. "You're not?"

"Are you kidding?" Grizzly baited her. "I'm not that stupid!"

"Don't sell yourself short," Athena said. "You're not as brilliant as you think you are."

"Okay," Blade interrupted. "That's enough."

Athena stared at the Warrior. "You're just going to stand there and take all this crap? How can you be so calm?"

"What would you have me do?" Blade asked. "Shoot Grizzly in the head because he doesn't think like we do? Because we don't share the same beliefs? Because he doesn't have faith in the Spirit?"

"That'd be a start!" Athena suggested. "You're supposed to be so religious! Do something! Anything! Prove he's wrong! Show him!"

Blade sighed. "Athena, it's not my business to meddle in Grizzly's personal life. Nor are his beliefs my concern, so long as they don't affect the rest of the Force. I know he's wrong, but I can't beat the truth into him. He'll have to find out for himself."

Athena shook her head. "Some spiritual person you are!"

"I told you before," Blade said. "I'm not a preacher or a

teacher. I'm a Warrior. Yes, I was raised in a religious environment. Yes, I consider myself a spiritual person, but I'm not qualified to preach. For one thing, I don't have the temperament. For another, I do have talent as a Warrior."

Athena laughed. "A spiritual Warrior! There's a contradiction."

"What's so unusual about that?" Blade inquired. "Read a bible sometime. Study Samson and David, to name just two. They were warriors and they were spiritual."

Athena pursed her lips, perturbed.

"Can we get this show on the road?" Grizzly inquired. "I thought I joined a military outfit, not a revival!"

Blade walked up to the cliff and stepped onto the ledge. "Let's go. Are you coming, Athena, or not?"

Athena gazed upward. "I'm not staying here."

Blade extended his left hand. "Then take hold. Grizzly and I will help you up. One of us will always have a hand on you."

"If you don't mind my touch," Grizzly noted. "Me being off my rocker and all."

Athena gulped and took Blade's hand. "I hope I don't live to regret this."

They began the ascent.

CHAPTER THIRTEEN

Havoc was waiting for the perfect opportunity to make his break. Dox was in front of him, Rhea behind. They were descending the west slope of the ridge toward the valley below, toward the Kingdom. The breeze was cool and refreshing, invigorating him after the arduous ordeal on the cliffs.

"Home," Dox announced happily.

Havoc could see several lights flickering in the valley.

"Tell me, human," Dox said, mocking him. "How does it feel to be on the verge of your doom?"

"Speak for yourself," Havoc retorted.

"Too bad we lost the female," Rhea commented, his voice distorted by his crushed nasal passages.

"That wasn't our fault," Dox said. "This human is to blame."

"Up yours!" Havoc snapped.

Dox looked over his right shoulder. "I just hope I get the brains."

"The brains?" Havoc repeated, puzzled.

"Your brains when we feast on you," Dox stated. "I like brains, and I shall relish consuming yours."

"Fat chance," Havoc remarked.

"I like fat too," Dox confirmed.

Havoc debated whether to make his break. There were only two of them now. Dox had ordered the other Hatchling, a

deviate named Syph, to stand guard at the top of the cliffs for a
while to insure no one was on their trail. Syph had grumbled but
assented.

"The Tower," Dox remarked cheerfully.

"What tower?" Havoc questioned. The middle of the valley
was too distant to perceive much detail, even with the full
moon.

"That's right," Dox commented. "You humans can't see
worth shit at night."

Havoc surreptitiously glanced to his rear, noting Rhea's
position. The hybrid was two yards away, repeatedly gazing at
the valley ahead as if he couldn't wait to reach their destination.
Dox was the same way. Neither mutant was expecting trouble,
and why should they? He had cooperated so far. They wouldn't
anticipate him being rash enough to attempt to escape in their
own territory, which was exactly why he should go for broke.
Once they had him in that Tower, he'd be at their mercy.
Getting away would be considerably harder.

"My nose hurts like hell," Rhea commented.

A dark figure unexpectedly emerged from cover 15 yards off.
"Is that you, Dox?"

"Who else would it be, idiot!" Dox replied.

As they drew nearer, Havoc discovered the figure was a
human guard wearing black clothing to blend in with the night.
The guard carried an automatic rifle of indeterminate type.

"That's no way to talk to me, Dox," the guard stated. "We
are brothers, after all."

"Don't remind me, Sadist," Dox said distastefully.

The guard, a short man with a pale countenance, came closer.
"Weren't you sent after a female? And where's the rest?"

Dox did not seem pleased by the interrogation. "Who are you
to question me? I report to Father. No one else."

"I was just wondering," Sadist said.

"Don't bother me!" Dox snapped disdainfully, marching past
the guard.

Havoc came abreast of the man in black. He noticed a scar
running down the left side of Sadist's face. The weapon he
recognized as a Heckler & Koch Model HK94, an excellent
piece of firepower.

Sadist returned Havoc's glance with a threatening scowl.

"Hi there, baboon-face!" Havoc quipped. "Were you born looking like that, or did you take a self-improvement course?"

The reaction was exactly what Havoc wanted.

Angry, stung by Dox's rebuke, and now insulted by the prisoner's effrontery, Sadist impulsively raised the HK94 with the stock toward the soldier, preparing to bash the noncom in the mouth.

Only Havoc had other ideas. As the Sadist lifted the HK94, he exposed his midsection and his groin. Havoc pivoted, executing a side stop kick to Sadist's genitals, his right leg a streak as the blow connected. Even as Sadist grunted and started to double over, Havoc closed in, ramming his elbow into the guard's nose, crushing it. As expected, Sadist's grip on the HK94 went momentarily limp, and Havoc wrested the weapon from his hands. The maneuver was accomplished in the twinkling of an eye, before either Hatchling could intervene.

Rhea responded first, hissing and charging.

There was no time to check the safety. Havoc swung around, leveling the HK94, and squeezed the trigger. The HK94 cut loose. Previously converted to full automatic and outfitted with a 30-shot magazine, the HK94 stopped the mutant in its tracks, the 9-mm Parabellum slugs ripping a pattern across Rhea's face and crumpling the hybrid to the ground.

One more to go!

Havoc whirled, finding Dox not two feet away, talons outstretched. He fired, the HK94 chattering, the rounds tearing into Dox's chest and propelling him backwards, the impact sending the mutant sprawling.

Sadist was trying to rise, his left hand over his ruined nose, his knees wobbly.

Havoc swiveled, pointing the HK94 barrel at the guard.

"No!" Sadist bleated, gaping at the end of the barrel not a hand's-breath from his face. "Don't!" he gurgled.

"Stand up!" Havoc commanded.

Sadist slowly straightened, blood pouring over his mouth and chin.

Havoc backed up several strides, allowing room in case the guard tried to jump him. He glanced at the lights in the valley, waiting for a hue and cry, some indication his shots had been heard. He guessed the lights must be a quarter of a mile off.

"What are you gonna do with me?" Sadist blubbered.

"Shut up!" Havoc snapped, listening. He waited several minutes, but nothing happened.

Sadist was breathing loudly through his mouth.

"Where are the other guards?" Havoc asked, his tone grating and hard.

"There are two patroling the area near the huts," the Sadist said. "Down there." He pointed toward the valley.

"What about up here?" Havoc queried.

Sadist wiped some blood from his lips. "I'm the only one."

Havoc wagged the HK94. "You expect me to believe you?"

"Honest!" Sadist wailed. "Just one guard is posted on this ridge!"

"Where are the rest of the Hatchlings?" Havoc probed.

"In the Tower, as far as I know," the Sadist said.

"Okay. Move your ass!" Havoc waved the barrel in the direction of a stand of trees to his left.

"I'm going!" the guard assured him, hurrying to obey.

Havoc cautiously followed Sadist into the trees. Satisfied they were concealed from view, he halted. "Stop!" he directed.

Sadist complied, his left hand over his nose. "Please don't hurt me!"

"Why shouldn't I?" Havoc demanded. "I know all about what you've done to the women here. You deserve to die, you prick!"

Sadist gasped. "Please! No! I'll do anything you say! Anything you want!"

"I want information," Havoc stated. "For starters, why did you call that Hatchling your brother?"

"Because he is," the guard replied. "Or was."

"I don't get you," Havoc said.

"We both had the same parents," Sadist divulged.

"Dox and you had the same parents?" Havoc asked skeptically.

"That's right," Sadist affirmed.

"The Spider was your father?" Havoc queried.

"You know about the Spider?" the guard responded.

"Why do you think I'm here?" Havoc retorted. "But how is it you both had the same parents?"

"Easy," Sadist said. "Sometimes the Spider's babies are

mutants, or part mutant, like the Hatchlings. They take after the Spider. But some of the babies are human, like me. We take after our moms."

"So the human guards here are all children of the Spider? All his human kids?" Havoc asked.

"Yep," Sadist confirmed. "The Spider doesn't let all the human babies live. Only the males, and only enough to keep his guards up to strength."

"What about the rest of the boy babies and the girls?" Havoc inquired.

Sadist hesitated.

"I asked you a question," Havoc stated stiffly.

"They're . . . eaten," Sadist responded hesitantly.

"And you don't do a thing to prevent it, do you?" Havoc asked.

"What could I do?" Sadist said fearfully. "The Hatchlings would eat me if I objected!"

Havoc's lips curled downward. "You make me sick!"

Sadist wisely kept his mouth shut.

"All right. Here's what we're going to do," Havoc stated. "You are going to lead me to the Tower. Any problems, and I'll blow your head off. Understand?"

"The Tower?" Sadist glanced toward the valley. "You don't mean it!"

"Want to bet?" Havoc countered.

"Listen, mister, I'll take you anywhere but the Tower," Sadist said. "Anywhere!"

"You'll take me to the Tower, or you'll die right here," Havoc declared.

"But *he's* in the Tower!" Sadist exclaimed.

"Which is why I want to go," Havoc said. "I'm going to kill the Spider."

Sadist shook his head. "You're nuts, mister! There's no way you can kill him!"

"Haven't you heard?" Havoc cracked. "A positive attitude can do wonders for your life." He motioned with the HK94 barrel. "Get the lead out!"

Sadist shuffled down the slope. "You'll never make it!"

"Let me worry about the Spider," Havoc said. "And keep your trap shut!"

Shaking his head, holding his broken nose, Sadist descended.

Havoc was alert for the slightest hint of danger as he dogged the guard's tracks. Since no alarm had sounded, he doubted anyone had heard the shots before. Which meant he might be able to reach the Tower of the Spider unnoticed. Once there, he intended to bring the mission to a speedy resolution by terminating the Spider. If the Spider fell, or so he reasoned, the Hatchlings might be easier to dispose of. The Spider was the leader, the brains behind the operation, and without him the Hatchlings and the human guards might come apart at the seams. At any rate, his plan was worth a try.

The trees on the ridge became sparser the lower they went, the tree line fronting a wide field between the forest and the middle of the valley. Huge nets were suspended above the field on poles, obscuring the parcels tilled during the spring and summer from aerial observation. Brown, dry, and broken corn stalks littered the field. On the far side a group of buildings, the huts and the Tower, were visible.

A path wound under the nets, and Sadist moved along it.

Havoc felt his muscles tense as they approached the center of the valley, the heart of the Spider's domain. He was bothered by the sensation of being watched, but he surveyed the field and the buildings beyond without spotting a soul. His instincts were prompting him to abandon his plan, to take cover in the forest and await a better opportunity. But he advanced anyway. He wanted to end the mission as quickly as possible, but he also wanted to prove something to himself and to Blade. Twice the Warrior had bested him at his own game. Twice! And one of those times had been at hand-to-hand combat, no less. His specialty! He wanted to redeem himself in Blade's eyes, to show the Warrior why he was considered the best damn soldier in the California Army!

And then there was the woman.

Havoc frowned as he thought of Leslie Reese. He'd failed her, failed her miserably, and as a consequence she had died. The sight of her lying broken and smashed on the rocks below the cliffs had been horrifying. He had felt like a branding iron had been imbedded in his abdomen. He still felt that way. To a man who prided himself on his perfection, failure was devastating. By terminating the Spider, he might atone, in some small way, for

Leslie Reese's death. He might assuage his burning guilt.

The huts were starkly defined by the moonlight. There were ten of them, one much larger than the others, each with a domed roof. Only the large hut displayed any light through its windows. Light also emanated from the Kingdom's centerpiece, the enormous, imposing, ominous edifice dominating the valley: the Tower.

Havoc stepped up to Sadist and prodded him in the spine with the HK94. "Slow down," he whispered.

Sadist imitated a statue.

"Where are the women?" Havoc queried.

"In their huts," Sadist said. "They're not allowed out this late."

"In what part of the Tower will I find the Spider?" Havoc asked.

"The top," Sadist revealed. "His chamber is way up at the very top."

Havoc gave Sadist a shove. "Head for the Tower. And no monkey business!"

The ground around the huts and the Tower had been cleared of all brush. There was no place to hide, and no one was in sight.

Havoc felt more confident as they walked between two huts toward the Tower. The large hut occupied by the guards was positioned to the north of the rest, perhaps 50 yards distant. They weren't expecting an attack and their security was lax. He couldn't believe how easy the job was.

That was when another guard appeared, coming around the corner of a hut to the right, whistling softly, an HK94 slung over his right shoulder. He abruptly halted, spotting the newcomers. "Sadist? Is that you?"

Havoc nudged Sadist with the barrel.

"Sure is, Jim."

Havoc was partially screened by Sadist. He held the HK94 low so the other guard wouldn't spot it.

Jim came toward them. "What the hell are you doing here? Aren't you supposed to be up on the east ridge?"

"I had to report," Sadist said.

"Report what?" Jim rejoined, now four strides away. "Why do you sound so funny? And who's that with you?"

Havoc waited until the second guard was almost to them

before he made his move. He shoved Sadist aside and performed a front snap kick to the second guard's chin, snapping the guard's head back, stunning him. Havoc instantly followed through with a jamming heel kick to the guard's right knee, then a front ball kick to the guard's face as the man doubled over.

The second guard dropped like the proverbial rock.

"Damn!" Sadist exclaimed, dazzled by the soldier's speed and power.

Havoc jerked his right thumb at the Tower. "Let's go!" he prompted, concerned the commotion might draw more guards.

Sadist hesitantly approached the Tower.

Havoc constantly scanned the huts, the field, and the Tower, amazed no one else was challenging him. But after decades of operating in the valley without any trouble from outside sources, why should the Spider expect any now?

"I don't want to do this!" Sadist whined.

"Do it or die!" Havoc snapped.

"You shoot me and everyone will hear it," Sadist said.

"Who needs to shoot you? You saw what I just did to your buddy. I can kill you with my hands or my feet. Take your pick," Havoc told him.

"I'll pass," Sadist muttered.

The Tower loomed above them, dwarfing the huts, seeming to reach the stars themselves. Two windows were in evidence, one near the domed roof and another about halfway up. A flickering glow radiated from both. At the bottom of the Tower was the entrance, a huge wooden door with light seeping under the lower edge.

Havoc was within ten feet of the Tower when the chill struck him, startling in its intensity, causing him to stop and gaze upward with a tinge of apprehension. Was his imagination over-reacting to the oppressive atmosphere in the valley, or was the air noticeably cooler near the Tower? He saw Sadist shiver. So his mind wasn't playing tricks on him. But what could be responsible for the drastic drop in temperature?

Sadist halted a yard from the door, trembling.

Havoc edged past the terrified guard to the door. He spied a rectangular metal latch on the right side of the door and walked over.

"Don't!" Sadist warned in a whisper.

Havoc glared at the man in black.

Quaking, Sadist lowered his chin to his chest and clenched his fists.

Havoc gingerly gripped the latch, the metal cold to his touch. The HK94 ready in his left hand, he tugged on the latch with his right, expecting resistance, assuming a door so massive would be difficult to open.

It wasn't.

The door swung wide on well oiled hinges, bathing Havoc and Sadist in a luminous golden halo.

And exposing them to the 13 Hatchlings waiting inside.

CHAPTER FOURTEEN

"I can't believe we made it!" Athena exclaimed, inhaling deeply, grateful to be alive.

"I knew we would," Blade said.

"I knew I would," Grizzly amended. "I wasn't so sure about you two, what with you being human and all."

"Don't start that again!" Athena snapped.

Blade stared at the stars above, then at the pool hundreds of feet below. They were perched on the very rim of the precipice, seated on a rocky outcropping, resting from the exhausting ascent.

"I don't scent any guards," Grizzly remarked, his face into the wind.

"And you won't," Athena stated. "I told you before. The guards are posted on the west side of this ridge. During the day there are two, sometimes three. But at night I think they only post one."

"Humans or Hatchlings?" Blade asked.

"Humans," Athena divulged. "The Hatchlings can't be bothered with such petty duty."

"Do you want me to go ahead and find the lookout?" Grizzly offered. "I'll slit his throat so fast he'll be dead before he realizes what happened."

"We'll stick together," Blade said.

"Can we make an exception in my case?" Athena inquired.

"An exception?" Blade repeated quizzically.

"I've got to visit the ladies'," Athena explained. "And I'll be damned if you two are going to watch."

Grizzly chuckled. "What are you worried about? You don't have anything I'd be interested in."

"The feeling is mutual," Athena countered, rising. She looked at Blade. "Give me a minute. That climb scared the piss out of me."

"Be careful," Blade advised.

Athena nodded. "I won't go far," she promised, and walked into the forest."

"I kind of like her," Grizzly declared. "She's spunky for a female."

"Females can be just as spunky as males," Blade remarked.

"Not many would do what she's doing," Grizzly observed.

"That's true," Blade concurred. He gazed heavenward, thinking of Thunder, hoping the Flathead had recovered. If the Indian had sustained brain damage, every moment they delayed in getting him to civilization, where he could receive the proper medical attention, was critical. But what other choice was there? Blade sighed. He couldn't call off the mission, not now, not when Sergeant Havoc and Kraft were prisoners or worse, not when the Kingdom was close at hand and their assignment nearly completed.

"You know," Grizzly commented, "at the rate things are going, if every job the Force is sent on is as dangerous as this one, then you'll be replacing Force members on a regular basis."

"I hope not," Blade said. "But if so, there's nothing I can do about it. Everyone on the Force is supposed to be a volunteer. They know the risks involved."

"I wouldn't want to be in your shoes," Grizzly mentioned.

"Oh?"

"You're the head of this outfit," Grizzly said. "When you get down to the nitty-gritty, our lives are in your hands. You make all the decisions. We have to follow your orders." He paused. "And I don't know as how I like that."

"Why? Because you don't like me, or because you don't like taking orders from a human?" Blade questioned.

"I never said I didn't like you," Grizzly stated. "Matter of fact, I admire you. You're the only human I've ever met capable of holding his own against me. But, no, I don't like taking orders from a human."

Blade stared at the mutant. "Listen, Grizzly, your service in the Force isn't set in concrete. If you want out, say the word. You can do whatever you want. You're not a slave like the women the Spider holds in the Kingdom."

"I'll stay for the time being," Grizzly declared. "I'm enjoying myself."

"I wish I could say I was," Blade mentioned.

"You're not?" Grizzly asked, sounding surprised.

"No."

"But why not? You're good at what you do. I saw you in action. You're one deadly son of a bitch," Grizzly said.

"Just because I'm good at killing doesn't mean I like to kill," Blade clarified. "You might laugh, but when I was younger all I ever wanted out of life was to live in peace and harmony with all creatures."

Grizzly laughed. "And then what happened?"

"I grew up," Blade stated soberly.

"Yeah," Grizzly philosophized. "Life does have a way of kicking you in the mouth every now and then, just to keep you in line."

Blade glanced down at the base of the cliffs, reflecting on the poor woman who had been killed, speculating on how his wife might react if he should suffer a similar fate. He shook his head, peeved by his morbidity, and stood. "I hope Athena hurries up," he commented.

"You don't know much about women, do you?" Grizzly joked, chuckling.

Athena was on her way to rejoin Blade and Grizzly, still 30 yards into the undergrowth, when she detected a rustling noise to her left. She paused, fingering the trigger of her M-16. Had the wind made the sound? No. The breeze had temporarily abated. An animal then? She was inclined to attribute the rustling to a nocturnal denizen of the forest, a fox or a skunk or a raccoon, because she knew the Spider did not post sentries above the cliff. But what if she was wrong? What if the Spider had changed his defensive setup? Or—and this thought produced goose bumps all over her flesh—what if it was one of the numerous *wild* mutants prowling the countryside, endowed with a ravenous appetite and inclined to attack anything moving?

She'd better get to Blade and Grizzly.

Athena hurried toward the rim of the cliffs, moving around and between all the obstacles in her path: trees, boulders, and impenetrable stands of brush.

The soft rustling was repeated, closer this time.

Athena searched the landscape to her left, but nothing was moving. Should she call out to Blade? Definitely not. She wasn't about to look like a wimp. Grizzly would never let her hear the end of it! She squared her shoulders and continued.

A boulder appeared ahead.

Athena purposefully skirted the boulder to the right, mentally chiding herself for a case of bad nerves, for creating monsters where none existed.

But one did.

She was alongside the boulder, not two feet away, when a squat shadow detached itself from the bottom and lunged at her. Athena tried to bring the M-16 to bear even as she opened her mouth to yell to Blade, but she was thwarted on both counts. A pair of hairy hands tore the M-16 from her grasp and flung the gun aside as another pair clamped on her, one hand covering her mouth while another applied pressure to her throat.

"Not a word!" snarled a tinny voice.

Athena could feel talons digging into her neck. She repressed an impulse to resist, to scream, knowing she would be dead in an instant.

A Hatchling had her!

"Do not move!" the hybrid hissed. It quickly stripped her of her pistols, then the knife in her right boot. It examined every pocket, every fold in her clothing, for a concealed weapon. Once convinced she was unarmed, it hauled her to her feet. "You will come with me! If you shout or try to warn your friends, I will kill you! Nod if you understand!"

Athena nodded, shocked not only by her capture but by discovering the Hatchlings could talk! During her years of captivity, the Hatchlings had not associated with the women prisoners, except to haul the captives off to the Tower now and then—and usually the guards discharged that responsibility in addition to

their other duties. The women were the Spider's property, and
his exclusively. While the human guards could mistreat the
women with impunity, they were not allowed to seriously harm
the women or abuse them sexually. Even to the Hatchlings the
women were taboo. Athena had seen the Hatchlings on countless occasions while she was a prisoner, yet not once had a
Hatchling so much as acknowledged her existence. Several times
she had seen them from the window of her hut, shambling off
into the night to abduct another unfortunate wretch, and heard
them clicking their talons. So for seven years she had mistakenly
believed they were mute, despite the testimony of some of her
fellow prisoners who had claimed the hybrids could speak.

The Hatchling holding her throat pulled her to the west,
deeper into the forest, away from the cliffs. After traveling 50
yards he halted and released his grip. "What I said still holds!"
he threatened. "Make a peep and you're dead!"

Athena swallowed hard.

"I recognize you!" the Hatchling stated. "You're the bitch
who escaped! What's your name?"

"Athena," she replied.

"Well, Athena, you must be as stupid as they come! You were
free, yet you came back. And you've brought others, professional soldiers! The Spider will not be pleased," the mutant
noted.

"The Spider will be dead before morning," Athena predicted.

Snarling, the Hatchling grabbed her throat once more and led
her in the direction of the valley.

Athena pondered whether to knock the Hatchling's arm aside
and scream. She knew Blade and Grizzly would hear her, but
she also knew the hybrid would make good its promise to slay
her before they came to her aid. What should she do? Common
sense dictated silence, and she opted to keep her mouth shut.

The Hatchling hurried down the west slope of the ridge, one
hand always on her neck.

At the sight of the Kingdom Athena stiffened and tried to drag
her heels.

"Move your human ass, bitch!" the Hatchling snapped.

Athena broke out in a cold sweat. What the hell had she done?
What if the Hatchling took her directly to the Tower? To the
Spider? *Any* fate would be preferable to confronting that hellish
monstrosity again!

They reached the field bordering the timber and headed for the middle of the valley.

The Hatchling, confident so close to home, released his hold. "I am Syph," he disclosed. "And I will ask Father for the honor of being the first to feed on your miserable body." He abruptly stopped and faced her, scowling, displaying his fangs. "Where are they?"

"Who?" Athena blurted.

The Hatchling slapped her across the mouth. "Don't play games with me, bitch! Where are my three brothers? Siad, Rehpes, and Sonnpec were to stop you from reaching the Kingdom, yet you and your two colleagues showed up." He waved the talons on his two right hands in front of her eyes. "Where are my brothers?"

"Two of them are dead," Athena answered arrogantly. "I don't know about the third."

"Damn you rotten humans!" Syph fumed. "You'll pay for this! All of you!"

"You're the ones who will pay!" Athena ventured to respond.

Syph hissed and clutched her left wrist, hauling her after him as he stomped toward the huts.

"Where are you taking me?" Athena queried in a sudden panic.

"What a dumb-ass question!" Syph said contemptuously. "Where do you think?"

Athena gawked at the lofty structure harboring the vilest fiend alive. "Not the Tower!"

Syph cackled devilishly.

CHAPTER FIFTEEN

"**D**rop your weapon!" the Hatchling nearest the entrance commanded. "You have until the count of three."

Havoc hesitated, bewildered by the unexpected turn of events. The HK94 was in his left hand. All he would have to do was elevate the gun, sweep his right hand to the trigger, and fire.

"One," the Hatchling said.

Four of the thirteen hybrids were likewise armed with HK94's.

"Two," the Hatchling counted.

Havoc frowned. All four were pointing their weapons at him.

"Thr—" the Hatchling began.

Havoc dropped his HK94 and raised his hands into the air. "Is this any way to greet a visitor?" he quipped.

"You don't like our welcoming committee?" the Hatchling rejoined, smirking triumphantly.

"I was hoping for a brass band and some cheerleaders," Havoc cracked.

The Hatchlings beamed. "I always have appreciated the human sense of humor." He paused. "Which is why my brothers think I'm somewhat strange."

"You knew I was coming," Havoc said.

"Of course," the Hatchling confirmed.

"But how?" Havoc wanted to know.

"Father felt you," the Hatchling revealed.

"Felt me?" Havoc responded, perplexed. "How? And who are you anyway?"

"Where *are* my manners?" the Hatchling asked rhetorically. "My name is Chanc."

"Where do you guys get your names?" Havoc queried facetiously. "Do you pull them out of a hat?"

"We do not wear hats," Chanc said. "Our names are bestowed on us by the Spider."

"I don't get it," Havoc stated. "If this Spider is your old man, why do you fruitcakes keep referring to him as *the* Spider?"

"Our father prefers to be addressed as such," Chanc explained.

"A great honor," Chanc replied. "You will meet our father. Follow me." He peered past Havoc. "You too, brother."

Sadist whined and retreated a step. "No! It wasn't my fault! He made me bring him!"

"The Spider is aware of the situation," Chanc said. "He wants to see you."

"Please! No!" Sadist begged.

Chanc motioned with one of his right arms, and immediately two other Hatchlings walked from the Tower and moved behind Sadist. "You will come, won't you?" Chanc requested politely.

Sadist appeared to be having trouble breathing. He weakly nodded.

"Excellent!" Chanc commented, looking at Havoc. "And what is your name?"

"Havoc," the noncom responded. "Sergeant Havoc."

"An appropriate name for a military man, yes?" Chanc remarked. "Come along, won't you?" He turned and headed off.

Havoc entered the Tower, his skin tingling. Now he was in for it! Trapped in the lion's den, with no angels of mercy to yank his fat out of the fire! Blade and the Force might arrive at any second, but he was doubtful. Who knew where they were?

"Father is in his chambers," Chanc mentioned, walking to the right, toward a spiral stairwell. "It's a bit of a climb, I'm afraid."

Havoc's forehead creased in confusion. What was with this hybrid? Was Chanc trying to smother him with kindness? "Are you the head Hatchling?" he asked.

"Dox is," Chanc answered, "by virtue of being the eldest. But he's not here at the moment." He stopped and glanced at Havoc. "You wouldn't happen to know where he is, would you?"

"How should I know?" Havoc lied.

Chanc nodded knowingly and started climbing the stairwell.

Havoc examined his surroundings, flabbergasted. The interior of the Tower was immense, spacious enough for an army, and the decor left something to be desired. From a human perspective, anyhow. Colossal beams latticed the edifice, projecting from the walls and crisscrossing the air space. Many of the beams came to an abrupt end in midair. Illumination was provided by lanterns suspended from hooks in the walls. Havoc's boots clumped on the stairwell as he ascended. Gazing upward, he spied the underside of a floor approximately 20 feet above his head. Why had they situated the lowest floor so far from the ground? Was the Tower only partially completed? Or did the beams serve a purpose?

"You are in for a treat," Chanc said over his left shoulder. "You are the first human male to lay eyes on the Spider in four decades."

"Lucky me," Havoc retorted.

"Sarcasm is so unbecoming," Chanc said.

"Why are you being so damn polite?" Havoc demanded.

"I attribute my courtesy to my genes," Chanc replied.

"Your genes?"

"Certainly. As you are no doubt aware, we are the offspring of a mixed mating. Human and mutant. And our parentage is displayed in our genes. Some of us possess slightly more human attributes than the others. Some, if you will, take more after our father's side of the family, while others tend to be like our mothers, more human. I am such a one," Chanc divulged regretfully.

"You don't sound too happy about it," Havoc noted.

"I'm not," Chanc admitted. "But I must bear the pollution in my bloodstream as best I can."

"What did you mean down there?" Havoc asked. "When you said the Spider felt me coming?"

"I don't quite know if I can explain it," Chanc said.

"Try," Havoc prompted.

"Are you familiar with mental telepathy?" Chanc queried.

"I know a little about it," Havoc stated. "Isn't it the same as mind reading?"

"Close, but not quite," Chanc replied. "Telepathy is a communication between minds, sort of like talking to someone else but conducting the conversation in your head instead of with your vocal apparatus.."

"And the Spider is telepathic?" Havoc inquired.

"In a certain respect, yes," Chanc confirmed. "The Spider can communicate with us, with each Hatchling, telepathically."

A dozen questions filled Havoc's mind. "Is this communication constant? Are you talking with him now? And what's the range?"

Chanc glanced over his right shoulder, grinning. "You possess a curious nature. What a pity."

"What is?" Havoc asked.

"Never mind," Chanc said, sighing. "No, the communication is not constant. The sensation is not easy to describe. When Father wants to contact one of us, we feel his thoughts in our head. By the same token, he can feel our thoughts."

"How close do you have to be?" Havoc probed.

"Father can project his thoughts to us up to a distance of fifty yards, and he can feel our thoughts at the same range," Chanc detailed. "Beyond fifty yards, we can not communicate telepathically."

"Can he do the same thing with humans?"

"No," Chanc revealed. "I don't know why. Perhaps human minds are too feeble. Perhaps humans lack the glands or whatever is necessary for telepathy. But the Spider can not project his thoughts in a human mind, although he can register the presence of a human up to the edge of the fields."

"How do you mean?" Havoc requested clarification.

"I'll use you as an example," Chanc said. "As soon as you entered our village, as you drew near to the first hut, the Spider felt your presence. He knew you were coming, even though he could not read your mind. He felt you. That's the best way I can explain his ability."

"And once he was aware of my presence, once he felt me coming, he had you prepare your welcome wagon," Havoc deduced.

"Exactly," Chanc verified.

They had attained the lowest floor. Walls and doors appeared to their left. The walls, though, were bizarre, designed with sharp angles and slanting upward instead of being aligned vertically. The material used in the construction was a dark wood.

"Are these your quarters?" Havoc idly asked.

"Our sleeping quarters, our storage rooms, our library . . ." Chanc said, itemizing them.

"You have a library?" Havoc queried in surprise.

"You were expecting maybe illiterate barbarians?" Chanc rejoined.

"Where do you get your books?"

"We have established trading relations with Reptilian," Chanc answered. "The booty that scaly bastard has amassed is incredible. He'll trade anything for some prime meat."

"Reptilian? Who's Rep—" Havoc started to inquire, but paused when an uncanny wail floated down from above.

The peculiar moaning ululation persisted for over a minute, rising and falling in intensity.

"What was that?" Havoc inquired, the hairs on the nape of his neck prickling.

"Father," Chanc said.

"The Spider?"

"Yes. He can not converse like you and I do. He can not speak. The Spider can communicate telepathically and with sounds, sounds unlike anything you or I could make," Chanc stated.

"I believe it," Havoc remarked. "Which reminds me. What's with the clicking you guys do?"

"We use the clicking of our talons to communicate when we're out in the field," Chanc said. "Our system is similar to your Morse Code."

Havoc nodded. So he'd been right!

They were approaching the top of the Tower, approximately 25 feet overhead. A landing became visible 15 feet up.

"We're almost there," Chanc announced. "I thank you for the pleasure of your company. I seldom am permitted to enjoy intelligent conversation, even with a lowly human."

"Why not?"

"Because we are not allowed to talk to the Spider's women," Chanc responded. "And my brothers, sad to say, have not refined the art of polite discourse."

Havoc couldn't help but grin. Chanc impressed him as the type of person, or thing, who unceasingly flapped his gums for the sake of hearing himself speak.

They climbed the remainder of the steps to the landing in silence. Fabricated of the same dark wood as the walls, the landing was ten feet square and bordered by a gray metal railing. A large door was located across from the stairwell.

Chanc moved to the middle of the landing and turned. "I will be going in with you to act as interpreter. The rest will remain here."

Havoc glanced to his rear. Six of the Hatchlings had accompanied them up the stairwell. Sadist was staring at the door in blatant fear, his lips quivering, his eyes wide.

Chanc walked to the door and gripped the metal latch.

"I imagine it's too late," Havoc stated.

Chanc looked at the soldier, puzzled. "Too late?"

"To ask you to surrender."

Chanc tittered, shaking his head. "Definitely a pity."

"Please!" Sadist interjected. "I don't want to go in there!"

"You must," Chanc said.

"No! I've been loyal all these years! This isn't fair!" Sadist shouted.

"The Spider wants to see you," Chanc stated. "Now calm down and come on."

Sadist retreated a step. "No! Please, Chanc!"

Watching the petrified guard, Havoc was struck by a thought. "Chanc, there's something I don't understand?"

Chanc released the latch. "What?"

"Why do you go to all the trouble of stealing your women from outside the Kingdom when you could raise them here? Sadist is a son of the Spider, right? All the human guards are. And if some of the Spider's offspring are fully human, like their mothers, why not let the girl babies grow into women?" Havoc asked.

"Because there have not been any female babies who survived," Chanc said sadly.

"None?"

Chanc shook his head. "Not a one. All of the female babies, whether human or Hatchling, die shortly after birth. We have tried everything to keep them alive, but nothing has worked." He paused. "Even many of the male babies perish. The inter-breeding of a mutant and a human has unforeseen complications."

Havoc indicated Sadist with a jerk of his left thumb. "But he told me all the girl babies and most of the boys are eaten."

"They are," Chanc confirmed.

"But . . ." Havoc began.

"They are consumed after they die," Chanc detailed. "After all, as much as we want them to live, we're not about to let good food go to waste."

Havoc felt queasy in his stomach.

"The genetic differential might account for the high infant-mortality rate," Chanc elaborated. "We count ourselves fortunate that some of the males do survive. Many mutants, we have learned, are incapable of breeding with humans. Their reproductive systems are incompatible."

"So I've heard," Havoc acknowledged.

"Now we really must go inside," Chanc stated, staring at Sadist. "If you will not enter of your own volition, I will have you carried."

Sadist extended his hands in a pleading gesture. "But I didn't *do* anything!"

"Father would like to have a word with you," Chanc said patiently. He took hold of the latch and opened the door. "Inside." With a wave of one of his left arms, he indicated they should proceed.

Havoc edged to the doorway. He was strongly tempted to bolt, but outnumbered as he was—and unarmed to boot—an escape attempt would be an exercise in stupidity.

Whining, Sadist shuffled toward the door.

Havoc gingerly stepped into the Spider's quarters. He anticipated outlandish architecture resembling the floors below; what he found exceeded his wildest imaginings.

The gloomy chamber was gigantic, 40 feet in diameter, and reached all the way to the domed roof. A pungent odor hung in the air. Another landing, a carbon copy of the one outside, was attached by beams to the north wall. Unlike the first landing, there was no railing. And occupying the rest of the Spider's quarters was a fitting symbol of the mutant's name and power, the only habitation perfectly suited for a being with arachnoid capabilities: a titanic web.

Havoc could scarcely believe his own eyes. His mind was boggled, overwhelmed by the seeming unreality of the sight before him.

The web was a dusky, dirty white circular pattern of enormous strands stretching from wall to wall. The center sagged, lending a cuplike aspect to its appearance. Each strand was as thick as a man's body, except for those nearest the walls. They were thicker. If size was any connotation, then the web was large enough for an elephant.

"Isn't it awe inspiring?" Chanc remarked to Havoc's left.

"I don't see the Spider," Havoc mentioned.

Chanc glanced up at the dome. "You will," he stated.

Havoc followed the direction of Chanc's gaze, but initially he didn't see anything out of the ordinary. The area under the dome was shrouded in shadow.

And then the shadow *moved*!

Havoc involuntarily gasped in astonishment as a tremendous inky form descended from the ceiling, slowly lowering toward the middle of the net. Vague at first, the shape solidified, acquiring distinct contours.

The creature's body was massive and segmented, consisting of two oval sections covered with fine black hair. Eight appendages, four on each side, protruded from the mutant's segments, and in contrast to the body they were not coated with hair. The limbs were a yellow tinge, and the skin appeared to have an elastic quality which was apparent as the appendages moved up and down. They were always in motion, always rising and falling, even when the creature was still.

"Sergeant Havoc," Chanc said. "I'd like you to meet my father. The Spider."

Havoc heard Sadist wimpering.

The Spider came to a stop abreast of the landing, dangling from the ceiling not ten feet from the visitors.

Havoc was riveted in place, staring in amazement at the Spider's visage. The skin was the same color and texture as the legs. Eight black, alien orbs returned his stare, capped by an expansive forehead. There was no nose, and the mouth was a vertical slit with two large fangs at the bottom and smaller fangs lining the gums.

"The Spider greets you," Chanc said.

"What?" Havoc mumbled.

"The Spider greets you," Chanc repeated. "He welcomes you to his humble abode."

"He's communicating with you?" Havoc asked.

"Of course," Chanc stated. "Telepathy, remember?"

Havoc spotted a strand of web connecting the Spider's posterior to the ceiling.

"Well?" Chanc said impatiently.

"Well what?" Havoc responded.

"You are being abysmally rude," Chanc noted. "The least you could do is say hi."

"Oh." Havoc shook his head, striving to organize his thinking. "Tell him hi for me."

"He heard you," Chanc said. "He may not be able to speak, but he can understand us."

"He isn't what I expected," Havoc remarked.

"What did you expect?" Chanc queried.

"I don't know," Havoc said. "I thought he would be smaller. Probably because he . . . mates . . . with human women."

Chanc seemed to be listening to an inner voice, his brow furrowed, all attention. "Father says his reproductive organ is no bigger than yours."

"What? As huge as he is?" Havoc commented.

"Father says many animals and insects have disproportionately undersized organs." Chanc chuckled. "Look at the whale. If a male whale had a penis commensurate with its bulk, it would sink to the bottom every time it got a hard-on. As for humans, their egos tend to greatly exaggerate their own sexual dimensions."

"I still don't understand why he picks on human women," Havoc said.

"What other reproductive source is there?" Chanc rejoined. "Like many mutants produced by the excessive radiation bombarding the atmosphere, he is one of a kind. He has no natural mate. Father considers the idea of mating with his inferiors, with animals and lesser mutants, revolting."

"But he mates with inferior humans," Havoc interrupted.

"Father says humans are inferior physically and mentally to mutants, but humans do have one advantage. Human females, that is. They are remarkably fertile, and their wombs are receptive to interspecies impregnation," Chanc explained.

"Wait a minute!" Havoc declared. "I just thought of something." He looked at Chanc. "If the Spider is the only one who can touch the women you capture, what do you do?"

"Me?"

"You and the rest of the Hatchlings," Havoc elucidated.

"Hatchlings do not possess reproductive potential," Chanc stated.

"You can't whoopee?"

"We can't reproduce," Chanc said.

"What about the human guards?" Havoc queried.

"Periodically one of the women is sacrificed," Chanc detailed. "Before we feast on her, the men are permitted to indulge themselves."

Havoc glanced at Sadist. "You bastard!"

"Father says to thank you for reminding him," Chanc said.

"Reminding him about what?" Havoc asked.

"Three guesses," Chanc remarked.

Havoc saw the Spider swivel, its malevolent face turning to his right, toward Sadist.

Sadist uttered a wheezing sound.

Chanc took a step forward, his eyes on Sadist. "Father says he is displeased by your performance."

Sadist dropped to his knees, pressing his palms together in an attitude of supplication. "I didn't do anything!" he shouted.

"Father says you led Havoc here," Chanc interpreted.

"I didn't have any choice! He would have killed me!" Sadist asserted.

"Father requires loyalty above all else," Chanc relayed. "Father believes you lack that essential quality."

"Please! Give me another chance! I promise I won't fail you again!" Sadist wailed.

"Father says you are right. You won't fail him again," Chanc said.

Havoc tensed, expecting the Spider to make a move, to do something decidedly lethal to Sadist. But when the move came, it astounded him.

A streak of white suddenly erupted from the Spider's hideous head, disgorged from its distended maw at a lightning velocity, the aim unerring. A thin, glistening strand, resembling the webbing but exceedingly slender, shot across the intervening ten feet and struck Sadist in the chest.

"No!" Sadist screamed, grabbing the strand and endeavoring to tear it from his body. But the strand, thin as it was, held fast.

"Observe this closely," Chanc casually commented to Havoc.

For his part, Havoc was fascinated by the tableau. He felt no compulsion to try and help Sadist; the son of a bitch deserved everything he got!

"Please! No!" Sadist protested. He went to remove his hands from the strand, but couldn't. "They're stuck!" he blurted in horror. "I can't get my hands loose!"

Spider uttered a protracted chittering noise.

"Father says you must excuse his uncouth manners," Chanc said to Havoc, grinning. "He is famished. He will not be able to share his repast with you."

"Fine by me," Havoc muttered in response.

Sadist screeched as he was abruptly hauled from the landing. He was pulled over the edge and plummeted toward the net below, but was brought up short by the strand adhering to his chest. The momentum of his plunge caused him to swing from side to side, a human pendulum, a tasty morsel for a hungry monster, like a fish on the end of a fisherman's line.

"Watch what happens next," Chanc stated excitedly.

The thin strand began to retract into the Spider's mouth, drawing its prey ever closer to its two-foot-long central fangs.

"*Nooooooo*!" Sadist shrieked.

The retraction seemed to take forever, but in reality was a mere three minutes, as the strand ever so slowly hoisted Sadist higher and higher. Alternately whining, yelling, and blubbering incoherently, Sadist gradually drew within range of the Spider's serrated fangs.

Havoc, mesmerized, saw what was coming.

Sadist became strangely quiet when he was within a yard of the Spider's head. He gawked up at the terrible features, petrified to his core.

Chanc laughed expectantly.

A few seconds more and Sadist was within range.

The Spider's two longest fangs clamped onto Sadist's head, one on each side, the sawlike edges ripping into the man's cranium.

Havoc heard a sharp crunch.

Sadist started convulsing as his body was drawn into the Spider's mouth. Additional smaller fangs were revealed as the maw was stretched to the maximum.

Havoc saw Sadist's head ease into the Spider's maw, and then those mighty jaws closed, the Spider's razor teeth neatly severing Sadist's head from his body. Crimson spurted over the Spider's chin and mandibles.

"I wish I could do that," Chanc remarked wistfully.

Havoc was appalled. What a way to go! How many people, innocent people, not scum like Sadist, had fallen victim to the Spider over the decades? Dozens? Hundreds? Thousands?

The Spider's mouth was working as he consumed his meal.

"Father would like to continue our conversation while he snacks," Chanc said. "If that's all right with you."

Havoc didn't respond.

"Father would like to know about you," Chanc translated. "How many more came with you? What unit are you with? Where are you headquartered? And how did you learn about the Kingdom?"

Havoc stared into the Spider's baleful orbs. He licked his lips and mustered all of his courage. "Go to hell!"

Chanc hissed. "What kind of attitude is that? Hasn't Father treated you with respect and dignity?"

Havoc glanced at the Hatchling. "Why don't you go take a swan dive off the cliffs?"

Chanc looked at his inhuman progenitor, then at the noncom. "You refuse to cooperate?"

"You're not so dumb after all,' Havoc rejoined.

"How can you be so obstinate after what you've just witnessed?" Chanc queried angrily.

"*Because* of what I've just seen, you can all get stuffed! You get nothing out of me!" Havoc declared.

"And there's nothing I can say to change your mind?" Chanc asked.

"Don't waste my time," Havoc replied arrogantly.

Chanc sighed. "Very well. You have made your choice. But Father will force you to talk, sooner or later."

"Bet me!" Havoc retorted.

"Don't say I didn't warn you," Chanc commented, moving toward the doorway.

Havoc gazed at the Spider. The mutant was engrossed in its meal, blood and flesh dribbling from the corners of its mouth as it chewed. For a few seconds Chanc was not in his field of vision. The Hatchling was behind him, heading for the door.

Or so he thought.

Havoc had a fleeting intimation of impending disaster when he detected the rapid pad of rushing feet, and then something slammed into his back, knocking him forward, toward the edge of the landing. He tried to throw his body back from the brink, but his combat boots slid over the rim, and with a sickening sensation in his stomach he hurtled toward the net below.

CHAPTER SIXTEEN

He was almost free!

Kraft grinned in delight as he felt the material binding his wrists about to give way. He had worked for hours, his arms developing a slippery layer of sweat to facilitate his effort.

If only the damn Hatchling would keep on sleeping!

Kraft had taken stock while the hybrid dozed. His M-16 and the Colts were gone, but he didn't know about his boot knife and his switchblade. He couldn't feel the boot knife rubbing against his skin, so he doubted the weapon was still there. The Hatchling must have searched him while he was unconscious. But, the hybrid might have missed his switchblade. When he quietly jiggled his legs, making as much noise as he dared, he felt a hard object gouging his right thigh. And the only hard object in his right front pocket had been his switchblade.

Not much longer!

The more he had worked on his bounds, the more convinced he'd become that whatever the Hatchling had used wasn't rope. The loops were too pliable for rope and not abrasive enough.

The Hatchling made a snorting sound.

Kraft renewed his frantic attempt to loosen his wrists. He could feel the material sliding down almost to his knuckles, but he couldn't quite extricate his hands. If he rolled onto his side, he might be able to apply more leverage. There was one hitch, however. If he moved, he might awaken the Hatchling.

To hell with it!

Kraft eased onto his left side, facing the hybrid. He extended his legs and peered down at his ankles. The moonlight revealed the material the Hatchling had used to bind him, a strip of camouflage fabric!

Where the . . .

Kraft glanced at his right leg and discovered a ragged tear in his pants. The damn Hatchling had torn two strips from his pants leg in order to tie him up!

Siad tossed in his sleep, shifting his body toward Kraft.

Was the Hatchling waking up?

Kraft held his breath, his eyes glued to the hybrid, but Siad slept on. Yeah! He grit his teeth as he exerted his muscles to the utmost, his face turning red, his veins bulging.

Go!

Go!

Go!

The fabric abruptly parted, taking him unawares, his right arm wrenching outward and his left thudding against the ground. He stared at Siad.

No reaction.

Kraft quickly unraveled a solitary loop clinging to his drenched skin, then bent forward at the waist to undo his ankles.

What an asshole!

Use the switchblade!

Kraft straightened, diving his right hand into his pants pocket, his fingers grasping for the switchblade. And there it was! His fingertips had just touched part of the knife, a smile of relief beginning to uplift his face, when the hybrid woke up.

No!

Kraft saw the Hatchling stir, its arm starting to raise as its body uncurled from its slouching position. Dammit! He swiftly laid down, on his back, his hands behind him, exactly as he'd been when the mutant had fallen asleep. Not a second too soon.

The Hatchling opened its eyes, gazing at the moon, then looked at Kraft. "Are you still here? I didn't think you liked my company."

"Up yours, Franky!" Kraft snapped.

"For the last time, my name is Siad," the hybrid stated archly.

"Sure, Franky," Kraft said, goading the Hatchling. "Whatever you say is cool."

Siad stood and walked over to Kraft. "When it comes time to eat you, I think I'll start with your tongue. You seem to have little intelligent use for it." He grinned.

"Get bent, mother!" Kraft retorted.

Siad returned to the tree and leaned down, taking hold of an object lying on the ground. When he rose, he pointed the object at Kraft.

"My M-16!" Kraft blurted out.

"And who says humans are dumb?" Siad quipped, chuckling.

"What did you do with my Colts?" Kraft demanded.

"I tossed them into the bushes," Siad answered.

"Only a mutant would pull a stupid stunt like that!" Kraft said, deliberately insulting his enemy. He needed to distract the hybrid somehow, to do something to divert the deviate's attention while he freed his ankles. Above all, he couldn't let the Hatchling roll him over. There was no telling what Siad might do if the mutant discovered his hands were loose!

Cool!

He had to play it real cool!

Siad sighed. "Why do all humans feel they must insult or kill all mutants?"

"Have you looked in a mirror lately?" Kraft cracked.

"You are a typical example of my reason for distrusting humans," Siad observed. "Mindless hatred is endemic to your species. Why do you think I discarded your pistols and the knife you had hidden in your boot? If you still had them, I'd be dead right now."

"You've got that right, dude," Kraft said.

Siad turned, staring to the north. "There must be a better place!" he declared passionately.

Kraft grinned. The dummy had its back to him! He began to slide his hands from under his back. "What are you babbling about?"

"Is it babble?" Siad asked, more to himself than Kraft. "I hope not. I've taken my life in my hands by deserting the Spider."

"Deserting?" Kraft repeated in bewildering. "Say! Where the hell are you taking me, anyway? The Kingdom?"

Siad shook his head. "No. The Kingdom is my past." He

pointed to the north. "Out there lies my destiny."

Kraft's hands were by his side. He inched his right hand toward the pocket containing his switchblade. "This is unreal! It isn't bad enough I get my butt captured by a mutant! It has to be a wacko mutant!"

"I wouldn't expect you to understand," Siad said.

"So clue me in," Kraft prompted. "I ain't going nowhere!"

Siad placed the M-16's stock on the ground and leaned on the barrel. "You're a human. You know nothing of what it's like to be a mutant. Why should I waste my time explaining my motives to you?"

"Suit yourself!" Kraft rejoined. "But you are lugging me with you, and I'm kind of curious about where you're taking me."

"I'm taking you north, into the area once known as the State of Oregon," Siad disclosed.

"What's in Oregon?" Kraft inquired, slipping his hand into the right pocket and gripping his cherished switchblade.

"Peace, I hope," Siad stated.

"Peace? On this world? You must be dreaming!" Kraft said, taking the switchblade out.

"Maybe I am," Siad said wistfully. "But I am tired of the status quo. Living in the Kingdom is torment. The Spider rules with an iron hand, and even his children must live under his complete control." He paused. "We can't make a move without Father knowing it. He even knows our thoughts! We're slaves just like the human females we seize, only my brothers are too dense to see the truth!"

Kraft quickly sat up and bent toward his ankles. Keep talking! All he needed was a few seconds!

"There must be some place where I can live in peace," Siad went on. "Somewhere I'll be free to make my own decisions. Somewhere where others won't want to kill me. Where I won't be labeled a mutant or a mongrel crossbreed. Part of me is human, you know."

Kraft didn't bother to respond. He'd never heard anything so ridiculous in his life! A groddy Hatchling wanting to be accepted as a person! What a laugh! He held the switchblade under his right shin to muffle the click, then pressed the release button. The five-inch blade snapped out.

"Am I asking too much out of life?" Siad was saying. "If I

look long enough, I know I'll find what I'm seeking. For starters, I'll stay with Reptilian. He won't mind putting me up."

Kraft applied the knife to the camouflage fabric securing his ankles. A few short strokes, and the material dropped to the grass.

"I've heard about this city," Siad continued. "Maybe you've heard of it too. A city where humans and mutants live in harmony, as brothers. It's supposed to be located far to the north of here. Do you know about it?"

Kraft kept his eyes on the Hatchling's back. "Nope. Doesn't ring a bell." He rose to a squatting posture.

"I heard about it from a human we captured fifteen years ago," Siad mentioned. "She had lived in the city for a while, knew it well, and Father forced her to tell him all about it. Several of my brothers and I were permitted to listen in, and they all suspected she was lying. But not me. I know she was telling the truth. I know there is a city out there, a utopia for mutants and humans alike. And I know I could learn to live with your kind if they accept me for what I am."

Kraft stood and cautiously crept toward the hybrid, his switchblade held low, near his waist.

"You probably think I'm insane," Siad said. "My own brothers believe I'm strange. Except for Chanc, of course. And the only reason Chanc understands is because, like me, his human half predominates emotionally."

Kraft grinned as he snuck to within a yard of the preoccupied Hatchling. The hybrid was a fool! Why was the jerk-face unburdening itself now, of all times? Kraft couldn't care less about the mutant's personal problems. He sensed the Hatchling was simply getting something off his chest, something it might have held inside for a long time.

"As for you," Siad stated, sighing, "I'm afraid I will be compelled to consume you to sustain myself. Whenever I get hungry, I'll take a few bites out of you to satisfy my appetite. Don't worry, though. I'll try and keep you alive as long as I can."

Kraft was two feet from his target. "You're all heart, shit-head!"

Siad whirled, stunned.

Kraft never gave the Hatchling a chance. He brought his switchblade up and in, sinking the blade into Siad's neck below

the chin and slashing the knife to the right, tearing a jagged line
in Siad's throat.

Siad gurgled, dropping the M-16, lunging at the human.

Kraft stumbled backwards a few feet with the hybrid's talons
clawing at his face. He felt a burning sensation in his right cheek
as one of Siad's swipes tore him open. Undaunted, Kraft yanked
his switchblade out of the hybrid's neck and drove it higher,
going for Siad's right eye, plunging the knife into the hybrid's
black orb.

Siad snarled and backhanded Kraft, sending him sprawling
onto his back, the switchblade still imbedded in his eye.
Doubling over in agony, Siad gripped the switchblade handle
and tugged, wrenching the knife free. "My eye!" he bellowed
shrilly, enraged.

Kraft rolled onto his hands and knees, knowing he had to do
something and do it fast! The Hatchling was going to rip into
him, no holds barred, and he was unarmed.

Siad glared at Kraft with his good eye, his lips twitching, drool
dripping from his fangs. "You'll pay for this, human! Oh, *how*
you'll pay!" He hefted the switchblade in his upper right arm.
"I'll carve you into pieces with your own knife! How's that for
irony?"

Kraft spotted the M-16 lying on the ground about four feet
behind the Hatchling. It was his only hope!

Siad took a step forward. "Where should I start?" he growled.
"Should I do to you what you did to me?" His mouth contorted
in a twisted grin. "Or should I start with your pecker? Isn't that
the word you humans use? Yes! I'll cut off your pecker and make
you watch while I eat it!"

Kraft rose to a crouch, watching the arm holding his switchblade. Concentrate on the arm! his mind warned. Nothing else!
The slightest slip and he was dead! He could not afford a lapse in
his attention, not for a second.

Siad was wheezing, spittle frothing his lips, yellow blood
flowing from his ravaged throat. "Are you ready, human?"

Kraft backed up a stride. The arm! Focus on the arm!

"Say good-bye to your pecker!" Siad roared, and charged.

Even prepared, Kraft was unable to avoid the Hatchling's
bullish rush. Two arms encircled his waist and lifted him,
propelling him rearward, while a third arm raked his forehead,

digging deep. The fourth buried the switchblade into his left shoulder.

No!

Kraft was conscious of blood trickling over his eyebrows and onto his eyes, and of an intense stinging in his left shoulder, and then he was brutally slammed into the trunk of a tree. Vertigo briefly engulfed him as he slumped to the earth. Somewhere, someone was laughing. His awareness returned with astonishing clarity, and he saw the Hatchling standing above him, snickering.

Siad wagged the switchblade. "That's just for starters, human pig! Before I'm done, you'll plead for mercy!" He paused. "I should thank you for showing me the error of my ways! How could I ever have expected to live in peace and harmony with humans? You are all alike! You're all ready to kill at any provocation! My brothers and father were right!"

Kraft was woozy, struggling to concentrate, knowing his life was on the line. It was do-or-die time! But what could he possibly do against the Hatchling's superior strength without his switchblade?

Siad suddenly coughed, more spittle seeping from the corners of his mouth. "Let's get this over with!" he stated.

Kraft's brainstorm struck at the very last instant. He saw the Hatchling leaning toward him, sneering, bending toward his genitals. Adrenaline coursed through his body, electrifying him, and he moved, reaching out and grabbing one of the mutant's left wrists. He yanked on the wrist even as he shifted to the right, with the desired effect.

Siad was pulled off balance, toppling forward, his other left arm carving furrows in Kraft's right forearm.

Kraft dropped onto his right shoulder, retaining his grip on the hybrid's left wrist, hauling on the wrist for all he was worth. He saw the mutant's face smash into the tree, and he released the wrist and scrambled to his feet. Move! his mind screamed. He ran toward the M-16, the weapon glimmering in the moonlight, and nothing had ever looked so beautiful as that gun, his sole hope of salvation.

Siad spun, shaking his head, snarling, then lumbering after the human.

Kraft didn't risk a backward glance. With a resolute singleness of purpose he raced to the rifle, launching himself into the air to cover the final yard, landing on his injured shoulder, and flinching as he scooped up the M-16. He twirled, leveling the rifle, releasing the safety and squeezing the trigger as the Hatchling hurtled toward him.

Siad screeched as the slugs tore through his body.

Kraft's lips were set in firm lines as he emptied half the magazine into the hybrid, pouring round after round into Siad's torso and head.

Siad went down to his knees, dropping the switchblade.

Kraft ceased firing. He slowly stood, the M-16 trained on his foe. The Hatchling, incredibly, was still alive, but barely. Swaying and bubbling yellow blood, Siad was on the verge of collapse. Kraft walked up to the Hatchling. "Eat my pecker, huh? Not fucking likely!"

Siad hissed. It was his ultimate, terminal act of defiance.

Incensed, Kraft raised the M-16 and bashed the stock into the Hatchling's face. Again and again and again, until the hybrid's grotesque features were a mass of pulpy flesh and dripping gore. Winded, he stepped back.

Siad, the mutant in search of a dream, the Hatchling seeking peace and harmony, pitched over into eternity.

Kraft's legs abruptly became unsteady and his hands started trembling. He staggered away from the corpse, then sank to the dank earth. Damn! He'd done it! This Freedom Force business wasn't so hard after all! He wiped his right sleeve across his forehead to stem the flow of blood. His eyelids were caked and the corners of his eyes were filled with blood, but his eyes were clear.

Now what?

Kraft took deep breaths, slowly recovering. What should he do next? He had to find the others, but which way was the right way? He didn't know where he was in relation to the spot where he'd been captured. Not only that, he didn't know in which direction the Kingdom was located. He guessed to the south because the damn Hatchling had mentioned they were traveling north, away from the Kingdom. But what if he was wrong? What if he went south, and wound up penetrating deeper into the forest? He could get hopelessly lost in no time.

So what the hell should he do?

He rose and crossed to the tree Siad had used. Rest. He required rest. Sighing, he slid his battered, bleeding body to the ground, propping his back against the trunk. His blood loss worried him. If he lost too much, he'd never make it out of the wilderness. The prospect of internal bleeding was another factor.

Of all the lousy places to die!

Kraft laid his head back, using the rough trunk for support, and idly gazed skyward. He recalled the course Blade had taught before their departure from the Force HQ, a course on determining direction in the woods. Part of the instruction had dealt with compass reading, but his compass had been in his backpack. Blade had also provided pointers on deducing direction at night.

What was it the big guy had said?

Something about one of the Dippers.

Kraft studied the stars. He didn't know one from the other, but he knew the Dippers when he saw them. The Big Dipper was easy to find, but it took several minutes to locate the Little Dipper. According to Blade, the North Star was part of one of the Dippers, situated in one of the handles. But which one? Was the North Star in the Big Dipper or the Little Dipper? The North Star could serve as a guide if he could only remember!

He couldn't.

Exasperated, he decided to wait until daylight. All he had to do then was note the sun's position and bear in mind the basic rule: the sun rose in the east and set in the west. If he aligned his right arm with the rising sun, then his left arm would be pointing west. North would be in front of him, south to his back. Easy as pie.

Except for one thing.

He still didn't know where the hell the Kingdom was! North? South? East? West?

Shit! Shit! Shit!

Kraft closed his eyes, fatigue pervading every pore. A little snooze and he'd be as good as new. Then he'd look for some clue as to which direction he should take to rejoin the others. His eyelids drooped and within seconds he was asleep.

CHAPTER SEVENTEEN

Athena felt the terror welling up inside of her, and she struggled to remain calm, to stay alert. She didn't want to give the Hatchlings the satisfaction of seeing her afraid.

"Father is eager to see you again," Syph commented from her right. He was holding her right arm, hauling her up the Tower stairwell toward the Spider's chamber. Another Hatchling held her left arm.

"What a pleasant surprise having you back," mentioned the hybrid who had greeted them at the Tower entrance and introduced himself as Chanc.

"You'll get yours soon enough!" Athena asserted. "Just wait!"

"Syph told us there are two others with you," Chanc remarked. "If you're thinking they will rescue you, you're wrong. Seven of our brothers have gone to take care of them."

"Good," Athena said.

"Good?" Chanc repeated quizzically.

"Yep. That means there will soon be seven less Hatchlings in the world," Athena taunted.

"Gloat while you can, woman," Chanc advised.

"I hope father lets us have you!" Syph declared eagerly.

Athena glanced upward, swallowing hard. The revolting memories of the times she'd visited the Spider's inner sanctum overwhelmed her. An irresistible urge to flee compelled her to strain against the hybrids.

Syph laughed. "It seems the human is reluctant to meet the Spider again."

"Humans are notorious for their lack of social grace," Chanc said.

Athena blanched when they reached the landing. Her eyes widened at the sight of the familiar door.

"There's someone inside you might like to see again," Chanc commented as they crossed the landing.

Athena assumed he meant the Spider. She tensed, her breath catching in her throat.

"Here we go!" Syph declared, opening the door and throwing it wide.

The two Hatchlings forced her inside.

Athena involuntarily gasped as her eyes alighted on the repellent fiend perched on the web on the far side of the chamber.

The Spider stirred at her arrival, shifting its body, those emotionless orbs boring into her.

Chanc smiled. "Father says it is nice to see you once more."

"Tell him to get screwed!" Athena snapped.

Syph tittered. "You've got it backwards!"

Athena was on the verge of panic. What had gotten into her? How could she have been so insane? Why had she volunteered to lead the Force to the Kingdom, knowing the risks involved as she did? She deserved the Moron of the Year Award for inanity above and beyond the call of duty!

"Father wants to know why you have betrayed him?" Chanc asked.

"Because he deserves to die!" Athena answered shrilly.

"Father is very disappointed," Chanc said. "You were always one of his favorites."

"Bullshit!" Athena responded angrily. "All any woman is to him is another womb he can use to satisfy his lust and create bastards like you!"

"Be civil!" Chanc said sternly. "Or your demise will come sooner than it would otherwise."

"Who cares?" Athena retorted. "Get it over with!"

"There's no rush," Chanc stated. "Father ate a short while ago. He's saving you for breakfast."

"Lucky me!" Athena quipped.

"First things first," Chanc commented. "I told you there is

someone here you'd like to see again."

Athena didn't understand. "Who?"

Chanc and Syph pulled her to the edge of the landing.

"You do know him, don't you?" Chanc inquired, pointing downward.

Perplexed, Athena ventured a look over the side. Amazement commingled with relief washed over her. "Havoc!" she cried.

Sergeant Havoc was caught on the web. He was on his back, his limbs spread-eagled. "Ms. Morris! They got you too!"

"Are you all right?" Athena called down.

"I'm fine," Havoc yelled up. "Except I can't move!"

Chanc smirked. The surface of the Spider's web was coated with an adhesive substance. Anyone caught in the web was hopelessly trapped, doomed to die at the Spider's convenience. Only the Spider and the Hatchlings could negotiate the webbing without becoming stuck.

"Hang in there!" Athena shouted.

"You should convince your friend to cooperate with Father," Chanc said. "If he doesn't, Father may start nibbling on him soon." Chanc hoped he could attend the interrogation. One of the Spider's techniques for eliciting information from prisoners was diabolically clever and supremely effective. The Spider would have one of the Hatchlings pose questions to the captive, and every time the prisoner refused to answer, or if the Spider believed an answer was a lie, there was a dire price to pay. For every unanswered question, for every lie, the Spider would take a bite out of the captive. Not a big bite, mind, but a nibble, tearing off the prisoner's flesh in bits and pieces. Very few questions went unanswered after the first nibble.

"Talk to your friend," Chanc urged. "We'll leave you alone now." He moved toward the doorway, Syph following.

Athena watched them leave, hearing the latch click and the scraping of a key in the lock.

There was no way out!

"Athena!" Havoc shouted.

Athena glanced down at the noncom, wishing she could extricate him from the webbings. But he was 20 feet below her, or thereabouts, and she had no means of reaching him. "Yes?"

"What about you? Are you all right?" Havoc queried.

"I'm fine," Athena replied, looking at the Spider 40 yards away. "So far."

"Are the others safe?" Havoc asked.

"Spader is dead," Athena informed him. "And Kraft disappeared. Thunder was hurt pretty badly."

"What happened?"

"We were ambushed," Athena disclosed.

"And the others?" Havoc inquired.

"They're okay," Athena said.

"Don't tell me where they're at!" Havoc cautioned. "The Spider can understand us."

"What?" Athena stared at the gigantic mutation, bewildered. All those years she'd spent in the Kingdom, and only now was she learning some of the best-kept secrets! She'd never known the Spider could comprehend English. But how was she supposed to know? The guards had never confided in the women. And the Hatchlings, on those few occasions when they had escorted her to the Tower, had never uttered a word. Why? she wondered. What purpose did they have in keeping the Hatchlings' vocal ability a secret?

"If that son of a bitch comes after you," Havoc yelled, "watch out for its mouth! It shoots something out of its mouth!"

More new information! The Spider had never shot anything at her. When the women were summoned to the Tower and raped, the Spider simply took them on the landing, holding them down while forcing their legs apart. But what about this mouth business? She vaguely remembered studying spiders in school. One type, if she recalled correctly, was known as spitting spiders. They possessed a pair of large glands enabling them to squirt a sticky thread at prospective victims. Perhaps the Spider was endowed with such glands.

"Don't worry, Ms. Morris!" Havoc called up encouragement. "We'll get out of this mess okay!"

"I hope so," Athena said, feeling obligated to respond that way although she was extremely skeptical. Blade and Grizzly probably knew she was in trouble, but what could they hope to do about it? Even if they deduced she was being held in the Tower, the two of them couldn't hope to defeat all of the guards, the Hatchlings, and the Spider, and then rescue her.

Could they?

CHAPTER EIGHTEEN

"**I** don't like this waiting!" Grizzly groused in a hushed tone.

"Neither do I," Blade whispered in response.

"Then why don't we go in now?" Grizzly asked.

"You know why," Blade said. "We don't go in until sunrise." He glanced over his left shoulder at the ridge to their rear. "It won't be long."

They were crouched behind a cluster of boulders bordering the field to the east of the Kingdom. The Tower and the huts were clearly visible in the spreading light afforded by the arrival of dawn. Birds were chirping in the forest around them.

Grizzly stared into the woods. "I still think we should have jumped those seven turkeys earlier."

"I didn't want to advertise our presence," Blade explained. "They might have been looking for us, but they didn't know we were this close to the Kingdom."

"But if they can track by scent, like I can, then they'll pick up our trail at the cliffs and come after us," Grizzly noted. "They'll show up here sooner or later."

"Hopefully later," Blade said. "And by then they'll be too late. We go in shortly. We know Athena and Havoc are in there, because that's where their scent-trails lead. If they're alive, they might be in the Tower."

They waited in silence for the sun to appear.

"There's something I'd like to ask you," Grizzly whispered after a time.

Blade glanced at the bear-man. "What?"

"Why didn't you send me instead of Havoc?" Grizzly inquired.

"Send you where?" Blade responded innocently.

"Don't play games with me!" Grizzly stated. "You know what I'm talking about! When you first spotted the Hatchlings, you sent Havoc to keep tabs on them. Why him? Why not me?"

"Havoc is a skilled soldier," Blade noted. "I didn't expect him to get captured."

"That's not what I meant and you know it!" Grizzly said, peeved. "You know that most mutants have heightened senses. We can hear, see, and smell better than humans. So why did you send Havoc to watch the Hatchlings when you could have sent me? My senses are just as good as the Hatchlings'. So why send a human to do a mutant's job?"

Blade shrugged. "It seemed like the right decision at the time."

Grizzly studied the Warrior for a moment. "I'm beginning to see through you," he said appreciatively.

"Oh?" Blade remarked, arching his eyebrows.

"Yep," Grizzly affirmed. "You've got more upstairs than I gave you credit for. You're one clever son of a gun."

"You think so, huh?" Blade said.

"I *know* so," Grizzly stated. "You correct me if I'm wrong. The way I see it is this. You knew you were taking a chance by sending Havoc after the Hatchlings because of their superior senses. You could have sent Thunder, but even the Flathead can't match a mutant. And you could have sent me, but you didn't. I've been wondering about that ever since. And do you know what I figured out?"

"What?" Blade whispered.

"You didn't send me because you don't trust me," Grizzly said. "You know how I feel about mutants and humans. You didn't think you could rely on me to get the job done. You thought I might turn, go over to their side. Am I right?"

"Wrong," Blade declared.

"Oh, yeah?" Grizzly responded skeptically. "Then why didn't you send me?"

"I didn't want you killed," Blade informed the mutant.

Grizzly did a double take. "Say what?"

"I didn't want you to do something foolish and get yourself killed," Blade mentioned. "You're right about one thing, though. I know how you feel about mutants and humans. You have a low opinon of most humans, but you've set mutants up on a pedestal. Our conversation at the cliffs confirmed your attitude. You were all too ready to justify the atrocities committed by the mutant army of the Doktor."

"What's all this have to do with getting myself killed?" Grizzly queried.

"You're too willing to give mutants the benefit of the doubt, even murderous vermin like the Hatchlings," Blade answered. "If I had sent you after the Hatchlings, there was the chance you might not perform up to par. You might have been careless because you might have attempted to contact them, to talk to them, to find out if they were really as bad as Athena claimed." He paused. "I was concerned the Hatchlings might take advantage of your gullibility and kill you."

"Why should you care what happens to me?" Grizzly asked gruffly.

"You're a member of the Force now," Blade observed. "I'm responsible for your life. Besides," he smirked, "I kind of like you. I'm hoping we'll become friends."

Grizzly stared at the buildings beyond the field, his forehead furrowed. "Well, I'll be!" he muttered.

Blade gazed at the ridge behind them, pleased to note the brilliant golden glow pervading the atmosphere. "Okay. It's not nighttime anymore. The Hatchlings won't have the advantage. We're going in."

"What about these?" Grizzly questioned, pointing at the M-16, pair of pistols, and the boot knife lying at his feet. Athena's discarded weapons, found when they had searched for her.

"I'm surprised they left those behind," Blade remarked.

"The Hatchlings might be like me," Grizzly said. "I don't like using guns and knives much, not when I have my claws."

Blade nodded at the pile. "Hand me the M-16."

"You're going to use two?"

"The more the deadlier," Blade punned.

"Here you go." Grizzly handed the rifle over.

Blade checked to insure the magazine was fully loaded, then clicked off the safety. He was as ready as he'd ever be. In addition to the two M-16's, he had two 45's under his arms, his Bowies on his hips, and the Panther survival knife under the belt circling his back.

Grizzly had an M-16 and his claws.

"All right," Blade stated. "The orders are simple. Except for the women prisoners, Athena, and Havoc, take down everyone and everything you meet. Got it?"

Grizzly nodded.

"Then let's go." Blade rose from concealment and calmly walked to the field, to a well-defined path leading toward the center of the valley. He took the path, Grizzly close on his heels.

A number of figures were moving near the huts.

Blade gripped the M-16's a little tighter.

"Ms. Morris!"

Athena's head snapped up, her eyes opening in shock. She had dozed off! How could she sleep at a time like this! She remembered sitting down on the landing to rest during the quiet hours preceding daylight, fatigued by the hardships of the night before: the ascent of the cliffs, being taken prisoner, and her confrontation with the Spider. She sat with her legs curled under her, her left arm braced against the landing for support.

"Ms. Morris!"

Athena slid to the end of the landing and peered down at Sergeant Havoc. She realized the entire chamber was illuminated by a diffuse light, and she glanced to the left, at a small window high up on the wall. The stars were gone, replaced by an azure sky. Dawn had arrived.

Sergeant Havoc was striving to break free of the adhesive coating the webbing. He had spent the night struggling, without any success, and he was caked with sweat.

"Hi," Athena greeted him. "Sorry I fell asleep on you."

Havoc was frantically heaving his body from side to side. "The Spider!" he shouted. "The Spider!"

Athena looked up, recalling in a rush the words of the Hatchling named Chanc the night before: "Father ate a short while ago. He's saving you for breakfast."

Dear God!

The Spider had not budged all night, had stayed perched on the web on the opposite side of the chamber, apparently in slumberland.

But as Athena stared at the massive monstrosity in stunned horror, she saw it was moving now.

Coming straight toward her!

The figures were men in black, four of them, each armed with an automatic rifle. They had formed into a straight line between the huts and the field, facing the huts.

"Rise and shine, bitches!" one of them yelled.

Blade was 20 yards from the row of guards when the door to one of the huts opened and a weary woman clothed in virtual rags emerged. The Spirit had smiled on him so far. The guards, engaged in rousing the women to another day of grueling labor, had not noticed the approach of the two Force members.

A second, then a third woman stepped from the hut. They started to form a line of their own.

This must be the typical morning ritual, Blade realized. He leveled the two M-16's in the direction of the guards, the stocks pressed against his sides.

"Move your asses!" one of the men in black bellowed. "We ain't got all morning, you know!"

The door to another hut to the left opened, disgorging four more women.

Blade was within 15 yards of the guards, their backs toward him.

One of the women in line spied the approaching giant and the mutant, and she craned her neck for a better view.

Women were coming from several huts now.

Blade reached a point ten yards from the quartet of men in black.

"What the hell are you looking at?" demanded the spokesman for the guards, gazing at the woman craning her neck.

Nine yards.

The head guard turned, wanting to discover the reason for the woman's odd behavior. His mouth went slack at the sight of the big guy in the black leather vest and the hairy bearish mutant.

"Son of a bitch!" he blurted out, trying to bring his rifle into play.

Alerted by the head guard's exclamation, the attending trio began to rotate.

Blade shot them. All four. He squeezed both triggers simultaneously, sweeping the pair of M-16's in a tight arc from right to left. His slugs stitched patterns across their chests, rupturing blood vessels, spraying crimson from their thrashing forms. They danced and tossed for a full five seconds, while the barrage lasted, and then toppled to the ground.

Some of the women were screaming. Others had dropped flat at the first sound of the M-16's. A few were fleeing.

"Take cover!" Blade commanded. "We're here to rescue you!" He was grateful none of the women had been hit. Several had been standing close to the four guards, in the line of fire. He would have preferred to avoid imperiling their lives, but he hadn't had any choice. "Take cover!" he repeated.

Grizzly came up on Blade's right, scrutinizing the dead guards. "I think I'll go take a nap. I don't see what you need me for."

Blade ignored the jest, making for the Tower, walking between two huts.

A guard abruptly appeared around the hut to the right, rifle in hand.

Grizzly sent a half-dozen rounds crashing into the guard's head, flinging the man in black to the dirt.

Where are the Hatchlings? Blade asked himself. The hybrids should be counterattacking soon. How many were left? he wondered. Initially, Athena had said there were 19. He'd slain one, and so had Grizzly. They'd found two more, dead, on top of the ridge, possibly terminated by Sergeant Havoc. Which accounted for four. And they'd seen seven Hatchlings climbing the ridge, heading at a rapid clip for the cliffs, undoubtedly sent to apprehend them. Four and seven made 11. So there should be eight Hatchlings somewhere in the Kingdom.

But where?

A huge door at the base of the Tower suddenly opened, providing a partial answer.

A pair of Hatchlings charged from the Tower, rifles in their hands, firing on the run.

"Look out!" Blade cried, throwing himself to the left, diving for the ground, the Hatchlings' rounds narrowly missing him.

Grizzly had already shifted to the left, crouching and firing from the hip.

The foremost hybrid was hit in the face, its dark orbs dissolving in a shower of lethal lead.

The second Hatchling went to fire at the giant, but it neglected to verify the weapon was off of safety. In the few seconds required to recognize the mistake, it died.

Blade blasted the hybrid with both M-16's, hearing the smack-smack-smack of the slugs, seeing the Hatchling hurled to the ground in a disjointed heap. He surged to his feet and raced to the Tower door.

Grizzly was a pace behind him.

Blade halted at the doorway and carefully peered inside. He saw a stairwell off to the right, and he heard the hurried pounding of footsteps from up above.

"What now?" Grizzly demanded, keeping his eyes on the huts.

"One of us should stay here and hold the door to cover our rear," Blade directed, "while one of us should go up the stairs." He expected Grizzly to offer to remain at the doorway.

Instead, the mutant whirled and sprinted for the stairwell.

Blade was about to call out, to clarify his meaning, to tell Grizzly to stay by the door, when five guards pounded into view between two huts to the left.

They spotted him and charged.

What was the Spider doing?

Why had it stopped?

The mutant had circled to the left of the center of the web, bypassing the dip in the middle, traversing the thicker strands nearer the walls, perhaps because it could move faster along the outer rim.

Athena had watched the loathsome creature with baited breath.

And then, inexplicably, the Spider had halted 15 yards shy of the landing.

Havoc was like a madman, bucking and straining in a frenzied effort to break free.

Athena couldn't understand the reason for her reprieve, not until she heard the chatter of gunfire from outside the Tower.

Blade and Grizzly!

It had to be them!

Her elation was eclipsed a moment later when the Spider resumed its approach.

"No!" Havoc shouted in desperation.

Athena stood and stumbled backwards, unable to take her eyes off those eight vile black orbs.

Grizzly took the stairs two at a bound, listening to the thumping of hastening feet on the stairwell above. From the volume, he guessed there were several foes descending en masse.

"Hurry!" someone barked from overhead.

Grizzly recognized the metallic tone. Hatchlings. He stopped, planning his strategy. The spiral stairwell wasn't very wide, able to accommodate just two persons walking abreast between its rails. There wasn't much room to maneuver, which worked in his favor. He crouched next to the inner railing, his blood racing, waiting in keen anticipation.

The drumming footsteps came closer.

Grizzly was struck by a fleeting moment of indecision. Here he was, primed to plow into some Hatchlings, some fellow mutants, without giving them the opportunity to explain their actions, to justify themselves. He'd seen the women emerge from the huts and heard the derogatory remarks made by the guards, all of which lent credence to Athena's story. Still, a flickering finger of doubt assailed him. But before he could dwell on his uncertainty, the first Hatchling was upon him.

A hybrid with a rifle burst around the curve above.

Grizzly instinctively fired, his hasty shot striking the Hatchling in the forehead and causing the hybrid to trip and plummet over the outer railing toward the bottom of the Tower, over 20 feet below.

Another Hatchling appeared, and this one was unarmed.

Grizzly deliberately dropped the M-16, rising, his claws popping out over his fingernails, wanting to give the hybrid a fair chance.

The Hatchling never missed a beat. It closed on the intruder in one vaulting stride, aiming a vicious swipe of its talons at the bear-man's face.

Grizzly's reflexes were astounding. He ducked under the hybrid's blow and came up with his claws extended, ripping them into the Hatchling's abdomen, then using his immensely powerful shoulder and arm muscles to slice his claws from the hybrid's stomach to its sternum.

The Hatchling screeched as its internal organs squished through the rift in its epidermis.

Grizzly lifted and heaved, sending the hybrid sailing over the railing after its companion.

Two more Hatchlings closed on him from above.

Grizzly spun to face them, pitting his claws against their talons in a savage, primal contest. The confines of the stairwell cramped their assault, slowing them down, as they both tried to get at him at once. He backpedaled down three steps, letting them assume he was retreating.

One of the pair, the Hatchling on the right, took the bait and lunged.

Grizzly twisted, evading the hybrid's streaking talons, and slashed his right-hand claws across the Hatchling's eyes. The hybrid drew back, covering its eyes with its hands, shrieking in torment.

The second Hatchling tried to do likewise to Grizzly.

Grizzly jerked his face to the rear as the Hatchling's talons flashed past his eyes. Before the hybrid could recover, he speared his claws into the middle of the Hatchling's neck, then wrenched his brawny arms outward.

The result was as if the neck had exploded. Flesh and hair flew every which way. Yellowish blood spurted. The hybrid gurgled and went down.

Grizzly finished them off with a quick one-two, imbedding his claws in their foreheads, impaling their brains.

Four down.

How many more?

Grizzly raced up the stairwell, alert for an ambush, but he didn't encounter another Hatchling until he reached a landing at the top of the stairs.

A solitary hybrid stood in front of a large closed door, its four arms casually folded over its chest. "Greetings, stranger."

Grizzly tentatively stepped onto the landing, his gory claws in front of him.

The Hatchling stared at Grizzly's claws. "I see my brothers were unable to stop you."

"I want through that door," Grizzly stated. "I want to look on the other side."

The Hatchling smiled. "That's not possible. Father is busy at the moment."

From beyond the door came the terrified scream of a woman. Grizzly started toward the hybrid. "I'm warning you. . . ."

The Hatchling unfolded its arms, holding its talons at waist level. "You will not interrupt Father."

"Who says?"

"I do. I am Chanc, and I will defend my father with my dying breath!" So saying, Chanc sprang.

Blade raised the M-16's and cut loose, downing two of the five onrushing guards in the blinking of an eye. He pivoted to shoot yet another.

The M-16's went empty.

Blade ducked into the Tower, to the left, flinging the useless M-16's aside and drawing the Colt 45's from their shoulder holsters. He darted into the open again, bent over, the pistols held in front of him.

The three guards were still coming. They opened up as soon as the giant appeared.

Blade felt a burning sensation in his left shoulder, and something creased his right side, and then he was firing the Colts, both guns together, aiming two shots at each guard.

The nearest one was hit in the head and catapulted onto his back. The second took two rounds in the chest and went down. And in a geyser of crimson, the third guard lost his nose and his left cheek.

The abrupt quiet seemed unnatural.

Blade straightened, watching the fallen guards for any indication of life. Satisfied they were dead, he turned toward the Tower, intending to help Grizzly if necessary, when a commotion to the east arrested his attention. He looked up.

The seven Hatchlings he'd seen earlier hurrying up the ridge had returned! And they were not more than 30 feet off, closing rapidly.

Athena gasped when she backed into the door.

There was nowhere to go!

The Spider had reached the edge of the landing and paused, its eyes roving over her body.

Athena placed her palms against the door, trembling, feeling dizzy. She wanted to shut her eyes, to take refuge within herself, but her fear-filled gaze was glued to the gruesome genetic deviate.

The mutant's leading appendages glided onto the landing.

"Leave her alone, bastard!" Havoc was shouting. "Take me! Me!"

The Spider slowly eased its head and front segment onto the landing.

Athena lost control. She tossed her head back and screamed at the top of her lungs, venting her despair and her terror.

Four of the Spider's limbs were now on the landing.

Athena knew what was next, and she sank to her knees, tears forming in the corners of her eyes, tears of frustration and severe annoyance at herself for being dunderheaded enough to return to the Kingdom when she had been safe and sound.

Something slammed into the door, startling her, jarring the door to its hinges.

Now what?

Athena glanced over her left shoulder, perplexed, wondering what new menace was about to assail her.

And the Spider was on her, its two front limbs, capped by talons identical to the Hatchlings', grasping her wrists and dragging her onto her back, pinning her to the landing.

"No!" she cried, kicking her legs, trying to strike the Spider with her boots.

The Spider shifted its bulk, aligning its body.

Athena tensed, knowing from experience what to expect. The monster would ease its rear segment onto the rim of the landing, and a slit would open on its underside. And then its . . . organ . . . would emerge, a slender whitish rodlike affair not much bigger than a man's. Her pants would be ripped off, and the Spider would . . .

The landing door rocked to a tremendous blow, shaking the landing itself, and a hairline crack appeared down the center.

Athena's hopes soared. It couldn't be!

But it was.

A series of pounding thumps shook the door, the crack widening.

The Spider had forgotten its victim. The eight emotionless eyes were regarding the disintegrating door with an aloof detachment.

Athena unexpectedly found herself released, and she quickly slid to the left, to the very edge of the landing, watching the door.

"Athena?" Havoc yelled. "Athena?"

The door suddenly crashed inward, splitting into two sections. And there, framed in the doorway, awesome and mighty in his rage, was Grizzly. Behind him on the floor was a decapitated Hatchling. He glanced at Athena, then at the Spider, his eyes simmering points of fury.

The Spider moved backwards until it was balanced on the rim.

Grizzly strode onto the landing, his facial muscles twitching. "You!" he bellowed. "You're no better than the humans!"

The Spider brought its two front legs up in a defensive motion.

"I was wrong!" Grizzly practically shrieked, and then he raised his head and roared.

The Spider seemed to recoil.

Grizzly's eyes narrowed as he brought up his hands, the fingers rigid. His claws snapped out. And then he did something so strange, so inconsistent with the circumstances, that the effect was immeasurably more chilling than anything else he could have done.

He grinned.

Athena would never forget what transpired next for as long as she lived. She saw Grizzly cover the distance to the Spider in two blurred bounds, and then he vaulted into the air, going for the Spider's head, for those eight black eyes. He landed on the Spider's face above the vertical mouth, the claws on his left hand sinking into the Spider's flesh and affording purchase as he swung his right arm again and again and again, the five inch claws on his right hand tearing the Spider's eyes to shreds within seconds. The Spider reached up with its two front appendages, striving to tear Grizzly loose, but although it buried its talons in Grizzly's broad shoulders it was unable to dislodge him.

Athena was spellbound.

The Spider's limbs were waving wildly as it tried to slide from the landing. Incredibly, it lost its footing and pitched from view, Grizzly still ripping at its head.

Athena scurried to the edge of the landing and stared down-ward.

The battling mutants had landed on the web about twelve feet from Sergeant Havoc. The Spider was partially on its left side, endeavoring to pry Grizzly from its head. But Grizzly seemed impervious to the Spider's rain of blows. Like a mutant possessed, Grizzly slashed and slashed and slashed.

Athena surprised herself by laughing as new tears, tears of pure joy and relief, moistened her eyes. She watched, enrapt, as Grizzly carved the Spider's head to shreds, and she knew she had never, ever, witnessed such a beautiful sight.

She laughed some more.

Thank the Spirit the Hatchlings were unarmed!

Blade aimed the Colts, the pistols booming, and the nearest hybrid was shot through the forehead. He managed to shoot two more, expending his ammunition in the process, and he tossed the Colts to the ground and drew his prized Bowies. The blades gleamed in the bright sunlight as the four remaining Hatchlings surged toward him.

Come and get it!

Blade dodged aside as the first of the four tried to gouge out his stomach, and the Bowies flashed as he cut the side of the Hatchling's neck open with a left-hand strike, then stabbed his right Bowie into the hybrid's ear.

The Hatchling stiffened and toppled forward.

Blade wrenched his right Bowie free in time to counter the assault of the next Hatchling, parrying a swipe aimed at his groin by blocking the talons with the flat of his Bowie.

The Hatchling hastily retreated and was promptly joined by its two fellows. They wisely stayed beyond the giant's reach, slowly circling him.

Blade crouched, trying to keep all of them in his line of vision. If he could keep them at bay, he stood a chance. His greater height and reach worked in his favor. But if one of them got under his arms and tackled his legs, he was in serious trouble.

Which was exactly what happened.

One of the Hatchlings feigned an attack, pretending to step forward but stopping in midstride.

Blade pivoted to thwart the perceived threat, and one of the other hybrids leaped, springing in from the right and wrapping its four arms around his legs. Before he could hope to react, he went down, landing on his left side.

The Hatchlings were on him in an instant.

Blade became the focus of a veritable whirlwind of slicing talons and Bowies. His arms, legs, and torso were ripped again and again, but he gave as good as he got, delivering stroke after stroke. He tried to roll erect, but there was a Hatchling in his path, and he reversed direction as his right shoulder was torn open.

The Hatchlings were hissing like incensed vipers.

Blade lunged to his knees as a hybrid tried to impale his throat, and he buried his left Bowie to the hilt in the mutant's neck, then twisted the knife.

Gasping, the Hatchling jerked free of the dripping blade and tottered backwards.

Another Hatchling went for the giant's eyes.

Blade felt talons ripping into his right temple. Instead of pulling away, as the hybrid would expect, he leaned toward the Hatchling, bringing his right Bowie up and in, sinking the ten-inch blade into the hybrid's abdomen.

The Hatchling threw itself to the left, the Bowie lodged in its stomach.

Blade lost his grip on the slippery handle. He surged to his feet, holding the left Bowie in front of him.

The Hatchling with the Bowie in its gut was to his left, doubled over, wheezing.

The hybrid with the ragged hole in its neck was to his right, upright but wobbly.

And the final Hatchling was before him, seeking an opening.

Blade slowly eased his right hand behind his back, his fingers closing on the Panther. The Hatchling was watching the left Bowie, undoubtedly assuming it was his sole remaining weapon. Blade made a mock swipe with the left Bowie, forcing the Hatchling to veer to his right. The hybrid was still concentrating on the left Bowie when Blade swung the Panther in a brutal arc, driving the point into the Hatchling's right eye.

The hybrid frantically retreated, but not before the Panther was imbedded all the way into its eye.

Blade tore the Panther loose.

The Hatchling fell onto its stomach, convulsing and tittering.

Blade glanced at the two injured hybrids, amazed they were on their feet. He had to finish them off and find Grizzly.

But someone beat him to the punch.

There was the blast of a heavy-caliber revolver and the crack of an M-16, and the pair of Hatchlings went down, each shot through the head.

Blade turned in the direction of the shots, to the east, a smile creasing his haggard features.

They were standing 15 feet away, both attired in buckskins, the Cavalryman with a smoking Hombre in his right hand, the Flathead with an M-16.

"Thanks for saving some for us," Boone quipped, walking over and inspecting the Hatchlings to verify they were dead. His M-16 was slung over his left shoulder.

"Are you okay, Blade?" Thunder queried in concern, stepping to the Warrior's side.

"Fine," Blade said, realizing he was drenched with blood from a dozen wounds. "What about you?"

"I am well," Thunder replied. "The Spirit-In-All-Things was not ready for my soul. I think I had a concussion, but I am recovering."

"We've got to get inside," Blade said. "Grizzly is in there, and maybe—"

"Not anymore," Boone interrupted, motioning with his Hombre toward the Tower entrance.

Blade faced the Tower.

Grizzly was in the doorway, caked with yellow from head to toe. Gore was plastered to his fur. He came outside, surveying the littered bodies, then looked at Blade. "And here I thought you were goofing off while I did all the work."

"The Spider?" Blade asked.

Grizzly beamed. "Anyone for roast Spider for lunch?"

Havoc and Athena appeared, both squinting in the sunlight, Havoc with his right arm draped over her shoulders, supporting her.

"Are you two all right?" Blade inquired.

"I'm fine, sir," Sergeant Havoc answered, releasing Athena.

Athena nodded. "Just a little weak, is all. I think everything caught up with me at once as we were coming down the stairwell." She took a deep breath. "I'm feeling better already! And I haven't been this happy in ages!"

Sergeant Havoc scanned the huts. "What's next, sir?"

Blade straightened. "We round up the women, then set our charges." He stared at the Tower. "I don't want one stick standing when we're through."

Sergeant Havoc nodded. "There won't be," he assured the Warrior.

"I wish I could have been here," Boone commented.

"I'm glad I was," Grizzly remarked, involved in picking bits of flesh and black hair from his fur. He extended the claws on his right hand and critically examined them. "Damn! Look at all this gunk on my claws!"

"Thanks for cutting me loose from the web," Havoc mentioned. "I owe you."

"And I owe you for saving my life," Athena stated sincerely.

"Don't make a fuss about it," Grizzly said brusquely. "I was just doing my job." He looked at Blade and grinned. "I like this line of work. Can we do this again real soon?"

What was that noise?

Kraft came awake with a start, momentarily confused, wondering where he was. And then he remembered and he sat up, glancing at the dead Hatchling, his eyes narrowing to minimize the glare from the bright sunlight.

Bright sunlight?

Kraft peered at the sky, surprised to see the sun well above the eastern horizon. Sunup had been hours ago! He sluggishly stood, a dull ache pervading his body. Squinting at the sun again, he mentally noted the proper directions for north, south, east, and west.

But he still didn't know which way to go.

Kraft frowned, facing north, then south, debating.

And from the south came the clue he needed. A succession of thunderous explosions shattered the stillness of the forest.

They could only mean one thing.

Kraft gripped his M-16 and hastened to the south.

EPILOGUE

Blade was in his chair, seated behind his desk with his boots propped on the edge, reflecting on their first mission. Despite the setbacks and the blunders, they had succeeded, they had accomplished the mission.

The Force had been back at the compound for two weeks, the members enjoying a much-deserved rest-and-rehabilitation period. Blade had demanded several weeks off for everyone to recuperate, and General Gallagher had reluctantly complied.

What would be their next assignment? Blade wondered.

Whatever it was, they would face the challenge as a team, as a legitimate fighting unit. The confrontation with the Spider had brought them closer together, with one exception. While Havoc and Athena couldn't seem to compliment Grizzly enough, Kraft's resentment of the mutant was stronger than ever. Kraft had refused to talk about his experiences after he'd disappeared, and Blade was curious to learn the reason.

Even Thunder, after lengthy discussions with Sergeant Havoc and Athena, had accepted Grizzly into the ranks. Blade recalled the conversation he'd had with the Flathead about omens. Thunder had been drastically wrong. Instead of being a bad omen, Grizzly's presence had been essential to the completion of the mission.

Speaking of omens. . . .

Blade suddenly remembered the California flag with the grizzly bear depicted in the center. If he didn't know better, he might be inclined to believe the flag had been an omen for him. But omens were only superstitions.

Weren't they?

A jeep rumbled to a stop outside.

Blade stretched, thinking of Athena. Why had General Gallagher permitted her to recover from her ordeal at the Force compound? Why had the general gone to all the trouble to have a temporary wall installed in the barracks, just so she could have some privacy and enjoy a small room of her own? Gallagher's actions didn't make any sense.

Without any advance notice, in strolled the man in question.

"Hello, Blade," General Gallagher greeted the Warrior cheerily.

"You're in a good mood," Blade noted.

"I should be," Gallagher said. "The governor is pleased at how the mission turned out. Even the Federation Council is happy with the results. And the press has been eating up the story. Having Athena supply releases to the media was a stroke of inspiration."

"I'd pat you on the back, but your hands are in the way," Blade remarked, grinning.

"What's wrong with good publicity?" Gallagher queried.

"Nothing," Blade stated. "Publicize all you want. If it will make you happy, why don't you find a writer and have a book written about our exploits?" He laughed at the ludicrous suggestion.

General Gallagher's face seemed to light up. "A book! Why didn't I think of that?"

Blade shook his head in disbelief. "I don't care what you do, so long as you leave us alone for another week. I like this peace and quiet. I get to see my family each night. And I don't want anything to ruin it."

General Gallagher cleared his throat. "I understand. But there is a little matter I need to bring up."

Blade stared at the officer. "Is it a major problem?"

"I don't see it as a major problem, no," Gallagher said.

"A minor problem then?" Blade inquired.

Gallagher shook his head. "No. You see, Governor Melnick

has already cleared it, and the Federation Council say they will agree if you do."

Blade sat up. "Agree to what?"

Gallagher appeared reluctant to broach the subject. "Maybe I should come back another time."

"What's wrong with right now?" Blade demanded.

"I should catch you when you're in a better mood," Gallagher mentioned.

"What's wrong with my mood?" Blade questioned irritably.

"You see?" General Gallagher said. "If I bring it up now, I know you'll blow your top."

"I won't blow my top," Blade assured him. "What is it?"

Gallagher shook his head. "No. I'll come back."

Blade suddenly stood, leaning his clenched fists on the desk. "I want to know what it is, and I want to know *now*!"

"Are you sure you won't blow your top?" Gallagher asked.

"I'm sure!" Blade vowed.

"Okay." Gallagher smiled at the Warrior. "How would you feel about adding a new member to the Force?"

"Is that it? You want to add a new member to the Force?" Blade asked.

"That's it," Gallagher confirmed.

"What's the big deal? We need a new member to replace Spader," Blade said. "If you have someone in . . ." He abruptly stopped, insight dawning.

"I do have someone in mind," Gallagher said.

"That's why you let her stay here?" Blade questioned in amazement. "You must have planned this weeks ago!"

General Gallagher grinned. "Then you like the idea?"

"You're nuts."

"What's wrong with the idea? Athena would make a great addition to the Force," Gallagher observed.

"No," Blade said.

"Why the hell not?" Gallagher inquired angrily.

"Because I said so, and I'm the head of the Force," Blade noted. "We may receive our assignments from you, but I have the last word."

"Just give the idea some thought," Gallagher urged. "It will grow on you."

"No."

"Come on! For me?"

"No."

General Gallagher sat down in the chair facing the desk. "I think it's a great idea. And I'm going to stay right here until you agree! There's nothing you can say or do that'll make me leave!"

Blade slowly sat down, then reached for the intercom linking his office to the barracks. He pressed the appropriate button, activating a buzzer at the other end.

"Yes?" Boone responded.

"Boone, is Grizzly there?" Blade asked. The mutant had been persuaded to take up residence in the barracks.

"Yeah. He's here. Do you want to talk to him?" Boone responded.

"Send him to my office. There's a job I have for him," Blade directed.

"Will do." Boone clicked off.

General Gallagher had a worried expression. "You're bluffing. You wouldn't dare!"

Blade leaned back in his chair, smirking. "Try me."

Gallagher glanced at the intercom, then the doorway. He nervously licked his lips. "I don't see why you have to involve Grizzly in this."

Blade didn't bother to comment.

"Grizzly doesn't have any say in the matter," Gallagher noted.

"Grizzly has taken quite a liking to Athena," Blade disclosed. "They're the best of friends. I wonder how he will feel about you wanting to put her life on the line?"

Gallagher stood. "This is dirty pool."

Blade glanced at his clock. "He probably won't get here for another minute. If you hurry, you'll just miss him."

"You haven't heard the last of this!" Gallagher promised, then stalked from the room.

Blade was still laughing when Grizzly arrived.

"You wanted to see me?" Grizzly asked.

Blade stared into the mutant's eyes. "Has anyone ever told you you're a good omen?"

OUTLANDS STRIKE

PROLOGUE

Dear God!

He was going to crash!

The pilot experienced the chilling realization as he watched the bluish-black smoke pour from the sputtering turboshaft engine. He knew the engine would die at any second, and the prospect of his helicopter falling to the ground among . . . them . . . caused a prickly sensation to erupt all over his skin.

"What's happening, sir?" asked a familiar voice behind him, a voice strained by obvious tension.

The pilot glanced over his right shoulder.

Hertzog, the young crewman, was framed in the cockpit doorway. His angular features were pale, a stark contrast to his blue uniform. "It sounds like the bearings are shot all to hell!" he commented.

The pilot nodded grimly. Hertzog might be young, but he was the best damn copter man in the California Air Force. "This old war-horse has taken its last flight."

As if punctuating the pilot's remark, the Stallion suddenly lurched to the right, the turboshaft engine coughing.

"Damn!" the pilot fumed, struggling to maintain control.

Hertzog clutched the door frame for support, his knuckles white. "We're going down, aren't we?" he asked.

"Yes," the pilot confirmed.

"Down *there*?" Hertzog queried, emphasizing the last word with a touch of horror in his tone.

"Afraid so," the pilot stated.

"Any chance of missing the city?" Hertzog questioned hopefully.

"Doesn't look that way," the pilot replied forlornly.

"I won't let those . . . things . . . get me, Major!" Hertzog declared. "I won't!"

"They won't get us, son," the major assured his crewman. "If I can ditch the Stallion without sustaining too much damage, we'll cut out and head for the river. There are a lot of trees along the bank. We should be able to lose them there."

"I hope so," Hertzog said.

"You'd better strap yourself in," the major directed. "This might be bumpy."

"Do you want me to bag a few before we hit?" Hertzog asked. "They might hold back and give us the time we need to reach cover."

The major reflected for a moment. A pair of .50-caliber machine guns were mounted on the Stallion. Just one would be sufficient to deter those creatures below, but the risk entailed was too great. "No," he responded. "You might hit some of the humans."

Hertzog frowned. "I'm way out of line saying this," he mentioned, "but I think you're making a big mistake."

"We can't endanger innocent lives," the major noted.

"How do we know they're innocent?" Hertzog countered.

"You saw those pikes," the major reminded the airman.

"What a way to end a mission!" Hertzog muttered.

"At least I got off a coded message to General Gallagher," the major said. "They'll know where to find us."

"Our bodies," Hertzog commented, then departed.

The major surveyed the landscape below, his keen brown eyes seeking a suitable landing site. He could feel perspiration on his forehead and soaking his brown hair under his helmet. If he could only set the big chopper down before the turboshaft crapped out on him! All he needed was a little time.

But there wasn't any to spare.

The engine abruptly belched a cloud of grimy smoke, shuddered, and died.

"Son of a bitch!" the major snapped angrily.

With a whining groan, the Stallion plummeted rapidly.

The major reached over and flicked a silver toggle switch on the instrument panel, activating the radio. "Little Red Riding Hood to the Big Bad Wolf," he announced, hoping his call was being monitored in Yreka. "Little Red Riding Hood to the Big Bad Wolf. Condition Red. Repeat. Condition Red. The Goose is crippled. Probable impact at Mother Hubbard's. Repeat. Mother Hubbard's. Goldilocks is in. The Pied Piper was correct. End of transmission."

There.

One last message, just in case his previous transmission had not been received.

For all the good it would do them!

The major was compelled to devote his total concentration to the task of aligning the angle of the helicopter's descent, but the Stallion seemed to be endowed with a mind of its own. He wanted to come down in a large clearing not far from the Rogue River, but the copter was heading toward a dense stand of trees between the clearing and the waterway.

"Come on, baby!" the major coaxed the craft. "Don't do this to me! Not after all we've been through!"

The Stallion's tail started to swing to the left.

"No!" the major cried, desperately striving to maintain some semblance of level flight.

The Stallion rocked violently, and then the helicopter was spiraling downward at a frightening rate.

"Brace yourself!" the major cried, wondering if Hertzog would be able to hear him above the rush of the wind and the grinding of the chopper.

The ground filled the cockpit window, the clearing and the trees beyond the clearing visible intermittently as the copter rotated.

"We're going to hit!" the major shouted for Hertzog's benefit, bracing himself for the collision.

With a terrific, resounding crash, the Stallion plowed into the trees, all twenty-three thousand pounds of her, striking with the force of a bomb, leveling the first trees she hit.

The major saw the front of the cockpit shatter in a shower of plexiglass and metal. Something seared his right shoulder. His body was jarred unmercifully, his spine lancing with torment.

Her momentum scarcely checked, the Stallion slammed into other trees, her fuselage absorbing the brunt of the concussion. Her frame cracked and buckled. The starboard side crumpled like a flimsy eggshell with a rending, grinding roar.

His body flouncing in his seat, the major felt his neck whip to the right. He accidentally bit his tongue. For a moment he was completely disoriented, awash in vertigo.

With a surprising swiftness all motion ceased. The Stallion became still.

The major's heart was pounding in his chest. He glanced at his right shoulder and discovered a six-inch metal shard imbedded in his flesh. The jagged fragment had torn through his uniform and pierced his shoulder, narrowly missing the bone. A ring of blood encircled the wound.

Damn his luck!

Grimacing in pain, the major used his left hand to unfasten the seat restraints. He rose, his legs wobbly, and took several seconds to catch his breath and regain his strength.

Where was his crewman?

"Hertzog?" the major called out. "Are you all right?"

There was no answer.

The major staggered to the doorway, noting the extent of the damage to the cockpit, amazed he was still alive. He stepped through the doorway into the main cabin, then froze, aghast.

Hertzog had not survived the crash. The airman was strapped in a seat on the starboard side of the helicopter, his torn and mangled form partially encased in a shroud of twisted metal and protruding tree limbs. One of the limbs had speared him through the neck, nearly decapitating him.

"Hertzog!" the major exclaimed weakly.

The exit door located on the forward starboard side of the cabin had been crumpled into an accordion shape and twisted to the rear, leaving a two-foot space and affording a glimpse of daylight and the boles of trees.

Somewhere in the distance arose the sound of shouting.

The major moved to the starboard exit door and peered outside. Not more than three feet below was the ground. He cast a last look at Hertzog, then hurriedly slid through the two-foot space and dropped to the weed-choked earth. His right shoulder was racked by an excruciating pang. He flinched, doubling over, wishing he could extract the metal shard and tend to his wound.

But they would find him if he delayed.

His lips compressed to preclude an involuntary cry, the major hastened away from the helicopter. He scanned the tops of the trees, taking his bearings according to the position of the sun. Due west was directly ahead.

More yelling was coming from the east.

The major jogged in the direction of the Rogue River. His left hand brushed the grips of his .45 automatic, a reassuring gesture. The automatic was secure in a black leather holster, its butt

forward in the time-honored military fashion. Even with his right
arm out of commission, he could draw and fire using his left hand
with a fair degree of accuracy.

"This way!" a man bellowed perhaps 50 yards to the east.

They were closing on the downed chopper fast!

The major skirted a wide tree trunk and entered a stand of dense
undergrowth.

"Over here!" someone else barked.

The major bent over at the waist to reduce his profile. His left
hand scraped against a thorn bush, drawing blood across his
knuckles. He reached a shallow depression and eased onto his
knees, then drew the .45.

They weren't taking him without a fight!

That much was certain!

There was a hubbub, a commingling of indistinguishable
utterances, in the vicinity of the Stallion.

The major stared to the west, trying to spy the river. How far
did he have to go? he wondered.

A new element was added to the commotion near the chopper
when a deep, flinty voice boomed above all the rest.

"Silence! All of you will return to your work stations immediately! Move your asses, you worthless rabble!"

What was happening?

Had one of those . . . things . . . arrived on the scene?

The major rose, keeping his body hunched over, and hiked
westward. After a hundred yards the vegetation thinned out. He
encountered piles of weeds and brush at regular ten-yard intervals.
Someone was in the process of clearing the area near the river. He
advanced cautiously, moving past a large oak.

And unexpectedly discovered one of the occupants of the city.

The major halted in midstride, leveling the automatic.

A short, stocky man dressed in tattered brown pants and a
brown shirt was standing five feet off, a sickle clutched in his right
hand, an expression of astonishment on his oval face.

"Don't move!" the major warned.

The man gazed at the pistol, his mouth widening in
stupefaction. "You have a gun!" he blurted out.

"And I know how to use it," the major cautioned. "So keep
your voice down!"

"But guns are strictly forbidden," the stocky man said. "The penalty for owning one is premature consumption."

"Premature consumption?" the major repeated quizzically.

The man in brown looked to the east. "I heard a crash."

"My helicopter went down," the major stated. "I need your help."

The man gaped at the major. "You're not from the Province! I knew it!"

"No, I'm not from around here," the major confirmed. "And I need your help!" he reiterated.

The stocky man shook his head. "I can't help you!"

"Why not?" the major demanded. "I won't hurt you."

"No," the man said fearfully. "You don't know what you're asking! The penalty for aiding illegal entrants is premature consumption."

"There you go again!" the major snapped, frustration engulfing him.

The stocky man closed his eyes. "Please! Get out of here! I don't want to talk to you! I don't even want to see you! Go!"

"I'll go if you'll answer one question," the major declared. "Are there any boats nearby?"

"Boats?" The man in brown opened his eyes.

"I know I'm close to the river," the major said. "I could use a boat."

"No!" the man said.

"Look, I don't want to cause you any trouble," the major assured him. "I have a fair idea of what's going on in this city. I saw a lot of people from the air, and I also saw a lot of the monstrosities obviously running this place. I want to get the hell out of here before one of those creatures shows up. Which is why I could use a boat. Is there one nearby?"

The stocky man shook his head vigorously. "I can't! I can't! The Reptiloids will report me!"

"The Reptiloids? Is that what those things are called?" the major asked.

The man closed his eyes again, his lower lip quivering. "I just can't! Can't! Can't!"

"Now listen, you—" the major began.

There was the retort of a breaking branch to the rear.

Startled, the major spun. His eyes narrowed at the sight of several dark forms moving through the undergrowth toward him.

They were not bothering to conceal their pursuit; they barged right through the thickest vegetation, tramping bushes and breaking any limbs in their path.

"The Reptiloids!" the stocky man wailed.

The major hesitated, debating whether to make a stand or flee. He decided discretion was the better part of valor and took off to the west.

"No!" the man in brown cried. "No!"

His right shoulder pulsing with pain, the major weaved a zigzag pattern toward the Rogue River, putting as many trees between himself and his pursuers as he could.

A terrified screech rent the woods behind him.

The trees abruptly ended at the rim of a gradually sloping bank. Twenty feet away was the gently flowing Rogue River.

Elated, the major dashed to the water's edge. He glanced to the left and right, seeking a boat.

There was one.

But it wasn't available for his use.

A sleek, red motorboat rumbled into life 40 yards to the north, alongside a small dock on the opposite bank. The craft surged from the dock and shot across the water, bearing down on the man in the blue uniform.

The major took one look at the three figures in the motorboat and turned, intending to evade capture by hiding in the trees. But his retreat was cut off.

Three more of the creatures were perched on the lip of the bank. One of them, the largest, poised between his two companions, hefted a gleaming silver pike, and smirked.

The major raised the pistol.

"Have a care, human!" the thing stated testily. "If you squeeze that trigger, you will be ripped to pieces. You can not hope to slay all of us."

The speeding motorboat was already halfway across the Rogue River.

"I'll get one or two of you," the major vowed.

"Perhaps," the creature said. "Perhaps not."

The motorboat's engine created a raucous din.

"Drop the weapon," the creature on the bank directed.

"I don't think so," the major rejoined, smirking. He kept his pistol trained on the large thing in the center. They hadn't tried anything yet, and he was confident he could hold them off long enough to reach the trees. His train of thought was distracted by the noise of the approaching motorboat. The thundering engine was making an earsplitting racket. If he didn't know better, he'd swear the boat was right behind him.

It was.

The major managed a solitary stride before he realized his mistake and started to turn.

The creature driving the motorboat had the craft at full throttle.

Taken unawares, the major was unable to avoid the boat's prow. He saw the thing at the wheel jerk the wheel to the left, and the motorboat angled sharply. The craft slewed up onto the bank, and he felt a tremendous blow in his midriff and on his legs. His body was hurled backwards, tumbling head over heels. Everything was a blur for a second, and then he slammed into a hard object, his left side bearing the brunt of the impact. The world swam before his eyes, a pinwheel of blues and greens and yellows and reds.

Was he dying?

Slowly, sluggishly, his senses returned. A hideous visage materialized above him. Sounding hollow and distant, the voice of the large creature penetrated his waning consciousness.

"Foolish human! We must teach you the error of your ways!"

The major flexed his lefthand, surprised to find his gun was gone.

"Rest easy, human," the creature said. "You won't die. Not now, anyhow. But it may be a different story after your audience with Reptilian."

Reptilian?

The major sank into oblivion.

PART ONE
OF MUTANTS AND MEN

CHAPTER ONE

The giant was immersed in reflection.

He stood on a grassy mound 20 yards to the south of the command bunker, his keen gray eyes surveying the bunker, his forehead furrowed, his hands clasped behind his broad back. The rising sun was just topping the eastern horizon and there was a slight chill to the early April air. But the giant seemed not to notice. His massive physique was clothed in a black leather vest, green fatigue pants, and black combat boots. Strapped around his lean waist were two Bowie knives, one in a sheath on each hip. He brushed at a comma of dark hair hanging above his eyebrows and sighed.

What was he accomplishing here?

Was all the aggravation worth the effort?

He frowned as he glanced at the structure to the left of the command post, a supply bunker.

Three months had elapsed.

Three whole months!

And what had the Force done to justify its existence?

The giant shifted his attention to the building to the right of the command post, a long concrete barracks housing the members of the Freedom Force. They would be rising soon, and would emerge and assume formation to receive their orders for the day.

What did he have to tell them?

Simply the same old thing.

Drills, drills, and more drills would be the order of the day. And he was sick to death of repetitive practice exercises, which was highly ironic. Three months ago he had worried about their inexperience in functioning as a unit. He had demanded more time to train them before leading them into the field. And now here he was, fervently wishing the Force would be sent on a mission. They had drilled until they could perform their duties with skilled precision, but after three months of practicing day after day, three months of being confined to the compound except for occasional trips into Los Angeles, the members of the Force were beginning to get on each other's nerves. There were animosities simmering below the surface, animosities which threatened to explode if the Force wasn't handed an assignment soon.

Real soon.

A lanky man stepped from the barracks and began walking toward the command post. He wore buckskins and a pair of 44 Magnum Hombre revolvers in matching dark leather holsters. His brown hair fell to his shoulders. He took a half-dozen paces, then spotted the giant on the mound. "Blade!" he shouted.

Blade raised his right hand to acknowledge the greeting. "Boone! What is it?"

Boone jogged up to the mound, his brown eyes alive with excitement. He stopped and stared up at the giant, who normally towered over his six-foot-three frame by seven inches, and now loomed larger because of the mound. "We just had a call," he said.

"Who from?" Blade inquired.

"General Gallagher," Boone answered. "He's on his way here from LA."

Blade's interest was aroused. "Did Gallagher say why he was coming?"

"No," Boone responded. "He just said it's important, and he would appreciate it if you stayed close to the command post. He doesn't want you out on a training exercise when he gets here."

Blade scratched his chin. "This could be what we're waiting for."

"An assignment?" Boone asked hopefully.

Blade shrugged. "Could be. I want you to have the others fall out within ten minutes."

"Will do," Boone promised, and began to turn.

"Any problems last night or this morning?" Blade queried.

Boone paused. "The usual," he said.

Blade pursed his lips. "Kraft again?"

"Yep," Boone stated. "He just isn't happy unless he's making other folks miserable."

"What happened this time?" Blade probed.

"Last night Kraft tangled with Grizzly," Boone revealed. "If you ask me, I think Kraft is trying to commit suicide. If he keeps messing with Grizzly, he'll succeed."

"Was it verbal or physical?" Blade questioned.

"Kraft started in on Grizzly," Boone said. "He was griping about Grizzly being in the barracks, as usual, and I reckon Grizzly just had enough. He lifted Kraft off the floor and threatened to gut him."

"What did Kraft do?"

Boone snickered. "The idiot laughed, like it was all a big joke. Grizzly let him go, but I don't know how long Grizzly can control his temper."

Blade sighed. "Anything else?"

"A few minutes ago Kraft and Sergeant Havoc had a minor disagreement. Havoc was using one of the sinks to shave. Kraft decided he wanted to use that particular sink and told Havoc to take a hike," Boone detailed.

"There are four sinks and four shower stalls in the east end of the barracks," Blade noted. "Why did Kraft want to use the one Havoc was using?"

"Beats me," Boone said. "Thunder was in the shower, but none of the other sinks were being used."

"How did Havoc react?" Blade inquired.

"I wasn't there to see the whole thing," Boone said. "By the time I got there it was almost over. Kraft was on his back on the floor, and Havoc was using the sink like nothing had happened. Thunder told me about the argument. He said Kraft took a swing at Havoc, and Havoc did one of those fancy karate moves of his with his legs. Kraft stormed out of the bathroom cursing a blue streak." He paused. "Do you want some advice?"

"I'm always open to suggestions," Blade said.

"Then get rid of Kraft," Boone advised. "He's a monumental pain in the butt. None of us get along well with him. If he stays in the Force, you're only inviting trouble."

"If I send Kraft back before his year is up," Blade mentioned, "I could antagonize the Clan."

"We don't need a bad apple in the bunch," Boone remarked. "Not when our lives are at stake."

"I'll see what I can do," Blade pledged.

Boone nodded and jogged toward the barracks.

Blade watched the Cavalryman disappear inside. He'd known Boone the longest of any of the Freedom Force members, and he had developed an abiding friendship with the gunman. He tended to rely on Boone's judgment, and he knew the Cavalryman was right once again; if something wasn't done about Kraft, the Freedom Force would be endangered by internal strife. If the members couldn't relate well personally, they certainly wouldn't be able to perform their missions as a tight-knit team.

The Freedom Force had been the brainchild of the Freedom Federation Council, and he mentally reviewed its brief history as he pondered a solution to Kraft's disruptive presence.

One hundred and five years after World War Three, the North American continent was in a shambles. Devastated by nuclear and chemical weaponry, the United States had ceased to exist. Instead, diverse factions now controlled portions of the country. In the east the Russians ruled a corridor between the Atlantic Ocean and the Mississippi River. Chicago was under the heel of oppressive technological autocrats known as the Technics. Houston was dominated by androids. And there were other malignant groups, each in its own way determined to subjugate everyone and everything under an iron rule.

Fortunately for the sake of humanity, a number of factions were devoted to preserving freedom, to fostering liberty and maintaining the positive aspects of prewar culture. Seven of these factions had formed into a protective association designated the Freedom Federation. The leaders of this Federation had decided to establish a strike force to deal with any and all threats to the existence of the Federation factions, and they had named this elite squad the Freedom Force. Each of the seven factions was required to send a volunteer to serve for a period of one year.

Initially seven men, including himself, had constituted the Force. One of those men had been killed on their last mission, and the Federation faction from which the man had volunteered, the Moles, had not yet sent a replacement. Blade speculated on a possible reason for the delay.

The Force members began emerging from the barracks bunker, one at a time. They formed into a straight line, their backs to the barracks, standing at attention, facing the mound.

Blade suspended his reverie and walked toward his unit. He scrutinized the line from right to left as he approached, musing on the individual volunteers, on their strengths and weaknesses.

First in line was Boone. A frontiersman, he hailed from the

Federation Faction called the Cavalry. The Dakota Territory was their home range. They were a hardy breed of superb horsemen and horse women who, rumor had it, were taught to ride before they could walk. Boone was one of the most universally respected Cavalrymen, and his reputation as a shootist was widespread.

The second man was a full-blooded Indian, a member of the Flathead Indian tribe. They controlled the former state of Montana, and they had sent an expert tracker and marksman as their representative on the Force. Thunder-Rolling-in-the-Mountain was his name, and he had long black hair falling past his wide shoulders and alert, dark eyes. He wore a fringed buckskin shirt and pants, and moccasins.

The third volunteer hailed from the Federation faction known as the Clan. They resided in northwestern Minnesota, not far from Blade's birthplace, the survivalist compound dubbed the Home. And the Clan had sent, in Blade's estimation, the worst candidate for a position on the Force. The perennial trouble-maker, Kraft, was a Clansman. At five-foot-nine he was hefty but muscular. His lengthy blond hair was slicked and shaped into projecting spikes. He was partial to black leather attire and also wore thin gold earrings. In his right-hand pocket on his studded leather jacket he carried a switchblade, a weapon he wielded with exceptional skill.

Fourth in line was Sergeant Havoc. As the best noncom in the California Army, he was all military. California was one of the few states to retain administrative integrity after the war. As a recent addition to the ranks of the Freedom Federation, and wanting to demonstrate its commitment and capability, the government of California had agreed to construct the special facility for the tactical force near Los Angeles and to place the state's military hardware at the disposal of the Force. In keeping with their commitment, a soldier with impeccable credentials was chosen as the California volunteer. Sergeant Havoc was a qualified marksman and weapons master, a professional trooper with black belts in karate and judo and a brown belt in aikido. Six feet tall, with two hundred pounds of muscle on his frame, he wore his black hair in a crew cut and possessed penetrating blue eyes. He typically wore combat boots, fatique pants, and a green T-shirt.

At the west end of the line stood the volunteer from the

Civilized Zone. During the Third World War, the government of the U.S. had been virtually wiped out in a preemptive strike on Washington, D.C. A few administrators and bureaucrats had made their way to Denver, Colorado, and they established that city as the new capital. The area in the midwest they governed was designated the Civilized Zone. As the largest Federation faction, both geographically and numerically, the Civilized Zone included a unique minority among its citizenry: mutants.

Their volunteer was a mutant.

Grizzly was his name, and he was the result of genetic experiments conducted by a deranged scientist. Prior to the war, genetic engineering had been all the rage. Geneticists competed amongst themselves to see who would enjoy the distinction of producing a new species. The U.S. Patent Office had even granted patents to scientists desirous of developing higher or altered forms of animal life. Animals with augmented, manmade characteristics were propagated. The genetic tampering with lifeforms was touted as a major scientific breakthrough which would reap untold benign benefits for humankind. Inevitably, however, the process was applied to human beings for militaristic purposes. By deliberately combining human and animal traits, by editing the genetic instructions encoded in the chemical structure of molecules of DNA, the scientist responsible for Grizzly's creation had hoped to produce a perfect assassin.

He'd almost succeeded.

Like others of his ilk, Grizzly was a curious hybrid of human and bestial traits. He was five-feet-eight in height and endowed with a thick body rippling with layer upon layer of muscle. His shoulders and upper arms were especially dense. He was covered with a coat of short, light brown fur, and he wore a black loin-cloth. His face was decidedly bear-like, with a pointed chin, concave cheeks, elongated nostrils, a receding brow, deep dark eyes, and small circular ears. Thin lips rimmed a wide mouth, and when he smiled or growled, those lips curled back to reveal a set of tapered teeth.

Blade absently gazed at the mutant, pondering the three varieties of mutations so prevalent since the war. Grizzly, the product of genetic engineering, was representative of only one type of mutation. The other two groups had been unleashed on the environment by the nuclear and chemical weaponry employed during the global conflict.

One of the more common forms included those wild animals born with their genetic code deranged. The enormous amounts of radiation which had permeated the ecological chain had warped the transmission of hereditary traits. Animals were born deformed with extra limbs or heads, or their features might be displaced on their bodies. Humans were also affected, but to a lesser extent. A few instances had been recorded in which a human embryo was radically modified by parental contact with food or water or land contaminated by the tremendous radiation levels.

The third type of mutation was the deadliest of all. It was comprised of mutates, former mammals, reptiles, or amphibians infected by the chemical toxins utilized during World War Three—specifically, the regenerating chemical clouds. Once they were infected, they changed from an average example of their species into insane, pus-covered horrors. They existed for one purpose: to kill and kill again.

Blade reached a point about six feet in front of the volunteers, then stopped to address them. "Good morning," he stated.

"Good morning," Thunder responded.

"Morning," came from Boone.

"Morning, sir," Sergeant Havoc said.

Grizzly simply nodded.

Kraft didn't bother to respond. He yawned instead.

Blade glanced from one to the other. "As Boone may have told you, we are expecting a visit from General Gallagher—"

"Good!" Kraft interrupted. "Maybe we'll finally get us some action, dude."

"So we won't conduct training exercises this morning," Blade went on, ignoring the Clansman's comment for the moment. "I want all of you to tend to your gear. Check your backpacks, your rations, and your weapons. We must be ready to leave on a moment's notice."

"Why don't we cut out now?" Kraft interjected. "We could split for LA and cop a little fuzz tonight."

Blade slowly moved over to the Clansman. "In case you haven't heard, discipline is essential to a military operation."

"I know that, man," Kraft said.

Blade leaned down until his eyes were inches from Kraft's. "Then perhaps you can tell me why you see fit to flap your gums while I'm addressing the men?''

"Give me a break!" Kraft rejoined. "It's not like we're out in the field. Besides, I'm sick and tired of all this chickenshit military garbage!"

"You volunteered to serve for a year, just like the rest of us," Blade noted. "You should have expected to be in a military unit. You should have expected there would be discipline and regulations."

"I didn't know it would get this bad," Kraft complained.

"It could be worse," Blade mentioned.

"Yeah? Like how, dude?" Kraft queried belligerently.

Blade's right hand lashed out, gripping the front of Kraft's black leather shirt. Before Kraft could so much as blink, he was hoisted bodily a foot into the air.

"Let go of me!" the Clansman exclaimed, grasping at the giant's fingers.

Blade's eyes were steely gray pinpoints as he unceremoniously dumped the Clansman onto the ground.

Kraft landed on his buttocks, his face turning livid. He made a grab for the switchblade in his right pocket.

But Blade was faster.

The giant's right Bowie swept up and out, the glistening blade sweeping to within half an inch of Kraft's nose. "Don't even think it!" he warned.

Kraft blinked several times in succession, gawking at the Bowie. His right hand stopped next to his pocket.

"I want you to listen to me, and I want you to listen real good," Blade stated angrily. "I have taken all the crap from you I am going to take! If you don't start shaping up, right now, you can pack your suitcase and return to the Clan. I'll even send a messenger back with you, carrying my letter to your leader, Zahner. I'll explain the reason you were mustered out of the Force, and I'll ask Zahner to send a replacement, someone who doesn't have bricks for brains, someone who doesn't act like he has a stick shoved up his ass all the time. Do you read me, mister?"

Kraft didn't move.

"Do you understand me?" Blade said in a gravelly tone.

Kraft, reluctantly, nodded once.

Blade straightened. "You've been a source of dissension since the first day you arrived. Months ago you promised me you'd toe the line, but your word obviously is worthless. You're constantly causing trouble, picking fights, and insulting the others. You don't seem to know how to function as part of a team." He paused and sighed. "I've tried to make allowances for you, Kraft. I know you were once a gang member in the Twin Cities. Before you became part of the Clan, you were forced to live by your wits. You survived because you were faster and meaner than your enemies. But your gang life is a thing of the past, and gang ethics won't hack it here. Either you learn to cooperate, or you can take a hike."

Kraft was glaring at the giant.

"Anything you want to say?" Blade asked.

Kraft shook his head.

"Fine. Then go check on your gear," Blade ordered. He stepped back and replaced his right Bowie in its sheath.

Kraft slowly stood, his rage readily apparent.

"You can return to the Clan if you want," Blade stated. "The choice is yours."

"No," Kraft said.

"Think about it," Blade directed. "It might be best for everyone if you did leave."

Kraft spun and stalked off toward the barracks. He slammed the door as he entered.

"If you don't mind my saying so, sir," Sergeant Havoc said in his low voice, "I hope Kraft leaves. We don't need his kind on the Force."

"We'll let him decide if he stays or goes," Blade said.

"Why don't you just boot him out, sir?" Sergeant Havoc inquired. "You'd be doing all of us a favor. Kraft doesn't know what it means to be part of a military unit."

"Everyone deserves the benefit of the doubt," Blade remarked.

"A noble sentiment," Thunder commented.

"And noble sentiments are just dandy," Boone chimed in, "except for one thing."

Blade glanced at the Cavalryman. "What's that?"

"If you're not careful," Boone observed, "noble sentiments can get you killed."

CHAPTER TWO

Blade was seated in a metal folding chair at his desk in the command bunker when the general arrived.

He was ruminating on his life at the Home, the walled retreat constructed by a man named Kurt Carpenter shortly before World War Three. The descendants of Carpenter and his followers still resided at the Home, over a century since the war had ended. As the head of the Warrior class, the expert fighters responsible for the preservation of the Home, Blade had spent most of his adult life safeguarding the lives of others. His fame had spread beyond the confines of the Home over the years, as stories about his lethal prowess were circulated among the Freedom Federation factions. He'd had to overcome countless threats to the security of the Home, and because of his demonstrated competence the leaders of the Freedom Federation had asked him to assume his new post as head of the Force.

Sometimes, he wished he'd turned them down.

His life was much harder now. Being in charge of the Force was a totally different experience from leading the Warriors. The Warriors were all devoted to their craft, they were able to discharge their duties proficiently, and rarely had they given him any grief. But the Force members, on the other hand, were a never-ending source of disciplinary problems, as in the case of Kraft, or else their attitudes left a lot to be desired. Grizzly was a bigot; the mutant had once referred to humans as "scum." And even Boone's attitude was deficient. The frontiersman had volunteered for the Force at the request of the leader of the Cavalry, not because he wanted to volunteer. Boone was merely killing time until his enlistment was up.

Blade abruptly sat up straight in his chair, listening.

The sounds of footsteps pounded on the stairs leading from his open office door to the bunker entrance. A moment later an officer appeared in the doorway, a brown briefcase in his left hand.

"General Gallagher," Blade said, greeting him.

General Miles Gallagher nodded curtly and entered the office. Gallagher served as the personal liaison between the Force and the governor of California, Governor Melnick. And it was Melnick who relayed information pertaining to threats against the Federation from the leaders of the Federation factions.

"To what do I owe this honor?" Blade asked.

Gallagher walked to a chair in front of the desk and sat down. He was a bulldog of a man, stocky, with brown eyes and crew-cut brown hair. A dozen ribbons decorated his barrel chest. His eyes narrowed as he stared at the Warrior. "Are you making fun of me?"

"Would I do that?" Blade responded, smiling.

"You don't like me, do you?" General Gallagher demanded bluntly.

"I never said that," Blade said.

"You don't have to say it," Gallagher stated. "I can see it in your face."

"I have nothing against you personally," Blade divulged. "But I do somewhat resent the way you feel about the Force."

"At least I'm honest about the way I feel," Gallagher said. "I opposed the formation of the Force, and I still don't think it's a good idea. Oh sure, I know all of the Federation leaders believe we need a tactical squad which can respond immediately to any perceived danger. But California has been taking care of itself for over a hundred years. We can handle our own problems. Funding and equiping a measely squad of seven so-called specialists is a waste of valuable resources. What do we need your squad for when we have an Army, Navy, and Air Force of our own?"

"We've been all through this," Blade mentioned. "The Federation leaders wanted a mobile strike force capable of dealing with isolated trouble spots before they developed into full-fledged threats to the security of the Federation. You just said you don't like wasting valuable resources. Think of the savings in resource material we achieve by having the Force deal with problems before they grow to the point where an entire army might be needed to deal with the situation."

General Gallagher reflected for a few seconds. "I never thought of it that way."

"Give the Force time," Blade suggested. "We'll prove ourselves to your satisfaction."

"You did handle the Spider affair nicely," General Gallagher admitted grudgingly. "Although you lost one of your men."

Blade frowned. "You don't need to remind me."

"Any word on a replacement yet?" General Gallagher queried.

"No," Blade said. "We haven't heard a thing from the Moles. I don't have the slightest idea why they haven't sent someone."

General Gallagher, oddly enough, grinned. "Well, we can't have the Force go out on a mission undermanned. But we'll get to that in a moment." He opened the briefcase on his lap, the lid concealing the contents from Blade's view. "You may have the chance to prove yourselves at hand."

"What do you mean?" Blade inquired.

General Gallagher gazed at the Warrior. "What do you know about Oregon?"

"Not much," Blade said. "We studied geography extensively in our schooling classes at the Home. So I know Oregon was once a state, and it was located due north of California. But, so far as I know, Oregon did not survive the war intact. You were the one who told me that Portland sustained a direct nuclear strike."

Gallagher nodded. "According to our records Portland was completely destroyed. A few rural radio stations in Oregon, those outside the blast radius, reported their employees could see the mushroom cloud. For a decade or so after the war California received a steady influx of refugees from Oregon, but they eventually were reduced to a trickle. Oregon is now consisted part of the Outlands, the regions outside the control of the Freedom Federation or any other known group. The Outlands, as you well know, have reverted to barbaric, savage levels of existence. Anything goes."

"Don't I know it," Blade said.

"I'm bringing all of this up because the Federation leaders want the Force to go into what was once southwest Oregon," Gallagher explained.

Blade rested his elbows on his desk and folded his hands under his chin. As the head of the Force he could accept or reject any mission; he had wisely stipulated such a condition prior to accepting the post. "I'm all ears," he stated.

General Gallagher's expression became somber. "We have reason to believe a confederation of mutants may be forming in the Outlands with the express purpose of dominating the country, if not the world."

Blade tensed. "What?"

"That's right," Gallagher asserted. "Let me give you the facts. From time to time we would hear rumors—just rumors, mind you—from refugees crossing our northern border. Tales about a mutant, a tyrant who'd set himself up like a pretty king somewhere in southwestern Oregon. We also heard reports that this mutant was in league with other mutants in the Outlands, and they were planning to establish a mutant alliance dedicated to eradicating or conquering all humans."

"Didn't you investigate these rumors?" Blade asked.

"No," Gallagher said.

"Why not?"

"Put yourself in our shoes," General Gallagher responded. "We hear all kinds of rumors concerning the Outlands. Everyone who comes from the Outlands seeking sanctuary in California has a tale to tell. There's the one about a mysterious group of renegades with a functional nuclear weapon somewhere in Nevada. And the one about the aliens from another planet."

Blade did a double take.

General Gallagher snickered. "The alien yarn is one of my favorites. There have been about ten people who claimed they were abducted by aliens in a flying disk, transported to a secret base on some mountain, and subjected to a physical examination. Later they were released unharmed."

"Someone has been pulling your leg," Blade said.

"That's what I thought at first," Gallagher concurred. "But then I noticed something strange."

"Which was?"

"None of the people making these ridiculous claims knew one another," Gallagher said, his brow creased. "And they all came from different areas in the Outlands."

"Did they say why these aliens were supposedly abducting them?" Blade inquired out of curiosity.

"Yep. And here it gets even weirder," Gallagher stated. "All of these kooks claimed the aliens were abducting humans to monitor us, to keep tabs on our biological development. The aliens were particularly interested in the long-term effects of radiation on our species."

"Very weird," Blade agreed.

"So you can see why we didn't believe the rumor about the
mutant in Oregon at first," General Gallagher said.

"Something changed your mind?" Blade questioned.

"Yes. About a month ago a man showed up at one of our
northern outposts. He was on his last legs, suffering from several
wounds and severe malnutrition. The lieutenant in charge of the
outpost took the man to Yreka," Gallagher detailed.

Blade knew about Yreka. It was a town of six thousand located
in north central California, approximately 20 miles from the
northern border.

"This man died," General Gallagher said, "but not before he
told us an incredible story. He claimed he'd been held captive by
the same mutant we'd heard about previously. He said he'd been
just one of thousands of enslaved humans. But he'd escaped and
managed to reach California." Gallagher paused. "And that
wasn't all he said. He also told us where we could find this
mutant."

"Where?" Blade queried.

General Gallagher reached into his briefcase and removed a
map. He extended his arm and handed it to the Warrior.

Blade noticed the map was folded into sections and the word
OREGON was printed on the cover.

"Open it," General Gallagher said. "Look in the lower left
corner."

Blade complied, discovering a circle had been drawn around one
of the cities in red ink. He read the name aloud. "Grants Pass."

"That's right," General Gallagher said. "Grants Pass. At last we
have a definite location."

"What did you do about it?" Blade asked.

"We decided to send in a reconnaissance chopper," General
Gallagher replied. "Grants Pass is about thirty miles from our
northern border as the crow flies. We figured it would be an easy
job. In and out." Gallagher frowned and stared at the floor.

"Something went wrong?" Blade deduced.

General Gallagher nodded. "We outfitted an old Stallion
helicopter with our most advanced photographic equipment. The
camera they used could pick up a fly on your nose from twenty
thousand feet. We used our facility in Yreka as the communi-
cations link."

"You were in touch with them the whole time?"

"No," Gallagher replied. "They were under orders to maintain radio silence unless an emergency arose." He paused. "An emergency arose. We believe they crashed in Grants Pass."

"What makes you say that?" Blade asked.

General Gallagher reached into the briefcase and withdrew a yellow sheet of paper. "Here. This is a transcript of the two transmissions the Stallion crew made before they went down. The messages are identical. I think Enright repeated his distress call to insure we received it."

"Enright?" Blade queried as he took the yellow sheet.

"Oh. Sorry. The Stallion carried a crew of two. We wanted the bird to be as light as possible. Major Enright was the pilot. An experienced chopper airman by the name of Hertzog was also on board," Gallagher said.

Blade was studying the yellow sheet. "None of this makes any sense. It's like a page out of a book of nursery rhymes. Little Red Riding Hood? Big Bad Wolf? Mother Hubbard's?"

"We arranged a code in case any transmission was intercepted," General Gallagher elucidated. "Little Red Riding Hood was the code name for Major Enright. Big Bad Wolf was mine."

"Does Condition Red stand for an emergency condition?" Blade questioned.

"Exactly. Do you see the part where Enright says the Goose is crippled?"

Blade nodded.

"The Goose was the code name for the Stallion," General Gallagher stated. "The next line is the critical one. Probable impact at Mother Hubbard's."

Insight dawned. Blade looked up. "Mother Hubbard's was your code name for Grants Pass?"

"That's right. So we know the chopper went down in Grants Pass," Gallagher said.

"What about the rest of this?" Blade inquired. "Goldilocks is in? The Pied Piper was correct?"

"Goldilocks was our code for mutant activity," Gallagher disclosed. "The Pied Piper was the name we gave the man who told us about Grants Pass."

"So Enright was confirming your informant's story," Blade noted.

"Yes," General Gallagher declared. "You see, there isn't just one mutant in Grants Pass. There may be hundreds. But one mutant is the brains behind the operation they have set up there."

Blade leaned back in his chair. "Why do you think the helicopter went down?"

"I wish I knew," Gallagher said. "The chopper could have been shot down. Or it could have malfunctioned. It was an old copter, but we checked and double-checked all the systems before we sent it up."

"Why did you use a helicopter?" Blade probed. "Why not use one of your planes or a jet?"

"Several reasons," General Gallagher said. "The jets move too damn fast to take high-resolution photographs while flying close to the ground. A jet at low altitude would have flown over Grants Pass in the blink of an eye. We could have used one to take a high-altitude run, but we wanted, if possible, visual confirmation by the crew. A plane would have been slower than a jet, but a plane can't hover for an extended period of surveillance."

"You could have used one of the Hurricanes," Blade mentioned, referring to the two exceptional aircraft the California military possessed. The Hurricanes were jets with vertical-takeoff-and-landing capability. The governor of California had graciously placed them at the disposal of the Force. When not required for a mission, the Hurricanes were utilized as a courier service between the Federation factions.

"We didn't want to disrupt their courier schedule," General Gallagher said. "Besides, a helicopter was ideal for our purpose. Because of California's size, being eight hundred miles from north to south and nearly four hundred from east to west, we've worked hard at keeping our planes, jets, and helicopters in serviceable condition. The Stallion we sent had been overhauled about three months ago."

"How long ago did it crash?" Blade queried.

"A week ago," Gallagher said. "We sent one of the Hurricanes to each of the Federation members with a report. The leaders have unanimously agreed on how they want to deal with this." He looked Blade in the eyes. "They want to send in the Force."

"How soon can we leave?"

CHAPTER THREE

The two Hurricanes were waiting on the pad.

Blade scrutinized the VTOLs for a moment, then glanced to his left at the hangar. He spotted General Gallagher and several other people near the hangar and angled toward them. As he strode across the northeast corner of the pad, he reflected on the expense the governor of California had invested in the construction of the Force headquarters.

Located northwest of Pyramid Lake, which was north of Los Angeles, the headquarters compound was surrounded by an electrified fence enclosing all 12 acres. The fence was patrolled by regular California Army troops and was crowned with barbed wire. Because the Hurricanes did not require a long runway, a concrete pad 50 yards square sufficed as their landing and takeoff space. The pad and the hangar were located in the southern section of the compound. In the central area were the three concrete bunkers: the supply bunker, the command post, and the barracks. To the north of the buildings the land was preserved in its natural state for training exercises. An asphalt road connected the headquarters facility to civilization, and entrance to the compound was afforded by a gate positioned in the center of the south fence.

Blade abruptly stopped.

A woman was with General Gallagher! A woman he recognized!

Damn!

Blade advanced slowly. He was dressed in his full battle gear: Around his waist were his prized Bowies; on his back was a backpack fashioned from a waterproof camouflage material, which contained his rations, an extra pair of fatigue pants, and a packet of plastic explosive, a timer, and a detonator; a canteen was affixed to his leather belt in the small of his back; and he sported a pair of Colt Stainless Steel Officers Model 45's in shoulder holsters, one under each arm. And instead of an M-16, he carried an M60E3 general-purpose machine gun in his left hand. Two ammo belts crisscrossed his chest.

General Gallagher gave a little wave of his right hand as the Warrior neared his group. "The Hurricanes are fueled and ready to go," he stated.

Blade halted four feet from the general. He glanced at the woman, who stood slightly to the general's left. "Why is she here?"

General Gallagher cleared his throat. "I need to talk to you about her. And these other two."

Blade stared at two men standing behind the general. They were both professional soldiers in camouflage fatigues and outfitted with their field gear. He gazed at the woman again. "We have nothing to discuss concerning her," he said crisply to Gallagher.

General Gallagher appeared to be uncomfortable over the awkward circumstances. "At least hear me out."

Blade's lips tightened. "We've already covered this. And you can forget it! Take her with you when you go."

The woman finally spoke up, anger in her voice. "I have a name, you know! Or have you forgotten it, Blade?"

Blade faced her. "I haven't forgotten, Athena."

Athena Morris had her hands on her hips, and her lovely features conveyed her extreme annoyance. She was athletic and slim, with fine brown hair down past her shoulders and brown eyes which projected an aura of inner confidence. Her high, prominent cheekbones and thin lips accented her inherent toughness. Like the two soldiers, she wore camouflage fatigues and had an M-16 slung over her left shoulder. "So you two have been talking about me behind my back?" she demanded.

"I've broached the subject a few times," General Gallagher admitted sheepishly.

"At least a dozen," Blade corrected the general. "And I've given him the same answer each time. No way!"

Athena studied the giant for a moment. "What do you have against the idea?"

"I don't have all day to list my reasons." Blade snapped.

General Gallagher looked at Athena Morris. "Give it up. We've lost. There's no way he will let you on the Force."

"You've got that right!" Blade confirmed.

"I think I have a right to know why," Athena stated.

Blade stared at her, his mind awash with vivid memories of their last association. Once, Athena Morris has been a journalist, a top reporter for the *Times*. Seven years before, she had taken a plane from LA heading for Yreka to cover a story on a destructive flood. The small plane had crashed, and Morris had found herself taken prisoner by a degenerate mutant known as the Spider. She'd later escaped, and volunteered to lead the Freedom Force to the Kingdom of the Spider hidden in the Marble Mountain Wilderness. After the mission had been completed, General Gallagher had proposed assigning her to the Force.

"We'll discuss this after I get back," Blade now told her. "The Force is about to leave on a mission."

"Why do you think I'm here?" Athena rejoined. "I'm going with you."

Blade glared at General Gallagher. "She's *what*?"

General Gallagher mustered a feeble grin. "I said it would be okay."

"You said?" Blade stepped up to the general. "*I'm* the head of the Force! I make all the decisions pertaining to missions and personnel. And I explicitly informed you three months ago that I do not want her on the Force!" He paused, shaking his head. "You really take the cake, you know that, General? You've tried every trick in the book to try and convince me to accept her. You claimed I would be doing Governor Melnick a favor, because Athena could write favorable press releases after each mission and bolster his image. You even conned me into letting her live in the barracks for a few weeks after we returned from the Spider assignment, claiming she needed to rest up from her harrowing ordeal. And now you bring her here just as we're about to take off on a dangerous mission, hoping I'll accept your crazy idea!"

General Gallagher shrugged. "I try my best."

"Forget it!" Blade barked.

"You still haven't told me why I can't go," Athena interjected. "Is it because you don't believe women can be competent fighters?"

"No," Blade said.

"I didn't think so," Athena stated. "General Gallagher has filled me in on the place you come from, the Home. Your people, the Family, select a number of skilled fighters to serve as defenders of the Home, as Warriors. Right?"

"That's right," Blade acknowledged sullenly.

"And some of these Warriors are women, right?" Athena pressed him.

"Currently there are three female Warriors," Blade said.

"So why are you being so damn obstinate over my joining the Force?" Athena asked.

"The Force is supposed to be an elite team composed of a volunteer from each Federation faction," Blade elaborated. "Seven members and that's it. We don't have room for someone else."

"You're conveniently forgetting a little fact," Athena mentioned. "The Force has been undermanned for three months, ever since Spader was killed. And the Moles haven't sent someone to replace him. So you do have an opening, if only on a temporary basis."

Blade looked into her eyes. "We don't need you on this mission."

"I could be an asset," Athena declared. "You know I can shoot as well as most men, and I can live off the land without complaining."

Blade scrutinized her for several seconds. "Tell me something. Why all this fuss? Why do you want to join the Force so badly?"

"I'll be honest with you," Athena said. "Joining the Force would be a tremendous boost to my career. I'd get the scoop on all of your missions. I could report everything firsthand. The papers and the other media fatheads would be eating out of my hand. And my reports would be great PR for the Force and Governor Melnick. General Gallagher has told me how he feels about the Force, and I know there are some other people who feel the same way. My stories could be just the thing to convince them the Force is essential, that Governor Melnick is right about the idea."

"Your reports would bolster Melnick's political career," Blade remarked.

"What's wrong with that?" Athena rejoined. "Haven't you ever heard the phrase 'You scratch my back and I'll scratch yours'? What harm can it do to help Governor Melnick? The original idea for the Force was his, after all."

"I don't see what harm it can do," Blade admitted. "But you still can't come on this mission. It promises to be extremely dangerous. We will need all of our combat skills to stay alive. And while you might be a good shot and can live off the land, you're not a seasoned soldier. You don't have any military training."

Athena Morris smiled triumphantly. "That's where you're wrong."

"What?"

Athena glanced at the general. "Tell him."

"She has spent the past two months in intensive training with our Ranger Corps. They're the best we have, Blade. And they've put her through the wringer. She passed all of her courses, everything from Survival Techniques to Clandestine Termination," General Gallagher divulged. "She wouldn't be a burden from a military aspect."

Blade pursed his lips. "My compliments. You two seem to have covered all the bases."

"Thank you," Athena stated, grinning.

"But I only want seven permanent members in the Force," Blade said. "The Force is designed to strike swiftly, to go in, accomplish the objective, and get out as quickly as possible if need be. Additional members would only reduce our effectiveness. Any strike force functions best when it is just big enough to get the job done. The more members you have, the greater the odds of something going wrong, of someone making a mistake and endangering everyone else. Seven permanent members is all I want and need."

Athena saw her opening. "Seven permanent members, yes. But what about temporary members? What about temporary additions to the Force?"

"Temporary?" Blade repeated quizzically.

"Sure," Athena said. "Like now, for instance. You're one person short. You could use another pair of hands."

"We *are* one short—" Blade began.

"There! See! Why don't you take me on this mission as a substitute for the missing Mole?" Athena urged.

"Athena has touched on an issue I wanted to bring up," General Gallagher commented. "You've trained your men well, and each of them has certain areas in which they excel. But it wouldn't hurt, I think, to take along a specialist from time to time. Let's face it. Some of your missions might require the talents of someone with an expertise your men don't have. Like this one to Grants Pass."

"This one?" Blade repeated doubtfully.

"There could be hundreds of mutants in Grants Pass," General Gallagher said."You need some added insurance." He turned and indicated the two soldiers behind him. "These men are your insurance. They're both Rangers and they are experts at guerrilla tactics. I strongly suggest you take them with you."

"Why don't we just take the entire Army?" Blade muttered. He gazed at the Hurricanes. Each aircraft could transport five passengers. If he took the Rangers and Athena, counting himself there would be nine.

"The Hurricanes can carry all of you," General Gallagher said, as if he guessed the Warrior's train of thought.

"Come on! Say yes!" Athena prompted. "We can be useful. We won't get in your road."

Blade hesitated. General Gallagher and Athena had presented logical reasons for taking the Rangers and her. But he balked at having to be responsible for the lives of three more persons. He was the head of the Force; their lives, in the final analysis, were in his hands. He'd already lost one man on a mission, and he didn't want to lose anyone else. Every time he lost someone, even if they died because of a boneheaded blunder on their part, he felt a certain degree of guilt.

One of the Rangers, a tall, lean man with a square chin and a set of bushy brows, stepped forward and saluted Blade. "Sir! We would be honored if you would agree to take us with you. We have heard a lot about the Force." He grinned. "Some say you're almost as good as the Rangers."

Blade couldn't help but smile. "What's your name, trooper?"

"Lieutenant Clayboss, sir," the Ranger responded.

"And you?" Blade asked, swiveling his attention to the second soldier.

The other Ranger snapped a salute. "Sir! Sergeant Rivera."

"And you two have experience in guerrilla tactics?" Blade inquired.

"Yes, sir," Lieutenant Clayboss replied. "We put in five years along the southern border."

"The southern border?" Blade said.

"Sí," Sergeant Rivera answered. "There are many bandidos along the border between California and Mexico. Bands of them like to cross the border and prey on the Yanquis."

"Do you speak Spanish?" General Gallagher interjected, speaking to Blade.

"No," Blade said. "Some of the Family members do. I've wanted to learn a second language, but I can never seem to find the time to learn."

"Sergeant Rivera is bilingual," General Gallagher stated. "He could come in handy on this mission."

Blade stared from face to face, noting the eager expectancy on each one. He sighed, knowing he couldn't rightfully refuse them. "Okay," he said. "The three of you can come."

"Out of sight!" Athena Morris squealed in delight.

"But," Blade declared forcefully, "I want certain things understood right here and now. I am in command. When I give an order, it is to be obeyed instantly. I don't want anyone grandstanding behind my back."

"Sir," Lieutenant Clayboss said. "Rivera and I are Rangers. Any orders you give will be carried out or we'll die trying."

Sergeant Rivera nodded.

"Good," Blade said.

"And you know I would never dream of giving you a hard time," Athena mentioned, smirking.

"See that you don't," Blade advised.

"Here come your men," General Gallagher remarked.

Blade glanced over his right shoulder. Boone, Grizzly, Sergeant Havoc, Thunder, and Kraft were approaching across the northeast corner of the concrete pad.

Athena Morris beamed and ran toward them with her arms outstretched. "Grizzly!"

Grizzly came forward to meet her, grinning, a backpack on his back, an M-16 over his left shoulder. He reached out as they met, gripped her under the arms, and lifted her into the air, spinning in a circle. "Athena! What a surprise! Don't tell me you're coming on the mission, gorgeous?"

Athena nodded as he set her on her feet. "Yep. The Big Guy just gave the okay."

Blade gazed at the unlikely pair of friends. Grizzly had become attached to Athena during the Spider assignment. The mutant had saved her life, and she had become quite close to him after the Force had returned.

Sergeant Havoc was walking toward the Rangers with a big

smile on his face. "Clayboss! Rivera! Don't tell me I'll have to
baby-sit you two yo-yos this time around!"

The two Rangers shook hands with Havoc warmly.

"You three know each other?" Blade queried.

"Yes, sir," Havoc answered. "We go back a long ways. We
were in the same squad when I was in the Rangers years ago."

"You were a Ranger? I didn't know that?" Blade commented.
"I was under the impression you were Regular Army."

"Sergeant Havoc has a broad military background," General
Gallagher chimed in. "He started his career as Regular Army,
then he transferred to the Rangers for four years. After that, he
was assigned to Special Forces. And now he's in the Force."

"Special Forces? The Rangers? What's the difference?" Blade
asked.

"They're both elite units," General Gallagher replied. "The
Rangers specialize in guerrilla warfare and engage in more
generalized military activities. The Special Forces are employed
on special missions, like their name implies."

Blade surveyed the men, woman, and mutant. "All right. Let's
get this show on the road. Boone, I want you, Thunder, and Kraft
in Hurricane number one with me. Sergeant Havoc, take the
Rangers, Athena, and Grizzly in the second Hurricane. I want us
out of here in five minutes." He stalked toward the VTOLs.

Sergeant Havoc, Lieutenant Clayboss, and Sergeant Rivera
headed for the second Hurricane.

"So tell me," Lieutenant Clayboss said. "Is this Blade as good as
they say?"

Sergeant Havoc nodded. "Better. I've never met anyone like
him."

"That says a lot, amigo, coming from you," Sergeant Rivera
mentioned.

"What's the scoop on the others?" Lieutenant Clayboss
inquired. "We've met Athena before. We even supervised part of
her training. The lady has guts."

"That she does," Sergeant Havoc agreed. "As for the rest,
they're a mixed bag. The Indian, Thunder, is a hell of a tracker.
Boone, the guy in the buckskins, is one of the fastest people I've
ever seen with a handgun."

"And the mutant?" Lieutenant Clayboss questioned.

"He's a moody cuss," Sergeant Havoc revealed. "Don't say

anything to rile him or you'll regret it. And watch those claws of his."

Sergeant Rivera peered at the mutant, at the mutant's hands. "Claws, amigo? All I see are fingers and nails, just like yours and mine, only covered with hair."

"Grizzly's claws are retractable," Sergeant Havoc detailed. "I don't understand everything about them, but I know he has a set of wicked claws on each hand. They're housed above his big knuckles, and there are tubes or sheaths of some kind just under the skin, extending from his knuckles to the inner edge of his fingernails. There's an opening covered by a small flap behind each nail. All Grizzly has to do is straighten his hand, make his fingers go rigid, and those claws pop out. He can make mincemeat out of anything with them."

"You've seen him in action?" Lieutenant Clayboss asked.

Sergeant Havoc nodded grimly. "He goes wild. I know I wouldn't like to take him on." He paused. "Blade did once, and he won."

"How's that, amigo?" Sergeant Riviera inquired.

"Blade took on all of us," Sergeant Havoc mentioned. "It was part of our training. He wanted to evaluate how good we were, so he took on each of us." He grinned at the memory. "And he whipped us."

"Blade beat you?" Lieutenant Clayboss asked in disbelief.

"He sure did," Havoc confirmed. "Like I said. I've never met anyone like him before. If all the Warriors where he comes from are like him, they must be the meanest bunch of sons of bitches on the planet."

Lieutenant Clayboss studied the giant's broad back. "This mission should be one I'll never forget."

"Just so we live through it, eh?" Sergeant Rivera said.

"With the three of us together, it's just like old times," Lieutenant Clayboss declared. "What can possibly go wrong?"

Although Havoc didn't respond, a silent answer arose unbidden in his mind, an answer based on the circumstances of the last assignment the Force had handled.

What could go wrong?

Everything.

CHAPTER FOUR

The two Hurricanes were twin streaks of gleaming light as they arced to the north, rending the California sky with their shattering roars.

Blade used the flight to think about his new post, his family, and his future.

At last the Force would see some action! He hoped the mission would work as an emotional catalyst for those under his command. The perils they faced might bring them closer together as a team. Confronting danger often had such an effect on people. In any event, this mission would be Kraft's last chance to redeem himself. Either the Clansman began owning up to his responsibilities, or Blade was going to boot him all the way back to Minnesota.

He thought of his family, of his wife and son. Jenny and Gabe were trying to adjust to the vast difference between life in LA and life at the Home. Living in Los Angeles was a nerve-racking experience for them. The pace of life was unbelievably hectic. Los Angeles had been spared from a nuclear hit during the war, and the life-style of its inhabitants had altered only slightly. Oh, there were far fewer luxuries, and even some of the necessities, like fuel, were rationed. But the citizens of LA all seemed to constantly be in such a great hurry. The metropolis bustled with activity 24 hours a day.

The residents of the Home, by contrast, led an almost idyllic existence. Less than 100 people lived in the 30-acre compound. Led by the Family's wiser Leader and guided by the prudent Elders, they continued to uphold the beliefs of Kurt Carpenter, the man they referred to as the Founder, and to realize his exalted ideals in their day-to-day life. The pace of life was as slow as the proverbial molasses.

Blade knew his beloved wife was not happy living in Los Angeles. She missed the simpler existence at the Home, and she was worried about the negative impact LA might have on young

Gabe. The children in the city were hardened at an early age. They were belligerent and inconsiderate, and they exhibited a startling disrespect for their seniors. Flaunting authority was a typical trait. None of these deplorable attributes had prevailed at the Home, and Blade could readily appreciate his wife's concerns.

A voice in his helmet intercom roused him from his thoughts. He was wearing an Air Force helmet similar to the pilot's.

"Are you awake back there, Blade?"

Blade grinned. The Hurricane was designed with the pilot seated at the forward end of the cockpit. Next came two seats for passengers, which Blade occupied on the right, Boone on the left. Behind them were two more seats, currently containing Thunder and Kraft. In the sole rear seat was their radio and their piled backpacks. "What's up, Laslo?"

Captain Peter Laslo was one of four pilots assigned to Hurricane duty. The quartet rotated their schedules to insure that at least two of them were always standing by to transport the Force on short notice. "I've been meaning to ask you," Laslo mentioned. "How is your wife taking to LA?"

What was he? A mind reader? Blade idly stared at the ground far below. "Jenny misses our Home. She may change her mind after we acquire some friends we can socialize with. And I haven't helped matters much because I haven't been spending much time with her and my son. I've been too busy training my unit."

"If you want my advice," Captain Laslo said, "you'd better get on the stick and make time to spend with her, or she might just decide to head back to the Home, with or without you."

"She wouldn't do that," Blade stated.

"You never know about women," Laslo offered. "I should know. I'm an expert. I've been married three times."

"Why so many?" Blade queried casually.

"The first two wanted a homebody," Laslo responded. "A military man makes a lousy homebody. Duty first, and all that."

Was that the real root of Jenny's unhappiness? Blade wondered. Was she upset mainly because of his prolonged absences?

"Say, Blade," Captain Laslo said. "General Gallagher gave us your destination, but he didn't tell us exactly where to drop you off. Do you want us to deposit you in Grants Pass or outside of the city?"

"Just a moment," Blade remarked. He reached into his right

front pocket and removed the map General Gallagher had provided. Where should the Force set down? Certainly not in the city. If Grants Pass was swarming with mutants, landing there would be suicide. He unfolded the map on his lap.

Nearly twenty thousand people had resided in Grants Pass prior to the war. Thousands more had lived in the town of Rogue River, five miles to the east. A number of major highways had passed through Grants Pass, including the primary north-south artery in western Oregon, Interstate Five. Would the highways still be in passable condition? He was doubtful. Vehicle traffic in the Outlands was practically nonexistent. Few automobiles or trucks were functional, and gas was a precious commodity.

What was this?

Blade leaned over the map, studying a section to the west of Grants Pass. "I think I've found it," he said.

"A place to drop you off?" Captain Laslo queried.

"Yes. According to this map, about eight miles west of the city is an area once known as the Siskiyou National Forest. No settlements or communities are listed. It's uninhabited wilderness. I think our best bet would be to find a clearing and land," Blade stated.

"How far into this Siskiyou National Forest do you want to go?" Laslo asked.

"The farther, the better," Blade replied. "We don't want anyone in Grants Pass to spot the Hurricanes. Why don't you swing to the northwest when we reach the Oregon border, then bank around and approach Grants Pass from the west. We should be able to avoid detection if we're dropped off about ten to twelve miles from the city."

"Ten to twelve miles it is then," Laslo stated. "After the drop, we'll fly to Yreka and wait to hear from you."

"Hopefully this mission won't take very long," Blade commented. "I'm looking forward to getting back to my wife and apologizing for being such a neglectful idiot."

"Don't sweat it," Captain Laslo advised. "This mission will be over before you know it," he asserted optimistically.

But, as subsequent events unfolded, he was proven wrong.

Very wrong.

They were seated in the pair of seats immediately to the rear of the pilot in the second Hurricane, conversing as they watched the clouds flash past.

"I don't know how much longer I can stick with it," he confided to her, the person he viewed as his one true friend.

"What's wrong?" Athena asked him. "You've never impressed me as the quitter type, Grizzly."

Grizzly lowered his voice so only she could hear. Neither of them wore helmets. "It's the same old story," he told her. "None of the others want me on the Force. Why should I stay where I'm not wanted?"

"I think you're exaggerating," Athena said.

"Am I?" Grizzly responded. "You haven't seen the look in Kraft's eyes when he stares at me. He hates me, Athena. I can feel his hatred in my bones. He's always pushing me, trying to cause trouble. Sooner or later he'll force me to gut him."

"I know Kraft doesn't like you," Athena acknowledged. "But he must have a reason."

"How much of a reason does a bigot need?" Grizzly retorted.

"If you don't mind my saying so," Athena observed, "you're a fine one to criticize Kraft. As I recall, you're on the bigoted side yourself. You don't think very highly of us humans." She paused. "I'm somewhat surprised we've become friends."

Grizzly's dark eyes studied her for a moment. "It's true I don't think much of humans. Look at what humans did to the planet! The chumps tried to destroy it, for crying out loud! They unleashed a nuclear Armageddon and came close to wiping themselves out. In the process, they've perverted nature by creating a horde of freaks like me. Most of the humans I've met are vain and arrogant."

"If you have such a low opinion of humans," Athena brought up, "how come you think so highly of me? Or are you just playing games with me? I thought we were friends."

Grizzly looked her in the eyes. "We are," he assured her in his low, raspy tone. "Never forget. I'm a half-breed. Part of me is animal and part is human. And the human part of me, I'll admit, craves companionship sometimes. I want to have friends, just like anybody else. You're my friend for two reasons. First, because of what happened in the Kingdom of the Spider. Second, because I can talk to you without sensing any fear or revulsion. You're the only human who relates to me as a person."

"Now I know you're exaggerating," Athena reiterated.

"Why do you say that?" Grizzly asked.

"Not all humans hate mutants simply because mutants are different," Athena noted. "Take Blade, for example. You might try opening up to him sometime. He doesn't hate you, and he sure as hell isn't scared of you. That man isn't scared of anything."

Grizzly stroked his chin thoughtfully. "I don't know what to make of Blade," he confessed. "He's the only human I know, other than you, who treats me like an equal. I don't understand what makes him tick. I know he's deeply religious, which confuses me even more. How can he be such a deadly sucker and still believe in God?" He shook his head. "I just don't get it."

"I asked him about that once," Athena divulged.

"What did he say?"

"Blade said the spiritual must protect themselves from the unspiritual, or something to that effect," Athena stated.

"I still don't get it," Grizzly said.

"What about the others?" Athena probed. "How are they treating you now? You've been working together for three months. Surely at least one of them could be considered a friend?"

"Nope," Grizzly responded. "Boone treats me decently, but I can't tell if it's all a front or if he's serious. Thunder is real reserved around me. I know he's on the superstitious side, and I suspect he sees me as some kind of bad omen. It's all a lot of Indian nonsense."

"What about Sergeant Havoc?" Athena inquired, lowering her voice to almost a whisper.

"Havoc keeps his feelings to himself," Grizzly answered. "I don't think he dislikes me, but I don't think he's crazy about having me on the Force either."

"Give them time," Athena suggested. "They'll come around."

"Who cares?" Grizzly rejoined. "I don't need them. I don't need anyone."

"Oh, really? I'll bear that in mind," Athena remarked.

Grizzly reached out and placed his right hand on her forearm. "I didn't mean that to come out the way it sounded."

Athena decided to change the subject. "General Gallagher briefed me on this mission. We could be biting off more than we can handle."

"Don't you worry," Grizzly said. "I'm not going to let

anything harm you."

"What if Gallagher is right? What if there are hundreds of mutants in Grants Pass?" Athena commented.

"I have nothing against mutants," Grizzly quipped.

Athena gazed at him for several seconds. "How do you feel about having to fight other mutants?"

"I learned a lesson during the Spider affair," Grizzly replied. "Some mutants can be as bad as humans. They're an insult to my species." He raised his right hand and wiggled his fingertips. "And I don't like being insulted."

"I've been meaning to ask you about those claws of yours," Athena mentioned.

"What about them?"

"When you lock your fingers, the claws pop out those holes behind your nails, right?"

"Yeah. So?" Grizzly responded.

"So do you have to keep your fingers straight when you're using your claws?" Athena inquired.

"Yep," Grizzly said. "If I relax my hand, the claws automatically retract. But when my fingers are rigid, they stay out. It's weird. I've never heard of anyone or anything with retractable claws just like mine."

"Neither have I," Athena declared.

"When we get to our destination," Grizzly advised, "stay close to me."

"I don't need a protector," Athena said. "I can take care of myself, thank you."

"I know that," Grizzly stated.

"Then why do you want me to stay close to you?" Athena wanted to know.

Grizzly grinned. "So you can keep an eye on me. You never know when I might need some protecting."

Athena laughed. "That'll be the day!"

The Hurricane began banking to the northwest.

PART TWO
OF MEN AND REPTILOIDS

CHAPTER FIVE

The Hurricanes rose vertically for several hundred feet, then hung motionless in the Hover Mode. Captain Laslo waved.

Blade returned the gesture.

With a rumble of their mighty engines, the Hurricanes shifted into horizontal flight and winged higher and higher, bearing to the south.

"We're on our own," Athena commented.

Blade turned. His team was waiting for their orders. They were strung out in a line in the middle of a huge field in the Siskiyou National Forest. By his estimation, they were 11 or 12 miles west of Grants Pass. Athena was first, then Grizzly, Boone, and Kraft. Thunder came after the Clansman, followed by Sergeant Havoc, Lieutenant Clayboss, and Sergeant Rivera. Kraft was carrying their radio.

"I'll take the point if you want," Boone offered.

"No," Boone said. "Grizzly, you take the point. Stay alert. Head due east, and try to stay within fifty yards of us."

Grizzly nodded and jogged to the east.

"The rest of you!" Blade declared. "Keep on your toes! We don't know what we'll find here. And Kraft, don't let anything happen to the radio."

The field radio was strapped to the Clansman's back alongside his backpack. Kraft, like the others, carried an M-16 and wore a pair of Colt automatics strapped around his waist. "Chill out, dude," he rejoined. "Nothing will happen to the squawk box."

"See that it doesn't," Blade cautioned. He glanced to the east. Grizzly was fast approaching the treeline. The mutant and Boone had both declined the use of a pair of Colts, Boone because he preferred his Hombre revolvers at close range, Grizzly because he relied upon his claws for the "personal touch," as he put it.

"Move out!" Blade directed, heading after Grizzly.

The Force members followed on the heels of their leader, with the Rangers bringing up the rear.

Athena scrutinized the Warrior's machine gun. "Say, Blade. What's with the change in firepower? Did you get tired of using an M-16?"

"No," Blade said. "We might need some extra punch on this trip, so I brought this along."

"What is it?"

"It's an M60E3," Blade disclosed. "General Gallagher provided it. This gun will put out ten rounds a second, and it allows me the option of mixing armor-piercing, ball, and tracer rounds in the belt. The stopping power and range are both greater than the M-16."

"I noticed that ammo belt you have in there is dangling down to your ankles," Athena commented. "I hope you don't trip over your own feet."

"I'll try not to," Blade said, grinning.

The Force quickly crossed the field and reached the trees.

Blade held up his right hand, then twisted to face them. "From here on out there will be no talking." He looked at Athena. "And I do mean no talking. Watch for my hand signals. Let's go!" He moved into the dense forest, hoping the system of hand signs he had developed would serve them in good stead. Far ahead he spied Grizzly, waiting for them to get within a range of 50 yards. After a few seconds the mutant melted into the wall of vegetation.

Blade led his team ever eastward, his senses primed, alert for an ambush. A prolific assortment of trees and shrubs furnished ample cover, screening the Force from observation. But the undergrowth could work against them as well by harboring an enemy force lying in wait. He wasn't about to take any chances.

Within a mile they came to a creek.

Grizzly was waiting on the bank, scanning the opposite side.

"Why did you stop?" Blade asked in a hushed tone as he neared the mutant. He held up his right fist, indicating the Force should halt.

Grizzly stared at the giant. "I wanted you to know."

"Know what?" Blade queried.

"I think we're being watched," Grizzly stated.

Blade surveyed the trees on the far bank. "I don't see anything."

"Neither do I," Grizzly affirmed.

"Then what makes you think we're being watched?" Blade questioned.

Grizzly frowned. "I'm not sure," he said uncertainly. "A feeling I have."

Blade was surprised by the mutant's vacillation. Grizzly's animal instincts were normally unerring, his eyesight and hearing were hyper-sharp, and his scenting ability was uncanny. "Have you seen any tracks?"

"Just wildlife," Grizzly replied.

"Have you heard anything out of the ordinary?" Blade inquired.

"Nothing," Grizzly responded. "I told you. I have a feeling."

"Well, we won't take your feeling lightly," Blade said. "Head out, but keep within ten yards. I don't want to lose eye contact."

Grizzly nodded, then promptly forded the creek.

Blade motioned for Athena to join him on the bank.

"What's up?" she asked, her M-16 cradled in her arms.

"You know some of the hand signals we use because you were with us on our last mission," Blade observed. "But I've developed a few more since then. I don't have the time to teach them all to you now, so when necessary I'll relay my instructions verbally." He paused. "We could have company. Pass it down the line. And whisper."

Athena nodded, then turned and walked to Boone.

Blade entered the creek, the water swirling up to his knees. He crossed quickly and posted himself on the bank to cover the others.

Athena waded into the water.

Blade felt a peculiar prickly sensation on the back of his neck and pivoted, examining the nearest vegetation.

Grizzly was right.

Someone . . . or something . . . was out there . . . somewhere.

Watching them.

Was it friend or foe?

Blade touched his finger to the trigger of the M60. What could possibly elude Grizzly's enhanced senses?

Athena reached the bank and stepped up to the Warrior's side.

Boone was starting into the creek.

Blade checked on Grizzly. The mutant was ten yards into the forest, watching them ford.

Boone crossed and Kraft gingerly stepped into the river.

A strange whistle sounded from the woods to the northeast.

And all hell broke loose.

Blade was turning in the direction of the whistle when Athena suddenly cried out.

"Kraft!" she yelled in alarm.

Blade spun.

Kraft was in midstream. He had dropped his M-16 and was clutching at a red object partially imbedded in his neck. His arms seemed sluggish and weak, and his eyelids quivered as he tottered to the right.

Thunder jumped into the creek, going to Kraft's aid.

Blade took a step into the water, planning to assist the Flathead.

The forest abruptly rocked to the blasting of automatic weapons as Sergeant Havoc, Lieutenant Clayboss, and Sergeant Rivera opened up from the west bank. They were standing near the creek, their M-16's trained on the vegetation on the east bank, firing into the trees.

Athena and Boone joined in.

Blade saw Thunder stiffen and twist. A bright red object had appeared on the Indian's left shoulder. He tried to grasp the thing, but his fingers went slack and he stumbled and almost fell.

Just then Kraft sprawled into the creek, on his back, his arms and legs spread-eagled, and began to drift downstream.

Something buzzed past Blade's right ear, and he automatically threw himself to the bank. He landed on his left side and rolled to a squatting posture, the stock of the M60 pressed against his stout thigh.

There was a hint of movement in a large tree 30 feet away.

Blade squeezed the trigger, the M60 thundering and bucking, the heavy slugs ripping into the foliage and sending leaves flying in all directions, the tracer rounds showing he was right on target.

A harsh shriek greeted the Warrior's volley, and an indistinct shape dropped from the tree into the undergrowth below.

Blade risked a hasty glance at the creek, and he was appalled to see Thunder and Kraft floating from view around a bend to the south. "Cover me!" he bellowed, and lunged to his feet.

The Force members continued to pour lead into the woods.

Blade raced along the bank after Kraft and Thunder. Kraft had been floating on his back, but Thunder had been face down, and

Blade was worried the Flathead would drown if he didn't reach
them in time. He crashed through a bush bordering the creek, his
legs pounding, and reached the bend within seconds.

And stopped cold, astonished.

Where were they?

Blade looked to the right and the left, perplexed. The creek ran
straight for several hundred yards. There was no sign of the
Flathead and the Clansman, but they couldn't possibly have
covered the distance to the next curve in the brief span it had
taken him to reach the bend.

Dear Spirit!

Where *were* they?

Blade advanced a few yards, scouring the terrain for some
indication of their whereabouts, baffled.

How could they just disappear?

The underbrush grew right up to the creek here and there, but
the vegetation was untrampled and still.

Damn!

Blade whirled and raced back to his companions.

Athena, Lieutenant Clayboss, and Sergeant Rivera were still
firing into the trees. Boone and Sergeant Havoc had ceased and
were scanning the vegetation. Grizzly wasn't in sight.

"Cease firing!" Blade ordered as he drew alongside Boone.
"Cease firing!"

The forest became abruptly, eerily silent.

"Where's Grizzly?" Blade demanded.

Athena looked around. "I don't know. I saw him just a minute
ago."

Blade motioned for Havoc and the Rangers to ford the creek.

"Where is Thunder?" Boone queried, surveying the water.
"And what happened to Kraft?"

"I wish I knew," Blade said. He waited for Havoc and the
Rangers to reach the east bank. "Okay, people. Listen up. We've
got to—"

"There's Grizzly!" Athena exclaimed, pointing.

Blade pivoted in the direction she was indicating.

The mutant was near the large tree 30 feet away. He extended
his right forefinger and jabbed it at the ground three times.

"He's found something," Boone remarked.

Blade moved toward Grizzly. "The rest of you stay here. And

stay alert!"

"You don't need to tell me twice," Athena quipped nervously.

Blade hastened over to the mutant. "What's up?"

"I saw you shoot into this tree," Grizzly said. "And I saw something fall. I came over to see if I could find a body."

"Did you?" Blade inquired hopefully.

"Nope," Grizzly replied. "But I did find something else. Something srange."

"Like what?"

"Come see for yourself," Grizzly stated, and moved to the base of the tree. He knelt down. "Take a look at this."

Blade crouched next to the mutant, his eyes narrowing as he beheld a small puddle of greenish fluid on the ground. "What's this?"

"I think it's blood," Grizzly said.

"Green blood?" Blade declared skeptically.

"What else could it be?" Grizzly rejoined. He pointed at another puddle to the north. "I think you hit whatever was in this tree."

"It looks that way," Blade conceded.

"Let me go after it," Grizzly urged.

"No," Blade said, rising.

"No?"

"Come with me," Blade directed. He led the mutant to the bank. "All right. Here's what we're going to do. Grizzly, I want you to find Kraft and Thunder. They fell into the water and were carried downstream around that bend. I couldn't find any sign, but you're a better tracker than I am. You can track by scent." He paused. "We'll follow the trail of blood. It should be easier."

"Grizzly shouldn't go alone," Athena stated. "He can't cover his back and watch the trail at the same time."

"Okay. You go with him," Blade instructed her. "Move it! We'll meet right here in three hours. Understood?"

"Understood," Athena confirmed.

Blade watched the pair jog to the bend and vanish around the curve in the creek. "Follow me," he directed, and returned to the large tree and the puddle of blood.

"That's blood?" Boone queried doubtfully when he saw the liquid.

"It could be," Blade said. "There's some more of it." He

OUTLANDS STRIKE

pointed at the second puddle. "I think I hit one of our attackers. We're going to follow this blood, or whatever it is. Boone, stay with me. Havoc and Clayboss to the right, Rivera to the left. Ten-yard spreads. Move!"

Sergeant Havoc and Lieutenant Clayboss headed to the right, Rivera to the left.

"Keep your eyes on them," Blade instructed the frontiersman. He knelt and tentatively placed the tip of his left forefinger in the fluid. The blood, if such it was, was exceptionally thick and sticky.

"What do you figure hit us?" Boone whispered.

"I don't know," Blade said. "But we're going to find out. Right now." He rose and hastened to the north, going from one greenish puddle to the next."

"Whatever the blazes it is," Boone commented, "it's sure losing a lot of blood."

Blade had to agree. He searched the ground for tracks, but the turf was densely packed and covered with grass and weeds. He found sections where the vegetation had been flattened by the passage of a heavy body, but no clear prints. His mind was racing. What in the world had hit them? What type of weapons had their assailants used? And what had happened to Thunder and Kraft? Were they alive . . . or dead? He wondered if he should have sent one of the Rangers with Grizzly and Athena, but it was too late to be second-guessing his own strategy.

The five men cautiously proceeded to the north, covering over half a mile. The thick vegetation hemmed them in, limiting their field of vision. They came to a boulder-strewn hill.

Blade halted, peering upward. The trail of green blood went straight up the middle of the hill, right between two huge boulders. The site reeked of an ambush.

"I don't like this," Boone mentioned.

Blade went to signal for the others to close ranks when he realized the Rangers did not know his new signal for the maneuver. Not unless Havoc had informed them on the flight from Los Angeles. He remembered the Rangers had stopped, along with the rest of the Force when he had given the fist-high sign earlier. So either Havoc had explained the hand signals, or like the professionals they were, the two Rangers had keyed their actions on his. In any event, he didn't have time to waste, so he simply waved the trio in.

They obeyed instantly.

"The blood leads up this hill," Blade whispered. "And it's an ideal spot for a trap. I want a volunteer to go ahead and check."

Sergeant Havoc went to open his mouth, but Lieutenant Clayboss was faster. "On my way," the officer said, and started up the slope.

"Take cover," Blade advised, positioning himself behind a tree, his gaze locked on Clayboss.

The others were secreting themselves behind boulders and trees.

Lieutenant Clayboss climbed slowly up the hill. He held his M-16 in front of him, at the ready. His head swiveled from side to side, and his whole body was tense.

Blade admired the Ranger's courage.

Clayboss reached a point 20 yards up the hill. He was almost to the two huge boulders. He glanced back once and grinned, then stepped higher, his body hunched over to minimize the target he made. He paused and inspected a fresh puddle of green blood, then stopped at the base of the boulders.

The space between the boulders was three feet wide and obscured by shadows.

Blade angled the M60 up the slope, searching for the first trace of trouble.

Lieutenant Clayboss edged into the space between the boulders and disappeared.

Blade waited expectantly.

Seconds elapsed.

The seconds became a minute.

Blade was growing impatient. If Clayboss had been jumped, the Ranger would have had time to get off at least one warning shot. But the hill was shrouded in a deathly quiet.

Another minute dragged by.

Blade was about to break cover and go after Clayboss when someone beat him to the punch.

Sergeant Rivera unexpectedly came around a tree and jogged up the hill toward the boulders.

Blade's lips compressed in annoyance. He knew Clayboss and Rivera were the best of buddies, but their friendship did not justify Rivera's breech of discipline. He went to call out, to call Rivera back, but changed his mind. The shout might alert their enemies.

For a moment it appeared that Rivera's indiscretion had not been a costly mistake.

But the moment passed.

Sergeant Rivera was ten yards up the slope when a streak of red, resembling a miniature arrow in flight, sped from the vicinity of the two huge boulders and lodged in the right side of his neck. Rivera jerked with the impact and dropped to his left knee. He managed to squeeze off a few rounds at the boulder, then toppled backwards, tumbling head over heels for three or four yards and becoming immobile.

Blade wanted to fire but couldn't find a quarry. He detected a blur of red out of the corner of his right eye, and one of the tiny shafts shot past his face. He swung to the right, but all he found were more trees.

This was no good!

There had to be more than one foe, and whoever, or whatever, they were, they evidently knew where the Force fighters were concealed.

"Fall back!" Blade barked, suiting his actions to his words. He sent a half-dozen rounds into the trees to discourage their mysterious adversaries, then retreated for over 40 yards. He finally halted and crouched in the shelter of an enormous log.

Boone and Sergeant Havoc did likewise.

"Why did we run, sir?" Havoc asked in disgust. "We shouldn't have deserted Clayboss and Rivera."

"We had no choice," Blade defended his tactic. "We would have suffered the same fate if we'd stayed there."

"What are they using on us?" Boone queried anxiously. "Guns? I haven't heard a single shot on their side."

"I don't know," Blade responded.

"Are we going back for Clayboss and Rivera?" Sergeant Havoc inquired.

"Yes," Blade assured the noncom. "We're going to circle around that hill and come at these things from the rear. It might give us the element of surprise."

"I don't reckon it will be necessary for us to go to them," Boone commented.

"Why's that?" Blade questioned.

Boone nodded his head to the north. "Because they're coming to us."

Blade glanced to the north.

A half-dozen shadowy figures were skulking toward them through the forest!

CHAPTER SIX

"Do you hear it?" Grizzly asked, his head cocked to one side.

"Hear what?" Athena replied, puzzled.

"The shooting," Grizzly told her. "From the north."

Athena listened, and to her ears wafted the metallic retorts of automatic gunfire. "Blade! It must be Blade!"

"Yep," Grizzly said, then continued to the east.

"Where are you going?" Athena demanded, hesitating for a moment before hurrying to catch up with the mutant.

"I'm following orders," Grizzly stated. "Blade said to find Thunder and Kraft, and that's exactly what I'm going to do."

"But Blade and the others could be in trouble!" Athena declared. "We should help them."

"No way," Grizzly rejoined. "Blade is a big boy. He doesn't need our help. And he's the one who's always drumming into us the importance of following orders. So we're going after Thunder and Kraft."

Athena's anxiety etched lines in her face. "I think we should go to Blade."

"You're here to cover my butt, not to think," Grizzly remarked bluntly, pulling ahead of her.

Athena wavered. The sound of the shooting had ceased, but she was filled with an intuitive feeling of dread for Blade and the rest. Grizzly did have a valid point, though. They were under orders, and Blade was a real stickler for having his orders obeyed. And the lives of Kraft and Thunder were equally as important as the Warrior's. But what if . . .

"Come on!" Grizzly hissed. "We don't have all day!"

Athena reluctantly increased her pace.

"I don't want to lose this trail," Grizzly muttered.

"What trail?" Athena asked. "I don't see anything."

Grizzly snickered. "No offense, but when it comes to tracking, most humans are worthless. They waltz around with their heads up their asses."

Athena smiled sweetly. "No offense, but go shove a grenade up yours."

Grizzly smirked, then knelt to examine a faint impression in the earth.

"What is it?" Athena whispered.

"They're still heading due east," Grizzly informed her. "Towards Grants Pass. There are three of them, moving fast. Two of them are carrying extra weight. Kraft and Thunder."

"How can you tell all of that?" Athena inquired in disbelief.

"Trust me," Grizzly said, standing and resuming their trek. He skirted a tall pine tree. "I found where these three fished the Indian and the shithead out of the water, and I haven't lost them yet." He paused. "And I'm not about to," he added meaningfully.

"You're taking this personally," Athena noted, surveying the landscape.

"Damn straight!" Grizzly snapped. "That ambush was my fault."

"You're nuts," Athena stated.

"I'm serious," Grizzly insisted. "If I'd been on the ball, we would never have been jumped by these turkeys. But I blew it, and Thunder and Kraft have paid the price."

"How did you blow it?"

"I should have picked up an unusual scent, seen a track, something," Grizzly said. "But I didn't."

"Have you picked up a scent yet?" Athena questioned.

"No," Grizzly replied. "But at least I found some tracks. Not complete prints, mind you, but partials. Whatever these things are, they're big, yet light on their feet. I have a feeling I wouldn't have found their trail if they weren't carrying the extra weight."

"What do you think we're up against?" Athena asked nervously.

"That should be obvious," Grizzly answered. "Mutants."

"I know," Athena said. "But what *kind* of mutants?"

"Who knows?" Grizzly rejoined. "The radiation and the chemicals and the wacko scientists made all sorts of freaks. Mutants come in all shapes and sizes. For all we know, we could be after giant ladybugs."

"You don't believe that for a minute," Athena remarked.

"No, I don't. I . . ." Grizzly stopped and held up his right hand. He suddenly crouched.

Athena followed his example, perplexed. She strained her eyes
and ears to the maximum, but all she saw was the encircling forest
and all she heard was a slight breeze stirring in the trees.

Grizzly raised his head and sniffed the air, then grinned. After a
minute he rose and motioned for her to do the same.

"What is it?" Athena asked, her voice barely audible.

"We're close," he told her. "Real close."

"Did you pick up a scent?"

Grizzly nodded. "The wind shifted for a second. I could smell
Thunder and Kraft. Kraft's scent came in clear and strong. He
always wears that cheap, pukey cologne he bought in LA."

Athena's forehead furrowed. "Kraft bought cologne? Where did
he get the money? Cologne is expensive."

"I overheard him bragging to Boone," Grizzly detailed. "Kraft
said he bought the cologne on the black market. It's supposed to
be a bottle left over from before the war. He claimed it was worth
ten times what he paid for it. I saw the bottle. Part of the label is
missing. It was called LY-something-or-other."

"Never heard of it," Athena mentioned.

"It reeks," Grizzly said. "But if Kraft wants to walk around
smelling like piss, that's his business."

They wound through the undergrowth in silence for over a
hundred yards. The trail went into a weed-choked gully.

"Hold up," Grizzly advised.

"What is it?" Athena queried.

"I don't like this. It could be a trap," Grizzly informed her.

"What do we do?"

Grizzly nodded to the left. "We'll work around the gully on
this side. If it is a trap, they'll be expecting us to go straight
through the middle. So we'll circle all the way around the gully
and surprise these bozos."

"Lead the way," Athena said. She diligently stuck with the
mutant as he bypassed the gully, and she did her best to make as
little noise as possible. Once she inadvertently stepped on a small
twig and it snapped.

Grizzly paused and glared at her.

Athena grinned feebly.

Grizzly rolled his eyes and continued.

Athena chided herself over her carelessness. She must do better
if she ever hoped to convince Blade to accept her as a member of

the Force! And more than anything else, she wanted to join the elite unit. Considering the state of the country, of the entire world, what with all the wild mutants, the mutates, and the evil genetically spawned creatures, not to mention all of the roving bands of plundering humans and other menaces, she knew the Force would see a lot of action. And the Force was her ticket to everything she'd ever wanted. Fame and fortune would be hers! Every story she wrote, every report she filed on their escapades, would constitute another rung on her personal ladder to success. The public would constantly be clamoring for more, and only she, from her insider position, would be able to provide genuine scoops. She would be able to name her own salary!

Grizzly ducked under a low-hanging limb.

As Athena followed suit, she gazed at the mutant's back, at his rippling muscles. Life was strange, sometimes, she philosophized. Who would have ever thought she would strike up a friendship with a mutant? Mutants had always given her the creeps. Initially, she hadn't even liked Grizzly. His arrogance and superior air had rubbed her the wrong way. Besides which, he was an atheist. Although she wasn't nearly as religious as Blade, she did have a generalized faith in a Supreme Spirit, and she had always labeled atheists as egotistical idiots. But here she was, friends with an atheistic mutant!

Grizzly had been right earlier. Their experience in the Kingdom of the Spider had drawn them together. He had saved her life, had charged to her rescue with his claws flashing, and perhaps her overwhelming sensation of gratitude had enabled her to drop her prejudices long enough to see Grizzly for what he really was: a man who happened to be covered with fur and who could revert to a bestial savage at the slightest provocation. But underneath his gruff exterior was a person, someone who wanted companionship yet refused to acknowledge his own need. Grizzly was a hardhead. She would never tell him the truth to his face, but the mutant was exactly like the humans he so despised.

On second thought, maybe that was *why* he despised them.

Athena shook her head to dispel her reverie. Now was hardly the time or place to indulge in idle speculation. Not when there were . . . things . . . lurking in the forest.

Grizzly came to a jumble of fallen trees and effortlessly leaped to the top of one. He turned and offered his left hand to her.

"Take hold," he directed.

Athena reached her right hand up and felt his hairy fingers close on her palm. With startling ease she was hoisted onto the log. Before she quite knew what was happening, Grizzly scooped her into his steely arms and took off across the tumbled trees, vaulting from log to log. The trees had fallen years ago, perhaps downed during a violent storm, and many had lost their limbs. Grizzly's calloused footpads readily secured a purchase on their rough bark. Her breath caught in her throat as he executed a daring 12-foot leap and alighted with a feline grace on the ground.

"There you go," he said, depositing her upon the turf. He noted her expression and chuckled. "What are you trying to do? Use your mouth for a butterfly net?"

Embarrassed, Athena closed her mouth. "Don't ever do that again!" she blurted.

"Why?" Grizzly responded. "I didn't think you got nosebleeds at high altitudes."

"I'm perfectly able to take care of myself," Athena stated. "I didn't need your help."

"I know that," Grizzly said, starting to turn to the east.

"Then why did you carry me over those logs?" Athena demanded.

"Blade gave us three hours to rendezvous with him," Grizzly commented dryly. "Not three years."

"You're a real smartass, you know that?" Athena remarked with a grin.

"I was wondering where my brains were located," Grizzly said.

"It's nice to see you've regained your sense of humor," Athena whispered.

"Wasn't aware I'd lost it," Grizzly quipped.

They were skirting the northern portion of the gully, the verdant incline rearing above them to their right.

Athena raised her left foot to stride over a rock in her path.

Grizzly unexpectedly whirled and sprang, wrapping his right arm around her waist and bearing her to the grass.

"What the . . .!" Athena exclaimed, shocked. Something red streaked past her eyes as she fell.

"Move!" Grizzly growled, hauling her erect. "That way!" he snapped, shoving her in the direction of a stand of trees.

Athena promptly complied, racing for the trees, running a

zigzag pattern.

"Faster, slowpoke!" Grizzly goaded her from behind.

Athena grit her teeth and sprinted as swiftly as her legs would move. She reached the first tree and ducked to the rear as a small crimson shaft struck the trunk with a thump.

Grizzly rounded a tree to her left and pressed his body against the bark.

Athena could feel her legs trembling. She struggled to compose herself, realizing they had walked into another ambush.

"Damn it! They did it to me again!" Grizzly fumed.

"What were they shooting?" Athena queried apprehensively.

Grizzly craned his neck for a quick look-see, then darted from his tree to hers, made a swiping motion with his left arm, and jumped behind the tree again.

"What . . . ?" Athena began.

Grizzly smiled and held his left hand at waist height, palm up. A tiny red arrow rested in his hand.

"What's that?" Athena asked.

Grizzly carefully lifted the shaft higher, inspecting the metal tip and the feathers. "It's a damn dart! The sons of bitches have been using darts on us!"

"Can darts kill?" Athena questioned.

"They can if they're tipped with poison," Grizzly said. "But I don't think these are."

"Why not?"

"Why would these clowns go to so much trouble to lug Kraft and Thunder all over the countryside if they're dead?" Grizzly responded. "Nope. I suspect the bastards are using tranquilizer darts, just like the kind your species uses on animals."

Athena let the dig pass. "But why? Why don't they simply kill us?"

"They must want us alive," Grizzly speculated. "Makes you wonder about the fate they have in store for whoever they capture."

Athena involuntarily shuddered. "I don't want them to capture me!"

"I won't let them," Grizzly promised. He glanced around the tree for a second. "I don't see anything, but I know they're out there."

"I say we get the hell out of here," Athena declared.

"Blade gave us a job to do, remember?"

"We can return and report what we've found out," Athena said. "Then the whole Force can come back and blow these things away."

"We're not returning without Thunder and Kraft," Grizzly vowed.

"How do you propose we save them?" Athena asked. "We can't even get close to these things."

"With you along I can't," Grizzly stated. "I want you to stay put."

"Where are you going?"

"Guess," Grizzly replied, and instantly cut to the right, weaving and dodging, until he was enveloped in the forest.

Silence descended.

Athena gripped her M-16 and gulped. She didn't like this one bit! All the ambition and all the training in the world didn't matter at a time like this! Her life was on the line, and she had to face the simple truth of the matter: She didn't want to die.

Where the hell was that grumpy mutant?

Athena risked poking her head out to scan the gully. Nothing moved. Which didn't mean a thing. She jerked her head back.

Time elapsed.

Five minutes.

Ten.

Athena consulted her watched at 60-second intervals, chafing at the wait.

Come on, Grizzly!

Ten additional minutes went by.

Athena gnawed on her lower lip in frustration. Something was wrong. Terribly, terribly wrong. Grizzly would never leave her alone for so long.

Had the things taken him prisoner?

If they had, what should she do?

Athena pressed her forehead to the bark, suppressing an emotional upthrust of stark fear.

No!

No!

No!

She wasn't about to panic now! When she got down to the nitty-gritty, this was what being on the Force was all about. If she couldn't handle this situation, she might as well chuck her notion of being the ace reporter with the inside scoops on everything the Force did.

So think!

Athena cocked her head, listening, but the forest was quiet. Too quiet. Not even a bird was chirping. She recalled the words of her father, an avid outdoorsman, when he had taken her on her first fishing excursion at the age of ten. "You must always be on the lookout for mutants and worse. Learn to read the animal life. When you can see the small animals going about their business, and you can hear the birds singing, you know you're okay. But if you can't hear the birds, and if there's no sign of the normal wildlife, then watch out!"

Her dear dad had been so wise, so loving!

How she missed him!

There was a loud crack to her rear.

Athena instinctively ducked, the move saving her as another dart smacked into the tree where her head had been a fraction of a second before.

Not today, bozos!

She spun and squeezed the trigger, raking the foliage with a wild burst, chopping leaves from trees and shattering limbs. Without waiting to ascertain the results, she rose and ran in the same direction Grizzly had taken. She calmed her mind, forcing herself to evaluate the odds. There were three of those things out there, according to Grizzly. She knew one of them had circled around her and was now to her rear. The second one was probably on the rim of the gully. Which left one unaccounted for, and he . . . or it . . . was the greatest threat.

Don't blunder into him!

Athena abruptly stopped and crouched alongside a five-foot-tall boulder. Her palms felt sweaty on the M-16. She peered into the undergrowth ahead, hoping she could spot the thing before it spied her.

Show yourself, bastard!

She stiffened as a dark shadow flitted between two trees about 30 yards off. There it was! She waited to see if the thing would show itself, but nothing happened. The one to her rear might be after her, and she couldn't afford to stay in one place for long. She reasoned her best bet would be to keep moving. Her left knee twinged with mild discomfort as she straightened and bore to the left, putting more distance between the gully and herself. Once she escaped, she was going to hurry to the rendezvous point and get Blade and the others. Together they would show. . . .

What was that?

Athena froze at the sight of a furry figure 15 yards to her left, slumped across a low mound. The figure wasn't moving. With mounting trepidation she approached the form. The texture of the light brown fur was unmistakable. She reached the mound and groaned.

Grizzly was lying on his stomach on the mound, his arms draped below his head. Two red darts were imbedded at the nape of his squat neck. Whatever had shot him had probably done so from concealment and from the rear. But why did they use two darts instead of one? Was a stronger dose of their tranquilizer required to down a mutant with Grizzly's iron constitution?

Athena crouched and felt for a pulse on his right wrist.

Forgetting her own predicament.

There was an odd noise behind her, close at hand, resembling a hollow cough.

Athena felt a sharp jabbing sensation on her left shoulder, like being pricked with a pin only worse. She tried to turn, realizing she had foolishly let down her guard.

They'd shot her!

She knew one of the crimson darts was in her shoulder, and dread engulfed her, submerging her in an icy cocoon of fear. Her body abruptly became sluggish, her reflexes languid. The M-16 drooped in her hands, the weapon suddenly weighing a ton.

No!

It wasn't fair!

Athena dropped to her hands and knees, shaking her head to clear her numb mind. She was on the verge of being captured, and she was stunned by the horror of the unknown.

It just wasn't fair!

After spending seven years as a prisoner in the Kingdom of the Spider, to be captured again so soon after achieving her freedom was a travesty of . . . of . . .

CHAPTER SEVEN

Incensed by the ease with which his antagonists were downing his unit, exasperated by his failure to so much as clearly glimpse his foes for a second, and inflamed at being checked at every turn, Blade impulsively rose up from behind the log, leveled the M60, and commenced firing.

The six shadowy figures were over 30 yards away, their features obscured by the vegetation. All of them were toting guns, rifles of an indeterminate type. All of them dived for cover as the Warrior cut loose.

Only four made it.

Two of the creatures were struck by the powerful slugs, their bodies flung backwards. They crashed to the ground, one of them screeching and thrashing convulsively before expiring.

Boone and Sergeant Havoc added their weapons to Blade's, but their enemies were already in hiding.

"Down!" Blade barked, and dropped to his knees.

Boone and Havoc obeyed.

"We're too vulnerable here," Sergeant Havoc commented. "We need a defensible position."

"Or something similar," Blade said. He scurried to a nearby tree and stood, using the tree for cover. A hasty scan confirmed their attackers were nowhere in sight. He motioned for Boone and Havoc to join him.

They promptly complied.

"Stick with me," Blade directed, and ran to the south, retracing their route. He knew the things would be after them soon, maybe in two or three minutes at the most. He needed to find the spot he wanted by then if he was to entertain any hope of turning the tide.

Boone and Sergeant Havoc jogged on the Warrior's heels. They were hard pressed to keep pace with the giant's prodigious strides.

Blade's gray eyes probed the terrain for an ideal site, his mind reflecting on the mission. Pitiful was the only word to describe his performance. He'd led his team into an ambush, then lost two more in another trap. What manner of beings was the Force up against? he wondered. Undoubtedly the things were mutants. Nothing human could have decimated the Force with such uncanny skill. But whatever the things were, they could be killed. And if they could be killed, then the Force stood a chance of winning.

Not much of a chance.

But a chance.

Blade slowed and scrutinized the landscape directly ahead. A boulder approximately six feet in height was situated in a circular clearing ten feet in diameter. High weeds enclosed the clearing. To the right, ten yards from the boulder, was a tree. To the left, 15 yards distant, was another tree.

Perfect.

Blade halted and turned.

Boone and Havoc stopped.

"We're going to use a little reverse strategy," Blade told them. "We've been ambushed twice. Now we'll return the favor."

"What do you want us to do?" Boone inquired.

"I want you to climb that tree," Blade said, pointing at the one on the right. "Havoc, you take that tree on the left. When our ambushers show up, let them have it."

"And where will you be?" Boone asked.

Blade nodded toward the boulder in the clearing. "I'll be the bait to lure them in. If they concentrate on me, they might not notice the two of you in the trees. Wait until you have a clear shot."

"You're taking a big risk, sir," Sergeant Havoc commented.

"There's no other choice," Blade said grimly. "Either we get the upper hand or we're done for."

Sergeant Havoc headed for the tree on the left.

Boone hesitated. "Watch your back."

"I will," Blade promised. "Get going."

Boone dashed to the tree on the right, slung his M-16 over his right shoulder, and began climbing.

Blade hurried to the boulder and moved behind it. If his calculations were correct, there were four foes remaining. Numerically, at least, the odds were almost even. But the creatures evidently knew the country well, and their familiarity gave them a distinct advantage. He peered over the top of the boulder, studying the forest to the north.

The woods conveyed a deceptive impression of tranquility. No evidence of the enemy presented itself.

Blade became impatient for his adversaries to arrive. Over five minutes elapsed.

Four sparrows appeared to the north, flitting from tree to tree.

Five more minutes passed.

A Western Gray Squirrel traipsed along the limbs of a conifer to the northwest.

Blade allowed five additional minutes to elapse before stepping from cover, raising his right arm, and rotating his forefinger in a tight circle.

Boone and Sergeant Havoc descended their trees and hastened to the clearing.

"They should have been here by now, sir," Sergeant Havoc remarked.

"That's what worries me," Blade admitted. "It looks like they didn't come after us."

"Why not?" Boone questioned.

"Let's find out," Blade suggested. He trotted to the north again, feeling perplexed. Why hadn't the things shown up? Had killing two of them dissuaded the rest? He came to the site of the firefight and halted. "This is where I shot those two," he mentioned. "Find their bodies."

The trio searched the vegetation for several minutes.

"The bodies aren't here," Boone mentioned.

"They must have taken them, sir," Sergeant Havoc said.

"Where?" Blade scowled. "I don't like this. We've got to reach that hill as quickly as we can."

They jogged to the north.

"There's the hill," Boone noted as the slope came within view. "But I don't see Rivera."

Blade didn't stop until he was at the exact spot where Rivera had fallen. "They took him! Now they have four of us!"

"Maybe not," Boone said. "Maybe Grizzly and Athena are having better luck than we are. Maybe they found Kraft and Thunder."

"What do we do, sir?" Sergeant Havoc inquired. "Go after them?"

"We try to outguess them," Blade stated. "If I'm right, they're mutants. We know there are mutants in Grants Pass, so we can assume they will be heading there. If we go due east, we should strike their trail. I doubt they can move very fast while carrying the bodies of their dead, plus Rivera and Clayboss."

The three men jogged to the east, ever viligant for their phantom enemies. They covered over a mile, sweat caking their bodies. The temperature rose into the seventies. Without warning, they emerged from a stand of trees and found themselves at the top of a rise. Seventy yards below was a wide field, then more forest.

"Down!" Blade whispered, and flattened. He cautiously inched to the edge of the rise and peered downward.

Four dark green mutants were almost to the forest bordering the field, proceeding to the east. All four were burdened by extra weight; two were bearing a deceased comrade over a broad shoulder, while the other pair were lugging Lieutenant Clayboss and Sergeant Rivera.

"You were right!" Boone said from the Warrior's left.

"Do we take them, sir?" Sergeant Havoc inquired from the right.

"No," Blade said. "We'll follow them."

"If we let them reach Grants Pass, sir," Sergeant Havoc noted, "we might not be able to save Rivera and Clayboss."

"We're not going to let them reach Grants Pass," Blade said. He glanced at the noncom. "And will you stop calling me 'sir'? It's driving me nuts."

"Sorry, sir," Havoc responded.

"Call me Blade," the Warrior directed.

"Yes, sir, Blade. I will," Havoc stated.

Blade looked at the quartet of mutants, striving to distinguish features, but the distance was too great to differentiate precise details.

The four walked into the forest.

Blade checked his watch, calculating. There was still plenty of time before he had to rendezvous with Grizzly and Athena at the creek. Grants Pass was approximately ten miles away. All of which meant he could bide his time before jumping the mutants and rescuing the two Rangers. Consequently, he waited more than three minutes before crawling over the rim of the rise and descending to the field. He searched the woods for mutants before crossing.

The dash to the trees was uneventful.

Blade paused behind a large trunk and scanned the vegetation ahead.

Nothing.

Satisfied the mutants were still hiking eastward, Blade rounded the tree and resumed their pursuit. He toyed with the notion of working his way ahead of the mutants and jumping them when they least expected an attack. Surprise was his edge, and he intended to take full advantage of it.

A half mile went by.

Blade noticed a puddle of greenish fluid on the ground. Was one of the quartet injured, or was the blood from one of the dead mutants? He pressed on until he reached the base of a low hill.

There was no activity on the hill.

Blade walked up the gradual slope, speculating on whether he would find the quartet on the other side.

They were much closer.

Blade, Boone, and Sergeant Havoc were a third of the way up the hill when they heard a scratching noise to their left. As one, they turned.

A trio of green forms had popped up from concealment in a thick stretch of undergrowth, their rifles against their shoulders.

Blade saw a crimson dart flying toward him, and he threw himself to the right in an effort to evade the tiny shaft. He was unsuccessful. The dart caught him high on the left shoulder. He aimed the M60, and as he did so his limbs turned to mush. Whatever the mutants used was fast-acting.

Sergeant Havoc and Boone were down, Havoc to his knees, the frontiersman on his stomach.

Blade grimaced as he forced his right hand to obey his mental command. He squeezed the trigger and the M60 boomed.

One of the mutants was hurled from its feet by the burst.

Two additional darts pierced the giant's skin, one on the neck, the second on his right arm. Blade sagged, swaying from side to side. The M60 fell from his nerveless fingers.

Damn!

He'd blown it!

He'd met his match at last!

Would the mutants slay him while he was unconscious, or did they have a worse fate in store for the Force?

Blade pitched onto his face, engulfed by an equal mixture of guilt and lassitude.

Somewhere, something laughed.

PART THREE
OF REPTILOIDS
AND REPTILIAN

CHAPTER EIGHT

"Wake up, you rotten scum! Wake up!"

Blade became dimly conscious of a grating voice bellowing in his left ear. Slowly, so slowly, he regained awareness of his surroundings. He opened his eyes, finding himself on his right side, his wrists bound by heavy rope in front of him. His weapons and his packback were gone.

"So! You're awake at last!" the grating voice barked. "About time, asshole!"

Blade rolled onto his back.

A tall, heavyset man stood three feet away, his face rimmed by a stubbly beard. He sported a thin mustache. His eyes were dark, his cheeks sallow. He wore black pants, a black shirt, and a wide black leather belt. In his right hand was a wooden club two feet in length. "On your feet, bastard!"

Blade's gray eyes narrowed. "Where are my friends?"

The man in black scowled and lashed out with his left foot, his black boot connecting with the giant's ribs.

Blade bent sideways, contorted by the pain.

"I do the talking here!" the tall man declared. "Now on your feet, slime-bucket!"

Blade grit his teeth and straightened. He realized his legs were untied.

"On your feet!" the man shouted. "Or you'll be eating this cudgel!"

"Eat this!" Blade retorted, twisting his body and sweeping his legs up and around. He caught the man in black at the ankles and sent him sprawling onto his back. Blade surged to his knees and pounced.

The tall man was trying to rise when the Warrior slammed into his chest, knocking him to the concrete floor. He attempted to bring his cudgel into play.

Blade, his knees straddling his opponent's chest, blocked the swing of the cudgel with his left elbow. He clasped his hands together, forming a ponderous fist, and savagely smashed the man in black across the chin. Once, twice, three times in all, and the tall man, rocked by Blade's malletlike blows, went limp, his eyelids fluttering.

"Well done, human," someone said to the Warrior's rear.

Blade rose and spun. His eyes widened in amazement and his mouth inadvertently slackened.

"What's the matter, human?" queried the figure near the open wooden door. "Haven't you ever seen a mutant before?"

Blade had, but never one like the dark green figure with a silver pike in its right hand.

The mutant was over six feet in height and conveyed the impression of awesome strength. His skin was a dark green, leathery and muscular. Green pants of the same shade covered its legs. The face and head resembled a reptile's; the eyes were red and emotionless, the nose was elongated, the ears circular. When the creature spoke, pointed teeth were disclosed. Its head was totally hairless.

"What are you?" Blade asked. "Where am I?"

"How original," the mutant quipped.

Blade surveyed the room he was in, noting the four brick walls and the two barred windows. A cot was positioned along one of the walls. "Where am I?" he repeated.

"In the Province," the mutant answered.

"The Province?" Blade repeated, puzzled. "How close am I to Grants Pass?"

The mutant cocked its head and studied the giant for a moment. "You are in Grants Pass," it stated. There was a sibilant accent to its voice. "The Province was once known as Grants Pass. This was decades ago, before the Mutant Era began."

"Where are my friends?" Blade asked.

"They are being held elsewhere," the mutant said. "Reptilian wanted you separated from the rest."

"Who is this Reptilian? And why does he want me separated?"

The mutant grinned, the expression oddly sinister because of its tapered teeth. "All in good time. Reptilian will answer all of your questions during your audience."

"When will I have this audience?" Blade inquired.

"At Reptilian's discretion," the mutant replied. "Perhaps tonight. Perhaps in two days."

"How long was I unconscious?" Blade wanted to know.

"I don't know," the mutant said. "You were unconscious when you were brought to the Imperium."

"What's the Imperium?" Blade queried.

The mutant nodded at the prone man in black. "Revive Prine. He has been assigned as your Indoctrinator." So saying, the creature turned and exited the cell, closing the door behind him. There was a loud rasping noise as a bolt was secured on the outside.

Blade frowned, contemplating his dilemma. He needed answers, lots of answers, and there was only one way to obtain them. He leaned down and retrieved the cudgel from the floor, then shook the man in black.

The man moaned.

Blade shook him again. Harder.

Prine's eyes snapped open. He stared up at the giant, recognition dawning. "You!" he growled, starting to sit up. "I'm going to . . ."

Blade wagged the cudgel in Prine's face. "You're not going to do anything! Make one false move and I'll split your skull!"

Prine looked at the club, then into the giant's eyes. He observed the flinty anger in those gray eyes, and he noted the incredible muscles contouring the giant's shoulders and arms. Somehow, the giant had not seemed so huge while lying on the floor.

"What's it going to be?" Blade demanded. "Do you cooperate or do you die?"

"I don't want to die," Prine said.

"I was told your name is Prine," Blade mentioned.

Prine's forehead creased. "Who told you that?"

"A mutant was just here," Blade disclosed. "He looked like he was part lizard."

Prine blanched. "A mutant? Was it Reptilian?"

"I don't know Reptilian," Blade said.

"Did he see what happened to me?" Prine asked, glancing at the door.

Before Blade could respond, Prine jumped up and moved to the door. He tried to shove it open, to no avail.

"He locked me in here with you!" Prine declared, sounding shocked. "It must have been Reptilian! I'll be slated for premature consumption for sure!"

"Come over here," Blade directed.

Prine gazed at the giant. "Why should I?"

"Because I need you to untie the knots on this rope," Blade said. "I won't harm you."

Prine edged from the door. "What's your name?"

"Blade."

"Listen, Blade," Prine stated nervously. "About the way I treated you earlier . . .."

"What about it?" Blade asked.

"It was nothing personal," Prine said. "I'm expected to treat all new arrivals the same way. If I don't, the Reptiloids will schedule me for premature consumption."

"What is this premature consumption you keep talking about?" Blade inquired. He extended his arms, the cudgel clutched in his hands.

Prine walked over and inspected the rope. "Premature consumption means I'll be eaten ahead of schedule."

Blade did a double take. "Eaten?"

"Sure," Prine confirmed, applying himself to the knots. "The Reptiloids use humans as a food source."

Blade stared at the door. "That's why the mutants capture humans? To eat them?"

Prine nodded while working on the knots.

"I need to know everything there is to learn about this place," Blade stated.

"I'll tell you everything I know," Prine offered. "It's my job as an Indoctrinator to fill all newcomers in."

"That thing with the red eyes said Grants Pass is now called the Province," Blade began.

"Red eyes?" Prine repeated, grinning. "The mutant you saw had red eyes?"

"Yes," Blade verified. "Why? What difference does it make?"

Prine was visibly relieved. "It makes a world of difference. If the mutant you saw had red eyes, then it wasn't Reptilian. His eyes are blue."

"The Reptiloids don't all have the same color eyes?" Blade asked.

"Do humans all have the same color eyes?" Prine countered.

"Tell me about these Reptiloids," Blade said. "Where do they come from? How long have they been in control of Grants Pass?"

Prine tugged on one of the stubborn knots. "The Reptiloids have been here for decades. I don't know exactly how long. Reptilian is their leader. He's the one who renamed Grants Pass as the Province."

"Why the Province?"

Prine shrugged. "Beats me. You can ask him at your audience."

Blade pondered for several seconds. "How many humans are there in the Province?"

"About two thousand," Prine replied.

"And how many of these Reptiloids?"

"About twelve hundred, I think," Prine said.

"If the humans outnumber the Reptiloids, why don't they revolt?" Blade queried.

Prine looked up. "Are you serious? Two thousand unarmed humans wouldn't stand a prayer against the Reptiloids."

"The Reptiloids are well armed?" Blade questioned.

"They have an armory of confiscated weapons," Prine answered. "And some of the sentries carry machine guns. Most of the Reptiloids, though, carry pikes. Those pikes are all they need."

"I don't follow you," Blade confessed.

Prine stared at the giant. "How did you end up here?"

"My unit was captured," Blade disclosed. "We never even saw what hit us." He didn't bother to mention the fact that two of his team, Grizzly and Athena, were still free.

"So how can you wonder why the humans don't revolt?" Prine rejoined. "The Reptiloids don't need to carry guns. One of them is the equal of ten humans. They have super senses. They can hear and smell better than any human. They're twice as strong. And they have their heat-detecting ability."

"What's that?" Blade asked.

"I don't know all the details," Prine said. "But I know the Reptiloids can sense body heat from far off."

"Sense body heat? How?"

"I told you I don't know," Prine emphasized. "Ask Reptilian."

"Why haven't you ever asked Reptilian?" Blade queried.

"I've never had an audience with him," Prine said.

"Why am I the lucky one?" Blade questioned.

Prine paused in his effort to undo the knots. "You must be special."

"In what way?"

"Reptilian only sees the special humans," Prine stated. "The ones with the qualities he wants."

"What qualities?"

"Ask him," Prine said. He rose and nodded toward Blade's wrists. "There you go."

Blade glanced down to find the knots untied. He deftly swirled his arms and the rope fell to the floor.

"Now you owe me one," Prine declared.

"I'd say we're about even," Blade said, disagreeing.

"I have to rough the arrivals up," Prine asserted. "If I don't, I'm in deep shit."

"Are there other Indoctrinators?" Blade asked.

Prine nodded.

"For someone who's supposed to fill me in," Blade remarked, "you haven't told me a lot."

Prine shrugged. "I've done the best I could. The Reptiloids don't blab all their secrets to humans, you know."

"How long have you been here?" Blade inquired.

"About eleven years," Prine revealed.

"You've lasted that long without being eaten?" Blade commented.

"If you serve the Reptiloids without giving them any hassles," Prine stated, "you last longer. The average is about five years."

"So you're a good little slave," Blade said, his tone registering his disgust.

Prine was offended. "What do you expect me to do? Fight back? What chance would I have? I'd be eaten tomorrow. And I sure as hell wouldn't be stupid enough to try and escape. I wouldn't last two hours out there with a Hunter Squad on my trail."

"What's a Hunter's Squad?"

"That's probably what bagged you and your friends," Prine mentioned. "The Hunter Squads go out after humans. They use tranquilizer darts."

Blade nodded. "A Hunter Squad caught us, all right. But we got in a few licks of our own."

Prine placed his hands on his hips. "How do you mean?" he inquired idly.

"I killed two or three of them," Blade divulged.

Prine's mouth fell open. "You killed Reptiloids?"

"Yes," Blade said.

Prine shook his head. "I wouldn't want to be in your shoes."

"Why not?"

"Killing a Reptiloid is a cardinal offense," Prine stated. "It's certain death."

"Then I have nothing to lose," Blade commented. He walked over to the wooden door and examined the jamb.

"What are you talking about?"

"If killing a Reptiloid is certain death," Blade said, "then I'm as good as dead. Unless I escape."

Prine snickered. "No one has ever escaped from the Province!"

"One man has," Blade corrected him. "He escaped and reached California. That's why I'm here."

"California?" Prine said excitedly. "I was on my way to California from eastern Washington when the Reptiloids caught me."

"I was sent here to free the humans," Blade detailed. "And to terminate Reptilian."

"You're doing a great job so far," Prine cracked.

"I'm just getting started," Blade assured him. "I take it you know where I'm being held?"

"Sure," Prine responded. "You're on the top floor of the Imperium, at ground level."

Blade gazed at the barred window to his right. "How can the top floor be on ground level?"

"Because most of the Imperium is underground," Prine explained. "The Reptiloids prefer to live underground. They don't much like the bright sunlight. Oh, they'll send out Hunter Squads for a day or two at a time. And they guard us during the day when we're tilling the fields and working on their projects. But, generally speaking, they like underground better."

Blade looked at the floor. "So the Imperium is under our feet?"

"Yep," Prine confirmed. "It goes about ten stories underground. That's not counting the Arena."

"What's that?"

"Believe me," Prine said. "You don't want to know."

"Where are my friends being held?" Blade asked.

"Probably on this level," Prine replied. "This is where they hold all the new arrivals."

"Good!" Blade smiled. "Get set."

"Set for what?"

Blade stared at the door. A barred window, six inches square, was situated near the top. He peered out the window at a gloomy corridor, insuring none of the Reptiloids were in sight.

"Set for what?" Prine reiterated.

Blade turned and stepped to the far side of the cell. He faced the door and squared his shoulders.

"Set for what?" Prine demanded in annoyance.

Blade grinned. "For this." He charged toward the door at top speed, his left shoulder lowered to absorb the brunt of the collision. His huge body smashed into the center of the door with a tremendous crash, jarring the door to its frame. The door buckled outward and cracked down the middle but remained in place. His shoulder throbbing, Blade drew his right leg up and delivered a shattering kick.

The door splintered and toppled into the corridor.

Prine was gaping at the doorway. "How'd you do that?" he blurted in astonishment.

"Let's go!" Blade ordered.

"Go? Where?"

"You're going to find my friends," Blade directed. "Now!"

"The Reptiloids will kill me!" Prine protested.

Blade lowered his voice and hefted the cudgel. "And what do you think will happen to you if you don't?"

Prine balked, obviously terrified at the prospect of resisting the Reptiloids.

"Move it!" Blade snarled.

Frowning, reluctant to comply, Prine shuffled forward.

Blade grabbed the man in black by the left elbow and pushed him into the corridor. "Move it! Or else!"

Prine nervously glanced in both directions. "They must be in one of the larger holding cells." He took off to the right.

Blade stayed close to the Indoctrinator. He didn't trust the man for a second. Prine would turn him in or betray him at the first opportunity, and Blade wasn't about to give the man the chance.

The floor of the corridor was composed of brown tile and the walls were plaster. Illumination was supplied by regularly spaced lanterns affixed to metal holders on the walls. There were no windows, but other cell doors were spaced at 20-yard intervals.

"It shouldn't be far," Prine said.

Blade looked to the rear. He was surprised none of the mutants had shown up yet. Surely they would have heard the racket when he busted out of his cell? Why hadn't they sent someone to investigate?

"This way," Prine stated, taking a turn to the left.

Blade cautiously followed, alert for the first hint of treachery. He disliked relying on the Indoctrinator, but what choice did he have? Searching the entire floor by himself was out of the question. The mutants would find him before he was done.

"It should be two doors down," Prine commented.

Off in the distance was a loud shout.

Prine reached a closed door. "Here it is!" he declared, grabbing the doorknob and yanking the door open. "Your friends are in here!"

Eager to find his companions and concerned for their welfare, Blade hastened past Prine and entered the cell without bothering to verify the cell was occupied.

It wasn't.

Blade realized his mistake as he heard the door slam shut behind him. He spun and rammed his right shoulder against the inner wooden panel, but the door held.

Prine's triumphant face filled the small window in the door. "You should be saving your strength! You're going to need it when you see Reptilian."

Blade was about to try and break down the door when three Reptiloids materialized behind the man in black.

Prine threw back his head and laughed.

CHAPTER NINE

Why were his wrists hurting so much?

Sergeant Havoc opened his eyes, and for a moment he was under the impression he was dreaming. He was in a square cell, his wrists in shackles, chained to a brick wall with his boots dangling six inches above the floor. No wonder his wrists hurt!

"Welcome to the world of the living," commented someone to his left.

Sergant Havoc twisted his neck. At the sight of Boone, who was also shackled to the wall, his memories returned in a rush. He recalled the drop in the Siskiyou National Forest and the subsequent fight with the unseen assailants.

"How are you feeling?" the frontiersman asked.

"I feel okay," Havoc answered.

"I've been awake for a few minutes," Boone said. "Blade isn't here, but we do have company."

Sregeant Havoc gazed to the right.

Other Force members were likewise chained to the wall. Thunder was to the noncom's right, then Kraft, then Sergeant Rivera.

"Where are the others?" Havoc inquired.

"We don't know," Boone said.

"They could be dead," Kraft interjected.

"We must find them," Havoc stated.

"Yeah, sure! How are we supposed to do that, Joe Army?" Kraft snapped. "In case you hadn't noticed, dude, we're not going anywhere! All of our guns are gone and they took our backpacks! And how are we going to get out of these chains? Gnaw through them with our teeth?"

"Where there's a will, there's a way," Sergeant Havoc stated.

Kraft laughed. "What a crock!"

"Pay him no heed," Thunder said, addressing the noncom. "He speaks with the voice of youth and immaturity."

Kraft glared at the Flathead Indian. "Who the hell are you

calling immature, turkey?"

Thunder smirked. "If the moccasin fits . . ."

Sergeant Rivera finally entered the conversation. "Hey! Do you guys argue like this all the time?"

"Not all the time," Boone answered. "Just when we're awake."

Rivera glanced at Havoc. "I thought you were in an elite unit. If you ask me, the Force isn't worth spit."

Kraft bristled. "Yeah? Who asked you, greaser?"

Sergeant Rivera's face turned a faint shade of red. He glowered at the blond youth in the black leather attire. "Greaser? Nobody calls me that! You just made the biggest mistake of your life! When I get down from here, I'm going to stomp your sissy white ass."

"You and what army?" Kraft retorted.

A new voice intruded on their dispute, a low, sibilant, mocking voice. "Such togetherness! The human species is one big, happy family, isn't it?"

As one, their eyes focused on the opposite side of the large room. As one, they gaped at the creature framed in the doorway, at his dark green hide, his red eyes, and his grotesque lizardlike features.

The mutant motioned with the gleaming pike he held in his right fist. "Are we having fun?" he taunted them.

"Who are you?" Sergeant Havoc demanded. "Why are you holding us like this?"

"Please," the lizard-man said condescendingly. "Don't insult my intelligence. You know why we are holding you. Because you, and your associates, were engaged in a hostile act of aggression against the Province."

Havoc went to speak, but the mutant cut him off.

"Don't deny it!" the creature stated. "Why else would an armed group be heading toward our city? We were fortunate one of our Hunter Squads intercepted you."

"Who are you?" Sergeant Havoc asked.

"I am called Gat," the mutant replied. "I am the Prefect here, second in command to Reptilian and his principal adviser. I wanted to observe you for myself. This is a very exceptional case."

Havoc didn't understand half of what the mutant was saying, but he needed information and wanted the creature to keep talking. Tact and diplomacy were called for. "There were others with us. Do you happen to know what happened to them?"

"I saw one of your colleagues a while ago," Gat revealed. "The big one. Your leader, I believe."

"Blade?" Kraft interjected. "Where is he?"

"Elsewhere," Gat replied. He studied the five humans for a minute. "You would make interesting contestants. I will recommend such a disposition to Reptilian."

"Will you let us down from here?" Havoc queried.

"In due time," Gat answered. He turned to leave.

Two more mutants appeared in the hallway. They exchanged whispers with Gat, who then reentered the cell.

"We need a volunteer," Gat stated, grinning.

"For what?" Havoc inquired.

"It seems the first one we took was not sufficient for our needs," Gat declared. "Another one of you is required."

"You took one of us?" Havoc asked, perturbed.

"Yes," Gat said. He indicated an empty set of shackles to the right of Sergeant Rivera with a jab of his pike. "A soldier. He said his name was Clayboss."

Rivera was all attention. "Lieutenant Clayboss? You know where he is?"

"Indeed I do," Gat confirmed, absently rubbing his abdomen with his left hand.

"And you need a volunteer to join Clayboss?" Sergeant Rivera questioned hopefully.

"Yes," Gat said.

"I'll go," Rivera offered.

Gat smiled. "Are you certain you want to go?"

"Sí," Rivera assured the mutant. "Yes. I want to join Clayboss."

Gat smirked. "Just so you're certain." He nodded at the pair behind him and they walked toward the Ranger.

Havoc looked at his friend. "I don't think this is such a good idea."

"I must find Clayboss," Rivera said. "Us Rangers stick together. You know that."

Sergeant Havoc watched the two lizard-men release Rivera. One of the mutants retrieved a small stool from a corner of the cell. He used the stool to stand on while unlocking the Ranger's shackles.

Rivera dropped to his feet, wobbled for a moment, then straightened.

"You will follow me," Gat directed, exiting the room.

Rivera glanced up at Havoc as he walked across the cell. He grinned and winked confidently.

Sergeant Havoc felt his stomach muscles inadvertently constrict as the cell door banged shut.

"I wouldn't trust those things as far as I can throw a horse," Boone commented.

"What a dork!" Kraft stated sarcastically. "I would never have done that."

Sergeant Havoc's chains rattled as he faced the Clansman. "No, *you* wouldn't!" he said bitterly. "And do you know why? Because you don't know the meaning of the word friendship! You don't know what it means to commit yourself to others. The only duty you have is to yourself. It's you first, and everyone else second. You're selfish and you're stupid. You don't deserve to be on the Force."

"Do you think I want to be in this bullshit outfit?" Kraft countered. "I didn't come all the way to California from Minnesota to get snuffed by a bunch of lizards! I knew there'd be fighting, but I like to rumble. I didn't expect all this military garbage. I could be lying on a beach right now, a fox on each arm, instead of hanging here and waiting to get my balls racked."

"This constant bickering must stop," Thunder remarked, gazing from the noncom to the Clansman. "We are a team, remember? We must put our personal animosities aside." He locked eyes with Kraft. "None of us are happy about being here. All of us miss our homes. I know I miss the forests of western Montana. Life there is relatively peaceful. We have mutant problems, but who doesn't?" He paused, a faraway look to his dark eyes. "I miss the smell of the pine trees in the early morning and the cool breeze off of Flathead Lake. I miss hunting and trapping and the aroma of a blacktail buck roasting over an open fire. I miss my family, my father and mother, two sisters and three brothers, and the happy times we shared. I am not comfortable living in the white man's world." He sighed. "No, Kraft. You are not the only one who is unhappy here."

"I miss Dakota," Boone mentioned wistfully. "I miss the feeling you get when you're on your favorite mount, galloping over the plains with the wind in your hair. I miss sitting around a campfire at night, slinging the bull with my friends. I miss those wild Dakota women, who can teach a man things about himself he never suspected existed. I miss the freedom I had there. In California I feel so hemmed in all the time." He glanced at the noncom. "What about you?"

"I was born and raised in California," Sergeant Havoc said. "My grandfather and my father were both career military men. I simply followed in their footsteps. The service is my life. I don't care which branch or unit I'm in. Being assigned to the Force, though, has been a bit of a letdown."

"Why's that, dude?" Kraft queried scornfully. "Aren't we good enough for you?"

Sergeant Havoc stared at the Clansman. "One of you leaves a lot to be desired. Guess who?"

"Up yours!" Kraft snapped.

"Here we go again," Boone muttered.

"I tried," Thunder stated.

They lapsed into an uncomfortable silence, each of them immersed in his own troubled thoughts. Periodically they strained at their shackles, a futile gesture because the chains were clearly unbreakable. They lost all track of the passage of time.

"I'm hungry," Kraft announced, breaking the silence. "When are those freaks going to feed us?"

"Leave it to you to think of eating at a time like this," Sergeant Havoc remarked.

"Don't start!" Boone interrupted them. "We should be working on a way to break out of here instead of squabbling."

The cell door abruptly flew open and in walked the mutant named Gat. He was attended by the same pair of mutants as before, both of whom were carrying trays laden with food.

Gat gazed at the prisoners, grinning. "You must be famished. I have brought some nourishment."

"All right!" Kraft said, elated.

"I'm not hungry," Havoc informed the mutant.

"Neither am I," Thunder said.

"I'll pass," Boone added.

"What a pity," Gat said. "I've brought meals for all of you. You really should keep up your strength for the Arena." He slowly moved closer to the captives. "Won't you reconsider?"

Sergeant Havoc, Boone, and Thunder did not respond.

"I'll eat!" Kraft declared. "Bring on the food!"

Gat stared at the Clansman. "You might not like the meal we have prepared."

"I don't care what it is," Kraft said. "I'm starving!"

"Very well," Gat stated, smirking. "Let him down," he said to the other two mutants.

The pair of attendants moved to a cot positioned along the right-hand wall and deposited their trays. They used the stool to release the Clansman.

Kraft fell the six inches to the floor, his knees buckling under him. He steadied himself before he could fall and stood. "Damn! My shoulders hurt!" he complained.

Gat waved his pike toward the cot. "Some sustenance will help you forget your discomfort."

Kraft grinned as he advanced to the cot, alternately rubbing his sore wrists. "Far out! What a feed!"

"Help yourself," Gat said. "You will find a pitcher of water. There are also potatoes, bread, and a rare treat. I had a can of peaches opened especially for this occasion."

Kraft sat down on the cot. He licked his lips as he regarded the feast. "This is great! Where did you get all this stuff?"

"The humans in the Province grow most of their own food," Gat detailed. "We also have a store of canned goods left over from before the war. The canned goods are quite remarkable. We discovered they will keep for ages if you store them in a cool area. We store ours in a subterranean level of the Imperium."

Kraft picked up a small circular roll containing a patty of cooked ground meat. "This smells funny. What is it?"

Gat smiled. "That is one of our specialties. It's called a burger."

Kraft raised the roll to his nose and sniffed. "What kind of meat is this? It doesn't small like beef or venison."

"It is a mixture of meats," Gat said. "We eat them all the time. Try it. You'll like it."

Kraft shrugged and bit into the burger. He chewed tentatively for a minute, then smiled and swallowed. "This ain't half bad! I could grow to like this."

Gat nodded, his lips upcurled. "Eat hearty. We want you strong and fit for the Arena."

"What is this Arena?" Sergeant Havoc inquired.

"You will find out soon enough," Gat said.

"Don't answer me then," Sergeant Havoc stated. "But don't expect us to answer any of your questions."

Gat looked at the trooper. "You will not be questioned. We already have all the information we require."

"Sure you do," Sergeant Havoc said.

Kraft finished cramming the first burger into his mouth and selected a second.

"We know all we need to know," Gat maintained. "We know your unit is designated as the Force. We know you were sent to free the humans held in the Province and to assassinate Reptilian. You will fail on both counts."

Havoc, Boone, and Thunder exchanged puzzled glances.

"How do we know so much about you?" Gat interpreted their expressions. "Simple. Lieutenant Clayboss and Sergeant Rivera gladly supplied the information."

"I don't believe it," Sergeant Havoc said. "Clayboss and Rivera are Rangers. You could never make them talk."

Gat smiled maliciously. "There are ways, Sergeant Havoc."

"You know my name?" Havoc asked, consternation creasing his brow.

"I know all of your names," Gat declared. "The Indian is named Thunder, the other one Boone." He swiveled and faced the Clansman. "And this simpleton stuffing his face is called Kraft."

Kraft had finished polishing off the second burger. "Get bent, freak!" He reached for a third burger.

Sergeant Havoc glanced from Kraft to the mutant. Something was wrong here. Terribly wrong. He could feel it, but he couldn't put his finger on it. Gat was too smug, as if he was privy to a fact the rest of them didn't know. "Where are Clayboss and Rivera now?"

Gat looked at Havoc. "We finished our interrogation, so I brought them back to the cell."

"Did you leave them in the hallway?" Boone queried.

"No," Gat said, his eyes twinkling. "I brought them back to this cell."

"What kind of game are you playing?" Havoc demanded. "Clayboss and Rivera aren't here."

"Ahhh. But they are," Gat asserted. He took several strides toward the cot. "Are you eating your fill?"

Kraft had taken a few bites from the third burger. "Yeah. These burgers are great."

Gat grinned. So did the other two mutants.

"May the Great Spirit preserve us!" Thunder unexpectedly stated.

Sergeant Havoc looked at the Flathead. "What's wrong?"

Gat snickered. "Your astute Indian friend has perceived the truth. My compliments, Thunder."

Kraft was listening to their discussion in evident confusion. "The truth about what?" he asked, his mouth full of burger.

Gat stared at the Clansman. "It seems I have been slightly remiss. Since you like those burgers so much, perhaps you would appreciate learning the ingredients."

"Who cares?" Kraft rejoined. "Just so they taste good."

"You might care," Gat said. "I was not lying when I told you Lieutenant Clayboss and Sergeant Rivera were in this cell. You see, they're on those trays. At least, parts of them are."

Kraft was about to take another bite from the burger. He paused, the roll and the patty inches from his mouth. "What?"

"When I said the burgers are a mixture of meats, I was also telling the truth," Gat remarked with scarcely suppressed mirth. "The burgers are an equal mixture of Lieutenant Clayboss and Sergeant Rivera."

Kraft let go of the burger like it was a scorching hot coal.

"There wasn't much of Clayboss left after the jail guards had their meals," Gat said. "But there was enough to mix with Rivera's meat to make a batch of delicious burgers."

Kraft's eyes widened in rapidly dawning horror.

"Dear God!" Boone exclaimed in revulsion.

Kraft reached his right hand up and touched his lips. "You're putting me on!" he declared weakly.

"Would I lie to you?" Gat responded. "I wouldn't want to be accused of being an impolite host." He started laughing.

The pair of attendants joined in.

"No!" Kraft cried. "Oh, no!" He rose from the cot and backed away, gawking at the trays.

"Oh, yes," Gat said, beaming.

Kraft's features were transformed by his overwhelming

loathing. He paled, his stomach churning.

"I love it!" Gat stated, and cackled. "They always act the same way!"

Kraft suddenly sank to his knees and doubled over, gagging.

Gat turned toward the doorway. "This is the disgusting part. I can't stand the sight of human vomit."

The three mutants walked to the door. One of the attendants handed a key to Gat.

"Here is the key to your shackles," the Prefect said. He tossed the key onto the cell floor. "When Kraft is finished, he can release all of you. We want you limber for the Arena." He laughed as he exited.

The cell door closed with a bang.

"Dear God!" Boone declared again, his eyes on the Clansman.

Kraft was gasping, his hands pressed to his abdomen, spittle dribbling from his mouth. "No!" he wailed. "No!"

Sergeant Havoc closed his eyes and swallowed. Hard.

Thunder averted his gaze from the Clansman.

For the longest while the only sound in the cell was that of a man in torment, a man whose anguish was unbearable, a man who was puking his guts out.

For the longest while.

CHAPTER TEN

He came awake instantly, his senses fully alert, and automatically leaped to his feet prepared to do battle.

"Calm down, Grizzly. I'm the only one here."

Grizzly slowly relaxed as he surveyed the cell they were in; the cement floor, the brick walls, and the cot along the left-hand side. A solitary barred window was to his right.

Athena was seated on the cot. "You were out a lot longer than I was," she commented, rising.

"Are you all right?" Grizzly asked her.

"Fine," Athena said. "Just worried."

Grizzly moved to the door and peered through the small barred window at the corridor beyond. "I don't see anyone."

"No one has been here since I woke up," Athena mentioned.

"We've got to break out of here," Grizzly said.

"That door looks pretty sturdy," Athena commented.

"We'll see," Grizzly said. He tensed, his keen ears detecting the pad of feet in the corridor. "We've got company." He gazed through the window and spied three figures approaching.

"Who is it?" Athena queried anxiously.

Grizzly retreated from the door, giving himself room to maneuver. He stood in the center of the cell with Athena to his left.

The cell door slowly opened and a mutant entered. He smiled at them, his red eyes flicking from one to the other. "Greetings. I am Gat. I'm pleased to see both of you have recovered from the tranquilizer." Two similar mutants were visible over his shoulders.

Athena calmly scrutinized the lizard-men. "Are you the one who captured us, ugly?"

"No. A Hunter Squad brought you in," Gat said. "All of you."

"All of us?" Athena repeated quizzically.

"Yes. Everyone on the Force has been taken prisoner," Gat revealed. He rested the shaft of his pike on the floor.

Athena shook her head. "I don't believe you."

"How else would I know all about you?" Gat queried. He stared at Grizzly. "We were surprised to find a fellow mutant among our enemies. We accorded you the privilege of having your female in your cell."

"*His* female?" Athena snapped, about to berate the lizard-man. Grizzly held up his right hand, hushing her. "I am Grizzly."

"I know," Gat said. "I know all of your names."

"How do you know so much about us?" Grizzly inquired.

"We interrogated two of the human sent to assassinate our leader," Gat explained. "Humans, as you probably know, are pathetically weak. They spilled the beans, as their kind would say."

"Why are you treating me so courteously?" Grizzly questioned suspiciously. "I too was sent to assassinate your leader."

Gat studied Grizzly for a moment. "You are a mutant, like us. You are of the superior species. We prefer to extend to you the benefit of the doubt. Perhaps your stay among the humans has warped your thinking. Perhaps they have succeeded in turning you against your own kind. We shall see."

"Are the other Force members still alive?" Grizzly asked.

"Some of them," Gat answered.

"*Some* of them?" Athena interjected apprehensively. "Which ones?"

Gat ignored her question. "You really must teach your female her proper place," he said to Grizzly. "Her arrogance is annoying. In the New Order such behavior will not be tolerated."

"The New Order?" Grizzly repeated quizzically.

"Reptilian will explain everything to you," Gat said. "You will have the option of joining our great cause or not."

"Reptilian is your leader?" Grizzly asked.

Gat nodded. "You will be granted an audience in a day or so. Until then, we are compelled to keep you in this cell. I apologize, but you must understand our position. We must test your loyalty to the mutant cause before we can grant your freedom."

"I understand," Grizzly said.

"Excellent," Gat commented. He cast a disdainful glance at Athena, then turned to leave. "Oh. Before I forget." He looked at Grizzly. "I will be posting a guard outside your door. If you need anything, let him know. And I will have a tray of food sent up."

"Thanks," Grizzly said politely.

Gat departed with his escort.

Athena waited until the cell door was closed before she vented her annoyance. "What the hell was that all about?"

"I don't know what you're talking about," Grizzly replied innocently.

"Like hell you don't!" Athena said. "Why were you so nice to that bastard? And why did you let him think I'm your woman?"

Grizzly walked to the window and stared out at an expanse of green lawn. "I had my reasons."

"I'd like to hear them," Athena stated.

Grizzly faced her. "We are in serious trouble here. All of us have been captured and some of us have been killed. . . ."

"If lizard-lips was telling the truth," Athena interrupted.

"I believe he was," Grizzly said. "I also suspect he would kill you without hesitation if he knew you're not my woman."

"So that's why you went along with him?" Athena said.

"Partly," Grizzly verified. "I didn't want to do anything to anger him or arouse his suspicion. We have to find the others, and we may get the chance if Gat grants me the run of this place."

"We're taking a big risk," Athena remarked. "The others could all be dead by then."

"What else would you have me do?" Grizzly queried. "If I made my play now, we would probably be caught again. And then the others would be worse off than before. This way, if I suck up to these scumbags, if they allow us to go free, we can find the others and help them escape."

"I hope you're right," Athena said doubtfully.

"At least we have an ace in the hole," Grizzly stated.

"We do?"

Grizzly held up his hands and straightened his fingers. Instantly his retractable claws popped out and locked in place, extending five inches above the tips of his nails. "These are our ace in the hole," he said. "Gat and his pals don't know about my claws. When the time comes, I'll be sure they get acquainted." He grinned wickedly, relaxing his fingers, and the claws slid from view.

Athena stared at him with an odd expression on her face.

"What is it?" Grizzly inquired.

"I just had a thought," Athena mentioned. "I think you're lying to me."

"You're my friend," Grizzly declared. "I would never lie to you."

"But you might fib to spare my feelings," Athena said. "And you're fibbing now. The real reason you're sucking up to these cruds is because of me, isn't it?"

"I don't know what you're talking about," Grizzly remarked.

"Bet me!" Athena countered. "You could break out of here any time you wanted. These lizard-men wouldn't be able to stand up to your claws. The real reason you're staying is because of me. I would be a hindrance if you tried to escape with me in tow. So you're sticking it out until you can get both of us out of here. Am I right?"

"That's the trouble with writers," Grizzly quipped. "You all have an overactive imagination."

"Yes or no?" Athena persisted. "Are you holding back because of me?"

"No," Grizzly said.

"I don't believe you," Athena told him.

Grizzly sighed. "Not to change the subject, but now I know why I couldn't pick up their scent earlier."

"Why's that?"

"They don't have any scent," Grizzly said. "Their body odor is virtually nil. I've encountered the same thing in snakes and lizards. It makes me feel a little better about myself. For a while there, I thought I was losing my touch."

The cell door swung wide, admitting two lizard-men. One bore a tray of food, the other carried a pike. The mutant with the tray crossed to the cot and placed it down. "Here. With Gat's regards."

"Thank him for me," Grizzly said.

The pair left.

Athena walked to the cot and examined the tray. "This doesn't look half bad. We've got some veggies and hamburgers."

"Hamburgers?" Grizzly repeated, coming forward.

"Yeah. That's right. You're not from California. You've probably never enjoyed a hamburger before," Athena said. She grabbed one of the burgers and handed it to Grizzly. "Here. Chow down on this."

Grizzly took the burger and lifted the roll to his nose.

Athena took one of the burgers and licked her lips as she raised it to her waiting mouth. "I'm so hungry I could eat a horse." She opened her mouth to take a bite.

"No!" Grizzly cried, lashing out with his left arm and knocking the burger from her fingers.

Athena gaped at him in amazement. "What the hell did you do that for?"

Grizzly's eyes narrowed as he examined his burger. "I didn't think you're a cannibal."

"What?"

Grizzly wagged his burger. "The meat here is human."

Athena's mouth went slack. "Human? Are you sure?"

Grizzly tapped his nostrils. "The nose knows."

Athena looked down at the tray, her shock showing. "They fed us burgers of humans?" she said, aghast.

Grizzly deposited his burger on the tray. "Afraid so. Maybe it's Gat's idea of a little joke."

Athena blinked rapidly several times. "I can't believe it! why?"

"The answer should be obvious," Grizzly responded.

Athena gazed at him, her eyes wide. "They eat . . . human flesh."

"Looks that way," Grizzly stated. He was startled when she unexpectedly stepped up to him and threw her arms around his neck.

"Dear Lord!" Athena exclaimed. "I almost ate one."

Grizzly could feel her trembling as she hugged him. "But you didn't."

Athena abruptly released him and moved back. "What if . . . it's one of the Force?"

"We have no way of knowing that," Grizzly said, trying to ease her mental anguish.

"Can't you tell? Your nose, I mean," Athena mentioned.

"Nope," Grizzly replied. "Cooked meat doesn't have the same scent as before it's cooked."

Athena gazed at the window. "We've got to get out of here!"

"We will," he assured her.

"What if they do that to me?" Athena queried, pointing at the tray.

"I won't let them," Grizzly promised.

Athena shuddered. "God! I wish I'd never come along on this

mission."

"We'll get out of here," Grizzly reiterated. "I'll stake my life on it."

"You may have to," Athena said somberly. "We both may have to."

Grizzly shrugged. "What's life without a little challenge now and then?"

CHAPTER ELEVEN

Blade paced his cell like a caged cougar. The longer he paced, the madder he became. He was furious at himself for his failure, and he craved vengeance on the creatures responsible for capturing most of the Force. By his estimation, he'd spent over 24 hours in the cell. Twice the Reptiloids had offered him a tray of food; each time he had declined. Four mutant guards had been posted outside of his door. Their first act had been to take his cudgel. Prine had disappeared after tricking him into entering the cell.

Prine would get his! Blade pledged.

What was that?

There was the scratching of a bolt being thrown, and seconds later the door opened. In strolled the mutant Blade had seen once before, the Reptiloid with the red eyes, his pike in hand.

"Hello, Blade," the mutant greeted him.

"Did Prine tell you my name?" Blade demanded.

"No," the mutant replied. "Lieutenant Clayboss did. My name, by the way, is Gat."

"Where is Clayboss?" Blade asked. "And the rest of my unit?"

"They are nearby," Gat said. "And they have not been harmed. You will be able to see them, in time."

"How much time? When do I get to see Reptilian?" Blade queried angrily.

"Soon," Gat replied. "Very soon."

"How do I know my people are all right?" Blade inquired. "How do I know I can trust you?"

"You must simply take my word for it," Gat assured the giant.

Blade scowled.

"The guards tell me you have not eaten," Gat observed. "Why not?"

"I haven't been hungry," Blade said.

"You must be famished," Gat disagreed. "We have not poisoned your food, if that's what you're worried about. And starving yourself to death would be a terrible waste."

"I'll eat when I'm good and ready," Blade snapped.

Gat, strangely, smiled. "You have fire in your veins. Such a commendable quality!"

Blade gazed past Gat at the corridor. The four guards were lounging near the doorway, apparently bored with their task. None of them, evidently, entertained the idea he might attempt to escape. Perhaps escapes were rare; all four had propped their pikes against the hall wall.

Their mistake.

"Well, when you are hungry, let me know," Gat was saying. He started toward the door.

"Say, Gat," Blade said.

Gat stopped and partially turned, his eyes narrowing slightly. "Yes?"

"Maybe I could use some food," Blade told him.

Gat grinned. "Fine. I'll have some burgers sent up." He strolled to the door.

Blade tensed, girding his massive muscles. He waited until Gat was between the jambs, until the mutant was in midstride in the doorway, blocking the view of the guards in the corridor. With their field of vision obstructed, he would be on them before they knew it.

He charged.

Blade plowed into Gat, driving his right shoulder into the small of the mutant's back and sending Gat flying straight into the guards.

Two of the guards were knocked to the floor with Gat sprawled on top of them.

The other pair closed on the giant, neglecting to use their pikes.

Blade knew the lizard-men possessed immense strength, but so did he. And he enjoyed the distinct advantage of superior size; each of the lizard-men stood about six feet in height, while he was a giant among men at seven feet. In addition, his long arms gave him the greater reach. Now, as they came at him from both sides, he employed his advantages to the fullest.

One of the lizard-men hissed as it lunged, the one on the right.

Blade whipped his torso in a tight arc, ramming his right elbow into the face of the mutant on the right. There was an audible crunch and the Reptiloid was catapulted backwards to crash onto its back, green blood spewing from its crushed nose.

The second Reptiloid grabbed the Warrior's left wrist.

Blade brought his right fist around and buried the knuckles in the mutant's mouth. Teeth shattered and greenish fluid spurted everywhere. Blade delivered another devastating punch, and the Reptiloid collapsed on the floor.

Gat was on his hand and knees, shaking his head to clear his benumbed mind.

The other two guards were scrambling to their feet.

Blade snap kicked his right boot into the face of the mutant in front of him. The Reptiloid actually became airborne, sailing into the opposite wall and toppling onto its stomach.

The last guard was erect, a pike in its left hand. With an enraged snarl, the Reptiloid speared the point at the Warrior.

Blade wrenched his body backwards, the pike missing his chin by inches. His right hand flicked out and gripped the shaft of the pike just below the sharp head and above the Reptiloid's left hand. He held onto the shaft, jerking the mutant up short, and planted his left boot on the guard's right knee.

The kneecap shattered with a pronounced snap and the Reptiloid began to buckle, stunned by the excruciating agony.

Blade fiercely yanked the pike from the guard's hand, then brought the pike down on top of the mutant's cranium.

With a groan, the final guard slumped to the floor.

Gat was almost upright and starting to lift his pike.

Blade closed in, swinging his pike like a club and catching Gat on the side of the head.

Gat staggered, green blood flowing from his wound.

Blade buried his right boot in the Reptiloid's crotch, and he was supremely gratified when Gat grunted and doubled over. Blade let the mutant have another boot to the chin.

Gat went down for the count.

Now which way should he go?

Blade paused, surveying the corridor in both directions. The hallway was deserted, but another Reptiloid could appear at any second and sound the alarm.

Where would he find the others?

Blade turned to the left and jogged in search of his companions. He wasn't leaving without the captured Force members. He'd die first!

A door materialized at the end of the corridor, a wooden door lacking a barred window.

Blade reached the door and opened it an inch, delighted to discover a stairwell on the other side leading downward. He threw the door wide and stepped onto a landing.

The stairs were wooden with a green metal railing. They seemed to descend into the bowels of the earth.

Blade scanned the landing, disappointed at not finding a door or window he could use to reach the outside. Either he used the stairwell or he returned along the corridor and risked being recaptured.

The shouting of agitated voices to his rear decided the issue.

Blade took the stairs two at a time as he hastened below. He needed somewhere to hide until the heat was off. But where? He came to another landing and continued lower. How many floors had Prine said the Imperium contained? Ten? Plus the Arena, whatever that was. There should be plenty of hiding places in such a vast structure.

If only he wouldn't run into more Reptiloids!

He did.

Blade was three steps from the next landing when a pair of mutants unexpectedly appeared, coming up the stairwell, talking quietly.

The Warrior and the Reptiloids reached the landing simultaneously.

Blade never broke his stride. He attacked, striking right and left with the pike.

Initially startled by the sudden onslaught of the giant, the Reptiloids reacted adroitly, separating to catch him in a pincer movement. Both toted pikes, and one of them, it turned out, was an expert at wielding the weapon.

Blade dispatched the first mutant, the Reptiloid on his left, with a minimum of fuss. He missed his rushing swing, sidestepped a counterthrust, and speared his pike into the lizard-man's throat.

Gurgling and clutching at its ruptured neck, the Reptiloid staggered backwards and fell onto the landing.

Blade spun to confront the second Reptiloid.

This one was holding his pike at chest height and regarding the giant with a calculating eye. "You are the one I've heard about," he said calmly. "The big human who killed three of my kind."

Blade nodded.

The Reptiloid smiled. "I will teach you a lesson you will never forget, human swine!"

"This year or next?" Blade retorted.

The Reptiloid closed on the Warrior, deftly handling the pike with consummate skill.

Blade blocked the flurry of stabs and thrusts, realizing he was up against a master. Only his power and speed enabled him to ward off the mutant's early assault. He was forced to retreat over a yard, and once the Reptiloid's pike nicked his left cheek.

The mutant abruptly stepped back and appraised the Warrior. "I understand now. No other human has ever lasted even this long."

"Why?" Blade responded. "Do you only pick on children?"

"For that," the Reptiloid stated, hefting his pike, "you will die a slow death."

"Anything would be better than listening to you flap your gums," Blade said, scrunching up his nose. "And you really should do something about your breath!"

With a snarl, the mutant tried to impale the giant's groin.

Blade narrowly avoided the blow. As a lifelong admirer of edged weaponry, he had spent many an hour in the enormous Family library perusing every book he could find on the subject. Volumes on knives had fascinated him from an early age. Ancient warfare books were also a special interest. The Founder had stocked over a dozen books on Rome and Greece. One of them, in particular, was devoted to a scholarly discussion of the Roman military machinery. The Roman soldiers had utilized a variety of weapons, but chief among them was the pike. And the Roman pike, according to the material Blade had read, corresponded in every respect to the type used by the Reptiloids. Both versions were simply heavy, formidable javelins, effective when thrown at a distance and decidedly deadly at close range. All of these thoughts flitted through the Warrior's mind as he swiftly backpedaled to evade a second sweep of the mutant's pike. At a range of only three yards the Reptiloid would likely be expecting him to fight by applying the stab-and-thrust techniques normally employed at such a short distance. But what if he reversed the tactics? What if he *threw* his pike instead?

Hissing angrily, the Reptiloid lunged, his pike held straight out from his waist.

Blade artfully ducked to the right, his steely right arm bringing his pike up and around in the traditional overhand spear toss.

The Reptiloid attempted to dodge to the left, but at a span of three yards there wasn't enough time to react. The glittering tip of the Warrior's pike penetrated the mutant's chest, passing through the lizard-man's body and projecting out his back. The Reptiloid stumbled sideways and collided with the landing wall, its eyes blinking at a fast clip, its mouth wide. Gasping for air, the mutant gazed at the giant in astonishment, then died, sliding down the wall and pitching onto the floor.

Blade scooped up the pike of the first Reptiloid he'd slain. He hurried down the stairs, wondering how much time he had before the Reptiloids on the upper level deduced he was in the stairwell.

A commotion at the top of the stairs served as his answer.

He was out of time!

Blade came to the next landing and angled toward a door to his right. Every landing below the upper level had doors, undoubtedly affording access to the inner passages of the Imperium.

Where would this one lead?

He yanked the door open and walked into a plush corridor complete with red carpet, paneled walls, and lanterns attached to gold fixtures on those walls.

The Reptiloids would find the pair on the landing at any moment!

He had to discover a hiding place, and quick!

Blade jogged along the hall, seeking a door, another stairwell, anything. After traveling 25 yards, he saw a door to his right. Throwing caution to the wind, he twisted the knob and stepped boldly inside.

And immediately regretted his rashness.

The chamber in front of him was huge, its spaciousness enhanced by a vaulted crystal ceiling. In the center reared an imposing marble throne perched on a circular series of gold encrusted steps. Reptiloids were everywhere. Between the doorway and the throne stood four dozen lizard-men, two dozen on either side, forming a living aisle to the throne. They were standing at attention, their pikes at their sides. All eyes were on the Warrior.

Blade frowned, exasperated at his stupidity. His gaze alighted on the regal throne as a stately voice rang out.

"Come in, Blade! I've been expecting you! But kindly drop that pike you're holding, or my personal guard will be constrained to use you for a pincushion!"

Blade released the pike and it fell to the soft, red carpet.

A towering figure stirred on the throne.

"I believe you have been eager to meet me," the figure declared, rising. "I know I have been eager to meet you. I've heard a lot about you, Warrior. My name is Reptilian."

PART FOUR
OF REPTILIAN AND MEN

CHAPTER TWELVE

"One of us should talk to him."

"You talk to him, Boone," Sergeant Havoc snapped. "If it was up to me, I'd kill the son of a bitch with my bare hands."

"He didn't know," Boone said.

Sergeant Havoc glared to his right, his lips tightening at the sight of the Clansman huddled in the far corner of the room. "That's no excuse! I'll never forgive him for what he did! Those men were friends of mine!"

Thunder, his arms crossed over his chest, gazed at Kraft. "Put yourself in his shoes. Imagine how he must feel."

"He brought it on himself!" Sergeant Havoc stated. "He can suffer the consequences by himself!" He turned and tramped to the door, staring through the window at the six mutants in the corridor.

Boone looked at the noncom's back. "Nothing we can say will make Havoc change his mind." He sighed. "And I can't say as I blame him."

"Then one of us must talk to Kraft," Thunder said. "As much as we dislike him, we are all on the same team, all part of the same unit. How many times has Blade told us we must stick together at all costs?"

"Blade wasn't here to see what Kraft did," Boone noted.

"Will you go, or should I?" Thunder inquired bluntly.

Boone reflected for a bit. "I'll do it," he offered.

"Are you certain?" Thunder queried. "I don't mind being the one."

Boone glanced in the direction of the despondent Clansman. "No. I'll do it. I've always been a glutton for punishment." He stared at the cot, at the putrid pile next to the cot. "I wish they'd clean up that mess! It reeks!"

"These creatures have no compassion," Thunder commented. "They are a violation of the natural order. They are an abomination to the Spirit-In-All-Things."

"Not only that," Boone said. "They're just plain ugly." He walked toward Kraft, thoughtfully chewing on his lower lip. The Clansman had withdrawn into himself after the incident with the burgers. Kraft had not uttered a word since. He simply sat there, his knees tucked against his chest, his arms around his legs, with his chin on his knees and a blank expression on his face. The man was obviously in shock. What can I say, Boone asked himself, to snap Kraft out of it? How do you deal with abject depression?

Kraft never bothered to look up as the Cavalryman approached.

Boone halted a few feet away. "Kraft?"

Kraft didn't budge.

Boone moved closer and squatted alongside the man in leather. "Kraft? It's me. Boone."

There wasn't the faintest hint of a reaction.

"Talk to me, Kraft," Boone urged.

Kraft said nothing.

Boone pursed his lips, studying the Clansman. Now what should he do? Slap Kraft a couple of times? "Kraft. Talk to me. I want to help," Boone said, scarcely believing he was saying the words. The last person in the world he would ever want to help was Kraft. Of all the people Boone had ever known, and he had known some real bastards, Kraft was the most obnoxious. "Is there anything I can do for you?"

The Clansman might as well have been chiseled from stone.

Boone extended his right arm and placed his hand on Kraft's left shoulder. "Kraft?"

The Clansman's lips moved, feebly mouthing a word.

Boone leaned forward. "What was that? I didn't catch it?"

Kraft repeated the word, his voice barely above a whisper. "Don't," he said.

"Don't? Don't what?" Boone inquired.

"Don't touch me," Kraft stated bleakly.

Boone withdrew his right hand. "Whatever you want. Would you like to talk?"

"Leave me alone," Kraft mumbled.

"I need to talk to you," Boone insisted.

"No," Kraft said.

"Yep," Boone countered. "You've got to snap out of this."

"Go away," Kraft murmured.

"I can't," Boone said. "We need you on your feet when we

make our break. We're going to try and jump these things if they ever come in, and we're not leaving without you."

"Leave me," Kraft said. "Who cares what happens to me?"

"Don't you?" Boone queried.

"Nope," Kraft replied sincerely.

"Why?"

Kraft's eyes finally blinked, moistening as he inhaled deeply and looked at Boone. "Don't ask stupid questions."

"You can't let it get to you," Boone stated. "Not now."

"I . . . I . . ." Kraft began, but he was unable to complete his sentence.

"Let it out," Boone suggested. "Get it off your chest."

"Why should you care?" Kraft declared testily.

"We're all part of the Force," Boone said. "We must help each other."

Kraft's shoulders slumped and he closed his eyes. "I . . . I didn't mean to do it," he said weakly.

"I know," Boone said.

"I just wanted to feed my face."

"I know," Boone reiterated.

Kraft groaned. "You have no idea how I feel. It's like I'm dead inside. I did the worst thing you could ever possibly do." He paused. "I *ate* someone else!"

"You were tricked," Boone observed. "You didn't know what you were doing."

Kraft didn't respond.

Boone frowned. This was getting him nowhere. They would need all the help they could get when they jumped the mutants. Kraft had to come around.

But how to do it?

"Suit yourself," Boone said, shrugging. "If you want to sit here and mope, that's your business. I just thought you might want to get even with Gat and his buddies."

Kraft opened his eyes. "Get even?"

"Sure," Boone stated. "You don't think we're going to take all of this lying down, do you?"

"How can we get even?" Kraft inquired.

"By doing as much damage as we can," Boone said. "They must have our weapons and backpacks around here somewhere. If we can get our hands on them, we'll show these jackasses a thing or two."

Kraft's eyes narrowed. "I would like to rack that prick Gat."

"You may get the chance," Boone commented. "But you must get your act together if you're coming with us."

Kraft's mouth compressed into a thin line as he wrestled with his emotions.

"We know Blade is here," Boone added. "We must hitch up with him and do a number on these mutants."

"What chance do we stand against all those freaks?" Kraft asked.

"What chance do we have if we do nothing?" Boone rejoined. "I doubt they'll let any of us live, and if they do we'll live as slaves. I'm not too fond of that notion."

"I'll never be their slave!" Kraft vowed. His complexion was slowly returning to normal.

"You're with us then?" Boone queried.

Kraft nodded. "I'm with you."

"Good. Come with me." Boone stood and ambled over to Thunder. "Now all we need is for them to open that door."

Thunder smiled at Kraft. "I am happy you have recovered."

"I'll never recover," Kraft said brusquely, then softened his tone. "But thanks."

Boone looked toward the door. "What's happening out there?"

"Nothing much," Sergeant Havoc replied. "The pissants are standing around shooting the breeze."

"Maybe we can outfox them," Boone proposed.

"How?" Thunder asked.

"Let's plan this together," Boone proposed. "Havoc!" he called out. "We need you."

Sergeant Havoc walked toward them, his flinty blue eyes riveted on Kraft.

Kraft averted his face.

"What is it?" Havoc asked.

"We need an idea to draw those mutants in here," Boone stated. "Once they're inside, we'll jump them."

"There are a half dozen out there right now," Sergeant Havoc divulged. "We'll be outnumbered, and they have pikes while we're unarmed."

"Does this mean you don't want to try and escape," Boone inquired.

"I was just noting the odds," Havoc said. "I'm with you one hundred percent."

"Then how do we draw them in here?" Boone asked. "Pretend one of us is sick?"

"That's the oldest trick in the book," Sergeant Havoc commented. "And they may not care if one of us is sick. We need something else."

"I have a suggestion," Thunder spoke up.

"What?" Boone inquired.

"The creature called Gat said we must keep our strength up for the arena," Thunder reminded them. "They are saving us for a special fate. If so, they would not want us to harm one another."

"You think we should stage a fight?" Boone deduced.

Thunder shrugged. "Unless one of you has a better alternative."

"But who should do the fighting?" Boone questioned. "You and I?"

"If you want the fight to be as realistic as possible," Sergeant Havoc said, "Kraft and I will go at it."

Kraft's head snapped up. "What?"

"I don't know. . . ." Boone stated uncertainly.

"A fight is a great idea," Havoc persisted. "Kraft and I will put on a good show and lure the guards in here."

"You and me?" Kraft said reservedly.

"Sure. Why not?" Havoc rejoined. "You aren't afraid, are you?"

"I ain't afraid of you!" Kraft snapped.

Havoc smiled and stepped to the center of the cell. "Prove it."

Boone clutched Kraft's right arm. "You don't have to do this if you don't want to. I'll square off against Havoc."

Kraft gazed at the noncom. "No. I'll do it." He walked toward the trooper.

Boone hesitated, reluctant to see the pair clash, worried their mock combat would turn into the real McCoy.

Thunder moved in the direction of the cell door. "Come on," he urged the frontiersman.

Boone, frowning, complied. He took a position at the small window with Thunder to his left. Together they looked at the duo in the middle of the room.

Sergeant Havoc adopted the Zenkutsu-tachi, the forward stance, with his fists clenched in the Oriental fashion. His thumbs were bent over the second joints of his first two fingers, instead of on the side of the fist as was the Western style. He grinned at the Clansman. "I'm ready when you are."

"This isn't fair," Kraft said. "You'll break every bone in my body."

"Not every bone," Havoc stated. "Just the major ones."

Boone glanced out the window. The six mutants were engaged in idle conversation. Three of them held pikes. The rest had leaned their pikes against the wall. He looked back at Havoc and Kraft. "Let's get this show on the road."

Sergeant Havoc grinned and snap-kicked his right foot at Kraft's face.

Kraft sidestepped to the left and assumed an uneven horse stance. He swung his left fist at the noncom's chin.

Sergeant Havoc easily evaded the blow, dodging to the right and countering with a spin kick. His right heel slammed into the Clansman's abdomen and doubled Kraft over.

Watching from the door, Boone decided the time was ripe. He raised his right hand and pounded on the glass. "Hey! Open up! There's a fight in here!"

The lizard-men gazed at the cell door, but none of them made a move toward it.

Come on! Boone's mind screamed.

Sergeant Havoc brought his hands around and in, boxing Kraft on the ears with the heels of his palms.

"In here!" Boone cried. "There's a fight!"

One of the mutants came up to the door.

Boone stepped aside and waved his left hand toward the center of the room where Sergeant Havoc was just delivering his right knee to the point of Kraft's chin.

The lizard-man took one look and reached for the bolt.

"Here they come!" Boone whispered to Thunder, who promptly flattened against the wall adjacent to the door's inner edge.

Kraft was on his knees with Sergeant Havoc standing over him.

The door swung out and three of the lizard-men entered, two of them with their pikes.

"You there!" the mutant in the lead shouted. "Stop fighting!"

Sergeant Havoc ignored the command. Instead, he kicked Kraft in the stomach and the Clansman went down.

"Didn't you hear me?" the lead mutant yelled. "Stop fighting this instant!" He headed for Havoc and Kraft, his two companions right behind him.

Boone stared at the doorway.

Where were the other three? They needed all six in the cell if their plan was to succeed.

The remaining trio walked into the room, all three bearing their pikes. They strode forward.

And Boone initiated the bedlam by stepping in close to the nearest lizard-man and hooking his left leg under the mutant's legs, catching the creature from the rear. The lizard-man toppled backwards, its arms swinging wildly in a vain effort to stay erect, its pike in its left hand. Boone snatched at the weapon, and to his amazement it came loose from the mutant's grip.

A second lizard-man caught the frontiersman's attack out of the corner of its left eye. It spun, leveling its pike.

Thunder vaulted from behind the door, tackling the second mutant around the waist and they both sprawled onto the floor.

With a deft flip of his wrists, Boone reversed the pike and plunged the razor tip into the first mutant's left eye.

The cell became a whirlwind of conflict as the Force members fought for their freedom.

Sergeant Havoc closed on the three mutants in the lead, executing a spectacular Yoko-tobi-geri, a side jump kick, and ramming his right boot into the head guard's face, bowling the mutant over.

Thunder and the lizard-man he'd tackled were wrestling on the floor.

Boone wrenched the pike from the dead mutant's eye socket and pivoted to confront two of the creatures coming at him with their pikes extended.

"Enough!" a familiar voice abruptly bellowed. "Cease this nonsense immediately!"

All action froze as all eyes, human and mutant, shifted to the doorway.

Gat stood there, his pike in his right hand, rage on his face. "Drop that pike!" he ordered, his lips split and puffy.

Boone balked at relinquishing the weapon.

Gat stepped to the right of the door and motioned toward the doorway. "Drop it or die!" His left ear was swollen and discolored.

Boone's eyes widened at the sight of two dozen mutants lined up in the corridor, each one armed with a pike.

"We came to escort you to the Arena," Gat declared. "But none of you will reach the Arena alive if you don't do exactly as I say. Now drop the damn pike!"

Reluctantly, Boone let go and the weapon clattered on the cement floor.

Gat gazed at the dead lizard-man. "You humans are more trouble than you're worth! I can't wait to see you torn apart in the Arena!" He looked at each Force member in turn, sheer fury radiating from his features. "Prepare to die, you miserable slime!"

CHAPTER THIRTEEN

Reptilian was an awesome mutant. He possessed the characteristic traits of his kind, the same dark green skin, the same elongated nose, the same round ears, and the same set of pointed teeth. But he stood a foot taller than the average Reptiloid, and his bodily proportions matched Blade's in every respect. Reptilian's eyes were a deep, eerie blue, animated by his devious genius intellect. Unlike the other male Reptiloids, who all wore a standard garment consisting of a pair of green pants, Reptilian adorned his person in a striking red outfit: a red shirt, red pants, red boots, and even a red cape. He smiled at the Warrior and beckoned with his right arm. "Come here. We have much to discuss."

Blade gazed at the mutants packing the throne room, his eyes narrowing at the sight of the first female Reptiloids he had seen. They were counterparts of the males in every respect, except their breasts, naturally, were considerably larger. The females wore green garments covering them from their ankles to their necks. He wondered why the Reptiloids preferred to wear green? Was it because the color matched their skin and afforded an excellent camouflage when they were on the surface?

Reptilian noticed the Warrior's scrutiny of the chamber and misconstrued the reason. "Don't worry," he declared. "None of my followers will harm you here. You have my word on it, and the word of Reptilian is inviolate."

Blade walked toward the throne, his skin tingling as he moved between the two rows of Reptilian's personal guard. He halted at the base of the golden stairs and looked up at the mutant leader.

Reptilian studied the Warrior for a moment, then smiled. "You're perfect."

"Perfect for what?" Blade asked.

Reptilian ignored the question. He sat down on his marble throne and motioned for Blade to ascend the steps. "Don't be shy. We have much to discuss," he reiterated.

Blade slowly climbed the stairs until he stood on the top level next to the throne. "What do we have to talk about?"

"I want to know all about you," Reptilian said.

"Why?"

Again Reptilian disregarded the Warrior's query. "I can see we have a lot in common," he commented.

"How do you figure that?" Blade remarked.

Reptilian rested his chin in his right hand. "You, obviously, are a giant among your kind. I, by the same token, am a giant among mine. We should thank our parents for the exceptional genes they bestowed upon us."

"My parents have already passed on to the higher mansions," Blade said.

"The higher mansions?" Reptilian repeated quizzically. "Don't tell me you believe in an afterlife?"

Blade recalled the teachings he had received from the Family Elders. "The afterlife is merely a continuation of this life," he stated. "If you have the faintest flicker of faith, then you never really die."

"This life is all we get," Reptilian disagreed. "There is no afterlife. Only simpletons believe that old wives' tale."

"I believe it," Blade asserted. "And there are dozens more like me where I come from."

"Is it true you come from Minnesota?" Reptilian asked.

Blade didn't answer.

Reptilian shrugged. "Suit yourself. But I already know everything of importance about you."

"Sure you do," Blade said sarcastically.

"I know you are the leader of the elite unit known as the Force," Reptilian said. "I know you were sent here to terminate me." He chuckled. "And I know you will singularly fail."

"I haven't failed," Blade said.

Reptilian encompassed the chamber in an expensive gesture. "No? Then what would you call this?"

"Planning my strategy," Blade commented.

Reptilian laughed. "I like you. A sense of humor is essential."

"You're not what I expected," Blade mentioned.

Reptilian cocked his head to the left. "Oh? What did you expect? An ogre with one eye and ten legs?"

"Something like that," Blade admitted.

"You humans are so predictable!" Reptilian declared. "If a species is different from yours, you automatically assume it is inferior."

"You're a fine one to talk," Blade countered. "I've heard about the way you treat humans, as slaves and food."

"Humans are mindless cattle," Reptilian declared. "I treat them the way they should be treated."

"Humans and mutants can be friends, you know," Blade noted.

"Friends?" Reptilian snapped, straightening. "You appear to be laboring under a severe misconception! Humans and mutants can never be friends for the simple reason humans can never be trusted!"

"That's ridiculous," Blade said.

"Is it?" Reptilian responded angrily. "Sixty years ago I tried to befriend your species, but they would have none of it! Instead they tried to kill me! And why? Just because I was different!" He scowled. "The irony of it all! I am different from your kind because your kind unleashed a holocaust of global dimensions and contaminated the environment with radioactive and chemical warfare toxins. I am different from your kind because massive doses of radiation drastically alter embryonic formation and development. And if the subsequent mutations mature and breed, they pass on their genetic traits to their offspring. The mutated strain continues to evolve over generations, becoming increasingly mutant with each one."

"I've never heard that theory before," Blade commented.

"It is not a theory," Reptilian stated. "It is an established fact. Permit me to elaborate. One hundred and five years ago, at the outset of World War Three, my ancestors were fully human. They lived near San Diego, which sustained a direct nuclear hit during the war. Although they were outside of the blast radius, they must have been exposed to the fallout, to the radiation. They migrated northward shortly thereafter, and about ten years later they had a child, a boy. This son was not quite human, nor was he completely mutated. He had pale green skin and red pupils, but his features were typical of your species. Over the span of decades, with each generation, his children, and then his children's children, and his children's children's children, all became increasingly mutant." He smiled. "You see the end result before you."

"All of which reinforces my point," Blade said. "If your lineage was once human, then your species shares the same ancestors. We should be able to share as equals and friends."

Reptilian pursed his thin lips and scrutinized the Warrior. "You truly believe that, don't you?"

"Of course," Blade replied. "At my Home humans and mutants live in harmony. You could do the same here."

"Not true," Reptilian said. "There may be a few exceptions to the general rule, but humans and mutants are destined to be implacable enemies. As a species we can never be friends because your kind will not permit us to attain our rightful destiny."

"Which is?" Blade asked.

"Why, to dominate the world, of course," Reptilian said sincerely. "The mutant species developed as a consequence of humankind's abysmal failure to manage this planet with wisdom and insight. Let's face facts. Your kind blew it. You had the opportunity to utilize the planetary resources to maximize peace and prosperity for all, but you weren't up to the task. You destroyed your civilization and you have only yourselves to blame." He paused. "The Mutant Era will be different."

"The Mutant Era?"

"Yes," Reptilian said, grinning. "The era of the ascendancy of my species over yours. The New Order I've established will eventually supplant the human species as the dominant species on this world."

"What is this New Order?" Blade inquired.

"The Province is not the only organized pocket of mutantkind," Reptilian disclosed. "And I am not the only leader of a budding mutant autocracy. I have sent out scouts and located other mutant outposts. Slowly but surely I am forming a mutant empire which will supplant the crumbling vestiges of human culture. Within another century we shall rule this globe."

"Don't hold your breath," Blade quipped.

"Mark my words," Reptilian insisted. "Mutants will one day subjugate humanity. We are the wave of the future."

"So how many other mutant outposts are in the New Order?" Blade casually inquired.

Reptilian grinned. "Nice try. Such information is confidential, you understand. Although you may be privileged to see the leaders of the New Order during the Arena festivities."

"Lucky me," Blade cracked.

Reptilian paid no attention. "The leaders of the New Order gather for periodic conclaves. They like to attend during Arena week. Every two months or so we like to put on a special entertainment in the Arena."

"What kind of entertainment?" Blade inquired.

"Can you read?" Reptilian unexpectedly questioned.

Blade's forehead furrowed. "Yes. Everyone in my Family can."

"I'm impressed," Reptilian said. "Reading is a lost art outside of the civilized territories and outposts. I encourage my subjects to learn to read at an early age. We teach the young Reptiloids to read by the age of five."

"What does all of this have to do with the entertainment in your Arena?" Blade asked.

"Everything," Reptilian responded. "When I was forming the Province, I researched all the ancient texts I could find on various types of government. I wanted to find the ideal form." He gestured at the royal chamber. "And I found it. Ancient Rome. I've patterned the Province after the Roman system of government. I've named our headquarters, our palace if you will, the Imperium. And, in keeping with the Roman style of entertainment, I had an Arena built."

Blade remembered reading about the Roman stadiums and the barbaric contests the Romans had sanctioned. The individual fighters had been known as gladiators. He recalled specific historical accounts; gladiators had been forced to battle starved lions, or a group of gladiators had fought against a pack of panthers. The Romans had delighted in having their gladiators fight with mismatched weapons. Such sickening cruelty had been exalted as the highest form of entertainment. "Do you have gladiators in your Arena?" he queried.

"Of what use is an Arena without gladiators?" Reptilian answered.

"Will I be one of these gladiators?" Blade asked bluntly.

"No," Reptilian said. "I have other plans for you. I will not run the risk of having you injured in combat."

"Why are you being so kind to me?" Blade asked with a tinge of derision.

"I will explain," Reptilian said, "in due time. First, though, I would like you to attend the Arena with me as my official guest."

"Don't you mean your official prisoner?" Blade corrected the mutant.

Reptilian slowly rose, his cape swirling to his knees. "I am doing my best to treat you with civility. The least you could do is reciprocate."

"You must be joking," Blade said.

Reptilian stared at the captive. "Your species has no class."

"You have no room to talk," Blade responded. "And I'm not going anywhere with you until you answer a few questions of mine."

"Why don't we talk while we walk?" Reptilian proposed, starting to descend the stairs.

"Now," Blade snapped.

Reptilian sighed. "Very well. What is bothering you?"

"Where is the rest of the Force?" Blade asked.

"You will see them at the Arena," Reptilian stated.

"I will?" Blade queried in disbelief.

"I have given my word," Reptilian said stiffly. "You will see some of them, anyway."

"Which ones? What happened to the rest?" Blade pressed him.

Reptilian resumed his descent. "If you want answers, you must come with me. If you don't want to attend the Arena, I will have you returned to your cell."

Blade realized he didn't have a choice. He wanted to see Boone and the others, to find out what was happening to them. "I'll come," he said.

Reptilian looked up, smirking. "How nice. Shall we?" He waited for Blade to reach him before continuing down to the floor.

"You must have it pretty cushy here," Blade commented. "Setting yourself up as a king and all."

"Not a king," Reptilian said. "An emperor. There is a fine distinction."

"Either way you cut it," Blade observed, "you're a dictator."

Reptilian grinned. "True. But I deserve to be a dictator."

"Why's that?"

They began moving toward the door, walking between the rows of guards.

"Greatness is inherently mine by virtue of my biological preeminence," Reptilian asserted.

Blade glanced at the lizard-man. "You must wear out a lot of mirrors."

Reptilian paused. "Mirrors?"

"Yeah," Blade said. "From kissing your reflection all the time."

Surprisingly, Reptilian threw back his head and laughed. "I must remember that line. Gat will appreciate it."

"Where is Gat?" Blade asked as they kept going to the door.

"He will meet us there," Reptilian said.

The Reptiloids in the chamber were conversing in a routine manner. They did not display any undue interest in Reptilian's Arena guest.

Blade was feeling increasingly apprehensive. Reptilian was being too nice, and there had to be an ulterior motive. But what? Why was Reptilian taking him to the Arena? What was the mutant leader up to?

Reptilian opened the door and nodded for Blade to proceed. Together they strolled to the stairwell with Reptilian's personal guard right behind them.

As they entered the stairwell Blade looked up. Were the pair he'd slain still up there? Or had the Reptiloids taken the bodies away? What would Reptilian do when he learned about their deaths?

"The two you killed on the landing above us have been taken to the crematorium," Reptilian mentioned offhandedly.

Blade glanced at the mutant. "Are you a mind reader?"

Reptilian chuckled. "Nothing so profound. I used deductive reasoning and prior knowledge. I knew you had killed two of my subjects on one of the landings above us, and when I saw you staring upward I guessed your train of thought."

"How did you know I killed them?" Blade asked. "And how did you know I'd escaped from my cell? When you first saw me, you claimed you'd been expecting me."

Reptilian reached up and tapped the right side of his head. "Deductive reasoning again. I was informed of your escape within a minute of its occurrence, and I was told about the landing incident seconds before you blundered into the throne room."

"You were informed? How?" Blade wanted to learn.

Reptilian slid his right hand around his back, under his cape. His hand emerged holding a small, square, black plastic device with dials and a little speaker on the front and a belt clip on the reverse. "These were once known as walkie-talkies. With the generator we obtained, and with our supply of rechargeable batteries, we find these walkie-talkies are ideal for communicating at distances up to a mile."

Blade knew about walkie-talkies; they were commonly used by the California military. "Where did you get your walkie-talkies and all the rest?"

"Where else? The black market. The Scarlet Clique does business with anyone, mutant or human," Reptilian divulged. "But then, you probably know all about the Scarlet Clique. Everyone does business with them."

Blade had never heard of the Scarlet Clique before, but he wasn't about to reveal his ignorance. "I imagine everyone does," he commented.

"They're the best supplier I know of," Reptilian said. He reattached the walkie-talkie to the back of his belt, then proceeded down the stairwell.

Blade stayed alongside the mutant. "Where do you suppose they obtain all the equipment and other items they supply?"

Reptilian shrugged. "I've never asked. Such a breach of etiquette would be unforgivable. If I foolishly pried into their affairs, they would sever our business relationship. And I need the merchandise they can provide." He paused. "I suspect they steal most of their goods from the Russians, the Civilized Zone, and California. Their network of thieves spans the country. I've even heard rumors it's international in scope."

An international ring of thieves? Black marketeering on a grand scale? This was information the Freedom Federation would consider crucial. How could he pump Reptilian without arousing the Reptiloid's suspicions? "I've heard the same rumors," he lied.

"You have?" Reptilian said. "You're the fourth one to tell me that. The rumors must have a basis in fact."

"Who do you think runs the Scarlet Clique?" Blade inquired.

"I don't know," Reptilian replied. "Trying to discover the identity of the head of the Scarlet Clique would be hazardous to your health."

Blade pondered for a moment. What else could he ask without giving himself away? "They like their secrecy, don't they?"

"Can you blame them? They work both sides of the fence, and they do so without stepping on anyone's toes. Their transactions are conducted in the utmost secrecy. To tell you the truth, I envy their superb organizational skills." Reptilian gazed over the railing toward the bottom. "We are almost there."

"Do you mind if I ask you a question?" Blade queried, recalling his conversation with the Indoctrinator, Prine.

"I may not answer it," Reptilian said.

"I know," Blade stated. "But I've been wondering about something. When your Hunter Squad fought with us in the forest, they seemed to be able to spot us even when we were concealed. And when Prime was talking to me, he claimed the Reptiloids have some sort of heat-detecting ability. Do you?"

"Yes," Reptilian confirmed. "Our vision is slightly better than human sight. I believe our range is extended further into the infrared spectrum than yours is. Have you ever seen a road on a hot day? Have you seen the heat reflecting off the road surface in seemingly wavy lines?"

"Yes," Blade said.

"Our vision works on the same principle," Reptilian explained. "Every body gives off a degree of heat. Mammals gives off more than reptiles, reptiles more than fish, and so on. Our vision enables us to see the heat being radiated by a physical form. If you were hiding behind a boulder, for instance, and even if I didn't actually see your body, I would be able to detect your presence by the heat your body was radiating. Our vision is not infallible. We can't see through solid objects, and on cold days physical forms give off less heat, which means they're harder to discern. But our ability is particularly beneficial when we are engaged in combat in rough terrain, as you discovered. We enjoy a decided advantage."

"I'll say," Blade agreed.

They came to the lowest landing. There was only one door, to the right.

"Prepare yourself," Reptilian said as he took hold of the door handle. "You have never beheld a sight like my Arena!" he boasted proudly.

Beyond the door was a long corridor painted entirely in red. They walked along it for hundreds of yards. In the distance a blue door became visible.

"What's that noise?" Blade inquired as a muted jumble of sound reached his ears.

"You will see," Reptilian responded, grinning.

The sound grew in volume, becoming a steady din.

Blade glanced over his right shoulder at the escort of personal guards. Their faces were impassive as they marched with their pikes aligned on their right shoulders in practiced military precision.

A thunderous roar shook the corridor.

Blade looked at Reptilian.

The mutant laughed. "One of my pets."

"What is it? A dinosaur?" Blade quipped.

"Close," Reptilian said. They walked to the blue door and he grabbed the knob. "There is nothing like the Arena. The Romans had the right idea all along." So saying, he turned the knob and pulled. "After you."

Blade stepped through the doorway, his gray eyes widening in amazement at the scene before him. "Incredible!" he declared.

"Thank you," Reptilian said from behind him.

The Arena was every bit as awe-inspriing as the Reptiloid leader had claimed. One hundred yards in length and 30 yards wide, the stadium was patterned after the Roman amphitheaters of old. The Arena floor was mere dirt, and countless dark splotches dotting the soil served as a silent testimony to the numerous lives lost during the games. A ten-foot wooden wall separated the spectators from the contestants. Rings of seats rose from the top of the wall in successively elevated tiers. The ceiling consisted of a latticework of huge beams braced by massive marble columns positioned around the outer row of seats. Over a dozen large doors were situated at regular intervals in the inner wall, affording access to the Arena floor.

Reptilian stepped up to Blade's left side. "Initially, I intended to construct an Arena only half this size. But when we were excavating for the Imperium, we found an enormous cavern adjacent to the Rogue River, under what was once Riverside Park. I decided the cavern would be perfect for the Arena."

Blade was surveying the stands, boggled by the sight of thousands of spectators. The Reptiloids occupied the rows nearest the Arena floor, the best seats for viewing the action. Blade estimated at least a thousand mutants were in attendance, but there were even more humans. They filled in the seats above the Reptiloids, and they were closely monitored by guards posted every few rows. The conversation of thousands of voices accounted for the racket he had heard in the corridor.

"Arena days are special," Reptilian mentioned. "Almost the entire population of the Province is here."

"You allow your human slaves to attend?" Blade asked.

"This is the only diversion they're permitted," Reptilian said. "They look forward to the games."

Blade gazed upward, spying a series of gigantic floodlights affixed to the wooden beams. "Your generator supplies the power," he deduced.

"Yes," Reptilian verified.

Blade noted his immediate surroundings for the first time. He was on a spacious platform located at the top of the inner wall directly above one of the doors. A half-dozen plush red chairs were lined up near the edge of the platform nearest the combat area.

"Watch this," Reptilian said, and walked out to the platform's rim.

The audience went wild, cheering and applauding. Chants of "Reptilian! Reptilian! Reptilian!" arose from the stands.

Blade was astonished to see the human spectators participating in the ovation. Why would the humans respond so enthusiastically? Had they been conditioned by the Reptiloids? Would they suffer a dire fate if they didn't applaud?

Reptilian was basking in the acclamation, his arms upraised, beaming. He turned and motioned for the Warrior to join him.

Blade slowly moved to the leader's right. He looked back and saw the personal guards filing from the corridor, one line branching to the right, the other to the left. They enclosed the platform on three sides, a living phalanx of protection for Reptilian.

"Reptilian! Reptilian!" the crowd shouted adoringly.

Blade glanced to his right, surprised to find a smaller platform twenty yards away. Seven chairs had been placed close to the lip of the wall, and in each chair sat a different mutant. These mutants were not Reptiloids; they were a diverse assortment of genetic deviates, each attired in splendid clothing. One was some sort of froglike man with bulging eyes and thick lips. Another resembled a cross between a bear and a human. The rest were a bizarre amalgam of traits, hideous creatures with alien aspects. Were they the leaders of the New Order? If so, why did they occupy a separate, smaller platform? Were they subservient in status to Reptilian? Was he the supreme mastermind behind the establishment of the Mutant Era?

"We should sit down," Reptilian directed, taking the centermost chair.

Blade complied. "Why are we the only ones on this platform?" he inquired, yelling to make himself heard above the crowd.

"Sometimes I invite guests to share the royal dais. Today, you have the honor," Reptilian said.

Blade nodded at the smaller platform. "What about them?"

"They are where they deserve to be," Reptilian stated brusquely.

"So much for mutant equality," Blade baited the Reptiloid.

Reptilian gazed at Blade with a condescending air. "I have no equals. Lesser mutants share equality."

"Now I know why you don't wear a hat," Blade taunted.

"A hat?" Reptilian repeated, puzzled. He reflected for a moment, then burst out laughing. "You really do have an excellent sense of humor."

"I'm sorry you took it so nicely," Blade cracked.

Reptilian faced the Arena. He raised his right arm, palm outward, and every voice was stilled. "Citizens of the Province!" he called out. "Another week of Arena festivities are upon us! The entertainment will be the best you have ever beheld! All human workers are hereby granted an executive leave of absence from toil until the games are concluded!"

The humans went wild, clapping appreciatively.

They certainly are well trained! Blade thought to himself. How could Reptilian exert such absolute control? Was his reign of terror that effective? How could the human population of the Province tolerate their enslavement? Especially when they knew they might be consumed without warning? Why did . . .

Hold it!

A striking inconsistency blossomed in his mind. "This doesn't make sense," he blurted.

Reptilian glanced at his guest. "What doesn't?"

"I was told there are two thousand humans in the Province," Blade said.

"More or less," Reptilian stated.

"And about twelve hundred Reptiloids," Blade mentioned.

"So?" Reptilian rejoined.

"So there aren't enough humans to suffice as a steady food supply for the Reptiloids," Blade said. "Not if each of you eats a human a day."

Reptilian laughed. "Where did you hear we eat a human a day?"

"I just assumed. . . ." Blade began.

Reptilian shook his head. "If we ate a human a day, our slaves would revolt en masse. Credit me with more intelligence than that! We consume a variety of foodstuffs, not just humans. Venison and elk meat figures prominently in our diet. They are our staples, along with fish. Human meat is a delicacy for us." He paused, scrutinizing the humans in the seats. "There are other factors involved. Our metabolism is not the same as yours. Humans must eat every day, but Reptiloids need only eat every three days. And the system I have established minimizes the stress on our human slaves."

"What system?"

Reptilian gazed at Blade and grinned slyly. "I will explain everything at the proper time. This is not it." He faced the Arena. "Let the games commence!"

A clamorous ovation greeted the announcement.

Blade stared at the Arena absently, speculating on what would be the first "entertainment" of the day. Lions against humans? Bears against women? Were there Reptiloid gladiators? Would the Reptiloids fight human "contestants"?

An answer was forthcoming when the door below the royal platform swung outward and four figures cautiously emerged.

Blade stiffened at the sight of the quartet. His hands gripped the arms of the chair until his knuckles were white. "No!" he exclaimed.

"Yes," Reptilian said calmly.

"Not them!" Blade stated.

But it was them: Boone, Thunder, Sergeant Havoc, and Kraft!

CHAPTER FOURTEEN

"It's Blade!" Boone cried as his gaze alighted on the platform.

The others swiveled toward the platform. They saw Blade rise from a red chair, his features contorted in rage, and take a step to the edge of the platform. The crowd started murmuring loudly.

"He's going to jump" Sergeant Havoc declared.

The immense Reptiloid next to the Warrior suddenly lunged, grabbing Blade's left wrist and wrenching him backwards. Blade stumbled into his chair and toppled over backwards. Before he could regain his feet he was ringed by a dozen Reptiloids, their pikes pointed at his chest. The Reptiloid in the red outfit said a few words to the Warrior, then barked a command at the row of guards to his left.

"What's going on?" Kraft asked.

Ten guards marched onto the platform and took up positions above the Force members. They hoisted their pikes and assumed a throwing stance.

Blade was on his knees, livid. He yelled something to the Reptiloid in red.

"What did he say?" Kraft queried anxiously. "I didn't hear him." The audience was growing louder and louder.

"I did not catch every word," Thunder said. "But I gather Blade intended to join us. The big one in red stopped him and threatened to have us speared by the guards if Blade tries it again."

"Who is that freak in the red threads?" Kraft questioned.

"My guess is it's the leader of the Reptiloids," Boone commented. "The one they call Reptilian."

"I wish I had my switchblade," Kraft remarked. He reached up and rubbed his bruised, swollen chin.

The door to the Arena abruptly closed.

"Uh-oh," Boone said.

"The bastards didn't even give us any weapons!" Sergeant Havoc stated.

"We should move away from the doors," Thunder suggested.

They edged to the center of the Arena, constantly scanning the doors, waiting tensely for the Reptiloids to unleash . . . what?

Sergeant Havoc glanced at the Clansman. "I have something I want to say to you."

Kraft snickered. "Get bent!"

"I want to apologize," Havoc said.

Kraft's mouth curled downward. "Apologize? After what you did to me back there? You beat the shit out of me, you son of a bitch! We were supposed to put on a good show for the muties!"

Sergeant Havoc pursed his lips. "I know that. I was out of place. I was venting my anger over what happened to Clayboss and Rivera on you. You can't help being a jerk."

"Shove your apology up your ass!" Kraft snapped.

"Enough, already!" Boone interrupted them. "This is not the time or the place to settle your differences. Wait until we get back to California."

"If we get back," Kraft amended.

"Look!" Thunder said, pointing.

A door to their right was slowly opening. The interior was plunged in shadows, obscuring whatever was inside.

"I wish I was in Minnesota," Kraft said wistfully.

Vague forms moved from the gloom into the light.

Kraft snorted. "What is this? Some kind of a joke?"

There were four of them, all women, all skimpily attired in leather harnesses, and all of them were armed.

"These clowns must be putting us on," Kraft said.

"I don't think so," Sergeant Havoc remarked.

Three of the women were white, one black. All of them were muscular, and all of them had cropped their hair short, to just below their ears. The black woman brandished a pike. The tallest white woman, a redhead, carried a short sword and a shield. Both of the remaining two were brunettes. One of them held a green mesh net in her left hand, a dagger in her right. The last woman was armed with a five-foot trident.

"They intend to harm us," Thunder said.

"I reckon so," Boone concurred.

"Give me a break!" Kraft declared. "They're just foxes. What can they do against all of us?"

"They're armed and we're not," Sergeant Havoc observed.

"So?" Kraft rejoined. "If they try messing with us, we'll kick their butts."

The four women walked toward the Force members, their tread steady and measured, their faces grim, their weapons held in front of them at the ready.

Boone glanced at Sergeant Havoc. "Do you have a plan?"

"I was hoping you had one," Havoc responded.

"Who needs a plan?" Kraft queried sarcastically. He stepped forward several feet and placed his hands on his hips.

The women halted 15 yards off.

"What do you want?" Kraft called out.

Extending her pike toward the Clansman, the black woman spoke a few words to her companions who broke out laughing.

"What's so funny?" Kraft demanded.

"You are, Pointy-Hair," the black woman replied. "You are in the Arena and you ask such a stupid question! What do you think we want?"

"You'd better not mess with us!" Kraft warned. "We've got a heavy rep!"

"I claim you for myself," the black woman told Kraft. "And before you die I will cut out your tongue."

The quartet advanced warily.

Kraft retreated until he stood next to Boone. "They're wacko!" he said.

"No," Boone stated. "They are professional fighters. I figure they have been in the Arena before. Many times before."

"Show them no mercy," Sergeant Havoc advised. "Just because they're women doesn't mean you should go easy on them. They'll kill you for sure if you do."

"I don't much like the notion of fighting a woman," Boone said. "But if it's a fight they want, then it's a fight they'll get."

With a shout of defiance, the four women charged their opponents. The black woman, true to her pledge, went after Kraft. The redhead bore down on Boone. Thunder was attacked by the brunette with the trident, while the woman with the net and dagger closed on Sergeant Havoc.

The noncom was determined to end his contest as quickly as possible so he could aid his comrades. He assumed the Kake-ashi-tachi, intending to spin-kick her into the middle of next week. But she had other ideas.

The female gladiator made an apparently reckless lunge with the gleaming dagger clutched in her left hand.

Havoc, surprised at her sloppy style, easily sidestepped to the right.

Which was exactly what the woman wanted. As the trooper was shifting his position and was momentarily off balance, she swept her mesh net around and in at ankle height. The upper third of the net wrapped tightly around the noncom's ankles, weighted by beads of metal stitched into the outer seam.

Havoc felt the constricting net enfold his ankles, and he desperately threw himself backwards, straining to extricate his legs. The net impeded his movement and refused to budge, and his momentum caused him to lose his footing. He tumbled onto his back.

With a cry of triumph, the gladiator sprang, going for a speedy kill, angling her dagger at the soldier's neck.

Havoc was ready. His ankles were tangled in the net, but he could still move his legs. He twisted and swung his legs to block her approach, his knees tucked against his chest.

The woman tried to circle to the right.

Havoc lashed out with his boots, his heels slamming into her left knee.

There was a distinct crack and the gladiator gasped and stumbled onto her right knee, her face contorted in anguish.

Havoc brought his legs up to his chest and struck again, planting both heels squarely on the point of her nose.

The gladiator's nasal cartilage crunched and she was flung onto her back, her right hand releasing the net.

Move! Havoc's mind screamed. He sat up and tugged at the mesh, swiftly unwinding the net.

Groaning, the center of her face a bloody ruins, the woman was striving to rise.

Sergeant Havoc tore the last of the mesh from his ankles and pushed himself erect. He saw his foe on her hands and knees, took one short step, and delivered a brutal kick to the right side of her head. She dropped, rolling onto her left side, exposing her neck. Without hesitation, he arced his right hand up and down, using the Tegatana, the knifehand, to finish her off. The calloused outer edge of his hand crushed her throat.

The gladiator gurgled, convulsed, wheezed, and died.

Havoc straightened and whirled, looking for someone to help.

Thunder and the brunette with the trident were ten yards away. The brunette was striving to impale the Indian on the three points of her weapon, but the Flathead was easily evading her.

Boone was also faring well.

The redhead was attempting to connect with a swipe of her short sword, and her frustration was clearly written on her features. Boone was always one step ahead of her, constantly backpedaling.

Kraft, though, was in serious trouble. The black woman seemed to be toying with him, playfully jabbing at him with her pike. Kraft darted to the right and the left, but he was never able to get out of the pike's range.

Sergeant Havoc ran toward them, a sense of guilt troubling his conscience. He shouldn't have treated Kraft so shabbily. Sure, the Clansman had no business being on the Force. And true, Kraft was a monumental pain in the butt. But Kraft wasn't totally responsible for his actions; he simply couldn't control his immature temper and his aggravating personality. Havoc wanted to make amends, somehow, if he ever got the chance.

He never did.

Kraft tripped and fell onto his right side. He surged to his knees, frantically scrambling to regain his footing.

Never missing a stride, the woman whipped the shaft of her pike around and pounded the Clansman on the temple.

Kraft was staggered by the blow. He bent backwards, sagging, unable to defend himself.

Cackling, the black gladiator raised her pike overhead.

"No!" Sergeant Havoc yelled in a desperate bid to distract her. "Try me!"

The woman's right arm descended.

Sergeant Havoc was five feet from them when he saw the sharp tip of the pike penetrate Kraft's chest squarely above the heart. The pike passed completely through the Clansman's body with deceptive ease.

Kraft screamed as he died.

The black woman glanced at Havoc as she tried to wrest the pike from her victim's torso.

Havoc felt a burning rage engulf him. He reached the gladiator in a single leap, crashing a Uraken, a left back fist, into her mouth. She released the pike and tottered backwards, bringing up her fists in a reflexive protective action. Havoc feinted with his left hand, and when she opened her guard by counterthrusting with her right, he used his right hand in a Nihon-nukite. His index and middle fingers stabbed into her eyes.

The gladiator backed away, blinking her eyes in an effort to clear her blurry vision.

His eyes blazing, Havoc leaped into the air and connected with a side jump kick. The ball of his right foot, reinforced by his combat boot heel, caught her on the point of her chin, snapping her mouth closed and her head to the rear. Her teeth splintered, blood and spittle spewing from her lips.

Whining, the woman staggered. "No! Please!" she blubbered.

Havoc paid no attention. Consumed by his fury, he rained a hail of blows on the gladiator, overpowering her feeble resistance, hitting her again and again and again. The world spun and tilted as his frenzy rose, then abruptly peaked. He suddenly realized he was on the ground, straddling the woman, his knuckles caked with crimson and pulp.

The woman was dead, her face a battered shambles, her tongue protruding from the right corner of her mouth, her eyes wide and glazing fast.

Stunned by his loss of control, Havoc stood. He turned, seeking the others.

Thunder and the brunette were less than four yards distant, the brunette continuing to try and stick him with her trident.

Boone and the redhead were likewise going at it, 20 feet to the left.

Sergeant Havoc dashed to Kraft. The Clansman was slumped on the dirt on his left side, a spreading pool of blood under him, his eyes closed, an odd grin on his face. The pike dangled from Kraft's chest, the shaft resting on the earth. Havoc leaned over and gripped the shaft, gazing for a second at the Clansman. "Sorry," he said softly, and then he yanked the pike out and straightened.

Three yards away the brunette with the trident was gaining ground on Thunder, her back to the noncom.

His lips a grim line, Havoc held the pike at chest height, extended the razor point, and sprinted toward the brunette. He aimed the tip of the pike between her shoulder blades, and in two strides he was close enough to spear the pike into her body.

Screeching, the brunette stiffened as she was impaled. The bloody point tore through her flesh between her breasts and jutted upward. She endeavored to turn, but her legs buckled and she fell forward.

Sergeant Havoc let her fall. He grabbed the trident from her lifeless left hand and pivoted.

Boone and the redhead were grappling on the turf, rolling over and over. The redhead had dropped her shield and they were wrestling for control of the sword.

Havoc raced to Boone's assistance. He reached them just as Boone succeeded in pinning the redhead. Boone's hands were clamped on the redhead's wrists, his legs aslant across her own. Havoc could see the woman's face over Boone's left shoulder. Her eyes flicked up toward him.

Thunder shouted from the noncom's rear. "Havoc! Don't!"

Havoc did. He buried the trident in the gladiator's face, the outer prongs piercing her startled eyes while the middle prong skewered her nose. She shrieked and bucked.

Boone rolled to the right and stood. He gaped at the woman, then at Havoc.

Sergeant Havoc held onto the trident until the gladiator ceased moving. He released the shaft and stepped back.

"You didn't need to do that!" Boone blurted. "I had her!"

Thunder joined them. "Havoc killed all four of them," he stated.

"What?" Boone responded, starting to turn, to scan the Arena floor.

"Kraft is dead," Thunder added solemnly.

"Kraft!" Boone spotted the Clansman and ran over. He knelt and examined the body.

Thunder stared at the noncom. "Are you all right?"

"I'm fine," Havoc answered, watching the blood flow from the last gladiator's eyes.

"What got into you?" Thunder inquired.

Havoc glanced at the Flathead. "I'm a soldier, remember? This is what I do best. It's what I do for a living. And it's about damn time we started acting like a military unit instead of a sewing circle!"

Thunder's features softened. "I regret Kraft's passing too."

"Kraft's death has nothing to do with this!" Sergeant Havoc snapped.

Boone walked toward them, downcast. "Kraft is dead," he said, as if he couldn't believe it.

"We'd better get set," Sergeant Havoc suggested. "They're bound to throw something else at us."

"Look," Thunder said, pointing at the big platform.

Reptilian was on his feet. He scrutinized the audience, which was strangely quiet. "Citizens of the Province!" his voice boomed. "It appears these games shall be more entertaining than we dared imagine! These outsiders have proven themselves valorous! They have defeated four of our favorite fighters, and in so doing have amply demonsrated their prowess! They deserve a round of applause!"

On cue, the audience erupted in applause.

Reptilian waited for the clapping to subside, then went on. "We salute you, outsiders!" he addressed the Force men.

Sergeant Havoc flipped him the finger.

Reptilian smiled. "Yes! These games promise to be the most exciting we have ever held! All thanks to you! But you must be fatigued after your bout. You will be permitted to eat and rest, to refresh yourselves for your next contest!"

Sergeant Havoc pointed at Kraft. "What about him, you bastard? We want his body buried!"

Reptilian smirked. "I'm sorry. Burial is not possible." He paused. "We never waste meat."

The door under the royal platform swung out, disgorging ten Reptiloids with pikes. Five formed a line to the left, five to the right.

"Again, we salute you!" Reptilian declared. He motioned toward the door.

"I say we stay here and fight!" Sergeant Havoc stated angrily.

"And commit suicide?" Boone remarked. "No way. We can all use a rest. We need time to plan."

"I agree with Boone," Thunder said.

Sergeant Havoc glanced at Kraft's corpse and bowed his head. "Okay. For now. But I won't take much more of this!"

They strolled wearily in the direction of the door.

Sergeant Havoc gazed up at Blade. The Warrior was in a chair, glaring balefully at Reptilian, surrounded by Reptiloids. "Some head of the Force he is! He just sits there while one of his men dies!"

Boone looked up at Blade. "He doesn't have any choice. Look at all those mutants."

"I see them," Havoc said. "But if I'd been up there, I would have done something. I don't know what, but something." He frowned. "You know, I used to admire Blade a lot. Now I'm not so sure."

"Don't be so hard on him," Boone commented, his tone laced with annoyance. "He did the right thing. What good would it have done him to be killed needlessly?"

"Well, while Blade sits up there doing nothing," Havoc said, "there's one thing you'd better keep in mind."

"What's that?" Boone asked.

"One of us has already died," Boone snapped bitterly. "Which one of us will be next?"

CHAPTER FIFTEEN

Not another one!

Dear Spirit, no!

Not another one!

Blade watched a detail of human slaves remove the bodies from the Arena. He noticed their rough manner as they handled Kraft, and his veins stood out on his temples. For the first time in his life he thirsted for vengeance with a powerful passion. Emotion ruled his temperament instead of his typical logic. He wanted to make the Reptiloids pay for their bloodthirsty tyranny! He wanted to see them suffer! Most of all, he wanted to get his hands around Reptilian's neck!

"Aren't you enjoying our games?" Reptilian asked. He was reclining in his chair, his features reflecting an attitude of smug satisfaction.

Blade's gray eyes bored into the mutant's. "I'm going to kill you."

Reptilian chuckled. "Really? Somehow I doubt it. If you make any hostile moves, my personal guards will slay you on the spot."

"I don't know when," Blade reiterated. "But I'm going to kill you. You don't deserve to live."

"Who are you to judge me?" Reptilian responded acidly. "Humans are hardly qualified to sit in judgment on mutants!"

"No matter which species is involved," Blade said, "murderous psychopaths are all the same. They all deserve a similar fate. Summary execution."

"You are judging me by human standards," Reptilian stated. "By mutant standards I am a paragon of virtue."

"Then mutants must have pitiful standards," Blade commented.

Reptilian studied the giant for a minute. "You are understandably upset about the death of one of your men. Perhaps you should not be here when they return."

"How long will that be?" Blade inquired.

"Several hours," Reptilian revealed. "There are other contests we must observe first."

"Which one will I be in?" Blade asked.

"You?"

"Surely you're not going to keep me on this platform during all the contests?" Blade queried.

"That's exactly what I am going to do," Reptilian said. "Except for when your men return. I may have you returned to your cell."

"I'm really not going to be in any of your so-called games?" Blade demanded.

Reptilian shook his head. "You may view them, but you will not participate."

"Why?"

"I will explain everything later," Reptilian said.

"I want to know now," Blade persisted.

Reptilian sighed. "Very well. We have a few minutes to spare before the next bout." He gazed out over the Arena. "Earlier we were discussing the different dietary requirements of humans and Reptiloids. I mentioned a certain system I've developed when it comes to the consuming of humans."

"I remember," Blade commented.

"As I mentioned, human meat is a delicacy for us," Reptilian said. "We primarily reserve the consumption of humans for special occasions. By intentionally limiting the number of humans we consume, we reduce the inevitable adverse reaction in our human slave population. They know if they cooperate with us, they may never be eaten. If they work hard and obey us diligently, they can live to old age. Once they do, they're safe, because we are not fond of consuming the flesh of the elderly. It's too stringy, and nowhere near as tasty." He paused. "To further reduce the prospects of a rebellion, I have established a system of selective consumption. We will eat outsiders before we touch a member of our core slave population. This explains why we send out so many Hunter Squads. We don't want to run out of outsiders. Unless our slaves violate one of our rules and regulations, they are relatively safe. This condition gives them a glimmer of hope on which to base their lives, and it reduces the risk of a rebellion."

"You have everything figured out, don't you?" Blade commented.

"I am Reptilian," the mutant said. "I can do no less."

"So what about me?" Blade inquired. "Why aren't you going

to throw me in the Arena?"

"Because I don't want you damaged," Reptilian said.

"Why not?"

Reptilian stared at the Warrior. "Because I am quite fussy about my food."

"Food!" Blade blurted.

"Of course," Reptilian said. "Did you think we would become bosom buddies?" He snickered. "I will not eat just any human. I prefer one with outstanding physical and mental attributes. You qualify as such a one."

"Lucky me!" Blade quipped.

"When I was informed about your fight with the Hunter Squad, I knew you were right for me," Reptilian said. "Very few humans can hold their own against us in the forest. But you did. You even killed several of my subjects. Only a human endowed with great strength and ability could have accomplished such a feat. You are just the sort of meat I like the most."

"If you intend to eat me," Blade said, "why are you being so nice now?"

"I enjoy getting to know the human I consume beforehand," Reptilian explained. "My meal is that much more delectable. Perhaps an analogy will suffice. I know humans in other parts of the country raise animals for food. Cows, chickens, turkeys, and the like. Imagine you had spent years raising a cow or steer to feed your family. When the time came to butcher the animal, you might be somewhat sad because you had grown attached to it. But at the same time, the meat from that steer or cow would be some of the best-tasting meat you'd ever eaten. Do you follow me?"

Blade simply glowered.

"So now you know," Reptilian said.

"You'll never succeed," Blade declared. "You know that, don't you?"

"At what? Consuming you?" Reptilian grinned.

"No. At establishing your Mutant Era, as you call it," Blade said. "We will stop you."

"Humans stop us?" Reptilian responded, and laughed. "Your pathetic species is on the eclipse and doesn't have the brains to recognize its own demise!"

"Don't count the human species out yet," Blade cautioned. "We will rebuild the world. We will produce a civilization better than the one which nearly destroyed the planet."

"It's a little late for that, don't you think?" Reptilian rejoined. "Your species had its chance and you blew it. Mutantkind will do better. We will fashion a Utopia."

Blade snorted derisively. "Is the Province your idea of a Utopia?"

"Utopian civilizations take time to construct," Reptilian replied. "They are not produced overnight. Rome, as the saying goes, was not built in a day."

Blade glanced at the small platform to his right. "Do the other leaders in the New Order agree with you?"

Reptilian gazed at the seven diverse mutants and frowned. "we do not see eye to eye on everything. But they will come around to my way of thinking eventually. If we can turn Grizzly around, we can turn any mutant."

Blade straightened, astounded. "Grizzly? He's here?"

Reptilian smirked. "How thoughtless of me. Did I forget to mention we had captured him and the lovely Ms. Morris?"

"Athena too!" Blade exclaimed.

Reptilian relished the Warrior's stunned countenance. "Did you honestly think they would elude us? I have given orders they are not to be harmed, not until Grizzly has demonstrated where his loyalties lie. Gat has held several profitable conversations with him, and Gat is of the opinion Grizzly will come over to our side. Grizzly, as you no doubt are aware, is not very fond of humans."

Grizzly turning traitor? The idea dazed Blade. He knew Grizzly disliked the human race, but would the bear-man actually betray the Force?

"So what is it going to be?" Reptilian inquired. "Do you want to remain here when your men return for their next contest, or would you rather go back to your cell?"

Blade slumped in his chair. "I'd like to return to my cell now, if you don't mind."

"Now? And miss all the fun?" Reptilian responded scornfully. "Very well. I find your attitude depressing. You may return to your cell." He glanced at one of his personal guards. "Tur, take this morbid excuse for a sentient being back to his cell. Take ten others with you to insure he doesn't attempt to escape. Leave four to watch the cell, then return. I wouldn't want you to miss the games."

"As you will, my liege," Tur said. He prodded Blade with his pike. "Let's go, human! On your feet!"

Blade slowly rose, the picture of depression.

Reptilian snickered. "Do you see him, Captain Tur? This is the man who claims humans will defeat us?"

Captain Tur laughed.

"I just hope when it comes times to eat him," Reptilian commented, "he doesn't give me indigestion! I hear Clayboss and Rivera were on the lean, stringy side." He cackled in sadistic glee.

PART FIVE
OF MEN AND MUTANTS

CHAPTER SIXTEEN

"Where have all the guards gone?" Athena asked.

Grizzly, seated on the cot, looked up. "What do you mean?"

"There aren't as many as there were before," Athena said. She was standing next to the door, gazing out the barred window. "There were six out there at one time. Now there are only two. I wonder where the rest went." She paused. "And there hasn't been as much traffic in the corridor."

"The Arena games must have begun," Grizzly mentioned.

"Those horrid contests Gat was telling us about?" Athena asked.

Grizzly nodded. He rose and moved to her side. "This could be the chance I've been waiting for."

"But how will we break out of here?" Athena questioned.

"We may not have to," Grizzly said.

"What?"

Grizzly nodded at the small window. "Here comes our gift horse."

Puzzled, Athena looked out the window.

The Prefect was approaching their cell, a pike in his right hand. He motioned for the guards to unlock the door.

Grizzly stepped back from the door and and drew Athena with him.

"Greetings," Gat said as he entered, all smiles. "Reptilian asked me to stop by."

"When do we get to meet Reptilian?" Grizzly inquired. "I was hoping we would before this."

"Reptilian has been busy with the preparations for the games," Gat replied. "He sends his regards."

"When will we be allowed out of our cell?" Grizzly queried.

"Not for a while, I'm afraid," Gat said. "Reptilian is still not convinced you can be trusted."

"What can I do to convince him?"

"Reptilian has a test in mind for you," Gat stated. "You must prove yourself to his satisfaction. He was most disappointed when you refused to eat your burgers."

"I don't much like humans," Grizzly said, "but I've never eaten one before."

"Try them. You'll like them," Gat assured him.

A biting retort was on the tip of Athena's tongue, but she held her peace. Grizzly had explained to her the necessity of not antagonizing the Reptiloids, not if they wanted to acquire their trust.

"What is this about a test?" Grizzly asked.

Gat smiled. "You will see. Very shortly."

"Any word on the other Force members?" Grizzly inquired politely.

"Why should you care?" Gat responded. "They are your enemies. You must never forget that."

Grizzly surreptitiously glanced at the cell door. Both of the guards were leaning against the far wall, pikes in hand, conversing. Gat was standing slightly to the right of the doorway.

"Reptilian is a patient mutant," Gat was saying, "but his patience has limits. Don't take forever making up your mind."

"Tell me," Grizzly urged. "Why is it so important for me to wholeheartedly embrace your cause? Why is Reptilian going to so much trouble to convert me?"

"Because of the propaganda value," Gat divulged. "You've lived among the humans. You've accepted their way of life. But if we can turn you around, if we can make you see the light, your conversion will help to convince other mutants living with our hated enemy. We know there are other mutants living in the Civilized Zone and elsewhere. Even a few of the leaders of the New Order harbor secret sympathies for the humans. We want you to tell them the truth. Tell them about the miserable treatment mutants receive at the hands of the bigoted humans. Tell them about the prejudice you have faced. Tell them the humans are a vile, wicked race, who deserve to be subjugated. Humans are only good for one thing; to function as slaves."

Athena couldn't keep quiet any longer. "Slaves? Why can't humans and mutants live as friends?"

"It will never happen," Gat asserted. "Think back on your human history. Human beings have never been able to live in peace with their own kind, let alone another species. The white race came close to destroying the red race and enslaved the black. The blacks despised the whites. The yellow race distrusted everyone." He laughed. "If humanity could not live at peace with itself, how in the hell do you expect your species to live in peace with us?"

"We've learned from our mistakes," Athena said. "As a race, we've finally learned the value of peace."

Gat shook his head, smirking. "We must not live on the same planet. Where on this world is your race at peace? The Russians control a section of what was once the eastern United States, and they are locked in a life-or-death struggle with your Freedom Federation."

"You know about the Freedom Federation?" Athena inquired in surprise.

Grizzly took a casual step toward the doorway.

"Of course," Gat answered her. "We have contacts in the black market and elsewhere who keep us informed. And the major we captured, Enright, told us a lot before he died."

Athena knew about Enright; General Gallagher had provided details of the major's doomed reconnaissance run prior to their meeting with Blade. "Enright is dead?"

"Yes," Gat verified, smacking his lips. "And he was quite tasty, I must admit."

Grizzly took another step in the direction of the doorway. He was now three feet from Gat, five from the door.

Athena bowed her head. "This is like a living nightmare," she muttered.

"Did I upset you?" Gat asked facetiously. "My! What a pity!"

Grizzly draped his hands at his sides.

"Well, I must be off," Gat said. "I don't want to miss too many of the contests."

"Will we get to see any of these contests?" Grizzly asked.

"Yes, you will," Gat replied, grinning wickedly. "Very soon, in fact."

"Before you go," Grizzly stated, "there's something I'd like to say to you."

"What is it?" Gat inquired hopefully. "Have you come to your senses at last? Are you ready to pledge your loyalty to the mutant cause?"

"What I have to say is this," Grizzly said, taking one more

stride, speaking softly. His features abruptly hardened. "You are, without a doubt, one of the most suck-egg sons of bitches I've ever met. If you expect me to turn against the Force, forget it, chump! When I joined up, I gave my word to serve for one year, to take on any threats to the Freedom Federation. My word may not mean much to you, shit-for-brains, but it means everything to me. If you don't keep your word, whether you're a mutant or a human, then you're not worth beans as a person. Of course, I wouldn't expect a scumbag like you to understand that."

Gat's lips were moving but he couldn't seem to find his voice. "You dare!" he finally bellowed.

The two guards in the corridor ceased their discussion and straightened.

"I will inform Reptilian of your allegiance to the humans," Gat told Grizzly. "I will recommend immediate execution."

Alerted by Gat's tone of voice, the pair of guards came toward the cell to see what was happening.

Grizzly raised his hands to waist high. "I don't think so."

"What?" Gat said.

"I don't think you're going to live long enough to tell Reptilian anything," Grizzly stated grimly, his hands rising to his chest.

Gat was clearly perplexed by Grizzly's confidence. "Don't try anything!" he warned. "The odds are three to one."

Grizzly grinned. "Which means I have the edge."

The two guards walked over to the cell door.

Gat glanced at them, and reassured by their presence he made bold to taunt Grizzly. "I knew it! I knew you couldn't be trusted!"

"I didn't fool you for a minute, did I?" Grizzly asked sarcastically.

"Not for a minute!" Gat replied belligerently.

"Sure I didn't," Grizzly said contemptuously, then sighed. "Well, I guess we've said all that needs to be said. Suppose we get right down to cases."

Gat gripped his pike with both hands. "Don't even think it!"

Ignoring the Prefect, Grizzly looked at Athena. "When I cut loose, don't move. Stay right where you are."

Gat snickered. "Cut loose? What the hell do you mean, cut loose?"

Grizzly beamed and held his hands out, palms inward. "Just

this." He slowly uncurled his fingers until his digits were fully extended, and as he tensed his hand muscles, as he locked his fingers in place, his claws snapped out, sliding from the hidden sheaths in his fingers and protruding from under the flaps behind his fingernails.

"What the . . . !" Gat exclaimed at the sight of the five-inch claws and lowering the tip of his pike.

Grizzly suddenly crouched and growled, his hands dropping to his sides. He took a menacing step toward the Prefect.

Gat reacted by taking a stride backward, inadvertently putting himself in the doorway between Grizzly and the guards.

"I noticed someone did a number on you," Grizzly said in a guttural tone. "I'm going to finish the job!"

Gat hissed and jabbed his pike at his foe.

Transfixed by the tableau, Athena watched with baited breath as Grizzly went into action. She saw him easily sidestep the pike thrust and close on Gat. Grizzly speared his right hand up and in, and those deadly claws of his ripped into Gat's throat below the chin, angled upwards.

Gat's red eyes widened in stark stupefaction.

Grizzly, his claws buried to the fingernails in the Prefect's throat, added insult to injury. "Just as I thought!" he declared scornfully. "You're a wimp!"

Gat dropped the pike and grasped at Grizzly's right hand, but he was unable to sustain his grip. Green blood was pouring from his ravaged neck, a virtual torrent. He gasped and gawked at Grizzly, his eyelids fluttering.

The guards were trying to enter the cell, but they were stymied because Grizzly was holding the Prefect's body as a shield in the doorway. They couldn't see Grizzly's claws in Gat's neck; they mistakenly believed Grizzly had hold of the Prefect's neck. Their misimpression was rudely shattered when the guard on the right glanced down and observed the Prefect's blood spilling onto the floor. "Prefect!" he shouted, and tried to shove past Gat's body.

Grizzly yanked his claws free and shoved, sending the Prefect staggering backwards into the guards. One of the guards caught the Prefect under the shoulders and eased Gat to the corridor floor while the second attacked.

Athena, as always, was dazzled by Grizzly's speed. He dodged the second guard's pike and brought his left hand up, his arm a streak as he imbedded his claws in the guard's eyes, then raked them to the right.

With a terrified screech, the Reptiloid released his pike and placed his hands over the ragged furrow where his eyes had been a moment before. He uttered a sobbing sound and stumbled to the left.

Grizzly finished the hapless Reptiloid off with two quick swipes across the guard's neck. Gurgling and gushing blood, the Reptiloid collapsed.

"Look out!" Athena cried as the other guard charged through the doorway.

Grizzly, watching the dying Reptiloid sprawl onto its abdomen, almost lost his life. The other guard's pike grazed his chest as he twisted aside, drawing a thin line of blood. Unable to check his pell-mell lunge, the Reptiloid swung his shaft at Grizzly's head. Grizzly ducked under the blow and rammed both arms forward, imbedding both sets of claws in the guard's stomach. With his massive shoulder muscles heaving, he swept his arms upward, opening the Reptiloid from the navel to the sternum.

Athena grimaced as the Reptiloid's internal organs oozed from the cavity.

"No!" the guard wailed, his horrified gaze riveted to his stomach. "No!"

"Yes, sucker!" Grizzly snapped.

The Reptiloid clutched at his organs in a vain attempt to tuck them inside his body. But the slimy jumble of tubelike intestines and other organs slipped through his fingers. He tottered and tossed his pike aside. "No!" he said weakly.

Grizzly glanced at Athena. "This is it! Let's go!" He ran from the cell.

Athena took a last look at the gutted Reptiloid as the creature sagged to the floor, then she took off after her companion.

Grizzly was ten feet away to the right. "Come on!" he goaded her. "Don't be a slowpoke!"

Athena's left foot bumped something and she gazed downward. Gat was on his back, his hands on his chest, his eyes open but empty.

"Come on!" Grizzly prompted.

Athena nodded and jogged after him as he led her down the

corridor to a door which she opened. "It's a stairwell! Which way?"

"Gat told us the Arena is on the lowest level," Grizzly reminded her. "That's where we should find the others." He started down.

Athena followed. They descended two levels when Grizzly abruptly halted.

"Sssshhh!" he cautioned her.

Athena listened but could hear nothing.

"Someone is coming up these stairs," Grizzly informed her. "Come on." He nodded at the door and waited impatiently as she opened it. "Quickly!"

They sprinted along the hallway for dozens of yards.

Athena happened to glance to her right, and the word she read on a sign on a closed door brought her up short. "Grizzly!"

Grizzly stopped and turned. "What?"

"Look!" Athena exclaimed.

Grizzly stared at the door, reading the sign. ARMORY. He grinned and stepped to her side. "Just what the doctor ordered."

Athena looked in both directions. "Why aren't there any guards?"

Grizzly shrugged. "Who knows? Maybe they're all down in the Arena watching the games. Maybe they don't post guards here. Maybe they've become complacent because the humans have never revolted. Who gives a damn? He grabbed at the doorknob, forgetting his claws were fully extended. When his fingers were rigid and his claws out, he was unable to use his hands for any other purpose than ripping and slashing. He could not bend his hand or employ his fingers for gripping objects. Only after he relaxed his digits, after his claws were automatically retracted, could he use his fingers to hold anything. "Damn!" he muttered as his claws raked the door.

"Allow me," Athena offered, seizing the knob and trying to turn it. "It's locked!" she informed him.

"Stand back," Grizzly directed. He took a pace backwards, then brought his right leg up, delivering a shattering kick alongside the doorknob.

The door shook but held fast. It was obviously reinforced.

"Someone will hear!" Athena stated apprehensively.

."Let them!" Grizzly declared. He kicked the door a second time and was thwarted again.

"You're making too much noise!" Athena protested.

"You need a weapon," Grizzly told her. "Unless you plan to use spitballs against the Reptiloids." He kicked the door a third time.

A fracture appeared next to the knob, six inches in length and a quarter of an inch wide.

"We're almost there!" Grizzly gloated.

"What's that?" Athena queried anxiously, glancing at the door at the other end of the hall, believing she had heard an indistinct sound.

She had.

Reptiloids were surging through the door at the end of the hall, all of them armed with pikes. Six. Eight. Ten. Fourteen. She lost count. "Grizzly!" she cried, distraught.

Grizzly kicked the door a final time. The fracture widened and lengthened but the door did not open.

"Grizzly!" Athena shouted, backing against the wall.

Enraged beyond his endurance, Grizzly faced the charging Reptiloids, raised his arms above his head, and roared his defiant challenge.

CHAPTER SEVENTEEN

Blade walked with his head bowed, his eyes downcast, behind the captain of the escort to his cell.

Captain Tur looked over his left shoulder at the prisoner and snickered. "Look at this wretch!" he stated for the benefit of his ten companions following Blade. "A superb example of Homo sapiens!"

Several of the Reptiloids laughed.

"Yes, sir," commented one of them. "They are saps. That's for sure."

More laughter.

They were walking up a stairwell, their captive a study in misery. Not one of them entertained the slightest notion their prisoner would cause them any trouble. He was too depressed, perhaps on the verge of an emotional collapse. Or so they reasoned.

But they were wrong.

Blade prepared himself. He estimated they were about four levels below the ground floor, below the cell block. The stairwell bothered him; although he wasn't positive, he doubted it was the same stairwell he had used before. The placement of the lanterns seemed to be different. How many stairwells were there in the Imperium? he speculated. Probably a large number. The Imperium was huge, a maze of corridors and rooms. But he should be able to find his way down to the Arena without any difficulty after rescuing the others. He . . .

Wait a minute!

Blade almost gave himself away, almost snapped his head up in consternation, but he suppressed the impulse. Maybe he was making a mistake! He planned to scour the cells above, find the Force members, then descend to the Arena and kill Reptilian at all costs. Reptilian was, as General Gallagher had said, the brains behind the operation. If Reptilian died, the New Order might very well come unglued. Without a forceful leader, any organization ultimately decayed and disintegrated.

But what if he was wrong?

What if Boone, Thunder, and Havoc were not in one of the cells? What if they were being held somewhere in the Arena, awaiting their next contest? Would the Reptiloids go to all the bother to take them all the way up to the cells between bouts? The prospect was not very likely. Still, searching the cells would not be a complete waste of time. Grizzly and Athena must be in one of them.

He hoped.

Captain Tur unexpectedly turned and prodded the giant with his pike. "Move your ass, human! We want to see the games!"

Blade gazed down at the point of the pike pressing against his stomach and exploded. He gripped the shaft below the point and wrenched, jerking the pike from Captain Tur's hands. With a savage swipe he rammed the butt end of the shaft into Tur's throat, then twirled the pike, swinging the tip outward, and spun.

The Reptiloids on the stairs below took a second to galvanize themselves. The first one mindlessly lunged at the Warrior and received the business end of the pike in his right eye for his effort. He screamed as the point penetrated his brain, and then he was flung backwards, his consciousness fading as his body collided with those below.

Three of the Reptiloids went down in a chain reaction, sprawling onto the stairs. The rest charged.

Blade met them with a grin creasing his features. His gray eyes sparkled as he avoided a pike and stabbed his own into the neck of a mutant. He wrested the tip free in time to block another blow, and retaliated with a sweep of his pike into the groin of one of his opponents.

The Reptiloid doubled over, screeching, and was knocked down the stairs by those striving to reach the Warrior.

Blade found the pike to be an exceptional weapon. Its length enabled him to keep the Reptiloids at bay; they didn't dare get too close for fear of being lanced. Conversely, his pike handily deflected their jabs. For a minute the conflict was in doubt, but he adroitly held his own.

One of the Reptiloids tried to stab the giant's right kneecap.

Blade dodged to the left to protect his knee and in so doing accidentally saved his life.

OUTLANDS STRIKE 153

There was the pad of rushing feet, and Captain Tur hurtled past the Warrior, narrowly missing him, flying through the space he had occupied but a fraction of a second before. Tur plummeted into his fellow mutants, bowling five of them over. Two of them lost their footing and sailed over the railing, shrieking as they fell.

Suddenly Blade had the upper hand.

Only one of the guards had retained his footing. The rest were struggling to disentangle themselves and scramble erect.

With a prodigious bound Blade was among them. He smashed the shaft of his pike into the Reptiloid still standing and sent the mutant tumbling down the stairs. Two more of the Reptiloids were speared in the face before they could get to their feet. Another mutant did rise, and promptly received the pike tip in his jugular.

Captain Tur was on his hands and knees, shaking his head, dazed.

The last Reptiloid stood with his pike in his right hand.

Blade took a stride and kicked Tur in the mouth. The captain collapsed. Blade was about to plant his pike in Tur's neck when he detected a motion out of the corner of his eyes and whirled.

Just as the last guard hurled his pike.

Blade tried to throw himself to the right to avoid the gleaming point, but he wasn't entirely successful. He felt the pike bite into his left shoulder and an intense pain shot through him. The tip gouged an inch-deep groove in his flesh, scraping the bone and tearing his black leather vest, but the force of the Reptiloid's toss propelled the pike ten feet past him. Blade instantly retaliated by flinging his pike, with better results.

The Reptiloid was scanning the stairs for another pike he could use when the Warrior's weapon caught him in the chest. He was flung backwards by the impact and clattered and thudded down the stairs.

Blade sagged against the railing, his shoulder throbbing, blood flowing from the wound, abruptly dizzy. He surveyed the stair-well, expecting another attack, but none of the Reptiloids were moving.

He'd done it!

Blade inspected his injury, frowning at the sight of the jagged tissue. The blood flow was not very great, indicating the pike had missed a vital vein or artery. He couldn't afford to expend precious time doctoring the wound now. It would have to wait.

First things first.

Blade walked to a fallen pike and retrieved the weapon. Grimacing in discomfort, he headed up the stairs toward the ground level. He would need to search each and every cell to find Grizzly and Athena. If only he knew where the armory Prine had told him about was located! With his left shoulder injured, his effectiveness in combat would be diminished. He flexed the fingers of his left hand, pleased his dexterity was not impaired.

But could he use a pike with the injured arm?

Blade halted and took hold of the shaft with both hands. He tried a few tentative swings. His left shoulder twinged with pangs of agony, but he could use his arm if necessary. Satisfied, he gripped the pike in his right hand and resumed his ascent.

What was that?

He was on the third-level landing when he heard the harsh clamor coming from the corridor beyond the landing door.

Voices were shouting.

There were screams and cries of torment.

What was going on?

Blade cautiously stepped to the door and gingerly opened it a crack.

A savage fracas greeted his wondering gaze.

A battle royal was being waged at the far end of the corridor between Grizzly and a detail of Reptiloids. Seven or eight of the lizard-men were down, and the rest were trying to impale Grizzly on their pikes. The confines of the corridor prevented them from rushing him all at once, so they came at him two or three at a time. Grizzly's claws parried thrust after thrust, and if a Reptiloid miscalculated and came a little too close, he ripped him open.

Athena stood against the hall wall midway between the stairwell Blade was in and the fight raging at the opposite end.

Blade threw the door open and raced toward them. Grizzly's back was to him, but several of the Reptiloids saw him approaching and renewed their efforts to slay Grizzly.

Athena, engrossed in watching the brutal brawl, did not realize anyone else was in the corridor until a heavy hand fell on her right shoulder. She involuntarily jumped and turned, relief washing over her features. "Blade!"

"Stay here!" Blade directed, and started to go to Grizzly's aid.

"Wait!" Athena cried, clutching his arm. "Look!" she said, pointing at the ARMORY door.

Blade paused. The armory! He glanced at Grizzly, noting the mutant was holding his own, at least for the moment. But the Reptiloids threatened to overwhelm him at any second.

"We've got to help him!" Athena urged.

Blade gazed at the armory door, noticing the cracks.

"Grizzly tried to kick it in!" Athena told him.

Blade leaned the pike against the wall and reached for the knob, intending to batter the door down, but his fingertips merely brushed the doorknob and the door unexpectedly swung inward. Blade hurried inside.

Athena followed, glancing at the lock. The inner side of the jamb in which the lock was imbedded was hanging in strips. Grizzly's last kick must have shattered it! She looked up, almost bumping into Blade.

The Warrior had stopped a few feet in the chamber. The armory was plunged in darkness, the light from the hallway revealing a few crates and the vague outline of gun racks.

Athena recalled seeing several lanterns in the corridor. "I'll be right back!" she declared, and ran out.

Blade moved toward the gun racks, his keen eyes probing the gloom. He needed something with firepower, and he needed it quickly. His left knee bumped against the edge of a wooden crate.

Damn!

Bright light illuminated the chamber as Athena suddenly returned, bearing one of the hall lanterns in her right hand.

Blade spied a table to his right, his eyes narrowing as he recognized the items piled on top of it. All of the guns and backpacks confiscated by the Reptiloids were spread out upon the table!

"Hurry!" Athena goaded him.

Blade reached the table in two strides. He scooped up the M60, found an ammo belt, and fed the ammunition into the machine gun.

Athena dashed over. "Can I help?"

Blade grabbed an M-16 and tossed the weapon to her.

Athena caught the M-16 with her left hand, deposited the lantern on the table, and swiftly checked the magazine. "Loaded," she said.

"On me," Blade stated, running from the armory, Athena on his heels.

Grizzly was in trouble. A Reptiloid with a nasty gash on its neck had its arms wrapped around his ankles and was holding on for dear life. Encumbered by the lizard-man clinging to his legs, Grizzly was on the verge of going down. He was twisted sideways, blood seeping from a half-dozen lacerations, his claws countering pike after pike.

One of the Reptiloids prepared to let fly with a pike.

"Grizzly!" Blade bellowed. "Down!"

Grizzly cast a fleeting glance in the direction of the Warrior and flattened, diving away from the Reptiloids, still ensnared by the lizard-man with the injured neck.

Blade cut loose with the big M60, the machine gun thundering, the gun bucking against his side.

Athena joined in with the M-16.

Caught with nowhere to take cover, the Reptiloids were decimated. The M60's heavy slugs tore through their bodies, stitching them with holes, blowing out large chunks of flesh from their backs. Torso after torso erupted in a geyser of green fluid and blasted tissue. The rounds from the M-16 added to the carnage. Many of the lizard-men shrieked in torment or anger as they were perforated. A few tried to flee, to retreat to the far stairwell, but they were mowed down before they could manage two strides.

Blade kept firing until the floor was littered with the dead and dying. He eased up on the trigger, his ears ringing.

Athena ceased shooting. "That felt good," she commented.

Blade walked toward Grizzly. "Are you okay?"

Grizzly tried to rise, a look of astonishment flitting across his face as he realized he was still being held about the ankles. He looked down at the Reptiloid holding his legs.

The lizard-man was wheezing, green blood spraying from its neck.

Grizzly brought both arms around and down, burying his claws in the Reptiloid's head, one hand near each ear.

With a protracted gasp the lizard-man went limp, his arms dropping to the floor.

Grizzly jumped to his feet, a sneer on his lips. "Serves you right, sucker! Nobody manhandles me."

Blade reached Grizzly's side. "Are you okay?" he reiterated.

Grizzly glanced up, grinning. "Never been better."

Athena hurried over. "You're hurt!" she exclaimed, staring at the crimson coating his chest.

"A few pricks, is all," Grizzly said. "It's nothing."

"You should be bandaged!" Athena persisted.

"There's no time for that," Blade declared brusquely. "We must find Boone, Havoc, and Thunder." He scrutinized the heap of Reptiloid forms. "We're going to pay these bastards back for everything they've done!"

Grizzly beamed. "Now you're talking!"

"What about Kraft, Clayboss, and Rivera?" Athena asked. "You didn't mention them."

Blade gazed at her and sadly shook his head.

Athena's mouth went slack. "Kraft too?"

"I saw him killed," Blade detailed. "In the Arena."

Grizzly held his gore-encrusted claws aloft. "I can't wait to meet up with more Reptiloids!"

"Back to the armory," Blade ordered, wheeling and going back in.

Grizzly knelt and wiped his claws clean on the pants leg of one of the deceased lizard-men. He slowly relaxed his fingers and his claws slid from view.

"I'm sorry," Athena apologized as Grizzly stood.

"For what?"

"I wasn't much help to you," Athena said. "I stood there and watched instead of trying to get into the armory. The door was busted and I didn't even know it."

"It's no big deal," Grizzly said.

Athena frowned. "I'm not doing very well on this mission. I thought I would be able to face anything after my Ranger training. I guess I was wrong."

"Hey!" Blade shouted, standing next to the armory door. "What are you waiting for? World War Four? Get over here right now!" He stepped back into the armory.

"What's gotten into him?" Athena queried as she hastened to comply.

"I don't know," Grizzly admitted. "But I like the change. He's pissed off about something. I have a feeling we're going to see a side of Blade we've never seen before."

"How do you mean?" Athena inquired.

"Wait and see," Grizzly replied.

Blade was sorting through the gear on the table. He discovered his Bowies in their sheaths and snatched them up. Moving rapidly, he unfastened his belt, aligned a Bowie over each hip, secured his belt, then drew the knives. They glittered in the lantern light. "If I'd had these earlier," he declared, "Kraft might still be alive."

"How do we play this?" Grizzly asked.

Blade faced them, sheathing his Bowies. "We're going to finish the job we were sent to do." He scanned the armory, noting crate after crate of explosives. "We're going to destroy this hellhole and put an end to Reptilian's insane ambition."

"Do you have a plan?" Athena questioned hopefully.

Blade nodded. "I have a plan." He looked from one to the other. "But I want one thing understood."

"What?" Athena responded.

Blade's features changed, becoming uncharacteristically, shockingly sinister. "Reptilian is mine!" he stated in a gravelly tone.

Athena did a double take. She had never seen this aspect of the giant's nature before.

Grizzly chuckled. "Now you're talking! Let's party!"

CHAPTER EIGHTEEN

"How much longer, do you think?" Boone asked.

"How should I know?" Sergeant Havoc snapped. "Your guess is as good as mine."

"He was only asking," Thunder interceded on Boone's behalf. "Why are you so angry at him?"

They were in a holding room located under the stands, not more than 20 yards from the Arena floor. Periodically they heard the roar of the crowd, the clapping and the cheering. Three trays of untouched food rested on a wooden bench situated to the right of the barred wall fronting the corridor to the Arena.

Sergeant Havoc sighed, gazing at Boone. "I'm sorry. I can't seem to control my temper. All I can think of is Kraft. I keep seeing that pike going through his chest!"

Boone and Thunder exchanged glances. They were standing near the bars. Havoc was leaning against the wall eight feet away, next to the bench.

"You can't blame yourself for what happened," Boone said.

Havoc's self-torture was transparent. He slowly shook his head. "Who else can I blame? I was the one who kicked the stuffing out of him. My beating hurt him, slowed him down enough for the gladiator to kill him."

"You don't know that," Boone disagreed. "Kraft was out of it ever since he ate those burgers. Like always, his big mouth got him into trouble. And remember, Kraft didn't possess your skill at hand-to-hand combat. Without his switchblade he wasn't much of a fighter." Boone paused, reflecting for a moment. "For that matter, without my Hombres I'm not all that great either."

Sergeant Havoc frowned. "I'll never forgive myself for what I did."

Thunder stared at the noncom. "If Kraft's time on this world was over, there was nothing you could have done to prevent his dying. We all have our alloted spans. When the Spirit calls you home, you must go."

"I'm not a fatalist," Havoc mentioned. "I believe we make our own destiny."

"To a limited degree, perhaps," Thunder said. "But my people know all life is ruled by the Spirit-In-All-Things. The Spirit rules in the affairs of men, guiding us, teaching us. And when our time is up, we head for the higher realms. The Spirit always prevails."

"So whose side is the Spirit on?" Havoc queried angrily. "Ours or Reptilians?"

Before Thunder could reply, a Reptiloid appeared on the other side of the bars. "You have five minutes," he announced, and departed.

Sergeant Havoc straightened and walked to the bars. "Good. I'm tired of waiting."

"What will they pit us against this time?" Boone wondered.

"I don't care what it is," Havoc said. "Just so I get a crack at Reptilian."

"Reptilian?" Boone scrutinized the noncom. "How do you plan to do it? Reptilian will be up on that platform. What is it? Ten feet high?"

"I'll find a way," Sergeant Havoc vowed.

"Just find a way to stay alive," Boone advised.

"Blade will find a way to help us," Thunder predicted.

Sergeant Havoc laughed, a short, bitter sound. "Blade? He'll sit on his butt and watch us die, just like he did with Kraft."

"Let's not start that again," Boone said.

They lapsed into an awkward silence, awaiting the lizard-men. Several minutes elapsed.

Boone broke the quiet. "We don't have much time, so there's something I'd like to say." He gazed at Thunder, then Havoc. "I know some of us haven't always seen eye to eye—"

"There's an understatement!" Havoc mumbled.

"But I've enjoyed being on the Force," Boone went on. "These past three months I've come to know each of you fairly well. In the Cavalry we place a high value on honor and respect. You are two of the most honorable men I've ever met and I respect both of you highly."

"The feeling is mutual," Thunder said.

Sergeant Havoc shifted uncomfortably. "I like you guys too. You're not very military, but we can't all be perfect." He cracked a smile for the first time in hours.

"Here they come," Thunder declared, gazing down the corridor.

Twelve lizard-men marched up to the cell and posted themselves outside, their pikes leveled.

"Are you ready for round two?" the head of the detail inquired, producing a key from his left pants pocket.

"What's it going to be this time?" Sergeant Havoc inquired. "Gladiators? Wild beasts? Scuzzy mutants like you?"

The head of the detail grinned, opening the cell door. "I don't want to spoil the surprise. Reptilian has a treat in store for you."

"Do we get to fight Reptilian?" Havoc asked hopefully.

The lizard-man motioned for them to exit the cell. "No," he replied. "Reptilian does not need to prove himself in petty combat. This time you will face another of the Arena favorites."

"I hope the fans won't be disappointed when we win," Havoc declared.

"Dream on, human," the lizard-man stated. He waved them along the corridor.

The three men walked toward a wide door at the end of the hall.

"I lost a bet on your first bout," the Reptiloid remarked as the lizard-men tramped after the trio. "I won't lose on this one."

"Care to make a bet?" Havoc asked.

The Reptiloid laughed.

Boone, Havoc, and Thunder halted six feet from the door. Four of the lizard-man walked around them and unfastened a pair of metal bolts, then shoved the door open. The ominous glare of the Arena spilled into the corridor.

Sergeant Havoc squinted as he stepped outside. "Here we go again," he muttered.

Boone and Thunder advanced slowly. The door closed to their rear.

A ripple of applause stirred the audience as the Force members appeared.

"Sounds like we've got some fans," Havoc remarked stiffly.

"Greetings!" boomed a voice above them.

They turned and gazed upward.

Reptilian stood on the royal platform, a mocking smile upturning his lips.

"Where's Blade?" Boone asked anxiously. "I don't see Blade."

"He is not up there," Thunder confirmed.

"Hey, ugly!" Sergeant Havoc shouted. "Where's Blade?"

Reptilian placed his hands on his hips and glowered at the noncom. "Your overrated leader could not stand the sight of blood. He is sulking in his cell until the games are concluded."

Boone leaned toward Havoc. "He's not telling the truth."

"Don't you think I know it?" Sergeant Havoc responded.

Reptilian indicated the stands with a sweep of his left arm. "We trust you will be as entertaining as you were previously. I have arranged a suitable challenge to test your skills and courage."

"Let me guess!" Havoc baited the mutant. "We fight your mother!"

Reptilian's blue eyes became slits of wrath. "Your insolence will cost you, human. It will cost you dearly."

"Promises! Promises!" Havoc retorted.

"Let us see if you are so arrogant after you meet your adversary!" Reptilian declared. He gestured with his right arm.

A door to the right of the trio opened.

"You two stay behind me," Sergeant Havoc advised the frontiersman and the Flathead.

"We can take care of ourselves," Boone said.

"I'm the martial-arts ace here, not you," Havoc reminded him. "Let me take on whatever it is. You can be my backup."

"We're a unit, a team," Boone stated. "We'll take on whatever it is together."

A bulky figure stomped into the Arena.

"Good Lord!" Boone exclaimed.

"What is it?" Thunder inquired.

"I don't know," Sergeant Havoc said, "but I don't like it."

Their foe was a repulsive monstrosity displaying a variety of hybrid traits. It was essentially humanoid, with two legs and two arms. But what legs and arms! The limbs on the creature were as thick as the trunk of a towering tree, rippling with muscles and power. Its squat body was clothed in a tattered deer hide from its broad shoulders to its wide hips. A brown leather cord girded the garment at the waist. Its legs and feet were naked. The facial features were particularly arresting: a low, sloping forehead under a shaggy mane of black hair; two dark eyes under bushy brows; prominent cheeks and extremely bulbous lips; a square chin; and a pair of pointed ears.

"I've never seen anything like it!" Boone said.

"Reminds me of a blind date I had once," Sergeant Havoc quipped.

"It doesn't have a weapon," Thunder noted.

"It doesn't need one," Boone said.

The creature shifted to face them.

"Gentlemen!" Reptilian yelled down. "I would like to introduce you to Narg."

Havoc glanced up. "Great name! What'd you do? Pick the letters out of a hat?"

"Did you expect us to use mundane human names?" Reptilian retorted.

"Reptilian sounds mundane to me!" Havoc said, ridiculing the mutant leader.

"Reptilian is not my given name," the Reptiloid declared. "I selected it because of the fear the name instills. It is my title. My given name, the name my parents bestowed upon me, is Sauga. We are in the process of developing an official Reptiloid language. One day, our language will supplant English, Spanish, and every other human tongue. Wait and see."

"You mean I'll get to live that long?" Havoc taunted.

Reptilian smirked. "You should be so fortunate!" He stared at the creature. "Narg! Kill!"

The hybrid shuffled toward them as a man in black shut the door.

"Let me take him," Havoc said. Before the others could object, he dashed forward.

"Havoc! Wait!" Boone cried.

Sergeant Havoc was not in any mood to wait. Here was a golden opportunity to vent his accumulated anger, his seething resentment. He reached full speed, his eyes on the creature, amazed the thing wasn't making a move to defend itself.

Narg plodded toward the humans, seemingly oblivious to any danger they might pose.

Havoc grinned in expectation of an easy victory. He would show Reptilian!

"Havoc!" Boone shouted.

Sergeant Havoc came within ten feet of the hybrid and tensed his leg muscles. Eight feet. Six feet. He uttered a piercing kiai and launched himself into the air, performing a flawless Yoko-tobi-geri, a flying side kick, his right foot extended, his left tucked under his crotch. The maneuver, delivered by a master, could kill.

Havoc was such a master.

Narg was wrenched to the left by the impact as the heel of the noncom's combat boot slammed into his left cheek.

Havoc, expecting the creature to be rendered unconscious, suffered a rude awakening. His left boot glanced off Narg's cheek and he alighted in the cat stance three feet to the right of the hybrid.

Narg growled, revealing sawlike teeth.

Confounded by his failure, Havoc gaped at the creature's cheek, at the split skin and the flowing blood. Was that all? His best shot, and all he had accomplished was to inflict a minor cut?

Snarling, Narg suddenly whipped his right arm outward, striking with astonishing swiftness for one so heavy, his knuckles catching the noncom on the chin and sending Havoc catapulting backwards to sprawl in the dust.

"Kill him!" Reptilian goaded from the platform.

Havoc was on his stomach, motionless.

Narg took a step toward the human. His dull mind was slow to register the sensation of hands encircling his ankles from the rear. He felt those hands tugging on his legs, and he dimly realized the other two humans had attacked him from behind.

"Now!" Boone yelled, and strained his shoulder muscles to the utmost, his fingers locked on the creature's right ankle.

Thunder, applying his arms to the same task on the left ankle, grunted and heaved.

Together they succeeded where Havoc had not.

Narg voiced a rumbling growl as he abruply pitched onto his face. He placed his palms on the dirt and tried to rise.

Boone leaped onto the creature's back and wrapped his left arm around Narg's squat neck. He squeezed, hoping to choke the hybrid to death.

To Narg, the assault was scarcely worth noticing, the feeble attempt of a human flea to do him harm. He simply stood with the human clinging to his back, then unexpectedly bent forward at the waist.

Boone, unable to keep his grip, flew over the creature's head and smacked onto the ground. Intense pain lanced his left shoulder as he struck. He rolled and rose to his knees, clutching his injured shoulder.

Narg, like a tireless engine of destruction, closed in.

"Ho!" Thunder shouted, waving his arms to attract the creature. "Take me!"

Narg hesitated, distracted by the commotion.

"Take me!" Thunder repeated, backing away.

The Reptiloids and humans in the stands were cheering Narg on, certain their favorite could slay the outsiders.

"Me!" Thunder bellowed at the top of his lungs to make himself heard above the audience. "Me!"

Narg pivoted and lumbered after the Indian. He would finish off the others in a bit. First he must attend to the noisy one.

Thunder backpedaled to put more distance between the creature and his friends. He covered 15 yards and stopped, squatting on his haunches.

Narg shambled after the Indian, eager to end the battle and return to his peaceful cell where no one tried to hurt him and he was fed regularly. He disliked the bright lights of the Arena, the tumult and the violence.

"Ho!" Thunder called. "Come to me, demon!"

Narg was within eight feet of the human when his brain belatedly noted several strange details. Why wasn't the Indian running? Why was he crouched there, waiting to be caught? Why were his hands playing in the dirt? None of this behavior made any sense. Narg was accustomed to humans who fled, or else they fought with the desperation of the soldier with the fancy feet. They never just sat there, playing in the dirt. He halted.

Thunder's eyes narrowed. "Come to me, demon!"

Narg hesitated, confused.

"Are you afraid of me, demon?" Thunder asked. "Do you fear me because the Spirit-In-All-Things is in me?"

Narg had never been afraid in his life, but he did not like being made fun of, and he suspected this Indian was mocking him. Doing what all humans invariably did to him. His years in the wilderness of central Oregon had taught him to mistrust all humans. They either wanted to harm him or poke fun at him. Only the Reptiloids had treated him differently, had treated him with respect. A Hunter Squad had found him, had downed him after using seven darts. When he had awakened, Reptilian had been at his side. The Reptiloid leader had assured him

that he had found a home at last. He was a mutant, like the
Reptiloids. He was welcome to live with them, to be treated as an
equal. All Reptilian had wanted was one service: Narg was to go
to the Arena every so often and punish the bad humans Reptilian
had captured.

And now this bad human was making fun of him!

"Come, demon!" Thunder said again. "Come to me!"

Narg lumbered forward. He saw the Indian smile. How could
the Indian be so happy when he was about to die? He also saw the
Indian's hands in the dirt, and he was watching those hands when
they swept up, when they flung dirt directly into his eyes.
Annoyed, he stopped and wiped at his eyes. They were blurry,
filled with tears, and stinging terribly. He did not bother to hurry.
The Indian, after all, could not harm him. He was Narg, the
indistructible.

Or so he had been told by Reptilian.

Narg could feel the tiny grains of dirt smarting his eyes, and
then he felt something else, something very odd.

Someone was fiddling with the leather cord about his waist.

Why would anyone do that?

Narg dabbed at his eyes, the tears dissipating, his vision clearing.
He noticed the Indian was gone, then glanced down at his waist.

His belt was gone too!

Perplexed, Narg looked up. Why would anyone take his cord?
He liked that sturdy cord, had worn it for years. Who could have
taken it? The Indian?

A length of cord dropped over his head from the rear and
wrapped itself around his neck.

What was this? Narg reached up, feeling the cord constricting
tightly and biting into his skin. He tried to slip the fingers of his
right hand under the cord, but his fingers were too stubby, the
cord too taut. He became aware of someone standing behind him,
not touching him, just standing there, and he put two and two
together and perceived the Indian was trying to strangle him.

How interesting.

No one had ever tried this before.

Narg lashed his elbows backwards. The Indian, somehow,
avoided the blows.

This was a tricky Indian!

With the cord sinking deeper and deeper into his neck, Narg

scratched his chin and worked on a plan. He needed to be as tricky as the Indian. An idea occurred to him and he smiled. He reached behind his head and gripped the cord.

The Indian pulled harder.

Narg jerked on the cord again and again, but his mighty sinews were unable to dislodge the Indian. He released the cord and dropped his arms, stumped.

What next?

He remembered the one on his back, the one he had tossed to the ground, and he immediately doubled over, hoping to duplicate the results. The Indian stumbled into his backside, and he swept his arms behind him and snatched at the Indian's legs. His left hand seized a handful of material, but the Indian pulled free before he could obtain a firmer grip.

Meanwhile, the cord was squeezing ever tighter and tighter.

Narg was becoming concerned. There was a pain in his throat, and he was finding it difficult to breathe. He glanced up at the royal platform and spotted Reptilian, his only true friend. Smiling, he indicated the cord encircling his neck and beckoned for Reptilian to come to his assistance.

Incredibly, Reptilian laughed.

Reptilian laughed?

Narg's forehead furrowed as he gazed at the Reptiloid leader. Why was Reptilian laughing? Why didn't Reptilian help him? Was Reptilian making fun of him like all the others? His mind balked at the thought. There was one way to find out.

Ask Reptilian.

With single-minded determination, Narg walked toward the wall below the royal platform. He could feel the Indian yanking on the cord, and he ignored this trivial distraction, concentrating on Reptilian. A look of astonishment flickered over the Retiloid's features, to be replaced by unbridled fury.

Why was Reptilian so mad?

Narg came within ten feet of the wall and halted. The cord around his neck had gone slack. He saw Reptilian rise and speak to one of the guards, and the guard handed over his pike. "Reptilian!" Narg called. "Why did you laugh?"

Reptilian moved to the rim of the platform, the pike in his right hand. "Why did I what?" he snapped.

The crowd was silent, collectively puzzled by Narg's peculiar behavior.

"Why did you laugh at me?" Narg asked.

"Why haven't you killed them?" Reptilian rejoined. He scowled and shook his head. "I am very disappointed in you."

"You laughed at me," Narg persisted, his mind focused on the single issue to the exclusion of all else.

Reptilian sneered. "Of course I laughed at you, you moron! Did you really believe I would come into the Arena to help you?"

"Why not help me?" Narg queried, flustered.

"You really are pathetic, do you know that?" Reptilian said derisively. "You have the intelligence of a turnip! I supply you with a place to live and I ensure you receive all the food you need. Why? Because I want you to do me a teensy-weensy favor. All you have to do is punish the bad people in the Arena when I tell you to. But do you obey me? No. I'm beginning to think I'm wasting my time with you. Why should I go to so much trouble if you won't do as you're told?"

"I'm tired of fighting all the time," Narg said. "I don't want to hurt people. I want to be happy."

"Be dead," Reptilian declared, and hurled the pike.

Narg saw the pike arcing toward him, and had his reflexes been commensurate with his awesome brawn he might have evaded the gleaming death. As it was, the pike struck him in the center of the forehead and burst out the rear of his cranium. He tottered for a moment, confounded by the tremendous headache he was suddenly experiencing, and then toppled over.

Reptilian gazed at the lifeless hulk for a moment. "Imbecile!" he said irately, and then shifted his attention to the Force members.

Thunder was ten feet from Narg's corpse, looking at the body with a sad expression. Boone was rising to his feet, rubbing his left shoulder. Sergeant Havoc was on his hands and knees, his head hung low, not yet in full possession of his faculties.

"I am through toying with you!" Reptilian shouted. "You have won your second bout by default. But there will not be any rest this time. You will face your next opponents now." He paused, grinning gleefully. "Are you ready to die?"

And from across the Arena a deep voice responded to the question, a voice with a menacing edge. "Are you?"

Reptilian swiveled in the direction of the voice, his eyes

widening as he beheld the giant human in the black leather vest and the fatigue pants. It couldn't be! He was supposed to be in his cell! But there he stood, next to an open door in the far wall, armed to the teeth, a large machine gun cradled in his arms.

"Blade!" Reptilian hissed.

Blade leveled the M-60 and raked the stands with his flinty gaze, finally focusing on Reptilian. The corners of his mouth curled upwards as he spoke. "Dying time is here."

CHAPTER NINETEEN

For ten seconds the Arena was perfectly still. Reptilian glared his hatred at the Warrior. The human section of the audience didn't know what to make of the giant's abrupt appearance. The Reptiloids were disconcerted, recognizing the threat the armed human posed and waiting for their leader to command them to action, to give the word.

He did.

"Kill him!" Reptilian bellowed.

A lizard-man on the wall above the Warrior lifted his pike overhead.

"Look out!" Boone shouted.

Blade was already in motion, spinning and tilting the M60's barrel upward at the Reptiloids in the stands. He squeezed the trigger and held it down, the big machine gun bucking and blasting with indiscriminate abandon.

Seated in the open, yards from the nearest exits, the vast majority unarmed, the Reptiloids were the proverbial sitting ducks. Some of the lizard-men attempted to let fly with their pikes, but they were cut down before they could complete the throw. Those in the stands were shown no mercy. The rain of slugs tore their bodies apart, bursting a chest here, a neck there, downing them in droves.

"Get that son of a bitch!" Reptilian shrieked, gesturing at his personal guard.

The guards started to head around the Arena, using an aisle near the wall. They managed less than ten yards.

"Not so fast, you pansies!" said a husky voice above and behind them.

Reptilian and the guards spun.

He was standing nonchalantly near the blue door, the door to the corridor connecting the royal platform to the stairwell, grinning and wagging the barrel of an M-16 toward the guards. His chest fur was caked with dried blood, he wore a camouflage backpack, and a web belt containing spare clips encircled his waist. "Going somewhere?" he asked sarcastically.

"Grizzly!" Reptilian yelled angrily. "You're a traitor to your own kind!"

"Sticks and stones," Grizzly quipped, then crouched and fired.

"Get him!" Reptilian directed his personal guard, and they sprinted toward Grizzly, never considering for a moment the futility of pitting their pikes against an automatic rifle.

Reptilian was perched on the lip of the wall. He saw his guards falling before Grizzly's withering fire, and he saw Blade drilling the Reptiloids in the stands with the M60, and he knew he was in trouble. Still, his subjects overwhelmingly outnumbered the accursed giant and the bear-man, and sooner or later one of them would cast a pike and end the fray. There was no way two assassins could hold all of the Reptiloids at bay.

On the far side of the Arena dozens of Reptiloids were swarming over the wall, bearing down on Blade. He was forced to back up as he tried to prevent any of the lizard-men from getting within pike range.

Grizzly had killed over a dozen of Reptilian's personal guard, and still they came on. His back was to the blue door, the M-16 chattering.

Reptilian smiled.

Any moment now and it would all be over.

That was when a new element entered the battle. Athena Morris raced into the Arena through the door in the far wall, her arms laden with weapons and ammunition. She was heading in the direction of Boone, Thunder, and Sergeant Havoc.

Reptilian leaned forward, his lips compressing. Blade must have had all of this planned! While the giant kept his subjects in the stands busy, and Grizzly did likewise with the royal guard, the woman was going to carry weapons to their companions. Once Boone, Thunder, and Havoc were armed, the Force stood an excellent chance of defeating the Reptiloids.

No!

He couldn't allow that to happen!

The woman must not reach the men in the Arena!

Reptilian cast a hasty glance over his right shoulder, astounded to discover Grizzly had discarded the M-16 and waded into the elite guard wielding some sort of long claws. Grizzly was slashing furiously, ducking and weaving to avoid the pikes, a smile on his face, as if he was thoroughly enjoying himself.

Athena was a third of the distance toward the three others.

Pandemonium reigned in the stands. The humans in the upper tiers were fleeing in stark panic out the exits, screaming and pushing and shoving in their eagerness to escape the Arena. Many of the Reptiloids, especially the females and the young ones, were also running away, contending with the humans to be the first to safety. Most of the male Reptiloids were converging on the Arena floor.

Reptilian leaped over the edge of the wall and dropped ten feet to the packed earth. He landed lightly and instantly took off toward Athena Morris. If you want something done right, he mentally observed, you must do it yourself! The woman must not reach her three male comrades, and he was the only one in a position to do anything about stopping her. And stop her he would!

Thunder and Boone had joined Sergeant Havoc and assisted the noncom in rising. They saw Athena running their way and moved to meet her halfway.

Reptilian, 15 yards behind the trio, poured on the speed. He covered ten yards and was rapidly gaining ground when he suddenly drew up short.

What was this?

Blade had inexplicably turned and was jogging after Athena.

Dozens upon dozens of Reptiloids were coming over the wall in pursuit.

Reptilian's forehead creased in confusion. What was Blade up to now? He perceived Blade would reach Athena and the others far ahead of his subjects. Was the Force planning to make a last stand in the center of the Arena? Or did Blade have an ulterior motive? Reptilian looked back at the royal platform.

A mad whirl of arms, legs, pikes and claws denoted the savage fight still raging.

Reptilian stared at Blade again, puzzled. A striking incongruity occurred to him: Why didn't Grizzly shoot when he'd had the chance? Grizzly could have shot him at any time up on the platform, but didn't. Why?

Athena Morris reached Boone, Thunder, and Havoc and began dispensing hardware.

Reptilian whirled and raced for the wall, angling to the right of the royal platform, heading for the door through which Narg had entered the Arena. The door was closed, but he was certain someone would be inside and could open it for him.

Blade spotted the Reptiloid leader and increased his pace. He glanced at his watch as he approached his colleagues.

Athena had handed out the weapons. Boone had his Hombres strapped around his waist. Thunder and Sergeant Havoc held M-16's and were checking the magazines.

"Havoc!" Blade shouted as he pounded up to them. "Take this!"

Sergeant Havoc was accustomed to taking orders. After years of military life, he was conditioned to obey an order instantly. He promply gave his M-16 to Thunder and took the M60 with no questions asked.

"I'm going after Reptilian," Blade said. "I want you to take care of the Reptiloids. Don't leave one alive." He paused. "And remember, we have seventeen minutes until detonation. When those charges go, the whole Imperium will come crashing down."

"Charges?" Boone repeated.

But Blade was gone, dashing across the Arena toward Reptilian. He saw the Reptiloid leader thumping on one of the Arena doors, apparently in an effort to have one of the lizard-men open the door from the inside. Blade gritted his teeth and ran all out. He was going to put an end to Reptilian's insanity or perish!

Reptilian was drumming on the door with both fists and yelling for someone to open it.

Blade's eyes flashed as he neared the mutant. He still had a dozen yards to cover. If the door wasn't opened, he would . . .

The door started to open.

Damn!

Blade ate up the distance with his lengthy strides. The door, much to Reptilian's annoyance, was opening very slowly. The lizard-man impatiently grabbed the outer edge and jerked the door outward.

Blade had ten yards to go.

Eight yards.

Prine appeared in the doorway, speaking to Reptilian. He glanced past the Reptiloid leader and pointed.

Six yards.

Reptilian rotated, his features distorted by rage. "Kill him! Kill him!" he thundered.

Prine was armed with a cudgel. He charged toward the Warrior, lifting the club.

Blade was in no mood to trifle with the Indoctrinator. He drew his Bowies as he ran, and when he came abreast of Prine he ducked to the right, avoiding the downward sweep of the cudgel, then moved in close. His left arm was a blur as he slit Prine's throat, and a fraction of a second later his right Bowie rammed into the Indoctrinator's stomach and twisted.

Prine released the cudgel, screeched, and clutched at his neck.

Blade yanked his right Bowie out and pivoted to face the door.

Reptilian had taken a step into the corridor beyond, wrongly assuming Prine would delay Blade long enough to permit him to escape. He froze as Prine lurched and sank to the ground, blood spraying from the Indoctrinator's severed throat and ruptured abdomen. A strategic withdrawal was now out of the question. Reptilian turned, smiling. Here was the human who presumed to challenge his authority! He would show the interloper the reason he was feared far and wide! He would show the fool the folly of his audacity!

Blade crouched, his bloody knives held close to his waist. "I was hoping you would stand and fight!"

Reptilian gazed over Blade's head at the carnage in the Arena. Piles of Reptiloid dead littered the earth, yet the Reptiloids continued to press their attack on the Force members. "Your people will soon be defeated!" he yelled to make himself heard.

Blade risked a look-see.

Sergeant Havoc was a few yards in front of the others, bearing the brunt of the Reptiloid charge. He swept the M60 with devastating effect, mowing the lizard-men down in rows. Thunder, Boone, and Athena were providing covering fire, guaranteeing none of the Reptiloids could outflank Havoc.

Blade stared at Reptilian and smirked. "You've got it backwards! Today is the day the New Order comes to an end!"

"Idiot!" Reptilian snapped. "Killing me will not destroy the New Order!"

"Let's find out," Blade proposed, taking a step nearer.

Reptilian's right hand vanished behind his back, disappearing in the folds of his cape.

Blade paused, unsure of what Reptilian was hiding under the red cape. It could be a gun.

Reptilian smirked, his right arm partially emerging. "What's the matter? Afraid?"

"I just don't like surprises," Blade responded. "What's under that cape?"

"Come closer and find out!" Reptilian suggested spitefully.

Blade's eyes narrowed. "You're bluffing! You don't have anything in your hand!"

"Come and see for yourself!" Reptilian baited him.

Blade cautiously circled to the left, hoping to glimpse the object. It could be a gun, but if it was a firearm, then why didn't Reptilian use it?

Reptilian turned, keeping his back hidden from view. "Why don't you leave while you have the chance?"

"I'm not leaving until you're dead!" Blade replied.

"You will be here forever!" Reptilian stated.

Blade took another stride. "I still say you're bluffing!"

Blade decided to call the lizard-man's bluff. He knew the Reptiloids did not issue firearms as standard ordnance. The sentries on the surface, those assigned to posts ringing the city, carried guns. But in the Imperium, pikes were the rule. Since Reptilian did not have a pike, the mutant must be unarmed. Such was the conclusion Blade reached, and he acted on his determination by springing at the Reptiloid leader.

Reptilian brought his right hand from under the cape and hurled an object at Blade's face.

Blade dodged, recognizing the walkie-talkie as it flew past his eyes. He vaulted forward, his arms outstretched.

Reptilian threw himself backwards, the tips of the Bowies missing his chest by a hair. He darted to the left, into the Arena.

Blade was not about to give the Reptiloid leader a moment's respite. He went after Reptilian, expecting the mutant to wheel and confront him.

Reptilian wasn't about to stop. He sprinted toward Narg's body, desperation lending wings to his feet.

Blade slowly slightly, mystified. He couldn't understand what Reptilian hoped to achieve by . . .

The pike!

Reptilian was going for the pike imbedded in the creature's

head!

Blade quickened his pace, knowing he would be at a severe disadvantage if the lizard-man got hold of the longer weapon.

Reptilian never looked back. He was nine feet ahead of the Warrior when he reached Narg's corpse, and he wrested the pike free with a powerful twist of his rippling shoulders. He twirled, bringing the pike up, and grinning in anticipation of his impending victory.

Blade stopped six feet from Reptilian, his arms out, the Bowies gleaming.

"How quickly the fortunes of war can turn!" Reptilian declared.

"Humans have a saying," Blade stated. "Don't count your chickens before they're hatched."

"And I have a saying," Reptilian retorted. "Death to all humans!" He hissed and jabbed the pike at Blade's knees.

Blade swatted the pike aside with a sweep of his right Bowie. He gave way, slowly backing up as the lizard-man pressed the onslaught.

Reptilian was extremely adept in the use of the pike. He had bested countless adversaries in pike combat during the years he was ascending to rulership of the Reptiloids. So he now employed every trick he knew, thrusts, counterthrusts, feints, frontal stabs, and side swings, and none of them worked. Blade parried every one, the pike and the Bowies clanging as they struck. Reptilian had never encountered a human endowed with such amazing strength and stamina, and his anger at being thwarted grew with each blocked strike. He considered throwing the pike, but what if he missed?

Blade was focusing all of his energy on simply staying alive. His arms were growing tired, and he hoped Reptilian would commit a fatal mistake before he did.

As they fought, as their weapons clashed again and again, Blade had continued to retreat, covering dozens of yards in the process.

Reptilian's shifty eyes spied a golden opportunity to end their contest. He renewed his assault, wanting to keep Blade's mind on their duel to the death, intending to prevent Blade from glancing to the rear.

Prine's blood-soaked body was five feet behind the Warrior.

Blade took one step backwards at a time. To rush would prove

deadly. Concentrate! he commanded himself. Concentrate! He
must keep his eyes on Reptilian's pike, his feet firmly on the
ground. If he lapsed for a—

His left boot collided with something.

Blade tried to raise his boot and step over whatever was below
him, but Reptilian suddenly drove the pike in a beeline for his
heart. Forced to jerk his body to the rear to evade the pike point,
he felt his boot slip on a wet substance. He tried to retain his
balance, but the very next moment he was falling backwards,
exposed and vulnerable.

Reptilian smirked as he surged forward, drawing the pike back
to his ear and spearing the tip at the Warrior's midriff.

Blade landed hard on his shoulders and twisted onto his left
side. The pike gouged a chunk of flesh from his stomach, but the
wound was superficial. He ignored the pain and sliced his left
Bowie across Reptilian's right leg.

Reptilian instinctively jumped back several feet, glancing down
at his leg to assess the damage. His pants were slit and his skin was
cut, but the leg was fully functional.

Blade used the reprieve to roll to the right and rise. He glimpsed
Prine's corpse and realized he was covered with the
Indoctrinator's blood.

"Damn you!" Reptilian fumed. "What does it take to finish
you?"

"More than you've got," Blade said.

"Would you leave, right now, if I agreed to spare your life?"
Reptilian unexpectedly asked.

"I'm not leaving until you're dead," Blade replied.

Reptilian scowled. "I will relish feasting on your flesh! I will
boil your gonads in butter and eat them for my evening meal!"

"You're forgetting one thing," Blade said.

"What?"

"You have to win first," Blade declared.

"And win I shall!" Reptilian asserted.

"Not the way you fight," Blade said, deliberately insulting the
Reptiloid. "If you're as good in bed as you are with that pike, the
female Reptiloids must laugh themselves silly!"

"Why, you . . . !" Reptilian bristled, snarling and lunging, aiming the pike at the Warrior's face.

Which was what Blade wanted. He was not making any head-
way using the Bowies. Eventually the pike's greater reach would
prevail. He needed to do something completely unforeseen, a
move Reptilian would never anticipate.

Like so.

Blade snapped his head to the right as the pike lanced at his face.
He abruptly released his Bowies and grabbed the pike shaft,
clamping his fingers and pulling, adding his power to the
momentum of Reptilian's thrust.

The lizard-man was unable to check his lunge. He stumbled
forward, struggling to keep his grasp on the pike. The Warrior's
left boot smacked into his shins, tripping him, and he fell to his
hands and knees, the pike torn from his hands. He growled and
stood.

Blade held the pike for a moment, letting Reptilian know he
could use it if he wanted. Instead, he tossed the pike aside and
crouched.

Reptilian seemed surprised by the move. "You're giving me a
fair fight?"

Blade nodded. "One on one."

"You are dumber than Narg," Reptilian commented, and
attacked.

Blade met the charge with a right to Reptilian's jaw. The
mutant was staggered by the blow, and Blade followed through
with a left to the gut and a right to the side of the Reptiloid's head.

Reptilian sagged, doubled over, gasping for air.

Blade formed a single fist from both hands and lifted them over
his head.

Reptilian suddenly uncoiled, driving his right knee up and in,
catching the Warrior in the groin.

Grunting, Blade bent over, his hands protecting his privates,
racked by excruciating misery. He felt Reptilian's fingers lock
onto his throat and he was rudely hauled erect.

Reptilian was smiling. "And so this farce ends!" he remarked.

"I agree," Blade said, wheezing, and swung his arms up and in,
his rigid thumbs plunging into Reptilian's eyes. He pressed with all
of his might.

Reptilian reflexively clawed at the Warrior's forearms,
endeavoring to tear them from his eyes.

Blade held on, using his iron grip for leverage as he brought his right knee up, returning the favor, smashing his kneecap into the Reptiloid's crotch. Once. Twice. And twice more. With each blow Reptilian gurgled and trembled. "This is for Clayboss!" Blade commented, kneeing the mutant again. "And this is for Rivera," he added, sweeping his right knee up one more time.

Reptilian appeared to be having difficulty breathing. Spittle dripped from his lips.

"And this," Blade concluded, "is for Kraft!" His shoulder and arm muscles bunched, becoming rock hard, his triceps and biceps bulging. He fiercely snapped Reptilian's head to the right, then the left, and twisted.

There was a loud crack, a popping retort, and Reptilian slumped in the Warrior's grasp.

Blade let go and stood back.

Reptilian had a particularly stupid expression contorting his features, as if he couldn't believe his demise was possible. His knees buckled and he sagged to the ground.

Blade took a deep breath, regaining control of his emotions. He stared at the dead Reptiloid in grim satisfaction.

"Not bad for an amateur," remarked someone to his left. "I couldn't have done better myself."

Blade suddenly realized the Arena was quiet. He looked up.

Grizzly was on the Warrior's left, his fur splattered with fresh gore.

Boone, Thunder, Athena, and Sergeant Havoc stood seven feet away to the right.

"Where . . . ?" Blade began, surveying the stands and the Arena floor. Dead Reptiloids were literally everywhere.

"We killed as many as we could," Boone said. "The rest headed for the hills."

"It couldn't be helped," Athena chimed in. "We tried to get them all, like you wanted."

Sergeant Havoc was gazing at Reptilian. "My compliments, sir," he stated in his typically military fashion.

Blade remembered the explosive charges and checked his watch. "Let's move it, people!" he directed. "We have seven minutes to reach the surface. If we're in the Imperium when those charges detonate, we're as good as dead." He ran to his Bowies and scooped them up.

The Force members fell in behind him as he headed for the open door.

"What if there are humans still in the Imperium?" Boone mentioned. "Shouldn't we try to warn them?"

"There's no time," Blade replied over his left shoulder. "We'll barely have time to retrieve the radio from the armory."

"What about the Reptiloids who got away?" Boone queried. "Do we go after them?"

"No," Blade responded. "They're nothing without their leader. They won't give the Freedom Federation any more trouble."

He hoped.

EPILOGUE

He was seated at his desk in the command bunker when she entered.

"Grizzly said you wanted to see me," Athena said.

Blade looked up from the report he was writing on the Reptilian affair. "Yes. Have a seat."

Athena sat down in the chair in front of the desk.

"Are you all packed?" Blade asked.

"Athena nodded. "General Gallagher will be picking me up in an hour to take me back to LA."

Blade leaned back in his chair and folded his hands. "Grizzly tells me you did all right on this last mission."

"I don't think so," Athena said, frowning.

"Oh?"

"I blew it too many times," Athena stated. "I wasn't as in control as I thought I would be."

"Staying calm in combat isn't easy," Blade remarked. "Like everything else in life, it takes practice."

"I don't see how you do it," Athena confessed.

Blade studied her thoughtfully. "Weren't you the one who wanted to do this on a regular basis? What happened to your ambition?"

"I don't know," Athena said reservedly. "I was shaken up out there. You may have been right."

Blade pursed his lips. "I don't know about that. You performed as well as any of the men."

Athena brightened. "You really think so?"

Blade nodded. "In fact, I have a proposition for you."

Athena grinned. "Aren't you married?"

Blade smiled and laid his hands on the desk. "You don't have to return to Los Angeles if you don't want to."

Stunned amazement was reflected in her countenance. "are you saying what I think you're saying?"

"If you still want to join the Force as a temporary member,"

Blade stated, "I'll go along with the idea."

Athena leaned forward, scrutinizing the Warrior intently. "What happened? Did Reptilian give you a concussion?"

"No," Blade replied, chuckling. "I'm serious."

"Wow!" was all Athena could think of to say.

"I need your answer now," Blade said.

"What's the rush?"

"We're leaving on another mission in three hours," Blade informed her. "I just got off the phone with General Gallagher."

"Three hours?" Athena repeated doubtfully. "So soon?"

"I'm afraid so," Blade said. "I haven't told the others yet. I know they like you, and they would be happy to have you stay. I figure I can give them some good news with the bad. So how about it? Will you sign on or not?"

Athena hesitated. Here was the realization of her dreams, the chance to write her own ticket. All she had to do was say yes.

"I'll understand if you decline," Blade commented. "This is a harzardous profession. In two missions we've lost four men. We're bound to lose more."

"What if I blow it again?" Athena inquired apprehensively. "I could endanger everyone else."

Blade shrugged. "We all run that risk."

"This situation reminds me of the motto my grandfather had," Athena said. "No pain, no gain."

"Does this mean you'll accept?" Blade asked.

"I must be out of my mind," Athena stated, her excitement rising, "but yes, I accept."

"Good," Blade said. "I'll let you break the good news to the others. Don't tell them about the new mission. I'll be over to the barracks in five minutes and fill them in."

Athena stood, beaming happily. "I wonder if I know what I've gotten myself into!"

"You're in an elite military unit," Blade observed. "The key word is military. We may not go strictly by the book, but there are rules and regulations you'll be expected to follow, just like the others."

"Military decorum and all that. Is that what you mean, Big Guy?" Athena inquired.

"I suppose so," Blade said. "And stop calling me Big Guy."

"We could have a problem with military decorum," Athena mentioned.

"What kind of problem?"

"What am I going to do on laundry days?" Athena queried solemnly. "Should I hang my undies on the line with the rest of my uniform, or would General Gallagher have a fit?"

Blade laughed and waved her toward the door. "Go break the good news to the others. I have a report to complete."

Athena scooted to the doorway, then paused. "Blade?"

The Warrior looked over at her. "What?"

"From the bottom of my heart," Athena said sincerely. "Thanks."

"You've earned it," Blade assured her.

"If you say so," Athena said. "But thanks just the same." She paused and laughed. "You Big Lug."